SWORD

OF THE

SEVEN

SINS

SWORD OF THE SEVEN SINS

A NOVEL

EMILY COLIN

Blue Crow Books

Publisher's Cataloging-in-Publication Data
Colin, Emily. 1975-.
Sword of the Seven Sins: A Novel / Emily Colin
p.____ cm.____
ISBN 978-1-947834-46-0 (Pbk.) | 978-1-947834-47-7 (Ebook)
1. Science Fiction. 2. Young Adult Fiction. 3. Fantasy Fiction. I. Title.
813.6 | LOC PCN 2020936255

Blue Crow
Books

Published by Blue Crow Books
an imprint of Blue Crow Publishing, LLC
Chapel Hill, NC
bluecrowpublishing.com
Cover Design by Lauren Faulkenberry

ALSO BY EMILY COLIN

YOUNG ADULT FICTION

Wicked South: Secrets and Lies: Stories for Young Adults
Sword of the Seven Sins

FICTION FOR ADULTS

The Memory Thief
The Dream Keeper's Daughter

PRAISE FOR EMILY COLIN

PRAISE FOR SWORD OF THE SEVEN SINS

A hot, fast-paced, beautifully written story you won't want to miss!

— CAITLIN SINEAD, AUTHOR OF *HEARTSICK*

Amazing characters and a fast plot that will keep you on the edge of your seat!

— S.E. ANDERSON, AUTHOR OF THE STARSTRUCK SAGA

PRAISE FOR THE DREAM KEEPER'S DAUGHTER

A splendid mix of time travel, romantic yearning, and moving on after grief.

— *PUBLISHERS WEEKLY*

A passionate and sweeping tale of a woman haunted by a loss she can't explain, and a future she can't yet choose.

— ERIKA MARKS, AUTHOR OF *THE LAST TREASURE*

This story immerses you in a time that should not be forgotten and explores the infinite rippling effect of decisions, guilt, accountability, and love.

— SAMANTHA SOTTO, AUTHOR OF *LOVE AND GRAVITY*

PRAISE FOR THE MEMORY THIEF

This absorbing first effort brings to mind the mountaineers of a Jon Krakauer read, the tenderness of a Nicholas Sparks novel, and the enduring love story of Charles Martin's The Mountain between Us, all sprinkled with a heady dose of passion.

— BOOKLIST

Mesmerizing . . . dazzlingly original and as haunting as a dream.

— CAROLINE LEAVITT, *NEW YORK TIMES* BESTSELLING AUTHOR OF *PICTURES OF YOU*

[A] richly emotional tale . . . a writer to watch.

— JOSHILYN JACKSON, *NEW YORK TIMES* BESTSELLING AUTHOR OF *A GROWN-UP KIND OF PRETTY*

To my family and friends whose support kept me super-glued together through an incredibly challenging year—you know who you are. And to my indefatigable aunt, Ellen Rappaport, fellow warrior, voracious reader, and creative soul...all the love and light in the cosmos.

EVA

The first time I condemned a man to death, I was ten years old.

I was standing with the rest of the Commonwealth of Ashes in Clockverk Square, beneath the giant clockwork tower that stood watch over us all. Lined up at the front of the crowd with the other children from the Nursery, I was there to bear witness, judged by the Commonwealth to be of an age to understand the dire consequences of rebellion and sin. We children stood at the edge of the square, dressed in white, vibrating with excitement. Our days had a familiar, soothing pattern—wake, eat breakfast, exercise, have lessons, eat again, complete assigned activities, cleanse, sleep, repeat. Today was different. Today we would see a man die.

The other children were thrilled at the prospect—had been chattering about little else all week—but I felt nothing but creeping dread.

Mother Erikson stood behind me, her grip on my shoulders tight and unforgiving, so I could not look away. She needn't have. I made it my policy to face as much as I could, so I knew where my weaknesses lay.

At the edge of the square, the condemned man between them, stood two of the Bellators of Light. The Bellatorum Lucis were the Commonwealth's defenders, mysterious figures who dressed always in black and carried razor-sharp blades in sheaths stretching the length of their spines. They were an elite fighting force, trained to protect the Commonwealth against Outsiders and administer justice when called for. They would put the man to death today.

The bellators brought the man into the square, one gripping each of his arms. It hardly seemed necessary. He wasn't a large man, and he was blindfolded. Plus, he was unsteady, tripping over the stones, so that the bellator on his right had to yank him upright. He wore the gray clothes of the accused. His skin was pale, his hair dark against the whiteness of his face. He blinked when they removed his blindfold, trying to accustom himself to the light of the rising sun. And then he looked out over the crowd, as if he was searching for someone. Again and again his gaze lit on people's faces, but they shifted and looked away, refusing to meet his eyes. He had been one of us, and now he was not. We could not afford for his wickedness to contaminate the rest.

In the middle of the square stood the High Priest, a thin man in heavy red robes. He nodded to the bellators, who stepped back, retreating to the edge of the square. In his familiar, sonorous voice, the Priest said the man's name and listed his crimes. This man, he said, was guilty of the sins of greed and gluttony. He had been responsible for tending the vineyards, making the ceremonial wine the Priests used for blessings and rituals. He had been found to be selling the wine on the black market, hoarding the best vintages for himself. I wondered if that was why the man seemed unsteady, stumbling into the square—if he had lost his footing because his eyes were covered or because he had been consuming too many of his own wares. Later, I wondered if it was because he was summoning the bravery to face his fate.

The Priest faced us, hands high, silhouetted by the dawning sun. Executions were always held at sunrise, a righteous death signaling a new beginning. For this man, he said, it would be a righteous death indeed, a punishment deserved. A chance to go before the Architect with his soul washed clean.

The Priest made it sound as if the man should be grateful to die, and everywhere I looked, I could see people nodding in agreement. Better to die this way, judged and absolved at the hands of the Commonwealth, than fleeing in exile toward the Borderlands.

I knew I should nod like everyone else, knew the Mothers were watching the children from the Nursery to make sure we showed the appropriate response. But within me, from some unknown and dangerous place, came a spark of resistance. I thought of the times I'd sat at the Mothers' feet, struggling to pay attention as strange, toothed shadow-creatures writhed on the wall. Of the disdainful way Mother Erikson regarded me, as if she knew the face I presented to the world was a mask, concealing the ways I was different from the rest. If I let something slip—if I told her about the shadow-beasts—what would happen to me? Would I wind up like this man, suspected of increasingly unacceptable behavior until one day I wound up exiled or sentenced to death?

Regardless of his sins, I did not believe the man should be grateful to die like this, no better than a slaughtered animal. And even at the age of ten, I couldn't nod and pretend. I have never been very good at lying.

So I didn't nod. I didn't shake my head, either. I didn't protest, but I didn't show my agreement, the way I could see the other kids doing. To my left, Rósný was nodding vigorously, her blonde pigtail bouncing. To my right, Jósefína was doing the same, so vehemently I was sure it would make her dizzy. I was a still point between them, a silent place of negation. It wasn't wise, I knew that. But I couldn't help myself.

The Priest's eyes scanned the crowd. They paused on Rósný, and his lips lifted in approbation. Then they passed over me and found Jósefína, who was still nodding like one of those bobbing paper birds the Mother had taught us to fold and perch on the side of cups, pretending to drink water. He smiled even more broadly. And then his gaze drifted back to me, pinioned between them, and I froze. Maybe, I thought, he'll forgive this. There is a man to kill. Surely that is more important than one small girl's nod.

I should have known better. The Priests never forgive.

He motioned me forward, to stand with him and the condemned man in the middle of the square. I looked behind me, to my left and right, but that was a formality; I knew the Priest was gesturing to me. Perhaps he had seen into my heart, the way the Mothers were always warning us Priests could do. Perhaps he could tell I was not worthy of a life in the Commonwealth, and would banish me to the

Borderlands—in the wreckage of the floods and the Fall, where the savages dwelt, waiting to attack.

For most members of the Commonwealth, exile was the worst thing they could imagine. Certainly, I had never found any reason to feel differently. But as the Mother relinquished her grip on my shoulders and I stepped forward out of the white-clothed line of my fellow students, I was not afraid. If this were my fate, then I would go to meet it, and come out the other side. *Fear is the enemy,* I told myself, even as I lowered my eyes, because to hold the gaze of a Priest is the highest insult. *Fear is the force that can break the strongest of men. But it will not break me.*

This was my mantra, found in an old, discarded book in the Commonwealth's library and repeated silently in the deepest hours of the night, when all the other children were asleep. I had never slept well; I saw creatures sliding in the shadows where there were none, heard voices chattering in the walls and beneath the windows until I had to cover my head with my pillow to silence them. I knew without being told I had to hide this—from the Mothers, certainly, but also from the other children, who would relish the opportunity to pass on such a juicy tidbit. There were Informers amongst my playmates, poised to report the slightest transgression, and I was determined they should have nothing to say about me.

My shoes crunched on the gravel, slid on the rain-slick stones, still wet with the morning's dew. As I came to the Priest's outstretched hand, my back ramrod straight and my head lifted high, I could hear the crowd's collective intake of breath. To be called onto the stones by a Priest was a great honor. Later, in the Nursery, I would hear the Mothers whispering, would know they found it as extraordinary as I did—though for different reasons. But now, I stood still, my body moving with the force of my breath, gaze fixed on the green line of moss that traced the cobblestone at my feet. I breathed, and shut my eyes.

The Priest's hand came to rest on my head. Even through the thickness of my braid, I could feel the cold, damp pressure of his fingers. "Speak your name, child."

"Eva Marteinn, Father." My voice came clear and high. I was pleased it did not shake.

"You'll not have seen justice enacted before, Eva Marteinn. How do you feel, to witness it here today?"

The question hung in the balance between us, and my life hung with it. Slowly, I lifted my head, looking not at the Priest but beyond him, into the eyes of the man condemned to die. The man met my gaze without flinching, and his mouth lifted in a smile. It wasn't the unfocused, wild grin of a madman, nor yet the grimace of a man who was resigned to his fate. The condemned man smiled at me with what I could swear was happiness, and in his eyes was that most dangerous of emotions: Pride.

For the life of me I could not figure out what there was for him to be proud of. In any other circumstances I would have dropped my own eyes, lest my expression give him away. But this man had already been sentenced to die. He could choose to fornicate on the stones, provided he could find a partner willing to sin with him, or drain a dozen bottles of wine to the dregs. Nothing he did now would change his fate, which had been sealed the moment the Priests discovered the truth.

I held the man's eyes with mine as I answered the Priest's question. It was all I had to give him, the only way I knew to show courage. *Fear is the enemy. Fear is the force that will break the strongest of men.* But it had not broken me today, and I could see it had not broken this man either. He would die with his spirit intact, and I found this mattered to me.

Before I could lose my courage, I looked away from the man, to the edge of the square, where the two bellators stood at attention. "He threatens the innocent who spares the guilty," I said, raising my voice for everyone to hear.

The crowd breathed in again, this time in horror. These were the Priest's words to say, words that signaled the death of the man in the square. They were a call to arms, and not for a child to utter.

I knew this. And yet I had said them, because I was suddenly certain the guilty party here was not the man, but the rest of us—the Priest, the Mothers, the bellators, the judgmental crowd. I had said them, but not with their usual intent—a trigger that would loose the blades of a bellator, severing the condemned man's head with a single vicious downswing. I wanted the man to know that, though he might not be innocent of the charges the Priest had leveled, all of us were implicated in his death. And I wanted him to hear these final words from someone who understood.

"Eva Marteinn," the Priest said, his voice inscrutable. "Look at me."

And so I lifted my eyes to his.

For what felt like forever, the Priest searched my face. And then he turned toward the bellators. "Answer her call," he said.

As one, the bellators' gaze fixed on me. When they spoke, it was in perfect unison. "Either by meeting or by the sword."

The Priest had made me the instrument of the man's destruction, lent me the power to command the Bellatorum. It was a heady thing —but I knew there would be a cost.

The bellators moved into the square, prowling toward us with a pantherlike, anticipatory grace. One forced the man down to his knees and held him still; the other freed his sverd and raised it, gleaming silver in the light. The man did not struggle. He closed his eyes, the sun's rays glinting off his dark hair, and I saw his lips move silently. "Do it," he said.

The blade came down, unerringly finding its target. The man made a terrible noise, and then we were standing in a pool of blood. It spread around my shoes, made squelching noises when I tried to lift my feet.

The man crumpled on the stones, the life gone out of him. I couldn't look at him anymore. So instead I looked straight ahead, at the children who had come with me from the Nursery. Their faces were as white as their uniforms, and they stared at me with big, shocked eyes. I couldn't tell which they thought was worse—my hubris in speaking the Priest's call, or the death of the man, which had not been the glorious, thrilling event they'd imagined. Either way, I had a sinking feeling I would be the one to pay the price.

I hadn't been afraid when the Priest called me into the square, or when the man had died. But I was afraid now, and I despised myself for it. The world faded into the background, the only noise the roaring of my blood in my ears. And then I saw his face.

He stood behind the line of children that had come from the Nursery, with a group of other kids—a tall, lithe boy whose face looked vaguely familiar. He was wearing a green uniform, to show he was in his last year of study at the Under-School, before he turned thirteen and began his preparation to be Chosen. I studied his face—a stubborn jaw, cheekbones that were beginning to take on the sharp definition of adulthood, lips that curved upward even in repose, belying the angularity of his features. His eyes were wide and green and fixed on mine.

I could appreciate the boy's beauty, but the notion held no significance. It was not as if I would ever be allowed to touch him. In the Commonwealth, romantic love—and, of course, lust—is forbidden. Our children are conceived in test tubes, then implanted in an unrelated carrier who gives birth to them, avoiding unnecessary attachment. From there, they go to the Nursery, where they are raised with interchangeable groups of other children their own age, supervised by a rotating group of Mothers.

So what drew me to the boy was not the hope of a future with him, however fantastic. I looked at him because he was the only one who looked back, without horror or shock or anything but a cool acceptance. Him, and one other. Standing in the second row, Instruktor Bjarki met my eyes, wearing an expression that might be interpreted as sympathy. Then she glanced down, disassociating herself from my foolishness—and how could I blame her?

But the boy did not look away. As I watched, he inclined his head toward me, and in the gesture I saw affirmation: *You'll do.*

I drew a deep breath, and sound roared back around me—the murmurs of the crowd, the Priest's benediction for the dead man. The bellators had retreated to the edge of the square, and the one who had killed the man was cleaning his blade. The other stood guard, contained and watchful.

These two were young—no more than twenty—and their bodies were pure muscle, honed to do battle and survive. Their faces were expressionless, identical in a bone-deep way that went beyond the differences in hair and skin and eyes. As I watched, the one who was cleaning his blade slid it back into his sheath without needing to look. If I had tried that, I'd have sliced off my braid.

There was no law saying only boys could join the Bellatorum. I didn't know why there were no girls among their ranks. Maybe none had ever wanted it—after all, life was easier almost everywhere else. Not more certain. Just...easier. Or maybe they had wanted it, and the Executor had refused.

I had seven more years until my Choosing Ceremony, but I knew what I hoped for: a career in comp tech, the field for which I'd already shown the strongest aptitude. There had never been a female bellator, so I didn't worry I'd be inducted into their ranks. Nonetheless, the rush that flooded me as the bellators stepped forward to do my bidding, the fleeting sensation that it was I who swung the blade, whistling through the air to cleave deep into flesh and bone—it disgusted me. How could I see the horror in such things, and yet delight in them? Surely taking pleasure in such things was a terrible sin.

There in the square, my feet soaked in blood and the sun breaking bright over the horizon, I felt cold certainty settle over me. The Priests and the Executor claimed to enforce these punishments in the name of creating a sinless society, of suppressing our base, savage instincts to prevent another Fall like the one that had destroyed the natural order of things centuries before...but staring at the body of the dead man, I doubted their convictions.

The Caretakers had always told us that the Executor held us to such strict standards to keep us safe—from our own failings as well as from the threat of the barbaric Outsiders who roamed beyond our gates—but the Priests' punishments were far more savage than any infraction we could hope to commit. As for the Bellatorum, they were meant to be the arbiters of justice—but in that moment, standing in the square, I saw them for what they truly were: murderers whose violence was sanctioned by the authority we citizens held dear. And when I spoke the words that belonged only to the Priest, when I held the black-clad warriors' power in my hands—I'd been just as guilty.

You are a monster, I thought, daring to glance back at the red-robed Priest, *a wolf covered in blood. You're no better than an animal. And now...neither am I.*

Sickened, I squelched across the stones of the square, leaving a trail of red footprints behind.

2

EVA

SEVEN YEARS LATER

W hen I wake up on the morning of Choosing Eve, the morning after my seventeenth birthday, I don't expect to see a woman's eyes sewn shut before breakfast.

I get up at six in the morning, heading for my temporary job in the comp lab. With luck, after tomorrow, the position will be permanent. Though it is forbidden for me to take pride in my work, I have excelled, solving challenges the others could not, unraveling tangled lines of code that kept machinery running for the medics and restored power more quickly during storms.

I make my white-sheeted single bed, one of nineteen others on the third floor of the Rookery. Then I rummage the communal dresser until I find clothes that will fit, walk to the bathroom, and step into one of the five white-tiled showers.

Showers are exactly three minutes in length. They are not meant for lingering. Lingering could lead to self-admiration, to pride in one's appearance and even lust, to the weight of rocks sewn into the hems of one's clothes and the scorch of flames on bare flesh. Take a step down that path and before you know it, you're on your knees in the square with your neck bared for a bellator's sword.

So, no lingering.

The water turns off and I dry myself with a rough white towel from the rack. I drop the towel into one bin and my nightgown into the other, adding to the growing pile of items the natural-born will deal with when they come to pick up the laundry. I am not supposed to pity their lot, but I do just the same. It's not their fault their parents were sinners.

At six-fifteen I head downstairs, pressing my palm against the scanner to identify myself as we must do when entering or leaving the Commonwealth's buildings. The door gives and I walk out of the Rookery and into Clockverk Square, integrating into the group on its way to breakfast: the children of the Under-School clad in white, third-formers in their olive-green uniforms, the rest of us in brown and tan. Career citizens weave among us: white clothes for medics, denim and cotton for gardeners, yellow for seamstresses, purple for the surrogate carriers, blue for teachers. Red for the High Priests. And black for the Bellators of Light.

It's rare to see a bellator at breakfast. Valentína, who has the cot next to mine, likes to joke that they probably catch small animals in the woods with their bare hands, skin them, and eat them raw. I doubt that very much. To be a member of the Bellatorum Lucis is to be disciplined in all things. It seems a waste to rob our woods of its squirrels and chipmunks, when you could sit down to a perfectly decent bowl of oatmeal and get on with your day.

The faces surrounding me are a sea of white, distinguishable mostly by the colors of their hair, eyes, and uniforms. They vary from porcelain to verging on olive—but there's no one in the Commonwealth who could be described as dark-skinned like in some of the old books we've read. Rumor has it that the Outsiders who invaded from the south were darker; when I was growing up in the Nursery, the other children used to tease me for my black hair and brown eyes, saying that perhaps I was descended from the barbarians. Certainly the Caretakers always showed preference for the little girls with the fairest skin, their hair like butter and their eyes like cut-out pieces of the sky.

I have always found this to be ridiculous—not to mention hypocritical, given that the Executor himself doesn't meet these standards. The more the other girls teased me, the more determined I became to find things to love about the way I looked—my eyes, I told myself, were the color of prized sipping chocolate; the hue of my hair matched the gleaming obsidian rock that lined the gorges. So what if I didn't meet their standards of what was beautiful—I had something more, the ability to slip in and out of the shadows, to show the rest of the Commonwealth only what they wanted to see.

All these years—ever since that moment of realization in the Square—this is what I've done. Pretended to fit in, to think and feel like the rest. It is exhausting—but second nature, too.

At the dining hall, I line up between a sixth-former and a man bound for work in the cannery, shuffle forward, press my hand against the identification pad. The light above the pad flashes green and I step over the threshold, into the large, high-ceilinged room with its long wooden tables, each flanked by benches.

No sooner has the last of us made our way inside than the Executor's face appears on the four vid screens that bracket the room and his resonant voice comes over the speakers: "Good morning, Commonwealth."

His face takes up the entirety of each screen, dark bushy brows and deep-set black eyes, a large, hooked nose and a mouth that always frowns, even in repose. Looking at him the morning before my Choosing, I feel as if I understand. He has a lot of responsibilities, especially today. If I were him, I would probably be frowning too.

The Executor clears his throat, the camera panning out until we can see his hands, folded atop the uncluttered surface of his desk. "Please join me as I recite the Sins, that we may be empowered by their knowledge and encouraged to remain pure of soul."

And so, together, we recite the Sins (pride, lust, sloth, envy, wrath, greed, gluttony) and after them, the Virtues (chastity, humility, diligence, temperance, kindness, patience, charity) along with their Latin translations, the language the Priests hold holy.

He regards us from the screens, his expression unchanged, as we deliver our daily recitation of the Oath of Loyalty. Save for the name of each Commonwealth, the Oath is the same for every citizen of the Empire. The other Commonwealths are scattered across the lands beyond our borders—or so the Priests and the Executor tell us. We will never have the opportunity to see for ourselves; our place is here. To leave is to die.

We pledge our loyalty to the laws of the Commonwealth of Ashes, and to the Virtues which make it strong, one Sinless society under the eye of the Architect, united through piety, discipline, and truth.

"Very well, citizens," the Executor says when the last syllable of the Oath dies away and silence falls. "Let us recognize the core of our strength, the tenets that have allowed us to survive when so many others perished after the Fall." He clears his throat. "With attachment comes tenderness," he says, the first words of our catechism.

"With tenderness comes love," we reply, our voices blending in a chorus that pleases the Executor. A smile lifts his lips.

"With love comes loss."

"With loss comes hate." The words are inflectionless, spoken in perfect synchrony.

"With hate comes chaos," he prompts, his smile widening.

"Out of chaos comes order." We stand taller, spines straight and hands at our sides, embodying the spirit of our creed, and the Executor nods with approval.

"It pains me to share that we have two sinners in our midst today," he says, and the crowd murmurs. The Commonwealth sometimes goes weeks without the commission of a single sin. To have more than one, in such short order, is a terrible thing. Sins cannot go unpunished.

Around me, people have fallen silent. I'm sure they are taking the same personal inventory I am, wondering if they are about to be held accountable for mistakes they can't remember making. Or mistakes they can, and hoped to keep hidden: a raised voice, a thrown water pitcher, an intercepted, over-long glance.

In the Commonwealth, you never know who is watching.

The vid screens go blank, and then an image appears—one of the seamstresses. It takes me a moment to recognize her, though, given the disfiguration of her face. Beneath her image, incriminating black letters scroll as the Executor speaks: "Pálhanna Lund. Guilty of the Sin of Envy. Crime: Coveting her neighbor's promotion to supervisor. Punishment: Eyes sewn shut for a month, for we cannot covet what we cannot see."

A shudder passes through me. The stitches are temporary, but the black thread against her white skin looks so barbaric—an accusation she cannot disguise. The fact that this woman's trade—the needle and thread—was used against her makes it even worse.

"If I may have your attention." The Executor's gaze drifts over the crowd. "We have a second penitent today. Convicted of the sin of gluttony, for taking more than her weekly quota of books from the Library without permission. It can be argued that such an individual is only endeavoring to educate herself, to share her knowledge with the innocent souls we have entrusted to her charge. But here in the Commonwealth, we have learned from the mortal errors of those who lived to excess before the Fall, confusing self-glorification with the purity of spirit that can only come from living unencumbered." His voice rises, his eyes glinting with fervor.

This is one of the Executor's favorite topics—how, in the time leading up to the Fall, humans' greed ran rampant, destroying the southern forests in search of timber and heating the seas so the fish choked and died. The southerners fled north, where a massive barrier was erected just in time to keep them out. They raged against it, scaling the stone and giving rise to a brutal war for land and resources. In the end, the northerners won—but at a terrible cost. The seas flooded and retreated; the climate teetered between flame and ice.

To protect those northerners who remained, the Priests formed a series of Commonwealths in the area of the Empire where military bases were the thickest. Ours—the Commonwealth of Ashes, named such because, like the mythical Phoenix, it rose from the ashes to thrive once more—is the oldest and biggest. Legend has it that the city on whose back our Commonwealth is built contained the word "Ash," which the Priests saw as a good omen.

The Commonwealth of Ashes is a seat of power, located high in the mountains, where it can be easily defended. Like all Commonwealths, it's designed to keep us safe from the hordes of barbarians who prowl beyond our fences, eager to make a meal of whatever exiles are cast out from our gates. And like all Commonwealths, it is also designed to keep us safe from ourselves.

I have no idea what the world beyond our gates looks like; probably, I will never know. But one thing about this story has always troubled me. If the southern forests were destroyed, where were its inhabitants meant to go? It only makes sense that they fled north, toward safety. I've always seen them as desperate, rather than savage —children holding the hands of their Caretakers, thirsty and tired, wanting only safe haven…and instead, being turned away to die.

No wonder they turned to barbarity once they finally made it over the barrier, only to be defeated. They probably hate us, as the descendants of the ones that abandoned them when they needed help most.

Such thoughts are treasonous to harbor at all, much less when the Executor is speaking. I clamp down on them with an effort, focusing on his face on the screens.

"It is our duty to guard the unsullied state of your souls, for the past has shown us that only too easily can they become corrupt. So easily can mankind indulge our animal nature." The Executor spins his chair to face us, steepling his fingers under his chin. "Citizens of the Commonwealth, it gives me no pleasure to acknowledge our final sinner, who shall be sentenced to serve you our finest food and drink today—and yet partake of none. Thus she shall experience deprivation that will return her soul to purity; thus she shall renounce her gluttony, to serve and sin no more."

The image flashes up on the vid screen and, like everyone else, I look. And then I suck in a surprised breath.

The sinner is Instruktor Bjarki.

Aside from her show of support that long-ago day in the square, she is the sole teacher who ever showed me kindness beyond what was required, noting my affinity for comp tech and finding precious volumes on the subject in the Commonwealth's library. She used her own book rations to let me borrow them—an act that, while not forbidden, showed a generosity bordering on preference. Looking at her image on the vid screen, my heart sinks.

The screen goes blank, the Executor's face winking out of existence. Numb, I follow the herd to the far wall and line up at the vitamin dispensary machines. Usually the wait annoys me—not that I let it show, patience being a virtue—but today I am depending on it to distract me. I don't want to see Instruktor Bjarki broken, reduced to the sum of her faults.

I suppose forcing us to witness her humiliation—as much as the humiliation itself—is the point. *Next time*, the Executor is saying, *this could be you.*

The line moves all too quickly this morning, and I press my hand against the outline on the dispensary's vid screen, rewarded by the message that flashes green: *Welcome, Citizen Marteinn. Your vitamins are being prepared. Please wait.* The machine grumbles and clanks, spitting out a small paper cup containing the usual three pills: green, red, and yellow. Alongside them is a fourth pill I have never seen before. This one is pink.

"Excuse me," I say to the machine, feeling foolish. "But there's an extra pill here—I think maybe someone made a mistake—"

The machine whirrs and clicks. Then a new message appears on the screen. *There is no reason for concern. Your recent metabolic analysis indicates you are suffering from an iron deficiency. This supplement will alleviate your distress.*

An *iron* deficiency? I think back to what I know about the importance of iron in the blood. The lack of it leads to anemia, the symptoms of which are difficulty breathing, extreme fatigue, and heart palpitations. I suffer from none of these—but perhaps the symptomology has yet to manifest. I ought to be grateful the metabolic check caught the imbalance before it became a problem... but I don't feel grateful. I feel suspicious.

Just as quickly, I dismiss my concerns. If the Commonwealth wanted to poison me, they could have done it a long time ago. I'm being ridiculous and paranoid, and I ought to be ashamed. "Thank you for your clarification," I say and move aside so the man behind me can take his turn at the machine. I pick up a glass of water from the counter, empty the pills into my mouth, and swallow.

The dining hall is normally noisy, filled with the low hum of conversation. Today it is silent, and as I make my way to the food line to grab my tray, I see why. Behind the stainless steel counter, clad in the gray robes of the penitent, stands the tall, slender form of Instruktor Bjarki. Her pale hair is pulled back in a bun, and in the light that streams in from the large windows, she looks older than usual, the lines that bracket either side of her thin mouth more deeply cut. She is flanked on either side by bellators. One of them, a stranger to me, has sandy hair and a pointed chin. The other, to my surprise, is Ari Westergaard, the boy who met my eyes that day in the square.

I knew he'd become a bellator. I was in attendance at his Choosing two years ago. Still, I have never seen him wearing the black garb of the warriors before, with a blade at his back and a weapons belt hung low about his hips. At nineteen, he is as beautiful as I remember—except now he is deadly, too, in the manner of the prowling tigers they have shown us in the vids from before the Fall, when the world was still full of forests and beasts. There is a stillness about him, as if he is waiting for the cue that will cause him to explode into action. But what action can he possibly anticipate from poor, maligned Instruktor Bjarki?

Ari shifts his weight, as if he can feel me staring, and I glance away, searching for somewhere safe to look. My eyes fall on the counter, heaped with delicacies—apples baked with cinnamon, stacks of smoked fish, eggs scrambled with asparagus from the gardens, and skyr made with milk from the goats. Next to this bounty sit cut-glass pitchers of grape juice, harvested from the arbors the little ones tend.

The Executor must truly be concerned for the state of Instruktor Bjarki's soul. Only on the eve of the Architect's arrival have I seen such a spread.

The dining hall workers are wide-eyed—usually breakfast is just oatmeal and eggs, with a side of herbed lamb sausage on Idle Day—but Instruktor Bjarki is stone-faced. She ignores the bellators, ignores everyone except the person in front of her. Again and again she asks them what they'd like, ladles food onto their plates, and turns to the next person.

When breakfast is over, the dining hall workers will eat, choosing whatever they want from the cornucopia. But Instruktor Bjarki will have to stand and watch. They'll give her a hard heel of stale bread, a cup of tepid water. They'll make her starve in the midst of plenty as her punishment.

Rage flashes through me, shooting through my limbs, the feeling sharp as needles. Taking a few extra books—how can that be so bad? She just wanted to learn so she could be a better teacher. I cannot understand why this should be a crime.

No one else seems bothered by her presence. But me—it's all I can do not to run behind the counter and drag her out of here. My senses ratchet up, heightening so I can parse every scent, delineate every spice, hear every whisper. The light that shines through the windows is suddenly too bright.

I breathe deeply, trying to calm myself, but it only makes things worse: The competing aromas of fish and soap fill my lungs, nauseating me. Compounding the miasma is an unfamiliar, acrid stench that evokes the sensation of pounding heartbeats and shallow breathing—as if I'm inhaling the scent of fear.

What is happening to me?

The line moves, and now I am in front of the Instruktor. I can't bear to look at her, to see her reduced to this. Instead my eyes fall on Ari, who is standing beside her, one hand resting on his weapons belt and the other at his side, inches from Instruktor Bjarki's gray-clad elbow. A cat about to pounce, given the slightest provocation.

I stare at him, at his regulation-cut dark hair and his clear green eyes, his over-confident stance and the way his lips quirk up at the corners—he doesn't meet the Commonwealth's aesthetic standards, either; what he lacks in outward appearance as far as they're concerned, he must make up for in skill—and I am furious that he's here, playing a part in her humiliation. The strength of the emotion takes me by surprise, so that I forget to lower my gaze. And then Ari speaks to me.

"I'm not serving food today," he says. "In case you were wondering."

I'm so startled, I almost drop my tray. It's a close call; my fingers loosen, and the wood slides from my grip. The tray is in free fall toward the floor when I manage to snag it, with sharp-edged reflexes that take me by surprise. I'm normally well-coordinated, but nothing like this. The water doesn't even spill. "What are you talking about?" I manage, glaring at Ari.

He stares back, wearing an inscrutable expression—doubtless suppressing his amusement at my clumsiness. My teeth grind as he raises an eyebrow, dismissing me. "You're looking at me like you expect me to take your order, which I assure you is not going to happen. So in the interest of time, I'd suggest you make your choice and pass it along to the appropriate party. Before you lose your grip on anything else."

I don't think I've ever heard Ari's voice before. It's low and gravelly, skirting the edge of arrogance. And I'm not the only one who notices, because the other bellator gives him a disapproving glance. "Don't fraternize, Westergaard," he says.

Ari lifts one shoulder and lets it fall. "Just trying to move things along."

"Yeah, well, don't," says the sandy-haired man.

"Whatever you say, Riis. Your wish is my command."

The man snorts. "Too bad lying isn't a sin. They'd have you strung up by sunset." His eyes fall on me, their expression empty, bored. "You heard the man, citizen. Move it along. You're holding up the line."

Controlling my temper with an effort, I look away from Instruktor Bjarki and her two guards. But that is a mistake, because my eyes fall on the cornucopia on the counter.

I know what I'm supposed to do, but I can't manage it. Instead I gesture to the customary tub of oatmeal. Next to it sits a rare shaker of cinnamon and another of brown sugar, along with a small container of raisins.

"What can I get for you?" Instruktor Bjarki says in an unfamiliar, flat voice, her eyes fixed on the counter.

"Just oatmeal, please," I say, louder than I should. "Plain."

Her head jerks up and she stares at me. "Plain? You don't want... anything else?" Next to her, I hear Ari make a small, amused sound, but when my eyes dart to him, he is standing at perfect attention, staring straight through me.

"Plain will be fine," I say firmly, and am rewarded with a twitch of her mouth that, under other circumstances, might have been the beginning of a smile. "My stomach's upset," I add for the benefit of whoever might be listening, lest they accuse me of sedition.

But Instruktor Bjarki knows better. She heaps the plain oatmeal in a bowl and hands it to me, and I don't think I'm imagining the fact that her spine straightens ever so slightly. Gratified, I take the tray and make my way over to the closest table, doing my best to ignore the assault on my senses, the buzzing in my limbs.

Maybe there was something peculiar in that pill after all.

3

ARI

I finish my shift in the dining hall, guarding that misbegotten soul of an Instruktor while trying to ignore the distraction that is Eva Marteinn, and make my way to the bellators' weapons gallery to sharpen my blades for tonight. I have no idea what will happen at the Trials, but it's best to be prepared. Efraím would have my neck under his knife if I wasn't, and the Architect alone knows what punishment he would devise. Of course, Efraím has never had to reprimand me for failing to rise to a fight. I am never happier than I am with a weapon in my hand and an enemy to defeat. I won't fail him tonight.

But honing my blades on the whetstone is mindless work, and my thoughts stray to the way Eva looked in the dining hall, spitting mad on the sinner's behalf and doing her best to conceal it. She was as alluring as she'd been on the first, fateful morning I laid eyes on her—in Clockverk Square, seven years ago. Her gaze met mine that day, part pleading, part defiance, and in it I saw myself. Try as I might, I wasn't able to look away.

Nor have I been able to look away in the years since, when I've stolen glimpses of her every chance I get. We are not supposed to notice girls, not to think of them unless we must on Donation Day, when we make our contribution to ensure the Commonwealth's survival. But I have always noticed her.

Pride aside, thoughts of Eva are my besetting sin.

Her beauty is a weapon, the only one that has ever been able to bring me low. It has as much to do with the fierce intelligence in her eyes as it does with that thick fall of black hair, always bound in its braid, and the opalescent sheen of her skin. In my darker moments, I've imagined what it might feel like to tug her hair loose from its bindings, if it would run like water through my fingers. If her touch would burn.

She might not resemble the abstract ideals of appearance we are meant to prize—but I have always found her to be singularly lovely. Every time she looks at me, it's like a barbed net sinks its hooks deeper into my heart—and the virtueless truth is, part of me wants to be caught.

When she'd lost her grip on her tray, I'd almost reached out to grab it. I'd imagined the contraband brush of her fingers against mine —a moment I could pass off as an accident and hoard in secret, polished to a fine, forbidden sheen. But then, with sinfully quick reflexes, she'd recovered the tray herself, righting it without spilling so much as a drop of water. It was all I could do not to gape. I've rarely seen an untrained citizen move that way.

I test the point of my dagur with a fingertip, trying not to think of how Eva's back had stiffened as she approached the Instruktor in the food line, of the flash of pity in her dark eyes. For an instant those eyes rested on me, and I saw fury in their depths, shot through with glacial contempt. *You are nothing,* that look said. *Nothing and no one. You guard this woman like it's your right. But she's innocent, and you're the one who has sinned.*

No one looked directly at Instruktor Bjarki the way Eva did. Certainly no one requested plain oatmeal and stared me down as if they'd like to gut me with my own blade.

I was simply carrying out orders. How could she hate me for that?

The question puzzles me, and so I do as I've been trained— slipping into the skin of those I hunt, the better to perceive the world as they do. Through Eva's eyes, I see Instruktor Bjarki diminished, silenced, subservient. Made to suffer, while those around her reveled in excess, oblivious. Did I blindly inflict punishment on an innocent woman who only wanted to do the best job she could?

I tighten my hand on the hilt of my knife, gripping hard to center myself. Questioning a sinner's punishment is ridiculous. The Executor's word is law. The woman sinned.

But what if she didn't?

I'm jolted from my inappropriate thoughts by the sound of Efraím's footfalls, soft but unmistakable on the wooden boards of the hallway connecting the weapons gallery to the training room. He'd never walk straight into a room where I'm sitting if he can attempt to take me by surprise. Still, I know the way he moves—slightly more weight on his left foot, steps as clipped as his speech—as well as I know the pound of my own heartbeat. I grab my shirt from the floor —they keep the training rooms hot as the nine hells to build our endurance—and yank it over my head. The shirt covers the marks on my back, courtesy of a public whipping the High Priests gave me three years ago, punishment for my chronic inability to curb my prideful tongue.

The Mothers tried to cure me of my arrogance, coating my tongue with soap, lecturing me about self-abnegation, making me do penance for hours on the cold stones of the chapel floor—to no avail. Disgusted, they handed me over to the Priests for punishment.

Tied shirtless to the whipping post, I felt the lash come down again and again, my lips pressed tight to keep the mounting screams inside. I can still feel it—the bite of the lash, the warm trickle of blood running down my skin. And the Priest's harsh whisper: "Why do you not cry out, boy? Why do you cling so tightly to your pride? It gives me no pleasure to mark you this way. Only show some humility, and all of this will be over."

I shook my head, hands gripping the post to support my weight. "This isn't pride," I managed. "It's discipline. Whip me if you must. I'll not beg for you."

And so he had, each stroke harder than the one before. By the time he was done, I had my arms wrapped around the post to keep myself upright. Sweat ran down my face in rivulets, and my back was a bloody, fiery mess. But I never made a sound, aside from a grunt when the lash drove the air from my body, and I never begged the Priest to stop.

I wasn't a bellator three years ago—just a sixteen-year-old citizen —but to this day I believe the way I refused to buckle under the lash, how I stood steady despite the pain, led to my Choosing. The Bellatorum Chose me despite myself, and Efraím never lets me forget it. The Architect knows he uses every virtueless opportunity to remind me of my scars. He considers them to be my shame, and it's clear enough he thinks I should, too.

When Efraím's not around, I train with my shirt off every chance I get, as a not-so-subtle reminder to the other bellators of what I withstood when they were still mewling supplicants in the Nursery. But I'm not stupid enough to flaunt my defiance in front of Efraím, so the moment I hear his footfalls nearing the weapons room, I clothe myself and merge into the darkness.

It's not hard to conceal myself. While the rest of the Commonwealth benefits from wind turbine-powered electricity, bellators enjoy no such luxury. Our rooms are lit by candles and torches, training us to operate in ascetic circumstances. I'm standing in the shadows, clothed and silent, when he comes, my sharpened knife in my hand and a smile on my face.

He pauses at the doorway. "Very good, Westergaard," he says to the empty space where I used to be.

I grin wider, employing the misdirection that's made me such a formidable opponent in training—whether Efraím cares to admit it or not. "Did you want to speak with me, sir?" I say, making my voice issue from the far corner, beneath the display of scimitars. Efraím sighs.

"You've made your point. Kindly come out of wherever you've secreted yourself this time. I've something to say."

I know better than to try him any further. Sliding the knife back into its sheath, I step out of the shadows. "Sir," I say.

He gives a grunt of amusement. "Well, at least you can hide when you need to. That's something. Even if you're a piss-poor swordsman."

My spine stiffens at the insult. When it comes to bladework, I'm the best we have, and Efraím knows it. But part of my training is to learn how to swallow these comments, and so I restrain myself, inclining my head in acknowledgment. "My apologies, sir. I'll endeavor to improve."

He grunts again, louder this time. "You do that, Westergaard. In the meantime, I've got a reconnaissance and retrieval mission for you."

"Recon, sir?" I say, my interest piqued. "For one of the new recruits?" We're not allowed to know anything about the Bellatorum candidates until we face them in the Trials—it's an unfair advantage, given their lack of training.

Efraím nods. "A quick study as always, Bellator Westergaard," he says with the barest hint of sarcasm. Sometimes I wonder if Efraím even likes me. Other times, I'm sure he doesn't. But what does it matter? I do my duty, always. Affection doesn't enter into the equation. As a child, shunned and punished for my repeated attempts to show preference for one Nursery-mate or another, I learned that lesson the hard way.

"It would be my honor, sir." I feel that familiar grin threatening to break through—the one that's gotten me in so much trouble over the years—and do my best to suppress it. But before I get very far, Efraím holds up a hand in protest.

"Go ahead and smirk, for all the good it will do. You've not yet had the experience of dragging a recruit from his bed; they may be easily subdued, but they don't come quietly. We'll see how long that smile lasts tonight, when you have a thrashing she-devil to contend with."

The grin fades from my face. "Come again, sir? I don't understand."

"Did I stutter, Westergaard?" He hurls the words at me, each syllable a javelin.

"No, sir," I say, careful to keep my tone as empty as my expression.

He braces one shoulder against the doorway, watching me. Assessing.

"So the new recruit," I say, one hand on my weapons belt in case defensive action is called for, "it's a *female*? But...why?"

Efraím makes a noise low in his throat, and then a metallic object is flying through the air. I duck and it misses me, embedding in the wall behind where my head used to be. I crouch, wary, blade in hand, but all he does is glare. "Does your opinion matter, Bellator Westergaard?"

Eyeing him, I straighten. "No, sir."

"These are our orders, and so we will fulfill them. It's not our job to question the will of the Executor. We are warriors, not intellectuals or politicians. He says the girl is to be recruited, and so she will be. Most likely she'll be more a kitten than a she-devil if she's taken the sedative like the rest of them; regardless, we'll do our duty without inquiry or complaint. Do you have a problem with that?"

"No, sir," I say, doing my utmost to sound humble. "It would be my privilege. Thank you for your clarity."

He stalks past me and yanks the knife out of the wall, leaving a hole the natural-born will have to patch. Then he backs away, keeping me in his sights until he clears the doorway. "Take care of that, will you?"

"Yes, sir," I say, even though his order means requisitions and paperwork, the things I hate the most. He looks me over for insincerity, but he won't find any tonight. I straighten and stand at attention, hands at my sides. My face is blank, revealing nothing, my heartbeat studiously slow. I am the perfect bellator, everything Efraím has trained me to be.

He nods, satisfied, and steps into the hallway. "Good enough."

"Sir?" I say, before I lose my nerve.

Efraím turns back, exasperated. "What is it now, Westergaard?"

"The female recruit. The girl. What's her name?"

He looks at me as if he's never seen me before. "Why does that matter?"

"It doesn't, I suppose, sir," I say.

Except it does, because I am suddenly convinced I know exactly who she is.

I stare at Efraím, and he stares back. The seconds spiral down three-two-one, like the aperture of a vid camera closing, and still he doesn't speak. I don't drop my eyes in deference, like I probably should. This is a battle of wills I cannot afford to lose.

Finally he clears his throat. "You're a stubborn son-of-a-bitch, Westergaard," he says with grudging respect. "Meet me here at one o'clock, and you'll have your answer."

He spins on his heel and is gone.

25

4

EVA

The hours in the comp lab drag, even though they are usually my favorite part of the day. After work, I eat dinner with three other girls from the Rookery, but we are too nervous about tomorrow's Choosing to say much. Freed from conversation, I glance around the dining hall—and feel my heart stutter. Is it my imagination, or has each detail sprung into sharper relief—a smudge on the white wall by the door, a scratch on the pine floor, a missed stitch in the hem of Thordis Risberg's white pants? The blinds are open, and through them I see the mountains, each peak and valley as clearly delineated as if I were staring at them on a vid screen. Surely they do not always look like this.

Maybe I'm getting ill. Perhaps this is the precursor to a fever, or pre-Choosing nerves. Either way, I have no time to indulge in it. I turn back to my companions, forcing a smile. We walk back through Clockverk Square in silence, perform our nightly rituals, and climb into our respective beds.

Once we are settled, Mother Northrup pulls a straight-backed wooden chair into the center of the room. Logs crackle in the big brick fireplace behind her. Above it hangs a painting of a kneeling man, a red-robed Priest behind him, whip in hand.

"Tonight," she says without preamble, "the last night of your childhood—the last before your Choosing—I will read you the cautionary tale of Lachlan and the Selkie one final time."

I have heard this story on more occasions than I can remember, and would be happy to never listen to it again. Having no choice, I set my face with rapt attention and fix my eyes on the Mother.

Mother Northrup's dress is the color of the forest's fir trees at sunset, growing darker in the fading light. Shadows hide in the fabric's folds, spreading outward into the room. And things hide in the shadows.

A shiver runs through me at the sight, and I fight the longstanding urge to bite down on the end of my braid—not a sin, but a bad habit nonetheless. I've had these visions since childhood, imaginings of creatures that lurk in the half-light and voices that mutter in a language I can't understand—but they've been getting worse lately, as if the closer I get to the Choosing, something within me is shifting, changing.

I look away, but that doesn't help. On the bare white wall behind Mother Northrup, the shadows of the flames leap and dance. From inside them something stares at me—something with *teeth*—

The Mother lifts a familiar leather-bound book from the floor and cracks it open. A nasty, underground smell drifts from its pages. "Long ago," she begins, oblivious to the shadow-beasts looming on the wall behind her, their claws sunk deep into the Priest's painted red robes, "after the Fall, spread far across the lands of the Empire, there came to be four great Houses: Montyorke, San Fraesco, Minneska, and Satrizona. Each had its own kingdom and its own spirit animal made flesh: Montyorke the avaricious falcon and San Fraesco the seductive selkie, Minneska the prideful wolf and Satrizona the panther, dark as night and twice as treacherous. They lived as royalty, vacillating between their human skins and the pull of teeth and wings and talons, surrendering to their animal natures as they would."

The shapeshifter bit is just a fable, of course—but the four Houses did exist, coming to power after the Fall when the world was in chaos. Every citizen learns about the Houses in history class. There's San Fraesco, built by an ocean at the Empire's western edge, in a city of hills named for a forgotten saint—a place where earthquakes shook the ground as punishment for one's sins and a bridge built of gold arched over a frothing bay; Minneska, a northern land of forests and deep blue pools, so cold that your breath froze and fell to the ground as icicles, where twin cities grew alongside each other long ago; Montyorke, an island once home to millions, grounded in gluttony and seeded with the corpses of half-sunk buildings the height of a thousand men; and Satrizona, sprung from a western desert land carved from rocks, so red that in the light of sunset, it looked as if they were painted with blood.

The Houses weren't ruled by animals, naturally—but they might as well have been. The royals that led them were prideful pleasure-seekers who considered only their own comfort, leading lives even more sinful than those of the people before the Fall. They thought only of themselves, leaving the villagers and Priests to suffer.

The villagers and Priests banded together to lead an uprising. They fought the royals, who had banded together with the barbarians from the south. It was a bloody battle, a war that spanned land and sea. When the fight was over, the royals lay dead. All was chaos—but the Priests led the surviving citizens to safety, founding the Commonwealths and keeping citizens safe from sin.

Between the Commonwealths lie the Borderlands, unknown places where exiles drift, mutant creatures prowl, and the Outsiders, descendants of the barbarian warriors, still roam in hordes, looking for a way inside our gates. I imagine the Borderlands as a vast wasteland, filled with monsters like the shadows on the wall surrounding each Commonwealth, lurking and waiting to pounce.

Mother Northrup leans forward, the book balanced on one hand. Her eyes gleam in the firelight—flat disks one moment, deep pools the next. "The shapeshifters of each House were the skúmaskot, named for the dark corners in which shadows lurked. Though they were sworn to defend their Houses against harm, when the frenzy of the change was on them they thought only of indulging their basest impulses. Beneath the moon they fornicated, gorging themselves on wine and sweetmeats while the people of their villages sickened and starved."

Around me, the other girls suck in their breath, horrified. Lust and gluttony, pride and sloth—four of the seven deadly sins. How odd, I think, as I have since childhood, that they should fear such things, and not the shadow-creatures that dance on the wall. How odd that I am the only one who can see the creatures, whose imagination does not obey the dictates of the Mothers and the Priests. It is a secret I have kept for as long as I can remember.

"The selkies were the most egregious sinners. Seals, they were, living in the cold waters that lapped San Fraesco's rocky shores. At will, they came onto the beaches and left their pelts behind, swimming in their human form. The man who lay with such a creature had to choose—go with her into the sea and abandon all he knew, or steal her skin and lock it away. For without her pelt, a selkie can never return to the deep." Mother Northrup's voice is filled with a strange satisfaction, and when I risk a glance to my left and right, I see the same expression on each of my Rookery-mates' faces. Surely there must be something wrong with me—for I feel only sadness for such a wild creature to be robbed of its very skin.

The Mother turns the page. "All in San Fraesco knew better than to approach a selkie when it emerged naked and shining from the sea. But one brave man, Lachlan, had a young daughter, Margret, whom he cherished above all things. Each day, Lachlan watched as Margret grew weak for want of food. It had been a hard winter, the ground iced with the frosts of the North and the ocean reluctant to relinquish its bounty. The snares the hunters set yielded little, and the cold nipped at the barley in the fields til it withered and died on the vine.

"The selkies ignored the villagers' suffering, wallowing instead in greed and pleasures of the flesh. All feared to approach them—save one. Lachlan raged against the skúmaskot, so filled with wrath his stone cottage shook with the force of his bellowing. Though his wife, Anna, begged him to stay, he made his way to the shore on the night of the full moon. There he cupped his hands to his mouth and shouted into the wind, daring the skúmaskot to show themselves.

"From the depths, in response to his call, came the selkie Iris. On the rocks of the shore she stood, hair streaming down her back like fronds of seaweed. Bitter cold, it was, so that Lachlan could scarce feel the tips of his fingers, and his breath rattled in his lungs—but the bite of the wind and the rimy spray of the sea affected Iris not. 'Speak, man,' she said, and hers was the voice of the sharp-toothed deep.

"Lachlan did as she bid. 'My daughter, Margret, is near death. She is a lovely girl, and the child of my heart. All in the village are desperate for food, and our efforts in the fields and sea have come to naught. How dare you frolic in the waters while we are starving in our homes?'

"In desperation he lunged for her sealskin where it lay upon the rocks. 'Do as I ask,' he commanded, 'or I shall take this as my own, and you shall pay the price of its loss.'

"'If you do,' the selkie replied, 'who will feed your precious daughter? For I cannot hunt for you, should you lock away my pelt.'

"Lachlan knew this to be the truth, and hopelessness swallowed his heart. 'If you will not help me, then you are indeed a soulless beast,' he said, and pulled his skinning knife from his belt, prepared to hack the pelt to bits."

Wind rattles the windows, and the flames cast ever-taller shadows on the wall. I sink my teeth into my lip and bargain with myself: *If I don't look for ten seconds, they'll be gone. If I don't look for fifteen, they'll never come back.*

"In her cunning, Iris offered Lachlan a bargain: One night with her, in exchange for a winter's food supply for his family. Despite the vows he had made his wife and all he knew about selkies' wily nature, Lachlan agreed. He spent the night diving with the selkie in the waves, as impervious to the cold as she, taking pleasure in her body once more and again." The Mother's voice is stiff, filled with discomfort at the necessity of discussing such things.

"When the sun crept over the horizon, Lachlan lay naked on the rocks, a reed-woven basket of salmon by his side. Exhausted, he staggered to his feet, dressed, and made his way home. He envisioned the smile that would light Margret's thin face when he came through the door, how Anna would roast the salmon with the cords of garlic that hung above the hearth and they would feast together, licking their fingers clean."

Gluttony, I think. If you are starving, is it still a sin?

"But as he came up the path to his house, he saw that all inside was dark. When he pushed the door open, the fire was a dead thing, burnt to ashes inside the hearth. The air hung heavy with the tang of salt and iron.

"Lachlan rushed from room to room, calling his wife's and daughter's names. He found them at last in Margret's bed, arms wrapped around each other, his daughter cold and his wife's wrists slit, the sheet beneath them soaked with blood. For Margret had gone to join the many-headed gods in the early hours of the night, and Anna, seeking to tell her husband of their daughter's death, instead found him engaged in sin. Faced with the loss of all she loved, she went to their cottage, lay down beside Margret, and took her own life."

The many-headed gods—a primitive fantasy, nothing like the clear dictates of the Architect and the Priests. Still, though I have no real idea what is meant by the words 'wife' and 'daughter,' I can't help but imagine the woman and child twined in each other's arms, cold and bathed in blood.

"Lachlan wanted only to follow his family into death—but the selkie had bound him with her magic, making him her human familiar. His soul was tied to hers, so that he was drawn again and again to the rocky shore, compelled to do her bidding. Her word was edged as a double-sided blade: Each night of that long winter, Lachlan opened his door to find a basket of fresh-caught fish on his doorstep. At last he had all he needed to feed his family—but his family was no more, and his neighbors, believing him cursed, would have no part of his bounty. By the spring, many of them had perished of starvation, and he was alone."

The shadows dip and sweep and bite, their jaws closing on nothingness. Justice, I think, fingers twitching with the desire to reach for my braid, can be a cold and empty thing.

Mother Northup snaps the book closed and drags the chair back to its accustomed place in the corner. "And now," she says, banking the fire, "goodnight."

Mother Truelson emerges from where she's been listening by the doorway, balancing a tray on each palm. She hands one to Mother Northrup, and the two come around with tiny white pills and cups of water. They pause by each cot. I can hear them murmuring to the girls, their voices soothing. My bed is in the corner by the window, and it takes a while for Mother Northrup to reach me. I close my eyes, feigning tiredness, until I hear her footsteps, soft on the wooden floor.

"Citizen Marteinn," she says, and I blink, scooting to a sitting position.

"Good evening, Mother Northrup," I reply.

She holds out the pills and the water. "These are for you."

"Forgive my curiosity," I say, "but what are they?"

Mother Northrup smiles, a curve of her pale lips that doesn't reach her eyes. "Just a little something to help you rest. We know how excited you girls must be on Choosing Eve. Why, I remember my own Choosing like it was yesterday. I wouldn't have slept a wink if I hadn't had a little help. And it's very important you be well-rested, of course."

"Of course," I say. "Thank you for your consideration."

She stands by the bed and watches as I toss the pill into my mouth, take a gulp of the water, and swallow. And then she gives me an approving smile and moves on to the next cot. I hear her talking to Valentína, and take advantage of her distraction to turn my face toward the wall as if seeking sleep. I open my mouth, lift my tongue, and spit the pill onto the sheet, quickly covering it with the pillow. After lights out, I will crush it to bits.

I've never refused a Commonwealth dictate. If I am caught, there will be serious consequences. But on this night, the last before the path of my life is defined, I want a clear head. I've taken these pills before, know how they leave you with muddied thoughts and the sense the world is wrapped in cotton batting. I'd rather not meet my Choosing that way. If sleep eludes me, so be it.

I watch as the rest of the girls obediently take their pills and model my body language after theirs—deep sighs, blinks, and a sudden settling, their bodies sinking into the mattress, chasing sleep. Through a tiny gap in my eyelids, I see Mother Northrup standing with her hand on the light switch, surveying us. "Lights out," she announces, and the room fades into darkness. She leaves, closing the door behind her. I hear her footsteps retreat down the hallway, toward the room she shares with Mother Truelson at the other end, near the stairs.

As soon as I can't hear her anymore, I open my eyes. It takes a second to get used to the darkness, but then I can see well enough. In fact, my night vision is far better than usual. The sodium streetlights stream through the white window curtain, illuminating the humped forms of the other girls beneath their covers, the angles of their bedsteads and the boxy forms of the wooden dressers lined against the far wall. All around me, girls grunt and sigh and shift, bed frames creaking beneath their weight. Valentína, closest to me, whispers, "Please, I don't want—I'm not suited—" and then falls silent, as if even in her sleep, she knows better than to protest.

Cautiously, I sit up and glance around. I am the only one still awake. But just in case Mother Northrup comes back in for a second round of bed checks, I lie back down, clutching my blanket to my chest. I watch shadows creep across the walls, puzzling at the restlessness that grips me. It must be my imagination, but I'd swear the silent room is filled with a cacophony of heartbeats—some faster than others, skipping beats and stumbling. I press my palms to my ears to drown out the noise, but it does no good.

I'm still lying awake at two a.m., hands fisted in the bedclothes, resisting the absurd urge to chew on the end of my braid, when the window creaks open. Two black-suited figures creep soundlessly through, landing on the wooden floor and scanning the darkness. At first I think they are one of my nighttime shadow-visions, half-dream, half-hallucination. But then the figures separate from the shadows and head straight toward me. This is new, and I feel a weary curiosity. Blinking, I struggle up on my elbows to see them more clearly in the glow of the streetlight. One is taller, broad-shouldered and lean. The other is a head shorter, and stocky.

As I stare, trying to figure out whether they can possibly be real, the streetlight winks out. Before my eyes can adjust, the taller one is on me, knife at my throat.

"Don't scream," he whispers.

I don't, not that it would matter; no one in this room would hear, what with the sleeping pills, and the last thing I want is for Mother Northrup to come running. The Architect only knows what kind of trouble I'll get into if I'm imagining things again. Besides, if I opened my mouth wide enough to let out a good yell, I'd probably wind up slicing my jugular.

So I don't make a noise, but I do struggle. I can't help myself—it's instinct to resist with a sharp blade against my neck. To my shock, I manage to throw the man off. His knife goes skittering under the bed, and I hear his muttered oath. Emboldened, I thrash and fight like the rabid fox I saw once in the alley by the marketplace, biting anything that comes near and head-butting the stocky figure when it bends over me.

"By the Virtues," the taller figure hisses, irritated. I could swear I recognize his voice. "She's a fighter, yeah, sir?"

The shorter man grabs my shoulders to hold me still. "Shut up," he grunts.

"Yes, sir. But you couldn't wake those poor devils with a rockslide." He leans on me, pinning me down. I sink my teeth into his forearm and he hisses again. "Quit that, would you? It'll go the same for you, either way. Better if you cooperate."

Adrenaline surges, flooding my muscles. I head-butt the one that's got hold of my shoulders, kick out at the other, race for the window, and fling myself out. I hear the taller one cursing in that familiar voice as I fall, hurtling through the night. The ground comes rushing up and up. I hit hard and roll, trying to catch my breath.

Miraculously, I seem to be undamaged. I struggle to my knees and run. But before I've gone more than a few feet, strong arms grab me from behind, getting me in a headlock, wrestling me to the ground. I land on my back and stare up at my captor—Ari Westergaard, blood dripping onto my face from the place where I've bitten him. He kneels on my arms, well out of reach of my teeth.

"Now," he says with satisfaction, "lie still."

Since I have no choice, I obey. The streetlight is still out, and by the dim glow of the moon, I see the shorter, stocky figure clambering down the side of the building. Stupidly, I realize there is a rope. I could have climbed down and spared myself a lot of trouble.

The other man stalks over to where Ari has me pinned and glowers. I recognize him now: Efraím Stinar, the lead bellator. His nose is bloody, and I feel an involuntary grin spread across my face. I try to stop it, but it's too late.

Efraím doesn't like the grin. "What are you smiling about, girl?" he snarls. I don't answer, figuring muteness is probably my safest course of action. Instead I return his glare in silence, which Ari Westergaard fills.

"Well, I'd imagine she's got a few things to smile about, sir. For one thing, she nearly bested two trained bellators. For another, she leapt from a second-story window and landed without a scratch. And for a third, she's not dead—which is more than most people can say, after they've experienced us up-close and personally."

"Humility, Westergaard," Efraím snaps.

"Oh, I'm feeling humble, sir," Ari says, not sounding it in the least. "You and I are bleeding, and she, as I have pointed out, is not."

Efraím snorts and prods me with his foot. "What do you have to say for yourself, girl? Or do you intend to let this bastard do all your talking?"

I drag air into my lungs and ask the only question that matters. "Are you going to kill me? Because if you are, kindly get it over with. I'd rather not lie here waiting to feel your knife slide between my ribs, if it's all the same to you."

Efraím looks surprised. "Courage," he muses, gazing down at me. "An unexpected virtue. And one that will stand you in good stead in the hours to come."

Courage isn't one of the Seven Virtues, not unless the Bellatorum lives by a different code than the rest of us. I regard him, confused. "What do you mean?"

He eyes me with pity. Clouds scud across the moon, and by its revealed light, I take him in. He is clothed in the Bellatorum's signature black and bristles with weapons—a sheathed blade at his back, the leather belt buckled around his hips studded with all manner of sharp objects I do not recognize. "You have been Chosen," he says.

The suspicion that has been rankling since I saw them come through my window blooms into full-blown panic. The Bellatorum's rituals are a closely-held secret, but people talk, and I'd heard rumors they took their recruits in the night, subjecting them to a terrifying initiation. I'd dismissed it as so much hyperbolic gossip, but now—

From my prone position on the ground, I shake my head as much as Ari's grip will allow. "No."

"Aye," he says in the formal speech I have heard the Bellatorum use when addressing the High Priests. "And you must accept our challenge, Eva Marteinn. *Fac fortia et patere,* eh?"

Do brave deeds and endure—the motto of the Bellatorum Lucis. I look into his shadowed eyes and tremble. "But I—I can't—I mean, I'm a girl, and you don't—"

Efraím's lips twitch with distaste, and I grind to a halt. If this is what the Executor has decreed, then I will have to accept it—but how? It is as if he has seen into my dreams and brought to life the future I feared the most.

That must be it. I'm dreaming.

The thought lends me the strength to hold Efraím's gaze and give the correct response. *"Acta, non verba,"* I tell him. Actions, not words.

"Indeed," Efraím says. He nods at Ari, who hauls me to my feet, an implacable grip on my upper arm. "Tonight we see what you are made of, girl. Tonight, you walk with us."

5

ARI

Eva doesn't say a word during the long hike through the Commonwealth and the woods to the gorges. Doesn't ask a question or complain, though the night is cold and she is wearing only her assigned sleeping clothes—an ankle-length white nightgown, which clings to her body in ways I do my best not to notice. She just sets her jaw and trudges alongside us, her arm unyielding under my grip, though the pine needles lining the forest floor must hurt her feet and the brisk fall air is less than welcoming.

Despite my careful observation of Eva Marteinn over the years, I hadn't expected her to fight. In fact, I'd expected to come upon her asleep—if not the unnatural rest of the sleeping draughts, at least the restless slumber that afflicts those of us who reject the pills on Choosing Eve. It's a common enough rebellion among the citizens selected for the Bellatorum. Even though we don't know about the Trials, we are hypervigilant and untrusting by nature, unwilling to swallow anything that might slow our reflexes in the days to come.

Efraím and I had been arrogant, that was the only excuse. There's no way she should have been able to best us, and I shudder to think what the Executor would have said if she'd been killed in the fall from the window. But now, on the way to the rapids of the Austari, the river that cuts through the Commonwealth, we are both on our guard. My fingers dig into the material covering her upper arm, holding her fast. She couldn't get away if she tried.

The wind shifts, and I breathe deep, inhaling the smell of the woods at night: sap and dirt and the heady scent of growing things. I hear the roar of water, growing closer, and the far-off howl of the Bastarour in the off-limits forest that rings the electric fence. The Commonwealth is a series of concentric circles, carefully cultivated after the Fall and fifty miles wide at its largest circumference—the City, with its buildings and squares and gardens, housing our 10,000 citizens; then the Bellatorum's training territory, woods and gorges which most citizens have no reason to explore; then rolling hills, and the forest, a thick, tangled sprawl of trees and brush where the Bastarour prowl, contained by buried electric lines and the animals' solar-powered collars; and finally the fence itself, a towering metal structure between us and the chaos beyond. I have never seen the fence, but I know from my security training there is a gate on each side and a keypad to match. Should the Executor or his guard need to depart for any reason, this is the route they take.

The Bastarour are particularly unnerving—genetically modified, species-blended beasts created in the gen lab for maximum savagery, endurance, and protection. If one of the barbarians were unfortunate enough to stumble upon the Commonwealth from the outside—and sufficiently resourceful to outwit the fence—the creatures would devour them the moment they landed on the ground. As for those who leave from the inside, none of the exiles banished to the woods have ever come out again. Not alive, anyhow.

The roar of the water grows louder, drowning out the Bastarours' howls, and within me, anticipation rises. I don't change my expression, don't vary my pace or the pressure of my hand on her arm, but I could swear Eva senses it anyhow. Her head turns toward mine, and in the dim glow of Efraím's flashlight I see her delicate nostrils flare, as if she is sampling my scent. Her eyes go wide, and she turns away, eyes fixed on the path.

I feel my own eyes narrow. We learn how to hone all our senses in training, how to detect the pheromone shift that marks anger or fear or joy. But there's no way Eva could sense such a thing. It has to be a coincidence.

Before I can consider this further, we emerge on the ridge above the rapids. The full complement of the Bellatorum are massed, two hundred strong, clad in black. Here and there, a blade glints in the firelight flickering from torches staked at the edges of the clearing. A thrill runs through me, seeing them. We are forbidden attachment, but the Bellatorum is different. Together, we are brothers in arms, the closest to the antiquated notion of family that the Commonwealth allows. Though I would never say such a thing aloud, I crave the sense of belonging membership in its ranks gives me. It is foolish, verging on sinful—a weakness I keep close to my heart.

The bellators stand at attention, their eyes fixed on us. In Efraím's absence, Kilían Bryndísarson, the lead interrogator, has point. He stands in front—the tip of an arrow made up of the thirty elite bellators that comprise Efraím's inner circle—blade unsheathed in his hand, his close-cropped red hair gleaming in the torchlight. The rest of the bellators fan out behind Efraím's Thirty, coiled and silent. It is the highest honor to be named one of the Thirty, who carry out classified tasks beyond those assigned to the rank-and-file. As an apprentice, membership is beyond my reach; but one day soon, I am determined to stand with them.

Kilían inclines his head when he sees Efraím. *"In girum imus nocte et consumimur igni,"* he says in greeting. *We enter the circle at night and are consumed by fire.*

Efraím smiles, a quick, fierce baring of teeth. *"Igne ferroque,"* he replies. *With fire and iron.*

Behind Kilían, the Bellatorum speak as one and I with them, our voices echoing over the ridgetop and down the gorge. *"Igne natura renovatur integra."* *Through fire, nature is reborn whole.*

Eva stands between us, silent and motionless, tension thrumming through her body. I can hardly blame her: Gathered like this, brotherhood or no, the Bellatorum are an intimidating sight. I am one of them, and I still feel the cold spot between my shoulder blades that alerts me to the presence of predators, my adrenaline jacked in preparation for a fight. I remember how it felt to be in her place, trapped on a mountainside by two hundred warriors with no knowledge of what was to come. It wasn't that long ago for me.

"Don't be afraid," I say to her, low-voiced. "It won't help you."

Eva turns those deep brown eyes of hers on me and doesn't say a word. She doesn't have to; the expression on her face is eloquent enough. I'd only meant to offer her assistance, but it's clear she thinks I'm condescending to her—or worse, posing a threat. She looks at me as if, given the opportunity, she'd like nothing more than to sink her teeth into me again.

Annoyed, I face front and push her forward, following Efraím to the edge of the rapids. The Bellatorum part, letting us through. They are too well trained to make a sound, but I can feel the incredulity and unease that rise from them when they realize Eva is a girl, feel the weight of their gazes as we pass through their ranks.

It is a relief when we emerge on the overlook alongside the other two recruits, flanked by a guard on either side. The other prospective bellators look likely enough—fit and strong. One of them has fifty pounds on Eva; the other, perhaps seventy. They both have the advantage of height and reach. Eva's head turns, taking the recruits in. Alarm flashes over her face, quickly subdued.

Kilían has followed us, and as we come to a standstill, he speaks. "These are all of them, Efraím? Just these three?"

"This is it," Efraím says. "A pitiful bunch, I agree, but what are we to do?"

A smile lifts one side of Kilían's lips. "Our duty, I imagine," he says.

"Indeed, Kilían. Step away," he says, motioning at the guards. We obey, retreating so the three stand in isolation at the lip of the cliff. Beside the others, Eva looks very small.

Efraím straightens and pulls a short blade from his belt. He flips it over his knuckles, the way he does when he's hypnotizing an intractable interrogation subject. The boys' eyes follow the blade, but Eva's gaze locks with mine, then fixes on Efraím's. And finally, she speaks, her voice low but clear. "What is this?"

I don't expect Efraím to answer, but he does nonetheless. "This," he says with exquisite kindness, "is your first Trial."

He pushes her off the overlook, sending her into the roiling water below.

6

EVA

I fall down into the gorge, a yawning chasm. The spray of the rapids is icy, stinging me through my thin nightgown like a thousand tiny needles. *I'm going to die,* I think. *They brought me up here to kill me.*

My eyes are squeezed shut. When I force them open, I see whitewater rushing toward my body at a terrifying speed. I don't see how I can survive this; if the impact doesn't kill me, surely I will drown or go into hypothermic shock.

Someone is screaming: I can make out the noise over the oncoming rapids, a high, reedy sound. I am afraid it is me—but my lips are shut tight, my jaw clenched so hard it hurts. It must be one of the other recruits—one of those boys, calling out in terror as he falls.

I never wanted this, but I'll be damned if I'll let them murder me. I will fight for my life. If I die trying, so be it.

I make my body into a straight line, hands against my sides and my toes pointed, the perfect arrow. The world streams by, faster and faster. Inside myself I have gone to a staticky, empty place. There is nothing but the thought that somehow, I will survive. I have a second to wonder if this is how the Bellatorum feel when they kill.

My feet break the surface of the water and I suck in a giant breath. The water gives, it must, but still I feel as if I am hitting concrete. *You survived a fall from a second-story window,* I remind myself. *You can survive this.*

And then the water takes me down.

For a moment I am disoriented. There is no air, and I am choking, spinning, the pull of the rapids sucking me deeper. I kick for the surface with everything I have, my lungs aching, and break through, getting my head above water long enough to heave another ragged breath. The water sucks me down again, a greedy, grasping hand that has my body in its unforgiving grip.

Pure stubbornness saves me. That, or an intervention from the Architect himself. I fight my way to the surface once more and see a branch from a nearby tree extending over the water. Desperate, I lunge and miss, scraping the skin off my palms. I gasp in pain as the rapids drag me under, inhale water, and come up sputtering. With my last bit of strength, I lunge for the tree limb again and catch hold. For a second I hang there, disbelieving. And then, hand over hand, I haul myself in toward shore, where I collapse, panting.

I lie there, coughing to clear my lungs and checking to make sure my limbs are still attached. My abraded palms ache. I'm freezing, shivering so hard my teeth clack together, narrowly missing my tongue. How will I fight if I am hypothermic?

I'm reassured that the other two recruits won't be able to fight, either—but when I'm able to lift my head, I see the two of them being towed to shore atop inflatable rafts. My mouth falls open. How did they rate a rescue? Would the Bellatorum have let me drown?

Indignation drives me to my knees, then upward. I grasp the trunk of the tree that saved me, ignoring the pain in my hands, and pull myself to my feet. At the top of the cliff I see the dark mass of the Bellatorum, edged by torchlight. They are up there, waiting—but for what?

I stiffen, feeling suddenly as if I am being watched—and not by the Bellatorum. There is no way they can see me, not at this distance, down here in the dark. No, there is someone else, closer. I can't hear him—but I know he is there. My back against the tree, I turn my head left and right, searching.

The other two recruits are onshore now, coughing and choking. They're not paying me a bit of attention, nor are the bellators who ferried them back. On slightly higher ground, concealed by a clump of sugar maples, I can see them, but they have no way to return the favor. Still, I can feel the weight of someone's eyes on me.

Slowly, I bend and pick up a rock from the dirt. My hands are trembling, but I tighten my grip and don't let go. "I know you're there," I say. "You might as well come out."

A figure materializes from the blackness under the copse of trees to my right: a lone bellator, not much older than I but deep-voiced nonetheless. "Put down the rock, girl," he says.

"No," I reply, with a confidence whose origins bewilder me. "Unless you'd care to surrender your blade."

At this, the man laughs, a rusty, unused chuckle that forces its way up from his chest. "Keep your pebble if you want, citizen. You won't get far with it, anyhow. You'll be needing both your hands for the task ahead."

"Which is what?"

With his chin, he gestures toward the hulking rise of rock to the right of the rapids. "You've got to get back up there somehow, eh?"

"You want me to climb—that?" I say incredulously. "In the dark? Barefoot? Wearing this?"

He shrugs. "I don't make the rules. You'll climb, or you'll forfeit your Choice, and pay the price."

I clutch my rock, feeling desperate, and resist the urge to snap that I didn't choose this situation in the least. I'd love to relinquish my recruitment to the Bellatorum—but I've seen what happens to citizens who fail their Choosing; they are reduced to little more than natural-borns. I'll be damned if I let that happen to me.

Still, cold and exhausted as I am, wearing this flimsy nightgown—unlike the male recruits, in their rough but serviceable cotton pajamas—I'll never be able to make it to the top of that cliff. I'll be scratched to the Sins and back before I go five feet.

Chastened, I bow my head. "I just—I don't think I can do it," I mumble, pitching my voice beneath the roar of the rapids.

The bellator takes a step closer, lured by the scent of surrender. "What's that you say, girl?" His voice is so condescending I want to punch him, a sin in itself. But I don't. I bide my time.

Likely, I will have to commit a sin far worse than throwing a punch before this night is done. I don't reflect on this. I can't. Right now, my priority is to survive.

"I'm cold," I say, trying to sound as pathetic as possible. "I want to go back to the Rookery. Could I borrow your shirt, just until I get home?"

He laughs again. "You want to borrow my *shirt*?" The way he says it, you'd think I suggested borrowing his skin.

"Please," I whisper. "I'm so cold. And look—I cut my finger. It's bleeding." Widening my eyes to look defenseless, I hold out my free hand for his inspection.

The man sneers. But as I'd hoped, he comes closer, bending his head to inspect my injured finger. This is my chance. I draw back and smash the rock into his skull with all the force in me. He lets out a surprised grunt and goes down hard, spilling blood. Lucky for me, the sound is camouflaged by the roar of the water, compounded by the coughing of the other two recruits.

I have never hit anyone before, much less clubbed them with a rock—but there is no time to dwell on what I have done. The moment the man hits the ground, I am on my knees next to him. I check his pulse to make sure he isn't dead, then undo his weapons belt and tug it free. What I really want is the big blade down his back, his sverd—but it's wedged into its scabbard by some kind of trickery. In the dark, I can't see how to pry it loose. So I shove the harness down his arms with the blade still sheathed, then yank his pants and shirt off, pull my sopping nightgown over my head, and exchange it for the rest of his gear. He lies there in his undergarments, motionless, a small pool of blood seeping from his head, as I roll up the sleeves of his shirt, cuff his pants, and cinch his weapons belt around my waist.

By a stroke of luck, he has a pair of gloves stashed in his pockets. They're too big, but I put them on anyhow. His shoes are hopelessly huge, and his socks won't give me the friction I need to climb, so I'll have to stay barefoot. Still, my clothing situation has vastly improved. I wring out my braid, which has somehow survived, and drag him by his legs into the copse of trees he came out of. And then I head for the cliff.

The climb is easier than I'd imagined. There are ropes fixed to the rock and decent footholds. The downed bellator's gloves protect my abused hands, and, fueled by adrenaline and my unexpected conquest, I climb faster than I imagined possible. The top of the cliff is ten feet above my head when I feel weight on the rope below.

My initial fear is that the bellator I hit has woken up and is pursuing me. But no—when I peer down the rope I see the pale face of one of the other recruits. I shouldn't be able to make him out at this distance, but I am sure it is him nonetheless. Still, I climb faster. I don't know if I'm competing against myself, the others, or the Bellatorum. Either way, it's foolish to cede an advantage.

Finally, I haul myself over the edge of the cliff and drop the rope. Even through the gloves, my palms are stinging, and my calf muscles burn. The Bellatorum are nowhere in sight. I am alone.

It is a trick, a trap. It has to be. I back away and scan the shadows, looking for movement. But before I get very far, I hear Efraím's voice, issuing from somewhere to my left. "Well done, girl. You've surprised me for the second time tonight."

Instinctively, my hand drops to my stolen weapons belt. "What do you want?"

"You," he says, his tone matter-of-fact. Now his voice is coming from the patch of darkness under the trees, but I could swear he hasn't moved. I would have heard him. "Tonight we hunt you, Eva Marteinn."

"And if you catch me?" I force my voice not to waver.

He snorts. "Oh, we will catch you. It's just a matter of when."

Behind me I hear the other two recruits making their way up the rock. Soon, my advantage will be lost—if indeed I have one to begin with. My heart pounds harder, and I shiver in my borrowed clothes. "There are two hundred of you, and one of me," I point out. "That hardly seems fair."

Another voice issues from the shadows, this one amused. "Actually, there are three of you. And we'll even give you a head start. Three minutes. Think of it as a game of hide-and-seek, Citizen Marteinn, if that makes you feel better."

Laughter rises from the darkness between the trees, and I bristle. "You'd better hope you're not the one who catches me, Bellator Westergaard." My words issue between clenched teeth, and the laughter cuts off abruptly, as if someone has flipped a switch.

45

"Oh?" Ari's voice is sharp-edged, drifting from the trees overhead. "Had I, little warrior? What will you do?"

I don't bother looking upward. I know he isn't there. From a deep well inside me there comes a surge of rage. I am tired of being ripped from my bed and chased out of windows, marched through the woods like a criminal and tossed off cliffs into a maelstrom of raging water. I'd requested a quiet career in comp tech, not this uncivilized insanity. Wrath is forbidden in the Commonwealth, but I do not care.

As contained as the Bellatorum may be when they stalk the Commonwealth's streets, tonight in the firelit forest I see them for the savage, wild creatures they really are—little better than the beasts all the fables warn us against becoming. I am not one of them—not a hired blade, nor a killer. But as my fury crests higher, burning away the chills that rack my muscles, a strange feeling rises alongside it, as terrifying as it is unfamiliar.

Facing a horde of invisible warriors who want to hunt me like an animal, at liberty to speak my mind and bare the ugliness in my heart, I feel…free.

The Architect damn Ari Westergaard, and all his kind.

"Chase me if you will," I tell him, the words coming from some unknown, careless place, as if the two of us are alone here in the woods at the edge of the world. "Catch me if you can. And we'll see who hurls the insults then."

There is a brief silence. Then Ari replies, his voice ice cold, "Challenge me and pay the price, Eva Marteinn. What say you, sir? Should she run?"

When Efraím speaks again, he sounds resigned. "Three minutes, girl," he says. "And pray to the Architect that my apprentice is in a giving mood."

He doesn't have to tell me twice. I run for the woods, straight through the column of bellators I'm sure are scattered in its midst. Behind me I hear the other recruits cresting the cliff, hear Efraím explaining the rules of the hunt to them. I couldn't care less, save for the distraction and the noise that covers my retreat. I run faster than I ever have, and the night opens for me, coming alive. It seems to me I can smell the creatures that call the forest home, see each tree and fallen log, so it requires no effort to avoid them. I count as I run, second by second, making my way ever closer to the three-minute mark. And then I shimmy up a tree, high as I can go, and crouch in its branches, waiting.

I haven't climbed a tree since I was a child, but the running is familiar enough. Three times a week, our physical trainers make us exercise—it forestalls bodily excess and calms the mind. In the weeks leading up to the Choosing, I've pounded the track harder and faster than usual, driven by anxiety. I've forced myself to hold back, to stay with the pack of seventh-form girls, lest the trainer note my heightened speed and divert my Choice to a path more suited for citizens with physical acuity.

But maybe he has noticed, and informed the Choosing Committee anyhow. It's the only explanation I have, and I curse myself for a careless sinner. Regardless, tonight my anxiety-fueled adrenaline is all that stands between myself and certain capture, and I give thanks for it.

I have no idea how much time passes. Enough for my bruised muscles to protest, for me to realize my feet are bleeding. Enough to wonder if this entire endeavor has been a fool's pursuit. I count the space between heartbeats and press myself against the trunk of the tree, a knife from the borrowed weapons belt in my hand. I'd love to examine the belt's contents more closely, but I don't dare make a sound or do more than pull this one knife free. Its handle feels strange in my hand, awkward. I have never held a knife like this before.

What will Ari Westergaard do if he catches me? I think, and have to suppress a shiver. *Will he kill me?* I'd been foolish to goad him into anger. I knew better. And now, as he warned, I will doubtless pay the price.

I can hear the bellators moving quietly through the woods, hear the occasional sound of a struggle. Perhaps they have captured the other two recruits? I feel almost sorry for the two boys, with their sopping clothes and their lack of weapons. Perhaps they will even be relieved to be caught.

I don't hear footsteps coming in my direction until it's too late. They stop at the base of the tree, and then I hear a familiar laugh. "Hello," Ari Westergaard says, conversationally enough. "Care to join me?"

By the Sins. "Not really," I reply.

"Ah. I thought you'd say that. Well, too late."

The arrogance in his voice pushes me over the edge. Forgetting my resolution to control my temper, I throw the knife—not at the place where his voice is coming from, but to the left, where a form shifts in the shadows beneath the tree. To my surprise, the blade flies true, and a second later, I hear his sharp intake of breath.

"You put a hole in my *pants.*" He sounds offended. "I'll have to requisition another pair."

"Attachment to items of clothing is a sin," I retort.

If I could see Ari, I feel certain he'd be rolling his eyes. "I'm not attached, citizen. One pair of pants is as good as another. I just hate paperwork."

I tug another knife loose from the weapons belt—this one heavier in my hand, weighted for throwing. "How do you feel about your shirts?"

He doesn't answer, and I let the second knife fly. This time it draws blood; I can smell the iron tang, clear in the crisp night air. "Not bad," he muses, sounding infuriatingly unharmed. "If only you could put an end to your opponents by shaving the skin off their forearms."

From my perch in the tree, I see him draw the sverd at his back. The blade glints in the thin stream of moonlight that filters through the trees. "Out of curiosity, whose knives are you throwing at me? I could have sworn you began this evening unarmed and wearing your nightclothes. Now there you sit, outfitted like a bellator, weapons and all."

I don't say a word, and he throws the sword high, letting it fall end over end until it lands, trembling, in the earth between his feet. One hand resting on its hilt, he lifts his face to mine. "What did you do, Eva?" he whispers.

"If you must know, I tricked one of the bellators by the water into believing I was cold and hurt. It wasn't that hard. I mean, I was freezing, and I'd nicked my hand on the branch I used to pull myself out of the rapids."

As soon as the explanation leaves my mouth, I want to take it back. What if my little ruse might come in handy again? Not for the first time, I curse Ari Westergaard and his virtueless ability to bring out the worst in me.

Beneath the tree, I see him go still. "You pulled yourself out? But we saw rafts—"

"Those were for the boys. I got out on my own, no thanks to any of your bellator brothers. If it had been up to them, I'd be fish food right now." I wrap one hand around the branch to steady myself. "But when that bellator told me I had to climb the cliffs, I knew I didn't stand a chance. So I told him I was bleeding. When he came over to see, I hit him over the head with a rock and stole his clothes and his weapons belt."

"I see. What did he look like?"

The question startles me. "I don't know. He had a deep voice. He was stocky, broad through the shoulders, maybe a few inches taller than I am. His hair was wavy—I remember noticing that, before I hit him."

Ari is laughing again, but this time I don't think it's at my expense. "That would be Bellator Reykdal Skau. He didn't save you, so you laid him out with a rock and disarmed him. I'd say you have a fair talent for revenge, Citizen Marteinn."

"Revenge?" I say, puzzled. "It wasn't like that."

"Of course it was," Ari says, pulling his blade from the ground and wiping it clean on his shirt.

"It wasn't," I say stiffly. "He had something I needed. I took it. That's all. Revenge didn't enter into the equation."

"I see," he says again, not sounding as if he believes me in the slightest. "Well, Eva, as enlightening as this has been, I'm afraid target practice is over. I'm going to have to ask you to come down."

My heart jolts, then starts racing. "No." The word leaves my mouth without volition, startling me.

There is a pause, and then Ari gives a low chuckle. "No?" he says, sounding as incredulous as I feel.

"No," I repeat, digging my free hand into the bark of the tree. "I won't. Come up and get me, if you want me so badly."

He exhales so loudly I can hear it, more of a snort than anything else, and in the silence that falls between us, I realize what I've said. Blood rushes to my cheeks, heating my face to a fever pitch, but I don't move an inch. Maybe it's terror that holds me in place, or pure pigheadedness. All I know is, if the Bellatorum are going to make me play this game, I won't make it easy for them.

"You want me to come after you?" Ari says. "And force you to the ground? Are you sure, little warrior?"

I grip the hilt of one of my remaining knives. "I don't want you to do a virtueless thing, except go away and leave me alone."

"Such language, Eva. And you know I can't do that." He sounds different now, closer. I glance down into the shadows and realize he is circling the tree, his feet crunching in the fallen leaves, determining the best angle of approach. My heart quickens, and I draw the knife.

"Come down. I won't ask again." It's his persuasive voice, the one I'd swear could talk one of the Architect's fire-demons into setting itself aflame. Bracing, I steel myself against its sway. He was easy enough to provoke before; maybe that strategy will work again, and distract him long enough that he'll make a careless mistake.

"What, are you afraid you won't be able to best me, Bellator Westergaard?" I say, imbuing my voice with as much scorn as I can muster. "I'm just a girl in a tree. Why the reluctance? Perhaps you're all talk, after everything."

He growls, a menacing sound that makes me shiver. The rustling of the leaves stops, and in the moonlight I see the glint of his green eyes as they measure the distance between us. "Ah, Eva. You really shouldn't have said that."

The tree shakes as he leaps, lunging for one of the lower branches and catching hold. Alarmed, I reach for the limb above me with the hand not clutching the knife, but the tree quakes under his weight and I lose my balance. The branch breaks, plummeting to the ground, just as Ari Westergaard's blade presses against my throat.

He gives a low hum of satisfaction as the metal creases my skin. With his free hand, he forces the knife from my grasp, sending it tumbling after the broken branch.

"Come down," he says.

7

ARI

I divest Eva of her stolen weapons belt and march her back through the woods to the rendezvous point, careful to touch her only with my blade. Whether it's because the point of my dagur is digging into her back or because she knows it's a fruitless endeavor, she doesn't fight me.

While her compliance makes my life easier, part of me wishes she would fight back. Something about her stubbornness, her raw courage and determination, draws me like a magnet to its pole. Thinking about her climbing out of the river, dark hair dripping down her back and her thin nightgown hugging the curves and angles I'd felt when I'd pinned her to the ground outside the Rookery —ah, how I wish Efraím had assigned me to be her recovery agent by the river. She wouldn't have gotten the best of me like she did with Skau—but by the Sins, how I would have loved for her to try.

I steal a glance at her through the thinning dark and realize she is staring over her shoulder at me, her dark eyes fixed on my face. I feel as if she sees right through me—all my thoughts and secret desires, the relentless ambition that drives me to train until my hands are calloused and my muscles aching, the nights I've spent picturing her face and denying myself, again and again. Never mind what I'm thinking right now.

Blood rushes to my face, burning, and I turn away so she can't see. "Keep moving, little warrior," I snap.

"Don't call me that." Her voice is low, threatening. It makes me laugh.

"You do know I've got a knife at your back, yeah?"

"I don't care. I'm not your pet."

"I'll call you what I want," I say, letting my voice drop into the cadence I use to coax subjects in the interrogation chamber into revealing their secrets—the one I'd used to make Eva tell me what she'd done to Skau, that hopeless sinner. Efraím will never let such carelessness pass without punishment. "Besides, it's a compliment. You're a fighter, for all you haven't got any training. That was a clever ruse, tricking Skau that way. And just look at what you've done to my clothes."

"Now you're mocking me."

"Maybe a little," I admit, stepping over a log.

"Well, don't." She's looking straight ahead, but I can still feel the fierce weight of those dark eyes on me. "This may be one big joke to you, but it's serious to me. This is the last thing I ever wanted. You're nothing but trained killers."

The accusation stings, and reflexively, I lash out. "Oh, really? What about that day in Clockverk Square? You took a man's life long before I ever did, Citizen Marteinn."

Eva stops dead. If my reflexes weren't honed to perfection, I might've run her through. I pull my blade back just in time, ease it upward. "You remember," she says.

"Of course I do," I say, my voice deliberately indifferent. "Who wouldn't?"

"That's not what I mean," she says, turning to face me. I draw the blade away and let her. By the nine hells, the look on her face—I am falling drowning going under. Here in the woods with my blade inches from her throat, her in those ridiculous too-big clothes—I am supposed to be delivering her to Efraím for the Reckoning, but all I want to do is stand here forever with her looking at me like that. As if she sees me—all of me. Not just what I show the Commonwealth, but who I really am. It is terrifying and wonderful and dangerous all at once, and I want it. I want *her*.

"You stood up for me," she says. "You didn't look away."

"Don't talk about that," I say, my voice a rasp.

"I never thanked you. I couldn't. But that day—you gave me courage. You were the only one who didn't turn from me."

She steps closer, into my blade, and now I can smell her—sweat and dirt and river water and a sweet, spicy scent I can't identify. "Step back," I say, forcing the words through the sandpaper of my throat, but she doesn't move.

"Thank you," she whispers. I can feel her breath on my face.

My hand shakes and the dagur shakes with it and I look at them both as if they belong to someone else. This has never happened to me before. I tighten my grip so Eva won't feel the tremble of the blade against her skin, but too late: I smell the blood before I see it, a thin line welling on her neck, black in the dim light.

"I warned you," I say, as if bleeding her is something I intended all along. "Step away."

Eva moves, and for a moment I believe she is actually going to do what I've asked. But then I feel the cold slide of metal against my belly, piercing unerringly through the tear in my shirt to press against my skin.

She has pulled a knife on me.

We stand there, my blade against her throat and hers against my stomach. And then I start to laugh. "Where did that come from?"

She doesn't answer, but then again, she doesn't have to. She took advantage of my pride, that I assumed I had control of the situation. I didn't search her, just took the weapons belt. I figured she'd realize there was no point in fighting.

I have underestimated her—again.

"My compliments." I disarm her and grab her by the shoulder, spinning her around. "You're full of surprises, little warrior. Now march, before I lose my patience and draw more than a line of blood."

Eva obeys, her back straight. I have never been so glad not to see someone's face in my life.

She *took* me—like Skau, like a common mark. She played me, assessed my reaction, and used it to distract me. No one else could have gotten the drop on me like that.

I'm mad at myself—but I'm also intrigued as hell. The rest of the way through the woods, I imagine training with Eva, hunting her, working her in the interrogation chamber. What would it take to break a girl like this?

It's been a long time since I've felt this kind of challenge, and something in me rises up, eager. Which just proves what a fool I am. She messes with my concentration, subverts my focus. Assuming she passes the Trials, someone else will mentor her, train her. She'll be assigned to one of the experienced bellators, the way I was assigned to Efraím. I'll only have cause to come up against her during sparring matches or competitions—and that will be temptation enough for me.

Occupied by these dark thoughts, I drive Eva before me into the clearing. The sun is breaking over the crags, and by its light I see the semi-circle of bellators, faces set in an expressionless mask. In the center of the curve stand the other two recruits. And in front of them stands Efraím.

He turns when he hears us approach. "Took you long enough," he says.

"I'm sorry, sir." I press the blade against Eva's throat, feeling more like myself. "She led me on a bit of a chase. But as you can see, it all worked out in the end."

"Hmmm," Efraím says. "And what of her threats, Bellator Westergaard? Does the kitten have teeth, after all?"

I shrug the shoulder that isn't attached to the hand holding the blade. "She attacked my clothes, sir. A vicious assault."

A low murmur of laughter spreads through the Bellatorum's ranks, choked off as Efraím swivels to glare at them. "What a shame," he says, turning his attention back to me. "More paperwork for you, Westergaard. We all know how you dislike that. I trust you paid her back in kind?"

I twitch the blade to the side, revealing the line of clotted blood at her throat. "Just a nick. No real harm done."

Eva doesn't move, but I can feel the indignation emanating from her all the same. My lips curve up in a smile. "To be fair, sir, she did draw first blood," I say, switching the knife to my other hand and holding up my sword arm so they can see.

Efraím makes a noise low in his throat, somewhere between amusement and annoyance. "And how did she manage that?"

"She was in a tree, sir. And she'd gotten Skau's weapons belt. I could have gone up there after her right away, but I was curious to see what she'd do first." I leave out the part where Eva refused to come down, how she goaded me into retrieving her—stubborn, infuriating citizen. "Her aim isn't bad, considering. I was impressed."

Now Efraím does laugh, a full-throated chuckle I've rarely heard from him. "You let her throw knives at you from a superior position, in the dark, with no sense of her ability? Fitting, Westergaard, very fitting. The two of you are well-matched indeed."

I stiffen. "Come again, sir?"

But he turns away from me, still laughing. "That's Skau's belt you've got strapped over your own, eh, Westergaard?"

"Yes, sir."

"Ah, well. At least you aren't as much of a fool as that sinner. Bellator Skau, front and center." He beckons, and the crowd parts. Two of the Thirty bring Skau forward, each gripping one of his arms. He stands there in his smallclothes, weaponless and shivering, his eyes downcast. A streak of dried blood runs from his temple to his chin, evidence of Eva's assault with the rock. The bellator to his right —Jakob Riis—tosses a shapeless pile of cloth to the ground in front of Skau, where it lands with a splat: Eva's discarded nightgown.

"Here's your conquest, girl," Efraím says. "Do you have anything to say to him before he receives the punishment that's his due?"

Eva starts to nod, then thinks better of it. Efraím waves his hand, as if he has only just realized I'm holding her at knifepoint. "Let her go, Westergaard. She's hardly a danger to us."

That's what you think. She was a danger to Skau, and very nearly a danger to me as well. But against a force of warriors two hundred strong—well, perhaps Efraím is right. What can she do?

I lower the blade and Eva steps away, throwing me a look of such loathing, I almost take a step back myself. She stalks toward Skau, unarmed and wearing his oversized clothes. She ought to look ridiculous, but she doesn't.

She looks like a weapon.

"On your knees, Skau," Efraím demands, and he obeys, sinking down dizzily into the rock-studded dirt. The stones must hurt his knees, but he gives no sign. He stares straight ahead, as if he is seeing something other than the scene unfolding in the clearing. I don't

EMILY COLIN

blame him in the slightest. To be bested by an untrained citizen—a girl, no less—and wind up bladeless and almost naked in front of the brotherhood…I can think of few more humiliating fates.

Eva comes to a halt in front of him, a little more than arm's length away. Her instincts are excellent, and despite myself, I am impressed. She fills his field of vision, so he has no choice but to look at her. One hand drops to her waist, where she has had to roll the waist of his pants up to make them fit, and with a shock, I realize what she is doing—emphasizing that his clothes are much too big for her. That she took him, despite the disparity in their size and training.

There are some among us who never learn the finer psychological nuances of combat, who have aptitude only for brute force and the blade. You can break a man without laying a finger on him, if you know his mind and heart well enough. Excellent instincts, indeed.

Skau's eyes refocus on Eva, and in their depths I see the burn of hatred. She has made an enemy this night. But he kneels there and doesn't move. He knows better.

"Last words, Citizen Marteinn?" Efraím prompts her. He has used her title on purpose—another dig at Skau's failure to do his duty—and I see a muscle near the kneeling man's jaw twitch.

Eva takes an infinitesimal step closer, forcing Skau to look up at her. And then her lips lift in a smile of surpassing sweetness. "Thank you for your shirt," she says. "I really was cold."

Skau lifts his chin. "Generosity is a Virtue," he says in his rumbling voice. "Even when coerced. It's as the master strategist Sun Tzu said: *All warfare is based on deception.* Tonight, you were the better warrior, Eva Marteinn."

The words emerge gritty, dragged from his throat—but he says them, and that is enough for Efraím. He turns his attention to the other two recruits, standing silent, dripping wet and filthy, in the curve of the circle.

"Daríus Elison and Hendrik Karsten," Efraím says. "Your performance in the Trials has been adequate at best. Both of you had to be pulled from the water, whereas Eva Marteinn devised her own rescue. You stand before me soaking wet and in your nightclothes, whereas Citizen Marteinn disarmed a trained bellator and appropriated his gear. She beat you to the top of the cliff, wounded

56

her pursuer, and avoided capture longer than both of you—despite provoking one of our best fighters into hunting her."

It takes a second to realize Efraím means me. But before I can savor this unexpected compliment, he is off again. "However, you did complete the Trials in the allotted time. We will therefore welcome you into the Bellatorum on a provisional basis, pending your formal recognition in the Choosing Ceremony and your performance during the initial training period."

Elison and Karsten look pleased to hear this news. If they take offense at being unfavorably compared to Eva, they give no sign. The heavier, blond one inclines his head, fighting back a self-congratulatory smile; the other one, who has a lot to learn about dealing with our head bellator, attempts to curry favor through obsequience. "Thank you, sir," he says. "I won't let you down, sir. You'll see—"

"Silence, Citizen Karsten." Efraím's voice rings through the clearing, echoing down into the gorge and out from the trees. The boy chokes on whatever he was going to say next, sputtering into silence. "When I want your opinion, citizen, I'll ask for it." His gaze rakes the two of them from head to toe. "Until then, you will be silent. Your mentors will be assigned after the Choosing Ceremony, provided the two of you make it that far. Understood?"

The two of them squeak out a garbled, overlapping version of, "Sir, yes sir!" Efraím ignores them, turning his attention to Eva. I feel my body tense, and will myself to relax. Her fate is of no consequence to me. In fact, I remind myself, the further away from me she is, the better. She is an interference, a distraction I can ill afford. Just look at what happened in the woods.

"Citizen Marteinn," he says, and Eva snaps to attention, copying the other bellators with eerie exactitude. For someone with such contempt for our kind, she demonstrates rare aptitude and skill.

"Sir," she says.

"You have performed well tonight, citizen. You've exceeded all my expectations. The Bellatorum is honored to welcome its first female recruit into our ranks."

It's the nicest thing I've ever heard Efraím say to anyone. Hearing it, I feel a harsh, unwelcome pang of jealousy. Eva's mouth actually falls open in shock before she remembers herself and shuts it, her teeth slamming together with an audible click. "Yes, sir," she says, each word sharp-edged as a shuriken—a throwing star. "It would be my privilege, sir."

For the Architect's sake. "A great privilege," I say before I can stop myself, "to have amongst our ranks the scourge of shirts and pants everywhere."

Efraím shoots me a disgusted glance. "Westergaard," he says. "Meet your new apprentice."

The air leaves my lungs. "Excuse me, sir. I must have misheard. I thought you said—"

"You misheard nothing, Westergaard. Those are my orders, come down from the Executor himself. Personally, I think it's brilliant. If ever I met someone who was able to put an end to that smart mouth of yours, this is the one. The Architect knows I haven't been able to do it."

I grit my teeth, a thousand objections jammed in my throat. *I'm too young. I'm not qualified. I'm still in training myself. What do I know about having an apprentice?* All of which pales beside the real reason I can't be Eva Marteinn's mentor: *When she's around me, I can't think. I forget myself. She'll compromise me. Every day, she will test my commitment and my vows.*

Maybe this is the reason for the Executor's decree.

Over the years, I have come to think of Eva as a challenge, my own personal temptation. What I imagine doing with her is the greatest of sins. Resisting it is good practice for my soul, like sparring with Efraím is good practice for my body. Both will keep me alive. But to have her in such close proximity, day after day—that will test my limits, and sorely. I cannot help but wonder if somehow the Executor has foreseen this. Maybe during one of the juniper smoke-induced trances the Bellatorum uses to train us to control our minds as well as our bodies, the interrogators have seen something untoward. Maybe they have made me forget.

I force myself to breathe, my heartbeat to still. The other bellators are all staring at me, predators who will exploit my smallest weakness. Like any pack, we will root out the vulnerable members and expose their soft underbellies. I cannot afford such a thing, especially now. And so I straighten my spine and meet Efraím's hard gaze. "It would be my honor, sir," I say.

"Glad to hear it," he says, and then, pitching his voice louder, "Dismissed."

The Bellatorum move as one to leave the clearing. I linger with Efraím like I often do, ensuring there are no final duties he needs me to attend to. He nods to me, and I take my leave.

Eva Marteinn stands still, her dark eyes locked on me like a bird of prey's, but I pay her no heed. Let her find her own way home. I'll be responsible for her soon enough.

The last thing I see before I fade into the woods is Skau, his back against a pine tree and his eyes fixed in the middle distance, standing stone-cold still as Efraím lances three blades at him in quick succession. They find their marks within seconds, pinning him to the tree by the throat.

It's a stellar lesson in sidearm, balanced bladework. Not that it makes much difference to Skau. He's just as dead.

8

EVA

Reykdal Skau died because of me.

Try as I might to spin the situation otherwise—it was a rigged game; I shouldn't have been able to get the better of him; there was no way for me to know what Bellator Stinar would do—I can't get Skau's white, set face out of my mind, nor his torn throat, pouring blood as his eyes dulled, his body kept upright only by the blades that held him to the tree.

I didn't care for the man. He was a condescending, arrogant sinner. But that doesn't mean I wished him dead.

Guilt grips my muscles, sends my stomach roiling with tension as I pass beneath the massive arch of the Great Hall later that morning on my way to the Choosing. The names of the Sins and Virtues are engraved in the stone arch, weathered by snow and wind, but I don't glance at them. There's no need. My sins are etched on my mind far more indelibly than they could ever be carved into rock.

I file into the huge room and have no sooner taken my seat with the other seventh-formers than the Executor begins to speak from the dais. He seems smaller in person than he does in the vids, but the authoritative look in his black eyes is no less intimidating.

The five High Priests stand behind him, their red robes in sharp contrast to his crisp white shirt and pants, flanked by armed bellators. One is Efraím Stinar, and the other is Kilían Bryndísarson—the red-haired man he'd left in charge, who'd greeted him when he and Ari brought me to the falls last night: *We enter the circle at night and are consumed by fire.*

A shiver runs through me, remembering, and I rub my upper arms, hoping no one has noticed. With luck, they will attribute it to nerves or awe at the Executor's presence. Many citizens worship him as they do the Architect. It is rare for us to see him in person, a privilege.

"Citizens of the Commonwealth!" the Executor says in his resonant voice. "I stand here before you today on this, our ninety-eighth Choosing Ceremony, surrounded by the cream of our society. I am but the Commonwealth's mouthpiece. The High Priests keep its conscience. The Bellatorum enacts its justice. And you are its beating heart, our hope and our light. Together, we continue to build a world governed not by strife and the pursuit of power, but by order and peace."

Next to me, my classmate Adelía clenches her fists on the tan material of her pants. I turn my head slightly and see her pupils dilated, her lips parted. I could swear I hear her pulse pounding—but that isn't possible, is it? Either way, there is no mistaking the ecstasy emanating from her.

It is the morning in Clockverk Square all over again.

I fold my arms across my chest, trying to ignore the racing beat of Adelía's heart and the sharp musk of anxiety that rises from the rows of my fellow seventh-formers. My defensive posture draws disapproving looks, so I unknot my arms and thread my fingers together, resting my entwined hands on my knee. *Breathe,* I tell myself. *Of course you can't hear Adelía's heart beating, and what you smell is probably your own sweat. You're just nervous, and who could blame you?*

The Bellatorum are a black-clad phalanx occupying row after row in the back of the hall. I can feel their eyes boring into me as I sit, my numb hands gripping each other, listening to the Executor begin to call out citizens' names and assignments: *Jon Kaase, Arborist. Georg Trygge, Comp Networking. Alix Soelberg, Carpentry Specialist.* One by one, the Chosen come up and accept the responsibility that is their due, shake the Executor's hand—an honor that causes some of them to go pale—and return to their seats. They will embrace their new roles, regardless of personal preference. To do otherwise is a violation of the highest order.

"Step forward, Eva Marteinn."

I push to my feet, feeling as if a puppeteer is controlling my limbs, and make my way toward the dais. Shaking, I turn to face the crowd.

"Today," the Executor says, pausing for emphasis, "is a very special day, unique in our history. Today we announce the induction of the first female apprentice to the ranks of the Bellatorum."

It feels like the whole room inhales at once. Surely they must, because there is no air left for me to breathe. The crowd blurs into a tossing sea of colors, and when my vision clears I see Adelía staring at me, open-mouthed. I look around and realize everyone is wearing the same expression—dumbfounded.

"Citizen Marteinn," a deep voice says. I turn and see Efraím standing on the Executor's other side, his clothes pressed and his face serene, as if the night in the woods never took place. He has stepped forward soundlessly, leaving the second bellator to stand with the Priests. *They will teach me to move like that,* I think, returning his gaze. *When I am one of them.*

Efraím clears his throat. "You will listen to my questions, and you will reply," he says. "With the Executor, the Priests, the crowd, and the Bellatorum as witnesses. Do you understand?"

The shaking has spread everywhere, even my lips. "I do."

At the back of the Great Hall, the Bellatorum rises to its feet. The bellators fall into formation, forming a circle around the citizens of the Commonwealth. The symbolism is clear: The Bellatorum surrounds us. It protects us. It guards the Commonwealth, even from ourselves, and keeps us safe.

"Do you enter into this solemn contract of your own free will?" Efraím asks.

I want to tell him I do no such thing. That the idea horrifies me, day after day of violence shaping me into the worst the Commonwealth has to offer. But then I think about Bellator Skau, bleeding out his life onto the pine needles because of me, and realize it is too late.

First the thief in Clockverk Square. Then Reykdal Skau.

Ari Westergaard is right; I am already a killer—and a coward, too.

Because if Bellator Stinar can take the life of one of his own men, someone he broke bread beside and trained with, surely he can do the same to me. I will be at his mercy—and from what I can see, he has none, not even for those he calls his brothers.

So I don't tell him he can take his 'solemn contract' and carve it to bits, the way he did Skau's jugular, for fear of what the consequences might be. Instead I lift my chin, and lie. "I do."

"Do you enter it with the understanding that this is a bond severed only by death, or the renunciation of your oath?"

"I do."

"Do you understand the renunciation of your oath will carry with it a sentence of irrevocable exile from the Commonwealth, into the Borderlands?"

"I do."

"Do you swear to protect the Commonwealth with all the service of your blade and to the last drop of your blood?"

I draw a deep breath and utter the words that will commit me irrevocably to his cause, the ones every recruit must say to seal their oath. "I do so swear."

Efraím turns to his right. "Ari Westergaard, step forward," he says.

As Efraím's apprentice, it is Ari's duty to be by his side, unless ordered otherwise. I should have known when the bellators took their places, he'd be next to his mentor. But when Ari steps out of the line, looking more presentable than I've ever seen him—his torn clothes replaced with spotless gear, his face freshly shaven, and his hair combed—I have to dig my nails into my palms to keep from gaping at the contrast. Try as I might, I can find no trace of the warrior who pursued me through the forest, taunting me until I sliced his arm with a stolen blade. In his place is the beautiful, stubborn boy I'd been drawn to despite myself all those years ago in Clockverk Square—expressionless save his eyes, which are fierce with an emotion I am hard-pressed to decipher, but which ignites a burn within me nonetheless. I look at him, and I want something *more*: To best him with words or a weapon, even—the Architect forbid—to kiss him.

By the Sins, what is wrong with me?

"Sir," Ari says. His lips are set in a grim line, a sharp contrast from his usual smirk. He isn't happy with this turn of events—that much is clear enough. All I have to do is think of him saying *the scourge of pants and shirts everywhere* to know that.

"Do you accept this citizen, Eva Marteinn, as your apprentice?"

"I do." Ari's voice is husky. He looks anywhere but at me.

"Do you vow to pass along your knowledge to her, to instruct her to the best of your abilities, to train her in the ways of the Bellatorum so she may live to protect the flock and confront the wolf?"

"I do."

"Do you promise to challenge her when she must be challenged, to avoid the interference of personal attachment in her training, to demand all she is capable of, so she may in turn dedicate her life to preserving all we hold dear?"

Ari's eyes flick to my face. His expression is unreadable when he says, "I do so swear."

"Then step forward, Bellator Westergaard and Apprentice Marteinn. Step forward and make your promises in blood."

Ari takes a step toward me and holds out his hand. For an inexplicable moment I think he is reaching for me, and my heart jolts, spurred by an emotion for which I have no name. But of course he isn't. He is holding out his arm for the slice of Efraím's blade. I turn my head and see it—a foot long and razor-sharp, gleaming in the light. Fear grips me, sudden and humiliating—how deep will it cut? How much will it hurt? What type of barbaric ritual is this, anyway?

Seeing my hesitation, Ari curls the fingers of his extended hand, beckoning. "A moment, Bellator Stinar," he says. "Apprentice, come to me."

It is his coaxing voice, the one that persuaded me to confess how I disarmed Reykdal Skau. As if his words have the ability to compel my actions, I obey, stepping toward him until we stand less than six inches apart.

"Bare your arm," he says, and I do, rolling the sleeve of my shirt up with trembling fingers. My gaze strays helplessly toward the knife again, and he gives a small shake of his head. "Look at me, Eva." His words bear the clear bite of command. "At *me*."

With an effort, I refocus on his face. His eyes hold mine, clear and green and bottomless. "Efraím," he says softly. "Now."

The blade comes down. Out of the corner of my eye I see it, a quick flash of silver that pierces my arm and withdraws before I feel the pain. Dark blood wells up as it descends again, this time scoring Ari's flesh. He never flinches, never takes his eyes off mine. "Good," he says, but whether to me or to Efraím, I have no idea.

Efraím sheathes his knife and produces a small copper bowl. He holds my wounded arm over it, then Ari's. Our blood mingles, and still Ari doesn't look away. Then there is a hiss of metal against leather as two hundred bellators draw their blades. One by one, they cut themselves, passing the bowl around the circle. When it finds its way back to us, it is brimming with our shared blood.

Efraím is last, drawing the sharp point of his knife along his forearm. He takes the bowl and lifts it high. The reek of iron fills the air as the Bellatorum speak in unison, their combined voices sending tremors through the hall. "Your blood to ours, our blades as one. Your strength is our strength. Your fight, our own."

Efraím walks toward me, the bowl cradled in his hands. "Kneel," he says.

I sink to my knees and he dips his fingers, marking my forehead, my cheeks and throat. "Repeat after me. I am Bellatorum Lucis. I walk in the light."

I do as I am told, a bone-deep misery undergirding every word.

As one, the Bellatorum reply, *"Transit umbra, lux permanent."* Shadow passes, light remains.

"Rise, Apprentice Marteinn, and take your place alongside your brethren." Efraím's voice booms through the hall, echoing from the rafters.

I get to my feet, follow Ari to the line of waiting bellators, and take my place at his side. My arm throbs, but it doesn't matter.

There is no turning back.

9

ARI

The sun beats down on the rough-hewn gray stone of the Bellatorum's headquarters, reflecting off the chips of mica embedded in the rock. The building's four towers loom above us, each flying the flag of a House from one of the old fables, emblazoned with its spirit creature: purple for House Montyorke, with a soaring brown falcon; gold and green for San Fraesco, with a gray selkie; black and crimson for Minneska, with a snow-white, howling wolf; turquoise and cream for Satrizona, with an onyx panther, faded by the elements but fierce nonetheless. The Bellatorum's sleeping accommodations are divided among these towers, whose flags are meant to remind us of our role as arbiters of justice, peacekeepers who prevent the Commonwealth's citizens from backsliding into savagery.

Eva follows in my wake as I press my palm to the identification pad and swing the heavy wooden door wide. I walk her through the first floor, with its sitting area and kitchen, its storeroom full of energy bars and water and first aid supplies, then up the worn wooden stairs to the second story, which houses the training facilities, the armory, and the weapons repair room.

She trails me silently as we make our way up to Minneska's tower. Pushing open the door to the third-floor dormitory, I try not to think about the rush of power when I'd called her to me and she'd come— the weight of those large dark eyes, locked on mine as Efraím pierced her arm and then my own. I'd never seen her give an inch, but in that moment she'd let me be strong enough for both of us. It had roused an unfamiliar sensation in me, protective and hungry. The feeling is with me still, twisting inside me every time I look at her face. I don't know what to do except attempt to train it out of my body. Maybe if I push myself hard enough, if I sweat and bruise and bleed, it will go away.

"This is the Minneska dorm," I tell Eva, addressing a spot somewhere over her head. "You won't be sleeping here."

She nods. "Where's my room, then?"

I shut the door behind us, obscuring the rows of white-sheeted single beds, and stride down the hallway, to the door Efraím showed me when we got back from the Trials this morning. "Here," I say, pushing it open.

She steps inside. There's not much to see—a single bed, a worn wooden dresser, a window that overlooks the outdoor training ground. About half the bellators are already out there, sparring. She stands and looks down at them. And then she turns from the window.

"Will you teach me to do that?" she says.

"What, fight? It's part of the job description. Just don't expect me to go easy on you."

The words come out rougher than I intend, and Eva's eyes narrow. "I would never expect that. And I don't expect you to like me either. Just train me well."

"I don't dislike you," I say, surprised into honesty.

She laughs, a humorless sound that fills the space between us. "They do say bellators are prodigious liars, Ari Westergaard. Is this my first lesson?"

"I'm not lying."

"Well, you would say that, wouldn't you?"

"Believe what you want," I say, irritated. "It makes no difference to me."

Eva smiles. "Now that I do believe. So. When do we start?"

I bare my teeth, a savage mockery of her smile that promises violence. Prisoners in the interrogation chamber have dissolved into hysterics at the sight of this expression, but Eva doesn't flinch—not then and not when I draw my throwing knife from my belt, weighing it in my hand before I hurl it toward her—aiming far enough away to miss, close enough to terrify.

I don't know what I expect Eva to do—maybe duck, maybe scream like the untrained citizen she is—but I am disappointed on both counts. Her eyes flick to the blade and she dodges it with a burst of speed that excites the predator in me, sending my heart into overdrive. I stalk toward her, watching her eyes widen, breathing in the wash of pheromones that roll off her body. And then I reach around her, our bodies inches apart, and yank the quivering blade out of the window frame.

"Now," I say.

10

EVA

Bellators don't kill small animals for breakfast. They eat protein-heavy meals in their own dining hall, not speaking much except for the occasional request to pass a dish across the table. I sit next to Ari, ignoring the sidelong glances of the other bellators, none of who seem pleased to see me—not that I have the energy to care.

The weeks after my Choosing are a blur of exhaustion and bruising, of fighting and running and commands I never obey fast enough. I spend hours in the training room with Ari every day, during which he drills me on the name and history of each weapon, sets up targets for me to pierce, teaches me how to spar and to use my momentum as leverage. He teaches me to fall, and I fall over and over, ending with him standing over me, the tip of his sverd against my skin. *Je me rends*, I gasp, watching his smile widen. *I surrender*. Only then will he back off, so we can begin again. And through it all he taunts me, his voice an omnipresent irritant, a needle buried beneath my skin.

As exhausted as I am, you'd think I wouldn't dream. But I do—elaborate scenarios in which I slip through the woods on the trail of prey I never manage to catch, then race through the shadows until my muscles cramp to avoid the clutches of a relentless predator. It's the nightmare scenarios from my childhood all over again, but this time—just as is the case when I'm awake—all my senses are amplified. I pursue the prey through the woods, following a complex pattern of its scent. My speed is a blur, the darkness of no consequence. And then I wake, my muscles aching, only to find the dream has not left me.

I am tempted to stop taking the small pink pill that arrives each morning with my other vitamins—after all, this bizarre augmentation of my senses began in the dining hall, right after I swallowed that pill for the first time—but if I really am anemic, I can ill afford to let my red blood cell count fall. How will I defend myself then?

So I do my best to ignore the way the world seems more sharp-edged than usual, every scent exaggerated, my reflexes and balance far better than they used to be. After all, I am training every day for this exact purpose. Perhaps this happens to every bellator around the time of the Choosing; maybe these exaggerated responses are what qualify a citizen for inclusion in the Bellatorum.

I consider asking Ari, then think better of it; the last thing I want is to give him a reason to mock me—or worse, doubt my abilities, attributing them to a performance-enhancing drug. But what if that's the truth? What if the Executor had a deeper reason for choosing me as a bellator—and he's given me those pills to make me faster, stronger? To help me keep up with the others so I don't fall far behind, humiliating myself and the Choosing Committee?

It's ridiculous, given I never wanted to be here—that I'm jealous, every second, of the comp techs who get to spend their days manipulating code, lost in the precise beauty of algorithms—but the notion I need a chemical edge to be on a par with these conscienceless savages infuriates me. Each night, I pray to the Architect to cleanse me of both emotions; jealousy is forbidden, fury an indication of weakness, a shameful lack of control. But each morning, as I gulp down my pill, the feelings are still there, churning in my belly. And finally they crystallize into a rock-solid sense of purpose that spurs me forward with every breath.

The bellators are just people. If they can do this, so can I. I will train harder than all of them put together. I will do everything Ari Westergaard demands of me and more, until no one can lay the credit for my success at the feet of those small pink pills.

So I do my best to exceed at my new life, with its hours of training, strict discipline, and daily tests of endurance. Efraím and Kilían, along with the elite group that Ari calls the Thirty, have us climb the crags that surround the Commonwealth, digging our feet into crevices and searching for handholds. They pair the two male recruits against each other and force me to fight the winner. They forbid us to sleep and make us complete an elaborate series of tasks involving memorization, physical feats, and problem-solving skills. Anyone who fails to complete their tasks in the allotted time winds up in the center of a circle of the Bellatorum as Efraím enumerates their faults, strips them of their dignity, and either uses them for target practice or hands them over to the Thirty for additional motivation, the nature of which I don't care to discover.

And so I train until my fingers bleed and then toughen where they grip my weapons. I ignore Ari's arrogant, annoying tone and do everything he says, on the theory he wouldn't have been given an apprentice at such a young age if he didn't know what he was doing. He lets me watch him fight; he is lightning-fast and graceful, never quite where his opponent expects him to be, with an ability to assess and manipulate that is on par with his physical abilities. As obnoxious as he can be, I couldn't ask for a better mentor—not that I would ever tell him so.

I haven't forgotten what he'd said that first night, at the Trials—*the scourge of shirts and pants everywhere*—or the appalled expression on his face when Efraím told him I was going to be his apprentice. He hardly looks at me unless we're training, and then only to pin me with a scathing glare: *Is that the best you can do?* It's embarrassing that a part of me wants to impress him with my progress, to earn one of his rare compliments—though even those are sheathed in admonishment, lest a word of praise go to my head.

Watching him cleave through the air, shirt off and blades in hand, driving his opponents to their knees—it rouses a peculiar feeling in me. I want to fight him myself for the pleasure of it, want to pin him to the ground and trace the silvered web of scars on his back, mapping his lithe body with my fingertips. The intensity of my desire hovers on the delicate edge of what I'm sure must be a sin.

Ari earned those scars as punishment for his pride—was chained to a pole in Clockverk Square and whipped for everyone to see. I was there. I watched his blood drip onto the ground, the High Priest striking him harder and harder when he refused to cry out. Those scars should be the mark of his mortification, a harsh reminder of what happens when citizens fail to obey the Commonwealth's dictates. The last thing I ought to want to do is touch them. Yet he doesn't seem ashamed of the scars as he trains, his back bared for all to see.

I do the only thing I can think of—I train harder, trying to exhaust myself, to drive the impure thoughts from my mind. To ignore the unmistakable spike of pleasure I feel when he smiles at me or tells me I've done well. That's *supposed* to make me happy. He's my mentor, no matter if he can't be bothered to focus on my face for more than two seconds at a time.

Other than Kilían and Efraím—who seem indifferent to my presence—the only bellator who has treated me with anything approaching kindness is Samúel Nystaad, an older man and longtime member of the Thirty who works in the interrogation chamber. When Ari took me down to watch him interrogate a prisoner—one of two market employees suspected of plotting to acquire extra meat rations —Samúel sat behind the one-way mirror with me, explaining the intricacies of Ari's technique.

"See how he ingratiates himself with the prisoner?" he said. "Sitting to make himself less intimidating, leaning away from her to give her the illusion of control over her space? Watch how he smiles— that's meant to put her at ease. Now he's got her right where he wants her; she thinks he's on her side, so she'll relax and let something slip. You'll see him start asking tougher questions, still with the smile so it seems like he hates to bother her this way, but he's got to, it's his duty. Soon enough, she'll crack. They always do, poor doves."

I glanced at him sharply, and he gave me a rueful smile of his own. "Ah, you don't think I should pity her, Bellator Marteinn? Well, pity her I do. She's no match for the likes of him in there." He gestured towards Ari. "That citizen is a prime example of a sheep, if I ever saw one. She wants to be led, and if it's Westergaard doing the leading, then she'll follow, no matter where he guides her. That one wouldn't know she was drowning until the water closed over her head. And then she'd expect Westergaard to throw her a lifeline, but he'd just let her sink."

"Is that what being a bellator is about?" I blurted. "Lying?"

"It's not an easy life," Samúel said, placing a hand on my shoulder. "Sometimes I think the only ones who stride a tougher road are the High Priests and the Executor himself, may the Architect forgive me if I speak in blasphemy. For we must lie, and pretend to act in good faith, and take the lives of men and women who are but the poorest sinners. We look like the citizens among whom we walk, but we're not like them anymore. We've given up something of ourselves to gain much, and only now, as I come to the end of the road, do I feel the loss."

"To the end of the road?" I said, puzzled. "What do you—"

But he held up a peremptory hand, hushing me as the woman dissolved in tears and Ari strode out of the room, giving a subtle thumbs-up to the vid camera that captured the whole thing. "Well done, Bellator Westergaard," Samúel said, and went to escort the woman back to her cell. Two days later, I saw her covered in animal blood outside the slaughtering grounds, drenched in the remains of the creatures whose meat she'd coveted, staggering back to the City with tears cutting paths in the gore that streaked her face and flies dogging her every step. This is the Commonwealth's justice: To take what sinners desire most and wield it as an instrument of torture. Such is the punishment of those who stray from the path of righteousness.

I've thought a lot about what Samúel said—about giving up part of himself to become a bellator and coming to the end of the road. Surely his words couldn't mean what they sounded like—not just the end of his formal service, but of his life itself? Today, a month after the Choosing Ceremony, on my way down to the training room for another brutal session of fight-or-flight, I resolve to ask Ari. I'm outside the room, the question forming on my lips, when I hear Jakob Riis—the newest member of the Thirty and the other bellator who'd flanked Instruktor Bjarki the morning of Choosing Eve—giving Ari a hard time. I listen more closely, and realize he's talking about *me*.

"Don't fool yourself, Westergaard," he's muttering. "That little girl will never amount to anything. It's an insult to the Bellatorum."

I freeze, half-expecting Ari to agree. But instead he laughs, a throaty chuckle that is half amusement, half threat. "Envy is a sin, Bellator Riis."

"I don't take your meaning, Westergaard."

"Oh, I think you do." I hear Ari's footsteps pad across the floor, hear the clash of metal on metal. "Eva's a fighter. A damned good one, as it turns out. Give her a few months, and she'll kick your virtueless ass to the Sins and back, Thirty or no. And with your unpleasant attitude, I don't think I'll be motivated to call her to heel."

My mouth falls open. But before I can process that he's actually paid me a compliment, Ari clears his throat. "You might as well come in, apprentice mine," he says, sounding resigned. "I know you're there."

I edge into the room to find Riis glaring at me, blade in hand. Ari, on the other hand, is grinning. "Here she is, Riis," he says cheerfully, gripping his sverd. "Care for a trial match?"

Riis's glare deepens. "I know what you're doing, Westergaard. It won't work."

"No?" Ari says, his expression innocent. "Seems like it's working just fine to me."

Riis swears and stalks out of the training room, leaving me alone with Ari, who rolls his eyes. "Don't get any ideas, Eva. I said what I did to get under his skin. You've got potential, sure, but you've got a long way to go. Today you get your first assignment, and I'll thank you not to screw it up. You've got guard duty at the gen lab. Rumor has it the Executor himself will be paying a visit today."

THE GEN LAB IS AN IMPORTANT PLACE—IT'S WHERE THEY KEEP OUR digitized medical information and complete the artificial insemination procedures. Everything is protected not just by handprints but also by key codes, as a fail-safe. The guard I'm assigned to shadow makes a big deal of positioning his body between me and the keypad, as if my secret goal in life is to break into the lab and make more little citizens. "Don't touch anything," he warns as the door swings open. "Not a thing."

I give him the look the instruction deserves and step through, hands resting on my weapons belt. Over my time in the comp lab, I grew to be one of their most talented code-breakers—not that there's much cause for such things; the supervisors assigned such hypothetical tasks to us as a measurement of skill. It's not pride but a simple fact to say that if I wanted to decipher the keypad's code, I could do so without undue effort—not that it would do me any good without the handprint to match.

Inside the gen lab, white-coated medics bend over microscopes, petri dishes, and other equipment I don't recognize, muttering about splicing and mutations and other medical lingo. They glance upward at the intrusion—and then stare, ogling me. One of them even goes so far as to elbow another who's looked back down at his work.

I stare back, feeling like more of a freak than ever. Yes, I'm a girl. Yes, I'm an apprentice bellator. They were doubtless all at my Choosing; this shouldn't be news.

It's one thing to know someone has sworn an oath to the Bellatorum, though, and another to see them dressed in black and bristling with blades. I'm an anomaly, and I know it. Still, I don't enjoy being stared at like one of the Bastarour's gotten loose and stormed their stupid lab.

In desperation, I'm about to ask the guard when we might expect the Executor to arrive when there is a commotion at the end of the hallway—the sound of multiple people, moving our way. With them comes a barrage of scents: I can smell the oil the Bellatorum use on our blades, the dull scent of regulation soap, and an undertone of fried sausage.

The group moves closer, and beneath the sound of their feet on the wooden floor, I hear their heartbeats—one slower than the rest, one whose rhythm is uneven, the remainder marching along in a staggered but steady tandem. I snap to attention, hands at my sides, as they come abreast of the doorway where the guard and I stand. Efraím has taken point.

"Bellator Marteinn," he says to me by way of greeting.

"Sir."

"Ah." It's the Executor's voice, as resonant as usual. "Our most unusual recruit. Step aside, and let me greet her properly."

Efraím's eyebrows creep upward, but he jerks his head and the bellators part like water, leaving me face to face with the Executor. He stares at me, dark eyes beetle-black underneath the caterpillars of his eyebrows. I can hear the pound of his heart, with its too-long space between beats.

"How is the Bellatorum treating you, child?" he says.

I am so stunned at being addressed directly by the Executor—not to mention his apparent concern for my well-being—that at first I don't reply. After a moment I stammer, "Very well, sir. That is—I've been training hard. I'm grateful to you for the opportunity."

His thin mouth curves upward in what appears to be a genuine smile. I've never seen such an expression on his face before. Out of the corner of my eye, I see Efraím twitch—a movement he stills when the Executor turns his way. "I've been speaking with Bellator Stinar about your progress. He seems satisfied—am I right, Efraím?"

"Yes, sir," Efraím says, staring straight ahead.

"I've been curious about your training," the Executor muses. "Most curious indeed." He squints at me, peering down his hooked nose, and I have to fight the instinct to squirm. It feels as if his eyes crawl over every inch of my skin. At last he sighs and steps back.

"Ah, well," he says, "I suppose it's of no consequence. Time will tell."

"Sir?" I ask, but he has already dismissed me. Motioning to his entourage, he sweeps past me and into the lab, bending over the comp at the front. Efraím stands by the desk, flanked by Daníel Eleazar—the best climber we have; he puts Ari to shame when we race up the crags—and Jakob, who cuts his eyes at me in a disgusted look he wipes off his face as soon as Efraím's gaze flicks in his direction. With the bellators blocking the windows and the door, they form a solid wall of black that protects the Executor from any possible threat.

I'd thought Efraím or the Executor might want to assess my skill— but so far, all I've done is stand on display. Is that why I'm here today —not to demonstrate my abilities, but for the Executor to observe the progress of his experiment? Does he think I'm not good enough?

Does he plan to drug me some more? Maybe my induction to the Bellatorum is a joke he and Efraím have devised at my expense—an elaborate ruse to test the mettle of the true bellators, to see how they'll react to the presence of a girl in their midst.

Fuming in silence—given wrath is a sin—I glance upward to hide any hint of emotion that might show on my face. Above me is a mirror, designed to reflect the activities of the lab and stem the possibility of malfeasance. In it I see the Executor's profile, bent over the comp—and something else.

I can see his hands.

All the bellators, even Efraím, are facing outward to protect the Executor's privacy. None of them are looking at him, or at me. But I am perfectly positioned to decipher the forbidden information they have turned around to conceal: The Executor's password.

Far away as I am, I shouldn't be able to see the reflection of the individual keys in the mirror. But see them I can.

It's not like I can do anything with that information, without his fingerprint. Still less should I want to. But knowledge is power—Efraím reminds us of that often enough.

I'm not useless, I think, narrowing my eyes to bring the keyboard into sharper focus. *I'm not an experiment or a joke. And I deserved to be a comp tech. I* earned *it.*

He hits the final key of the sequence, clearing his throat to cue Efraím, who swivels to face him. The head bellator's gaze skates over me, and I drop my eyes, resentment churning inside me like the whitewater of the Trials' rapids. I fume during the rest of my shadow shift, as the guard shows me his route through the building, the blueprints of the Lab and the network of ventilation tunnels that run throughout the Commonwealth, and his routine for double-checking the entrances and exits. I am still fuming hours later, when I am dismissed and wind my way back through Marketor Square, through the alley that cuts between the market and the garment workshop, leading to Wunderstrand Square and the way home.

My mood does not improve when I find Ari sitting on my bed, flipping his knife over his knuckles. He doesn't look up when I come in, as if no more mesmerizing task exists in all the universe. "How was it?" he says.

"What are you doing on my bed?"

"Sitting. Did you acquit yourself nobly?"

"I did fine. Get off my bed."

"Why?" he drawls, glancing up at me. "Do you have a pressing desire to sleep?"

"No!" I say irritably. "But it's my bed. Go sit on your own, if you must sit somewhere and have convinced yourself nothing but a mattress will do."

Ari's eyes narrow. Then he rises to his feet in one fluid motion and stalks toward me. I dodge, but he anticipates me and gets there first, pinning me to the wall with a knife through the sleeve of my shirt. His hands go above my head, caging me in. "Ah, Eva," he purrs, "I think your day was more difficult than you're letting on. Still, that's no way to talk to your mentor, is it?"

Pinioned to the wall as I am, I have little choice but to pay attention to him. "Let me go," I say, but it's a *pro forma* protest. I know he won't do a thing until he's gotten what he wants.

"I don't think I will," he says, confirming my suspicions. "It seems to me you need to be taught a lesson, apprentice mine. I'll ask again—is this any way to address your mentor?"

"No," I say, eyes on the ground.

"Look at me, Eva." It's a command, and like the day of the Choosing, I can't help but comply. I raise my head and see him looking at me from inches away, green eyes boring into mine. After so many weeks of avoidance, the intensity is painful. It's all I can do not to look away—but I'll be damned if I give him the satisfaction.

When he speaks again, his breath gusts warm against my face. It smells of rosemary and mint, herbs from the culinary gardens. "That's better," he says. "Now. No, what?"

"No, sir," I say, and he laughs.

"You say all the right things when you're suitably motivated, apprentice mine. But why do I have the feeling what you're really saying is, *Pull your virtueless knife out of my sleeve and get the hell out of my room?*"

I don't reply, just hold his gaze.

"What happened today, Eva?" He flattens his hands against the wall, careful not to touch me.

"Nothing happened."

"Liar. Something's gotten under your skin, and I'd like to know what it is." Beneath the honeyed shell of his voice runs a core of steel. There's no point in arguing, and so I don't bother.

"It was the Executor, if you must know. He talked to me personally, and it made me uncomfortable. There didn't seem to be a whole lot for me to do, and so I thought—" I shrug as much as I can manage, trapped against the wall.

"You thought maybe you were only there so he could look you over. Yeah? To see if you belong here, with us. And it made you angry. Don't worry, I won't tell." He runs his thumb down my face, his touch warm against my skin. "Your secret's safe with me, Eva."

His choice of words does not sit well. During the second week of my training, Ari took me down to the interrogation chamber and had Kilían confide a secret in me while he waited in a separate, soundproof room. Then he came into the chamber and did his utmost to extract it, by turns charming, threatening, and cajoling. The encounter has left me wary of his ability to manipulate, even when I'm on my guard. "I gave you what you wanted," I say, struggling not to flinch. "Now let me go."

The familiar sardonic grin lifts his lips. "You have no idea what I want."

"Why don't you tell me, then? Or do you plan for us to stand here all night? You'd better hope Efraím doesn't object to you spending the evening in my bedroom, strip you of your title, and leave you for the Bastarour in the woods."

Ari's face goes blank, like a hand has wiped it clean of expression. "Watch what you say, Eva."

"Why?" I say, annoyed beyond restraint. "Are you that afraid of the Bastarour? They're just cross-bred, genetically engineered creatures designed to kill—surely the great Ari Westergaard has nothing to fear from them."

His lips flatten into a thin line. "Shut up."

I've never seen anyone get to Ari like this. Intrigued, I press my advantage. "I hear they're monstrous. Part tiger, part leopard, part wolf—how could they not be? And fierce. Rumor has it they bring their kills to the edge of the woods for the Executor's inspection. How would they identify you, Bellator Westergaard? From the scars on what remains of your back?"

He takes a step closer to me, eyes narrowed in threat. I can hear his heart thumping faster than usual, smell the sudden change as his scent deepens, laced with a forbidden undercurrent of anger. "Be quiet," he hisses.

"Make me."

The thumb tracing my cheekbone slides lower, pressing against my lips. "Like this?"

Furious and unnerved by the feel of his body so close to mine, the heat of his breath on my face, I can only glare—which doesn't deter him in the slightest. He regards me, his head tilted as if the sight amuses him.

"You're in a rare mood," he says, sounding more like his normal, controlled self. "Pushing me like this—it's not a good idea. But I think I know what you need. I'm going to step back, and then you're going to stop fighting and trust me instead. All right?"

Without waiting for me to reply, he yanks the blade out of my sleeve, pockets it, and retreats to the doorway, out of reach. "Come on," he says, and leads the way down to the training room, where he tosses me a sverd and then spars with me for hours, dodging and feinting, lunging and goading, until all I can think about is what we're doing to each other, until sweat soaks my body and my numb fingers can no longer grip my blade.

The sun has faded from the sky and the stars are visible through the windows when he pins me against the wall, sverd pressed against my chest. He looks me over, gaze moving over me from head to foot, assessing. And then he says, "Enough." He pulls his blade back, sheaths it, and walks out without another word, leaving me to put the room to rights.

As the haze of battle lifts, I realize that, much as I hate to admit it, he'd understood. While we'd been fighting, I'd stopped thinking about my upsetting encounter with the Executor, and focused instead on survival. There'd been no room for anything else.

Sheathing my blade, I survey the wreckage—mats shoved askew, a scattered stack of weapons belts, the room's one chair turned upside down, a target knocked onto the ground. I'd made him work for his victory. He'd had to earn it. He hadn't taken it from me.

Enough, he'd said, but it hadn't been. Not nearly. Next time, I will be faster, a better strategist.

Next time, he will be the one against the wall.

11

ARI

I go for a long run while it is still dark, alone. All the way through the woods that stretch between the City and the rapids, I curse myself for letting her get under my skin.

I know she thought it was her comment about the Bastarour that pissed me off—had made sure she believed it, in an act of self-preservation—but I could give less than a damn about that. No, it was her dig about Efraím finding us together in her bedroom, as if she could see right through me. As if she knew the whole time I was sitting on her bed, waiting—and later, when I pinned her to the wall with my knife through her sleeve—I was thinking about things I shouldn't. That I am drawn to her despite myself, the way a child seeks to touch the blue heart of a flame.

I shouldn't be her mentor. I should renounce my claim, withdraw my oath. But I know I will do no such thing, sinful or no, and the knowledge is a dark shadow, nipping at my heels, weighing heavy on my soul. I push myself harder than I ever have, but no matter how fast I run, the shadow of my claim on Eva is always with me, driving me onward, chasing me home.

1 2

EVA

When I finally sleep that night, I dream. First I'm a wolf, the scent of the woods alive inside me, hard on the heels of elusive prey—then a falcon, soaring above the trees, searching for movement below. I spot a mouse in the tall grass and dive, wings pressed to my sides, beak closing on the creature with satisfaction as I take to the skies again. Hot, fresh blood spurts into my mouth as the bell rings, wakening us well before dawn.

In the bathroom, I run my tongue over my teeth, half-expecting to taste rust and iron. But when I spit into the sink, my saliva runs clean.

It was a dream, that's all. Just a product of the traitorous, wild imagination that has plagued me since childhood.

But I can't let it go.

I'm not an animal, I tell myself. *I won't let them make me into some kind of beast.* But what if it is too late for such empty promises?

My eyes burn and my head aches, heavy with exhaustion. To make things worse, Efraím calls an early assembly of the Bellatorum at the top of Black Falls, a massive cataract carved from ominous dark lava. With minutes to go until the first pale fingers of light creep over the horizon, I stand next to Ari, concealed in the shadow of a crag, wondering what we are doing here. The ground where we stand slopes sharply up from the drop, giving us an unobstructed view of the cascades and the churning whitewater below. Black Falls is far higher and more treacherous than the rapids we use for the Trials and training, the icy water plunging so far into its depths, I'm sure no one could survive the descent.

I stand, eyes fixed on the inky darkness between the pines, as Samúel steps forward from our ranks. He reaches Efraím's side, and the lead bellator raises a hand. Silence falls, and into it, Samúel speaks. "My time with the Bellatorum has been the greatest of privileges. It has been my honor to serve as one of the esteemed Thirty."

Puzzled, I glance at Ari, but his face gives me nothing. In perfect concert with the other bellators, he answers, "As it has been our honor to serve alongside you."

Samúel lowers his head in acknowledgment. "Thank you for your kindness. The privilege has been mine. But there's a time to take up arms, and a time to lay them down again. This dawn, I will surrender my soul to the Architect. I do so willingly, without hesitation. *Transit umbra, lux permanent.* We will meet again as brothers in the light."

Efraím's lips rise in a humorless smile. "Aye, we will. For the Bellatorum's way is to give the elders amongst us a choice: Live out their days in peace, reconciled to their bodies' decay, or offer them an honorable death in their prime. You've chosen bravely, Bellator Nystaad. We won't forget. The one who takes your place amongst the Thirty will fight in the shadow of your name."

Horrified, I gape at Samúel. I'd meant to ask Ari what Samúel had meant about coming to the end of the road, and had never gotten the chance. But this—surely he can't mean to sacrifice himself?

Samúel lifts his hood, shrouding his face from view, and hands his weapons belt to Efraím. Then he turns toward Kilían, who stands at Efraím's right hand. "I am ready."

"As you wish it, so shall it be." Kilían kneels at his feet, tying a burlap sack filled with stones around Samúel's ankles. Samúel stands stoically, his hands clasped behind his back. He doesn't fight them.

When the weight is secured, Kilían straightens and nods to Efraím. Moving in eerie synchronicity, they take his arms, and I see what they mean to do—lift him and cast him outward, over the sheer drop that lies beyond. I bite my tongue to stifle a scream.

As they hoist Samúel from the ground, his eyes sweep the crowd of black-clad figures, coming to rest on mine. He holds my gaze, and I think of the way the condemned man had done the same that long-ago morning in Clockverk Square, before I said the words that loosed the bellator's blade.

I must make some small sound of distress, because in the shadows between us where no one can see, something brushes my hand, warm and feather-light. I glance sideways at Ari, but he is staring straight ahead, his expression betraying nothing. Perhaps I have imagined it? But no—his hand grazes mine again, that same questioning touch. I feel his fingers playing over my knuckles, the tips calloused from hours of bladework, and know his touch is no accident.

Shock vibrates through me, paralyzing me so I don't pull away the way I should. After an eternity I come to my senses, only to realize something even more disturbing: I don't want him to stop. Everywhere he touches, my skin tingles, as if he's ignited a slow-burning flame along my nerve endings. The strange, prickling sensation lingers long after his fingertips have moved on, trailing a meandering but sure line along the back of my hand, crisscrossing my palm until they come to rest against the inside of my wrist. I jerk in surprise and his fingers press harder in admonition, demanding I hold still.

Though we are at the back of the crowd, apart from the rest of the bellators, I'm still terrified that one of the others will turn toward us and glimpse this small gesture. If someone sees us, it will surely mean our deaths.

My pulse pounds wildly against his fingers, a bird trapped in a cage, wings thrashing in an effort to get free. Humiliated at my body's betrayal, I do my best to bring my heartbeat to heel—but it gallops on, racing so I am dizzy. The forest swims before my eyes, trees blurring into a single column of green that tilts unrelentingly toward the plunge of the falls.

No one has ever touched me this way. Certainly I never felt the smoldering heat of a slow-burning fuse when the medics worked on me or the Mothers sluiced the shampoo from my hair.

I stand stock-still, caught between horror at what's happening at the edge of the falls and the impossible fact of Ari's hand in mine, as they raise Samúel higher, so his feet dangle in midair. He glances downward, and the expression on his face shifts, betraying the terror he feels, after all. Then the wind catches him, and I see his graying hair blow back from his face, see his body sway. The two bellators lean backward in unison to counter his momentum, and their eyes meet. Efraím nods once, gravely. Kilían bows his head in response. And they let go.

Samúel goes over the falls without a sound, plunging toward the rapids. The heavy weight drags him down, hands stretched above his head, his body a straight, taut line. I imagine his face as I last saw it—his eyes wide, searching ours, his mouth an O of surprise that belies all his training.

Ari's hand clenches tight on mine. Then he loosens his grip, and one of his fingers traces the veins on the inside of my wrist, outlining the riotous passage of my blood. As clearly as if he has spoken aloud, I feel the wry acknowledgement in his touch.

Pull away, I tell myself furiously, even though that is the last thing I want to do. I am seized with an unaccountable desire to turn toward him and press my lips to his, to twine my fingers in the dark silk of his hair and discover if it feels as soft as it looks. Gritting my teeth, I try to force the thoughts from my mind. *Where is your sense of self-preservation? Maybe he has a death wish; you don't. Step away from him now, before there's no going back.*

This is excellent advice. I ought to follow it.

But I don't move.

I don't dare turn my head for fear the movement will catch another bellator's eye. They stand stock-still around us, silent as stone. I'm desperate to make sure their attention is on the horror in front of us, and not the sin happening behind their backs.

But I'm frozen in place, too frightened to breathe.

Ari's hand turns in mine, guiding me so my fingertips find the inside of his wrist, the way his found mine moments before. His touch is unexpectedly gentle, imbued with a reverence I have only seen him display when handling a finely crafted weapon. I feel his pulse pounding in tandem with my own, settling into the same punishing rhythm.

It is an admission of the most treacherous kind.

I'm seized with sudden horror that the other bellators can hear us, that they will spin around, blades unsheathed, and demand to know what we are doing—but they gaze into the fading night, paying Samúel the respect that is his due, watching his figure grow ever smaller as it hurtles down the sheer drop of the falls.

A spark of indignation grows, flaming until it is a bright, hot core of outrage at the center of my being. Samúel could have lived on, as an instructor or tutor or a dozen other things. He was too old to fight —but that doesn't mean he was useless. What does it say about my new brotherhood, that this is how they value their elders?

Ari's hand turns again and his fingers intertwine with mine, gripping hard. Our palms slide against each other, damp with sweat, but he doesn't let go. I hear his breath hitch, barely audible over the commotion of the falls.

Shocked back to myself, I yank my hand free with a rush of terror —what if someone had seen us, shadows or no?—as Efraím gestures to the lightening sky, his head still bowed, palm up as if to contain the rising sun. We speak in unison, as he intends, as we are trained to do. "The Commonwealth grieves for you, Samúel Nystaad."

Our voices break the silence of the new morning, echoed by the piercing screams of the falcons that circle the gorge, roused by the dawn and our presence in their woods. They're hunters, like us—but they're scavengers, as well. When Samúel's body washes up on the shore, the falcons will pick the flesh from his bones, leaving them to whiten in the sun.

The benediction fades into silence and Efraím speaks alone. "The peace of the fallen and the blessing of the Architect be with you, Bellator Nystaad. As from the earth you came, so to the earth you shall return. *Integer vitae scelerisque purus.*" *Unimpaired by life and clean of wickedness*. It is the greatest compliment he can bestow, how all of us hope to meet our end.

As the sun breaks over the crags, Ari makes a low, uneasy sound —in regret? Warning? I cannot tell. The wind shifts, blowing from the south, and I breathe deep, the spray from the rapids hitting my face, washing me clean.

13

ARI

Alone with Eva in the gear repair room after the ceremony, I busy myself with a cracked weapons belt, trying to ignore the accusatory weight of her gaze. There at the verge of the rapids, her eyes fixed on Samúel, she'd looked miserable, lost. I'd wanted to comfort her—an unfamiliar impulse I tried to fight back as soon as I recognized it for what it was. And that was the only way I'd known how, sin or no sin.

What I'd done was dangerous beyond measure—but the sensation of her hand in mine was the purest rush I've ever felt. I would do it again, and hang the consequences. I just wonder if she regrets it, or if she feels the same.

She'd walked by my side through the woods afterward, spine straight and eyes ahead, every inch the perfect apprentice, revealing nothing. I'm sure I looked much the same. But the truth is now we share a secret, a dangerous one. If anyone had seen us holding hands in the forest, the consequences would have been swift and brutal. Likely death for one of us, and exile for the other, condemned to wander the ruins of the Borderlands, at the mercy of the hordes.

I look her over, an inscrutable small figure who is so much stronger than she seems at first glance, her blade slung over her back in its custom-fitted sheath and her belt dipping low from her hips. Leaning against one of the white brick columns that hold up the ceiling, wearing her black gear, she is a study in contrasts. I can't read her the way I can almost everyone else, and it maddens me.

By the Architect, though—her pulse pounding against my fingers, the way she'd dug her nails into my wrist, the feeling of her small, callused fingers threaded with mine, skin to skin—I've never felt so alive.

I would do almost anything to feel that way again.

The full measure of my transgression settles in my belly, heavy and uneasy. When Samúel went over the Falls, I should have grieved him—and then turned my attention to which of us might be named one of the Thirty in his place. It's a coveted position, one I cannot take for granted. Instead, I stood with my hand in Eva's, feeling the heat of her flesh against mine, wanting things I had no business thinking about.

It's maddening to have her so close, yet so inaccessible, and suddenly I am furious—with her, with myself, with the whole virtueless situation. I want her—and the temptations she represents—gone from my sight.

Schooling my expression to blankness, I jerk my head up, forcing myself to look at her. "Why are you staring at me? Is watching me use an awl and thread that fascinating, apprentice mine? Surely you have someplace more useful to be. Or are you that confident about your bladework, then?"

Her eyes flash to mine, and even with all my interrogation training, I have a hard time deciphering their expression. "What do you want from me?" she says, ice dripping from every syllable.

Frustration sharpens my tone, honing it to a fine, deadly edge. "What I *want* is for you to train harder, to be a worthy opponent for me the next time we face each other. The Architect help you if you end up at my mercy with no more skill than you showed last night. Next time, I won't be gentle."

I look up at her, my features set in an expression of utter boredom. She is glaring at me, her face white, those dark eyes filled with the rage she's not allowed to spill. I would love to fight her again, to channel the heat sliding unchecked through my veins into the familiar rush of battle, but I don't dare. To face her now with a weapon in my hand would mean to risk losing all my control. Who knows what I might say, what I might do. I can't take the chance.

"I gave you an order, apprentice," I say, my eyes flicking downward, toward the leather strap in my hand. "Why are you still here?"

I don't hear a sound to indicate her departure—not a footfall on the worn wooden floor or the creak of silver against leather as her weapons shift in their belt. But sure enough, when I look up again, she is gone.

I'M STILL SITTING THERE HALF AN HOUR LATER, SORTING MY WAY THROUGH belt after belt and trying not to think about the feel of Eva's hand in mine, when Kilían comes in. "So here you are," he says. "I didn't see you at lunch, or that intriguing apprentice of yours, either. Then I came upon her in the training room, dueling Karsten and Riis at once, blood in her eye and giving no quarter. It's quite a sight, actually. They're drawing a bit of a crowd."

His voice is mild, but I sit up, the belt in my hand forgotten. "Eva's fighting the two of them at the same time? One of the Thirty, and his apprentice? Is she crazy?"

Kilían shrugs. "As to that, who can tell? But one thing she is, and that's determined. I've never seen a recruit move so fast, or so viciously, either. What in the nine hells did you say to her?"

"What makes you think I have anything to do with it?"

"I know you, Westergaard. Better than you think." The words walk the edge of a threat, but he raises one red eyebrow, lessening the sting. "You've got a gift for seeing what makes people tick—what motivates them, what makes them afraid. What they're hiding. If you hadn't said something to provoke Marteinn, you'd be down there training with her, and she wouldn't be working herself into a frenzy at the expense of Riis and that poor recruit—not to mention making a fool of them both in the bargain."

"Oh?" I say, straightening in my chair.

Kilían smiles, an unexpected flash of white in his freckled face. "When I left, Karsten was bleeding from four different places, and

Riis had all he could do to fight her off. She has it in for him, I'd wager. Karsten is just collateral damage."

"Ah." I feel a grin creep across my own face. "Well, that makes sense."

"Does it, now? And why is that?"

I pull my dagur loose and reach for the whetstone, in case I'm called upon to enter the fray. "A couple of days ago, Eva overheard Riis saying she'd never amount to anything, that her being a girl was an insult to the Bellatorum. It seems she took it personally."

Kilían's smile widens. "It seems she did. But that still doesn't explain why she took on the two of them at once. Which brings me to my earlier question—what did you say to her?"

When I run my index finger along the edge of my blade, it bleeds, but not fast enough. I slide the knife against the stone again and give Kilían an acceptable version of the truth. "You're right, I did provoke her. I told her the next time she faced me in the training room, she'd better put up a more effective fight. That she'd give me a battle worthy of my skills and her training, or she wouldn't like what happened next."

He tilts his head, regarding me. "Upset about Samúel, were you?"

"I don't know what you're talking about," I say, my voice even. "He met his death bravely. It is our way."

The truth is, this is the third ceremony of its kind I've witnessed, and I still found it unnerving, not that I would ever admit it to Kilían. Samúel chose this fate of his own free will; no one forced his hand. The alternative was growing old and decrepit amongst his fellow bellators, unable to defend himself or the Commonwealth should the situation so require. But still—watching one of our own allow himself to be thrown backward into Black Falls with a weight tied to his feet makes my stomach churn.

Kilían scrubs a hand over his face. "I don't think less of you for it, Westergaard. The man died bravely, but there's still a horror in it. That you recognize such things speaks to your humanity."

Silver-tongued bastard, I think, looking him over. I shouldn't feel the way I do about Samúel's death, shouldn't have permitted myself to get attached to him. But if we'd been allowed such things, I would have considered the aging bellator my friend. He was always kind to me.

This is the virtueless nonsense I got in trouble for as a child—prioritizing one person above another, caring for them beyond the utilitarian dictates of what life in the Commonwealth demands. I've never stopped, and not for lack of trying, either. But that doesn't mean I have to let Kilían see it. My *humanity*, indeed.

I eye him without speaking, and he turns away, taking off his formal robe and grabbing needle and thread with which to mend a small hole in its hem. Satisfied I've deflected him, I finish sharpening my blade and set it down. "I'll be going, then," I say, pushing to my feet. "To see the sparring match of the century and all. Wouldn't want to hear about the whole thing secondhand."

"Wait, if you don't mind." His head is down, eyes fixed on his work, but there is no mistaking the air of command in his voice. "I came to find you while the rest of them were occupied for a reason, Westergaard. I have something to say."

"All right," I say warily. I'd been about to sheath my blade, but I think better of it and leave it bare in my hand. "What is it, then?"

He lifts his head and looks at me. His Adam's apple shifts, and his eyes slide from mine. If I didn't know better, I'd say he was spooked—but why would Kilían be apprehensive about anything where I'm concerned? He outranks me, has ten more years of experience. I don't like the feel of this situation at all, and my hand tightens on the hilt of my blade as he speaks. "I shouldn't be talking about this, but you need to know."

If he saw us at the Falls, the important thing is not to panic. I know my tells—the hand I run through my hair, the downward glance, the way my left hand automatically drops to my belt in search of weapons. I will show him none of these. If he wants a confession, he will have to drag it out of me with a needle in my vein. "And what exactly is that, Bellator Bryndísarson?"

He turns toward me, his expression solemn. "What I'm trying to say, Ari, is—" His mouth snaps closed mid-sentence, and he looks down at the robe in his hands. "By the nine hells, this is difficult," he mutters. "I knew it would be, but standing here, looking at you, I don't know if I can—except I have to—"

If I have only rarely heard Kilían use my first name, I have never heard him stammer like this. Eloquence and verbal manipulation are his stock in trade. His hesitation is scaring me, which in turn makes me irritated. "Spit it out already, Kilían," I say, deliberately brusque. "Or do I have to beat it out of you?"

"Not here," he says, glancing nervously around the room. "We have to talk, and sooner rather than later. But someplace more private—"

I'm about to lunge forward and grab him by the collar when Jakob Riis bursts through the door, Karsten right behind him. His face is scratched; his weapons belt, clutched in his hand, has been severed above the buckle. There's a savage look in his eyes, and before I can say a word, he grabs Karsten by the scruff of the neck like a puppy and shoves him forward.

"Look at what your girl did to him," he hisses. "Just look."

Karsten is a mess. He's bleeding from a deep scratch on the back of his sword hand, his forearms are covered with defensive wounds, and his shirt is torn to rags. I gape at him, on the verge of laughter.

Riis is not amused. "Say something, would you!" He shakes Karsten hard, and the boy winces, clamping his mouth shut to keep from crying out.

"Eva did all that? While fighting you?"

"She's a wild animal!" He shakes Karsten even harder, and the recruit lets out a moan. "She knocked the boy's blade right out of his hand and before he could pull another weapon, she was on him like it was a fight to the death. He barely got his arms up in time to protect his face. Look at those cuts!"

"I see them, Jakob. What do you want me to do about it?"

"What do you mean, what do I want you to do? I want you to control your apprentice. She almost took out my eye. She sliced my weapons belt right in half, and laughed when it fell to the floor. If Efraím hadn't called the fight, the Architect only knows what she would have done. It's training, Westergaard, not the Trials." He glares at me in disgust. "She's yours, damn it. You're responsible for her. Make her behave. What did you say the other day? Call her to heel. I don't care what name you give it, rein her in or I'll do it for you."

"If you could have reined her in," I say softly, "you would have done it. You wouldn't be standing in front of me with your ruined weapons belt in one hand and a half-mutilated recruit in the other. Perhaps there should be two open spots in the Thirty, rather than the single one Samúel left behind."

Riis's face goes red, then white. "You arrogant bastard." He lets go of Karsten so quickly the boy almost falls to the floor, draws his long blade, and lunges for me.

I get out of the way just in time, leaping up onto the wooden counter behind me. My dagur in one hand, my sverd in the other, I stare down at him, teeth bared. "If it's a fight you want, I'm happy to oblige. I'd have thought you'd had more than enough for one day, but obviously not. Come on, then. I'm right here."

He takes one step forward, then another. But before he can take a third, Kilían comes to stand in front of him, forcing him back. "Ease down, both of you," he says.

"Ease down?" Riis says, his voice a growl. "That girl is a risk, Bellator Bryndísarson. Tell him."

"She's a recruit," Kilían says, in the calm tone I've heard him use on volatile interrogation subjects a hundred times. "So is Karsten. You are not. In the absence of her mentor, it's your responsibility to bring her into line. If the girl bested you, then perhaps it's you who needs more training."

Riis doesn't take his eyes off me, but I see his spine stiffen. "Yes, sir," he says, spitting the words out as if they taste rotten.

"Take Karsten downstairs. Get him cleaned up. And don't blame others for your shortcomings. Marteinn may be wild, but that's why she needs training, is it not? If she can best you now, think what she'll do after her apprenticeship is at an end. If I were you, Bellator Riis, I'd stop wasting my time with Westergaard and focus closer to home." He turns his body halfway, so he can keep both of us in view. "As for you, Westergaard—arrogance is a sin. Humility, a virtue. Don't antagonize Riis. It doesn't help."

"Yes, sir," I echo, without moving an inch. I have the high ground, two blades in hand, and a functional weapons belt at my disposal. Until Riis leaves the room, I have no intention of ceding any of my advantages.

Kilían sighs. "The boy's bleeding all over the floor. Get him out of here."

Riis snaps to attention, cuts another furious look at me, and turns to go. In the doorway, he and Karsten pass Eva, who looks them over with such disdain, I have to suppress a snort of amusement. Her eyes fall on me, standing on the counter with my blades unsheathed in my hands, and one dark eyebrow rises.

Then she stalks into the room, her skin sheened with sweat and her hair coming loose from its braid. There's a clotted scratch across her forearm and another on the back of her hand, but other than that, she's unmarked—a fact I'd find hard to believe, if I weren't taking it in with my own eyes. "Sir," she says to Kilían with impeccable politeness.

"Marteinn," he replies, lips twitching.

I see her eyes flick from the ground to the counter, judging the distance. Then she leaps, landing in a crouch beside me. When she straightens, her throwing knife is in her hand. "Am I a worthy opponent now?" she says, and lets it fly. It hurtles across the room, straight and true, embedding in the doorway above where Riis's head passed through a moment before.

Kilían chuckles. "I'll leave you to it. Good luck, Westergaard." He takes a deep breath, and when he speaks again, his tone is as serious as I've ever heard it. "What I was talking about before—it's important. When you have an opportunity—come find me and we'll finish our conversation."

He looks like he wants to say more, but whatever's on his mind, he obviously can't voice it in front of Eva. Instead he bows to her, a startling gesture of respect, inclines his head to me, and strides out of the room, doubtless to make sure Riis has obeyed his orders.

"Well?" Eva says, and I realize she is waiting for my answer. I blink, dismissing my troubling discussion with Kilían. Whatever he meant, now is not the time.

She stands inches from me on the countertop, her dagur in one hand and a throwing knife in the other. In her eyes, I see the unmistakable glint of a challenge, and instinctively, I answer its call. Without taking my gaze from her face, I drop my hand to my belt and free my shuriken. I keep my throwing stars razor sharp, but this time

I'm aiming to disarm, not to kill or maim. A flick of my hand, and the serrated weapon soars across the room, hitting the handle of her knife and sending it tumbling to the ground.

"Meet me in the woods," I tell her. "Tomorrow before dark. And then we'll see."

14

EVA

We're standing in a small clearing at the base of an oak, the tip of my sverd pressed against Ari's chest. Dusk has just fallen, and the threat of a growing storm weights the air. With his free hand, he beckons me closer. "Come and get me, Eva. Or are you afraid?"

"Does it hurt?" I ask him, breathless.

He laughs at this, one side of his mouth curving upward in a facsimile of amusement. "Of course it does. Don't stop."

I frown, uncertain. "I don't want to hurt you."

As soon as the words leave my lips, I regret them, but it's too late to take them back. Ari regards me, and his expression hardens. "Are you a warrior or not, Bellator Marteinn?" he challenges, and steps closer, digging the point of my blade deeper into his flesh.

I know what he's doing—goading me, using his words as another kind of weapon. Still, I can't help but rise to meet him. "I am," I say, the syllables issuing from between gritted teeth.

"Then prove it," he says, and slides like water from my grip. Bewildered, I shift my gaze one way, then another, trying to figure out how he's vanished—but I can't see a thing.

From the darkness behind me, I hear a mocking chuckle. "*Acta, non verba,*" he chides me.

"By the Virtues," I mutter in irritation, turning in a slow circle. My only reward is an echoing laugh that issues from everywhere and nowhere at once.

"Close your eyes, Eva," he urges from wherever he is hiding. "Breathe deep. Use all your senses."

"I'm not stupid, Ari. I'll close my eyes, and you'll be on me in a heartbeat."

He gives a grudging sigh. "I won't, I promise. Now close your eyes and tell me what you see."

"How can I see if my eyes are—"

Ari growls. A second ago I could have sworn his voice was coming from somewhere to the left; now it hisses from the shadows beneath a cedar tree, a bright thread of irritation pulled tautly. "Stop arguing with me, for the Architect's sake! Am I your mentor, or not?"

I don't say a word, out of pure rebellion. That, and the more I aggravate him, the more distracted he'll become. Distracted people make mistakes. But my silence must nettle him further, because when his voice comes again, it bears the clear, distant tone of authority, each syllable needle-tipped. "That was a question. You'll answer it now, or you'll answer to me."

"I was under the impression I already had to answer to you. So I don't see the benefit," I retort, revolving one more time in pursuit. His voice is moving, shifting with the wind, and I close my eyes as he's ordered, breathing deep, sampling the air. I will find him this way, I am sure of it—but that's no more or less than what he expects. In order to have him carry a truly stellar report back to Efraím—a report that will elevate me from the tedium of guard duty—I cannot merely pinpoint his location. I will have to find a way to impress him, instead.

"Don't provoke me, Eva." It's a whisper, borne on the breeze, heavy with the scent of coming rain.

Beneath the moisture that thickens the air, I can make out a mélange of other aromas, as layered as the complex flavors of the ceremonial wine they make us sample in training. On top is the perfume of the pine trees, the bite of cedar, the humid fug of leaf mold. Beneath that I can smell my own sweat, the oil I used on my blade this morning, the mild, neutral trace of soap. And hovering at the edge of my senses, something else, flickering in and out of my perception.

If this is the case for all the Bellatorum—if they can feel the forest move through them like a tide, so they are at once riding the waves and awash in its depths—then they're truly a tribe apart. For the first time, I wonder if it might be worth compromising the state of my soul to stand among their ranks—but if I owe my heightened senses to those little pink pills, I'm only an unworthy sinner, guilty of the worst sort of hubris.

"I'm waiting, Eva." Ari's voice darkens, the promise of violence lurking in its depths. "You'll acknowledge me, or you'll pay the price."

There's warning clear in his voice—but anticipation, too, carefully veiled and tempered. All of the bellators live to fight, coming to life only when they have a weapon in their hands and an opponent to defeat—and to my shame, I'm no different. The intense, expectant feeling I feel when I take my blade in hand, sizing up the man opposite me for weaknesses before I strike, the adrenaline-fueled rush I feel when I dodge a kick or land a blow—it must be how the act of sex felt to the craven people before the Fall. Only then am I truly present in my body, a physical creature without thoughts of sins or virtues, discipline or deprivation. There's only the pure, animalistic joy of the fight, my body moving in tune to another's, seeking completion.

It goes without saying that thinking like this is forbidden. But we all have our secrets, and Ari Westergaard is no exception.

I know what he wants—for me to recognize his superiority, to accept the chain of command and surrender to him. Do that, though, and this dance is over. He will have won, and it will only be a matter of time until I feel his blade against my throat. If I can delay a little bit longer, I'll have a chance. And so I feint, and wait for him to parry.

"Bellator Westergaard," I call back, eyes still closed. "What will you do if I say no?"

His only response is a low growl that vibrates through the air, augmented by the rising wind. Leaves whip around my feet, lashing my legs, rattling in the trees, and I suck in a lungful of air, holding it, letting it slip silently back into the gathering energy of the coming storm.

This is my last chance. Apprentices do not refuse their mentors. It isn't done, and Ari cannot afford my insolence. Either I strike, or he will.

"Don't tempt me, Eva." His voice is closer, moving in for the kill. He's set aside his misdirection, abandoned it as an unnecessary strategy. Which means only one thing: He is near enough that by the time I figure it out, it will be too late.

Desperate, I let the last of the air sift from my lungs, inhale one final time. Luck is with me: The wind shifts again, and then I have it —the rusty tang of blood, coming from directly overhead. He's in the trees, moving from one to the next, using the coming storm to cover his approach. He plans to leap on me from above.

Now that I've found him, I let my eyes blink open, allowing all my senses to come alive. I am careful not to look upward, betraying myself. If I have any chance of catching him, it will depend on the element of surprise. I ready myself, muscles tensing, one hand dropping to my weapons belt, closing on the hilt of my dagur.

He must see me go for my blade, because I hear him laugh again. "Come, now," he taunts, his tone light, teasing. "We can fight if you want, but you know I'll win, and where's the fun in that? You're the prey and I'm the predator, plain and simple. I outweigh you. I have more training. You have no advantages, Apprentice Marteinn. Yield to me before the storm comes in and you can nurse your defeat in your nice warm bed."

The use of my formal title—emphasizing my subordination to him —is a deliberate insult, a final dig before he finishes me off. I know him well enough to envision the sleepy grin spreading across his face, darkening his eyes with that false emotion that walks the line between humor and hubris, disguised just enough to deny. Infuriated, I yank the knife free.

"Have some sense, Eva. Say you yield. Give it up to me."

The time for stealth has come and gone. Shoving my knife into its sheath, I launch myself into the branches overhead, pulling myself up hand over hand, chasing the ghost of his blood's scent, heedless of scratches or commotion.

Overhead, I hear Ari's startled gasp, feel the branches shake as he prepares to jump. We are ten feet above the ground; he won't land easy. But that knowledge is cold comfort, not nearly satisfaction enough.

The wind gusts harder, just as the sky breaks open and the rain pours down. Perfect cover. I palm the dagur and lunge, getting my arms around him as he leaps into the air.

We fall together, through the slanting sheets of rain and the eddying swirl of leaves. Ari shifts in my grip, trying to break free, but I have my knife in my hand and he can't afford to struggle. Still, neither can I direct my fall, protect myself the way I have been trained. We land hard, him twisting at the last minute so he comes down first, taking the weight of our landing.

The breath is driven out of me all the same, the world gone to streamers in the rain-soaked dusk. Ari's arms are tight around me, his hands fisted in my shirt. His chest is heaving. The metallic pungency of blood fills the air, mingling with the ozone scent of lightning striking far away in the valley and the peppery reek of adrenaline.

Miraculously, I am still gripping the dagur, its handle slick. I press the dull edge to his throat, and his eyes blink open, the look in them wary. He doesn't move.

"Who's the prey now?" I say, the words a ragged gasp. "You may be my mentor, Bellator Westergaard, but I answer to myself."

Ari draws one shallow, careful breath, then another. "You know," he says, his tone conversational, "rumor has it wrath is a sin."

"Hmmm. Well, so is pride, last I heard." I shake my head, splattering water deliberately onto his face. "They do say pride goeth before a fall, Ari Westergaard. And rarely have I seen a proverb so neatly illustrated, if I do say so myself."

He laughs soundlessly, so as not to disturb the trajectory of my blade. "Touché. I won't tell if you won't."

"You're hardly in a position to bargain," I point out. "But not to worry. My lips are sealed."

Even bloodied and breathless, my blade against his skin, he gives me that infuriating grin, quirking an eyebrow upward. "How did you figure out where I was?"

Despite myself, I feel a smile spreading across my face. "I did what you said. I closed my eyes. And—I smelled you. The blood, from where I cut you, before."

"Ah." He blinks up at me again, clearing the rainwater from his eyes. "You have a gift with edged weapons, Bellator Marteinn. I take back what I said."

"What, in particular? You said a lot of things." My fingers have begun to ache where they're wrapped around the hilt of my knife, and I am beginning to feel foolish, holding it to his throat—but with Ari, I'm never sure where a lesson ends and life begins. It would be unfortunate to drop my guard, only to have him best me now.

"Well," he says, his tone measured, "you do seem to have me at a disadvantage, after all. Training or no training." His gaze travels over my face, drops to the dagur in my hand, then traces the lines of my body where it arches over his. My knees dig hard into the mud on either side of his hips, centering my weight, and his fists still grip my shirt, pulling me down against him. One of my hands rests on his chest, giving me the leverage I need to angle the blade. It is an oddly intimate position, closer than I have ever been to anyone unless we were actively fighting. Something sparks to life between us, coiling in my stomach with the sharp-edged sensation of fear, the charged intensity of impending battle. Suddenly it's hard to breathe all over again, and I open my mouth, tasting rainwater, gasping for air.

Ari shifts beneath me, perhaps planning to roll me off him, blade or no blade—but then his eyes settle on my stomach, bared in the fall, and I see him swallow, the muscles of his throat moving beneath the pressure of my knife. His eyes drift upward, lingering everywhere my wet shirt clings to me, a second skin. His hands grip me tighter, fingers digging in hard enough to bruise, and he sucks in a sharp, pained breath. "Quite a disadvantage, actually," he says, his voice hoarse, and when his eyes find mine again, they are hot, burning with emotion.

Even though I am on top of him with a knife at his throat, I feel horribly vulnerable—all the more so because I can feel heat in me responding, rising toward his unspoken call. It unnerves me, more than the darkness and the hunt and the heady scent of blood. My knees are rooted to the ground, as solid beneath me as Ari himself— so why do I feel as if I am still falling?

I freeze in confusion and feel Ari do the same, his body moving in response to mine as it does when we are sparring. Reason comes to me then, borne on a tidal wave of relief: Perhaps we're still playing the game, even now. Perhaps this is just another lesson.

That must be it. This is a test. Ari himself, a temptation. One among many tests, and I will not fail it.

Clarity floods me, and I lean a little harder against the blade. His expression flickers, but he does not wince. "I am Bellatorum Lucis," I say, each word dropping slow and clear into the press of the storm. "I walk in the light. Do you walk with me, or no?"

Ari's eyes are fixed on mine, his body still. I wait, unmoving, for the words that will set both of us free: *Shadow passes, light remains.* But he does not speak. Instead he searches my face—surely another test, this one of my emotional control. I school myself to impassivity as I have been taught, and give him nothing in return.

Finally he blinks, his eyes shuttering closed. When they open again, they are a study in inscrutability, his pupils blown wide to admit what little light remains. "Eva," he says.

"Yes?" Under the palm braced on his chest, I feel the slow, studied pounding of his heart. It beats against me as surely as if I hold it in my hand, an unexpected intimacy that sends a shiver rippling through me, my muscles quivering from head to toe.

Ari shivers helplessly in return, his body shifting under mine, as if he has asked a question and I have answered. *"Je me rends,"* he says softly, and I feel his hands loosen, falling, palms open, into the mud at his sides. *I surrender.*

15

ARI

As soon as the words leave my lips, Eva rolls off me, blade still at my throat. "Get up," she says.

I get to my knees in the mud, then rise to my feet. Standing, I could disarm her—but the last thing I want is to sever our connection, no matter how treacherous it might be. And it is treacherous, I know that well enough.

I'd intended to let go of her after we landed. But I couldn't make myself, even though I knew we might not be alone in the woods... that other bellators, intent on a night-training exercise, might well come upon us unawares. To be Bellatorum means to control your impulses, to school your very heart rate into submission. But with Eva on top of me, her hand on my chest and her knife pressed to my throat, I couldn't control a damn thing. My body had responded to hers as if it were an animal she'd called to heel. The knife she's still holding to my throat is nothing compared to that.

I want to ask her if she feels the same, but I'm afraid to look at her. The way the moonlight illuminated the bare skin of her stomach, beaded with rainwater—the way her clothes mold to her body, outlining every curve—to think about these things is the greatest of sins. Worse still is what I want to do: I have to fight the urge to knock away the blade, take her face in my hands, and kiss her, the way the stories we're told as children warn us against. I do my best to shove the image away, but it won't go. The more I struggle against it, the more intense it becomes.

Thinking like this is wrong, I tell myself. *Stop. Remember who you are.* But when she holds the tip of her blade beneath my chin, I think not of blood and punishment but of how her skin would slide through my hands, rain-wet and slippery as a selkie, how much I would like to know whether her lips are as soft as they look. How she tastes.

By the Sins. I can't do this. I can't I can't I won't. If we are caught, it may well mean our lives. But I am not strong enough to resist, not alone with her in the woods, the rain coming down and Eva looking right at me, a challenge clear in those dark eyes. Worse still, I don't want to. My heart races and inside me everything is falling and finally I speak.

"What do you want from me?" I say, my voice rough. "Do you want me to beg? I will, if that's what you need. Just tell me, so I can get it over with and we can get the hell out of here."

Her eyes flicker downward, the first indication of surrender—but then they sweep upward again, meeting mine. "That's an interesting proposition," she says, one side of her mouth curving upward. "Go ahead and beg, then. I'd like to see you try."

It's my first instinct to take offense at this. But where Eva is concerned, pride is the least of my problems. If she wants me to beg, then beg I will, and hang the consequences. "All right," I say, and wrap my hand around the one of hers that holds the blade. I force it downward, gaze steady on her face, and flick the knife into the muck.

Eva takes a step backward, eyes wide with alarm. "I didn't mean—"

"You wanted me to beg, yeah? Then come here." The words come from everywhere and nowhere at once, but once I have said them, there is no taking them back. I tighten my grip, pull her toward me, and bend my head, brushing my lips against her cheek, then downward, along her neck to the sharp rise of her collarbone. The current between us rises and spikes and the last of my restraint shatters, washed away by the storm and the taste of Eva's skin. She smells like the soap all of us use, like sweat and rainwater—and a scent all her own. It's sweet, but with an edge to it—like the hot chocolate spiced with cayenne they give us on the eve of the Architect's Arrival.

"I underestimated you," I whisper against her skin. "Forgive me, please."

She shivers. "Ari," she says, warning clear in her voice, but—miracle of miracles—she doesn't push me away. I wonder what, exactly, we are doing—how far both of us will allow this to go. Lust is forbidden—chastity, a virtue. But if I have already sinned by wanting her, then perhaps what happens between us now doesn't matter.

Perhaps we are already damned.

The thought terrifies me—but it exhilarates me, too. I have never felt anything more powerful than the pull toward Eva, a wanting so strong my hands tremble with it—my hands, which never shake when I wield a blade.

"Forgive me," I say again, the words barely audible—but this time I'm not sure whether the entreaty is meant for her, or whether it's a plea to the brotherhood of the Bellatorum, to everything I have sworn to uphold.

Tentatively, she traces a finger along my cheekbone. Her touch leaves a line of heat behind, and it is my turn to shiver. I press my lips to the hollow at the base of her throat, and her breath catches once, then again. I can taste her, sweat and soap and that strange, spicy sweetness.

A moan vibrates through me, a hungry, eager sound I have never heard myself make, and she tenses in my arms. Attuned as I am to the smallest movement, trained to read deception in a smile, flight in the smallest shift of weight, still I have no idea what this means. She's not fighting me, not trying to get away—but knowing Eva as I do, perhaps she is merely calculating the odds, determining the most effective method of escape. Or perhaps she is horrified by my forwardness, stunned into immobility. I have no way of telling.

"Eva," I say, more breathless than I have ever felt after an hour of wind sprints or a bout of sparring. My heart is pounding, hard enough I am sure she can hear it. "Do you like this? Do you want me to stop?"

Her head jerks up, eyes wide, the expression in them unreadable.

And then she stands on her tiptoes, leans into me, and presses her lips to mine.

For a moment I am so shocked I don't move. Then her mouth opens and she nips at my lower lip with her teeth, tracing the sting with the tip of her tongue. I gasp, and she swallows the sound, her hands locked behind my neck, urging me down to her.

Something gives in me then, a final barrier, and I pull her tight against me, kissing her back, my hands roving over her body, all the places I have never allowed myself to touch. We stumble backward, not stopping until her back hits the trunk of a tree. My arms are braced around Eva, first to absorb the impact, then as a cage, framing our bodies. "Are you all right?" I say, my voice oddly breathless. "This—it's okay?"

In response she reaches up and twines her fingers in my hair, shifting against me, forcing a growl from my throat and a sharp cry from hers. I lift her, letting the tree take most of her weight, and she wraps her legs around my hips, drawing me in. Then her lips are on my collarbone, her other hand sliding under my sodden shirt to press against bare skin, and a shudder ripples through me. I slide my palms down the rough bark, take her face in my hands, and claim her mouth again.

I have no idea what I am doing—how could I?—but instinct drives me forward, a primal urge for which I have no name. Or maybe I do. Lust, that's what this is, the base desire the Priests have warned us against again and again. It has little to do with higher thought, with any of the virtues and behavioral codes drilled into us over the years. I feel myself moving against Eva, feel her body arch under mine, her heat burning into me even through the layers of our wet clothes. And I know that the High Priests are right—this is terribly dangerous. Because in this moment, I don't care about the rules of the Commonwealth, about anything other than the girl in my arms. All I want is Eva. And being as close as we are right now—it is nowhere near enough.

Wanting like this must be a great sin.

The thought is a cold dose of reality, dousing my desire. If someone were to see us this way—it's one thing to condemn myself to an eternity in hell, put to death or exiled and doomed to wander the Outside until I meet my final reckoning. It's another to drag Eva down with me.

I pull back from her, panting, loosening her grip on me so she's standing on the ground once again. The rain has slowed to a drizzle, but we are both too drenched for it to matter. "We have to stop," I say, my voice uneven. "We can't do this."

Her cheeks are flushed, her eyes dark pools. "I know," she says. But then she steps into me and kisses me again, hard enough to bruise. I feel my teeth cut into my lip, but for the first time I can remember, pain doesn't clear my mind. Or maybe it does, and when everything else falls away, all that's left is Eva.

Boldly, I trace my fingers down her spine, beneath the sheath of her sverd, let my hands fan out over the curve of her hips. And then I am moving again and she is moving with me and I feel as if I am at the top of one of those rollercoasters they used to have before the Fall, everything inside me coiling building surging toward her, inching closer and closer to a precipitous drop from which there can be no return.

Desperately, I try to think, to find my way back to some semblance of reason. I dig deep, searching for the famed willpower and restraint of the Bellatorum, but it has deserted me. I am a stranger to myself, and it is both unnerving and the purest thrill I've ever known.

Then Eva's hands rise slowly, as if countering a great weight, and frame my face between them. She pushes me away a fraction of an inch and holds me still.

We stand there, her leaning against the tree and me leaning against her, both of us shaking. Her hair is mussed, coming down everywhere, and I can feel the thud of her heart against my chest. Or maybe it is mine.

Eva gives me a trembling smile. "Wow," she says.

It takes me a couple attempts before I can pull myself together enough to speak. "You're not kidding," I manage at last. Seeing her pupils dilated, her dark hair disheveled, her clothes in disarray—and knowing it's because of me, because of what we did together...it ignites something unfamiliar inside me, a feeling for which I have no name.

Mine, I think with a fierceness that takes me off guard, troubling me even more than the wild, driving sensation of her body yielding to me, her mouth rising to meet my own. I grew up in the Nursery with communal teddy bears; what makes me think I have the right to an entire human being? I draw a deep breath, centering myself, and don't move a millimeter. For the first time in my life, I don't trust my own body, don't trust what I might do.

When I hazard a glance at her again, Eva is worrying at her lip, looking more unsettled than I've ever seen her. "That was—it was—well." Her face heats, a gratifying sight. I've rarely seen her blush before, nor be at such a loss for words. "They're right. It is a deadly sin. I could get lost in it. Lost in *you*. And I would forget everything else—what's right, what I'm supposed to do. Who I'm supposed to be." Color rises in her cheeks. "I did forget that," she accuses. "You made me forget."

"You know what?" I trace the beads of water in the hollow of her throat. "You made me forget, too...and I liked it. So if this is a sin—I say, let us sin, then, and be damned for it. I'll gladly go to the devil with you, Eva Marteinn. Although preferably not in a soggy pile of leaves."

Eva looks appalled. "You don't mean that. It isn't a joke, Ari. Not a game. You'd really risk everything—for this?"

"Oh, I would," I tell her, even though deep down, I'm not sure it is the truth. Still, right now bravado is all I have—and so I bluff, and hope Eva can't see through me. "I'm trained for battle and deception. What is this but another kind of fight?"

"You do look like you've been in a fight, Bellator Westergaard," she says, a slight smile curving her lips. "And lost."

I open my mouth to reply, just as she tilts her head, listening—and then shoves me, so hard I almost lose my balance and go sprawling in the rain-slick leaves. "Someone's coming," she says, voice thready with panic.

"What? How can you—"

"We have to get out of here," she hisses, fumbling in the muck for her dagur. "Straighten your clothes, for the Architect's sake!"

I pull my gear into something resembling order, tugging my shirt to rights, listening for all I'm worth. And then I hear it—footfalls approaching through the woods, a long way off, crushing small branches as they come. We're in no immediate danger, and I eye her, puzzled. "They're nowhere near us, Eva. How did you—"

Her face closes down, the smile gone. "It doesn't matter. What we did—if anyone found out—by the Architect, what do you think would happen? We can't just erase it with a confession to the Priests. The way you touched me—the things we said—we have to stop it now, before it goes any further."

She's only echoing my own thoughts, but the idea of never being with her like this again sends a sick, spinning bolt of loss through my stomach. "We could be careful." It's a stupid, dangerous thing to say —but worth it, to me.

"It's a *sin*," she says, brushing past me.

I pull her up short, one hand wrapped around her upper arm, and gentle my voice. "I know you're scared. But don't run away. We can figure this out together."

Eva's expression ripples like water, from regret to anger to something I can't decipher—before it settles into firm, determined lines. "Stay here all night if you want," she says. "I'm leaving."

Turning her back on me, she strides off through the woods, away from the sound of the footfalls, toward home.

16

ARI

After Eva leaves me in the woods, I storm off in the opposite direction until I can't hear her or the other bellators—assuming that's who they are—and spend a considerable amount of time punching a tree. The hell with all this—trying to train an impossible apprentice, struggling with temptation every time I turn around, Riis and his attitude problem, Kilían and whatever he'd started to tell me yesterday. The hell with my feelings for Eva, and the hell with her too. I am a bellator, bred and trained for fighting. What do I know about taking these kinds of chances, the ones that leave your body intact but lay your soul bare?

Nothing, obviously. I'd made myself more vulnerable for Eva than I'd ever done in front of another person, and she'd thrown it in my face. How will I train her now?

Wrath has never been one of my primary sins, but tonight is a different matter. I'm infuriated by the rules that confine and dictate my behavior, sick of people telling me what to do, and on top of everything else, my pride is injured—a lethal combination. I stalk back through the woods, rubbing my bruised knuckles, kicking leaves out of my way, and grateful that, close to midnight as it is, no one else stumbles across my path.

I stop periodically to listen, but the other bellators are gone. Doubtless they'd had the same idea I did—challenging each other to a lethal game of hide-and-seek in the storm-soaked dark, the weather upping the ante by playing havoc with their tracking skills. I'd be willing to bet the trajectory of our evenings diverged in dramatic fashion, though. Surely they hadn't ended up pinning their apprentices to a tree, her hands buried in their hair and her mouth— her *taste*—

It takes considerable effort, but by the time I've reached the edge of the Commonwealth, I've mastered myself again. My face is blank as I press my hand to the pad outside the door of the Bellatorum's headquarters and go in search of Kilían, who is known for the late hours he keeps. Perhaps that is one problem I can resolve tonight, hopefully with violence. My body trembles with the need for it, desperate for release. The Architect help Kilían—or anyone else, for that matter—if he crosses me.

He's not in the armory, or the kitchen, or the common area, all of which are deserted. At last I find him in the training room, alone, a sverd in his hand. When he sees me, he pauses mid-lunge. "Westergaard," he says by way of greeting. "What happened to you?"

I glance down at myself—rain-drenched, muddy, gear flecked with fallen leaves—and shrug. My voice comes even, betraying none of my frustration. "I was training Eva in the woods, and things got a little out of hand. She leapt out of a tree after me and knocked me in the mud. Landed with her knife to my throat. It was quite impressive, really."

Kilían's face breaks into a genuine smile. "So she turned out to be a worthy opponent, after all."

"It would seem that way. But I'm not here to talk about my apprentice, promising though she may be." I straighten, dropping a hand to the hilt of my throwing knife. Kilían's eyes track my movement, and he shifts his weight, body tensing. Primed for battle as I am, the sight gives me a visceral satisfaction. "Yesterday, you said you had something important to tell me. That I should come and find you. Well, here I am."

"Here you are," he echoes. "Looking more like you want to knock me on the ground than listen to what I have to say, but beggars can't be choosers, eh? Did you see anyone on your way up?"

"I did not. What's this all about, Kilían? Cut to the chase, if you don't mind. I'm well aware patience is a virtue, but to be perfectly honest, I'm running low on it tonight."

Kilían gives me a long, considering look. He strides to the doorway and steps into the corridor, looking left and right. And then he pulls the door closed behind him and turns to me. He draws a deep breath, turning his sverd so light reflects off the gleaming blade, and meets my eyes. "You're not a regulation citizen, Westergaard. You never were."

I freeze, staring at him in shock. Of all the things I expected him to say, this is probably the last. Regulation citizens are what we call everyone in the Commonwealth who was born by acceptable means. The alternative—well, the alternative doesn't make any sense in my case. How could it? I stare at Kilían some more, waiting for him to retract his statement or utter a comprehensible sentence, but he doesn't. He just stands there looking at me.

The shock retreats like the tide from the shore, leaving behind the sharp-edged wreckage of my shattered control. "What are you saying?" My voice comes low, dangerous. I almost recoil from it myself, but Kilían doesn't flinch.

"I'm not trying to insult you, Westergaard," he says. "Though by the time I finish talking, you might prefer it if I were."

I don't want to believe a word that's coming out of his mouth. But although Kilían is a spectacular liar—it comes with the territory, being Lead Interrogation Specialist and all—I don't think he's lying to me now. His face is grave, his expression sincere. He holds my gaze, lets me look him over, and on his face I see a flicker of something unfamiliar: pity.

It's that look that scares me more than anything else.

No one has ever pitied me before.

I hadn't been frightened when the bellators tied my arms to the post in the square and the lash came down, or when Riis put his blade to my throat on Choosing Eve and forced me to climb down the rope to the ground five stories below my dorm. I wasn't frightened the first time I leapt into the rapids, or when Efraím put a knife in my hand and told me to fight. But looking at Kilían's solemn face, seeing that hint of pity reflected in his eyes, I taste the bitter metal of fear.

"Start talking, then," I say roughly. "And I'll let you know."

He looks me up and down. I hold myself still, trying not to betray my discomfort, but knowing Kilían, he sees it anyhow. "Your parents," he says, "they were sinners. Your mother was a scholar; your father was a medic. They—well, they committed the sin of fornication. Your mother tried to hide it, but she was bearing heavily during the summer season, and that was impossible. The High Priests did what they always do—imprison the male, confine the female under guard in the hospital. She had you there, and then the two of them were sentenced to death, together."

The walls are wavering strangely, leaning in toward each other, compressing the room and taking all the air with them. I gulp, tasting tin. "And then?"

Kilían shakes his head. "They were sentenced to death. But the sentence—it was never carried out."

"How?" I'm amazed by how level my voice sounds. Efraím would be proud.

"They ran," Kilían says simply. "The night before they were scheduled for execution, they escaped."

I can't help it—I gape at him, open-mouthed. No one has ever escaped the Commonwealth. Who would want to? There's everything a person could want here: food, shelter, a sense of purpose to guide your days. Out there, in the Borderlands, there's only the wreckage of the War, the crumbled remains of abandoned cities long dead, the barbaric hordes, and—if they're lucky enough to survive—the occasional exiled wanderer, driven mad from solitude and extremity. Certainly none of the other Commonwealths would risk taking in an exile. "How?" I say, disbelief clear in my voice.

Kilían doesn't answer. Instead, he tugs another sverd off the wall and tosses it to me. "Here," he says.

"You want me to spar with you?" In my current mood, this is akin to picking a fight with one of the Bastarour. Kilían knows this, knew I was craving the release of a physical altercation before he even said a word. Yet here he is, placing a blade in my hand. "Is this some kind of test?"

"No, you moron," Kilían says, and sighs. "I want to create a plausible reason for the two of us to linger here so late at night, and this is the best option at hand. The noise will cover our conversation, and there's only one entrance to the room. Pay attention, boy. *En garde.*"

Ignoring the insult, I settle into my fighting stance, my eyes automatically flicking over him for signs of weakness. *"Gardez-vous,"* I reply, and lunge.

I am a better swordsman than Kilían, have always been, and I block his blows effortlessly, breaking through his defenses, then pulling back at the last minute to give him a chance to attack. "If you're lying to me," I say, my tone empty, "you and I will have a problem."

"I'm not lying," Kilían says, getting his blade up in time to block mine. The clash of metal echoes through the armory as I dance backward, out of reach.

"No? How did they escape, then? Did a little bird come down and fly them away?" I duck to avoid the downward slash of his sverd, roll underneath it, and come up on one knee.

"It's complicated." He's panting, a fine sheen of sweat on his forehead. I take in this evidence of vulnerability and exploit it as I have been trained, lunging upward to press the point of my sverd against his chest.

"You have my undivided attention," I say.

"Hmmm." He bats my blade away with his hand, then thrusts his sword forward in a textbook *seconde.* "I don't expect you to believe me, Westergaard, but there are those who are not in perfect accord with the aims of the Commonwealth. Those who seek to reclaim the freedoms—and the gifts—of the world we have lost."

His words take me off-guard, more so than any of the hits I have absorbed from his sverd. "What do you mean?" I say, forgetting to parry for an instant. "Like a rebellion?"

He is on me at once, his blade sweeping under mine, aiming for my throat. "No," he says. "Not yet. More like...a resistance."

I narrow my focus, retreating, parrying, and then lunging forward with a vicious *riposte.* "And you're telling me—what? That my parents were members of this secret resistance movement? How would you know, anyhow?"

"I know," Kilían says quietly, "because I was there."

I pause, my blade an inch from his chest. "You knew my parents?"

He nods. "I knew them both. Your father, especially—his cot was next to mine in the dormitory during my seventh-form year. I would never have guessed there was anything between him and your mother. They were distant in public, very proper. I hardly ever saw them speak. No one was more shocked than I when the verdict came down."

"But..." I say, for once at a loss for words, "how did they get through the gate without someone noticing? The Bastarour—"

"Not the gate," Kilían says, shifting his weight onto his back leg. Sweat soaks his shirt, and he pulls it over his head, dropping it to the ground in a sodden puddle. "There's another way."

"Another way out of the Commonwealth? You're kidding."

"I've never been more serious in my life."

"Well, what is it?" I say, kicking his shirt out of the way.

He regards me through narrowed eyes. "I'll tell you that one day, Westergaard. When I know I can trust you."

Fair enough. "Let me guess, Kilían. This resistance, whatever it is, is alive and well. And you're one of its starring members."

"It's a brotherhood, actually," he says stiffly. "The Brotherhood of the Wolf."

Unbelievable. One of Efraím's Thirty, a traitor.

His blade clangs off mine again, and I drive him backward with the force of my blows, letting the fierce joy of battle flood me. "No girls allowed, huh?"

"It is a sexist name. I'll give you that." He forces the syllables out from between clenched teeth. "What, are you feeling sensitive about your little protégée?"

"Just making conversation." I feel lightheaded, at once in perfect control of myself and as if some omnipotent force is urging me forward, directing my blade with unerring precision. Step by step, I force him to retreat. He gives ground reluctantly, but give it he does. He has no choice.

If he is telling me the truth—if I am natural-born—then how can I fight the way I do? We are taught natural-born are lesser...slower, ignorant, worthy of carrying out the most menial tasks the Commonwealth has to offer. Why would the Executor—for surely he knows the truth of my origins—appoint me to a position in the Bellatorum? None of it makes sense—except the desire I feel for Eva. That piece of the puzzle comes into stark relief with an awful inevitability, making me gasp for air. *The sins of the fathers*, I think, and shudder.

"Tell me about my parents," I say, and feel my lips rise in that smile I have that isn't really a smile at all. "They left me behind, then. They gave me up?"

"They were told you were dead," Kilían says, breathless. "By the Architect, Westergaard, I'm just the messenger. By the time we realized you weren't, it was too late. They were gone, and what had happened to you—well, it was already done."

My smile-that-is-not-a-smile widens. I know what I look like when I do this, have seen it in the mirror a time or two—not vanity, just standard practice for interrogators who need to be intimately familiar with every weapon at their disposal. I know, for instance, that when I widen my eyes and let one side of my mouth curve up in the grin that's two parts promise and one part threat, most people—especially women, though some men as well—will tell me anything I want to know, reprisal be damned. I know my sense of humor can disarm or incite, depending on the interrogation subject and the matter at hand. And I know when I smile like this, people start screaming before I even lay a hand on them.

Kilían doesn't scream. He has seen the smile before, although never directed at him. And he is a warrior. Instead he fights to keep what little advantage remains to him. It's admirable, but a pointless endeavor. With ruthless, unforgiving strikes, I propel him backward until he is cornered, the long length of his spine pressed against the wall by the door and the sharp point of my blade against his chest, above his heart. "Tell me about my parents," I say again. "What happened to me? What do you mean?"

He doesn't struggle. His eyes meet mine, clear and unafraid. "Your parents were taken to safety. They fight with the Brotherhood now, have ever since they escaped. As for you, at first you were isolated, the way it always is with the natural-born, placed in the quarantined nursery. And then—you suffered some kind of crisis and disappeared. The medics supposedly brought you back again a few days later—but the Minder who'd been responsible for you since you were born...she swore they'd given her a different baby."

He is silent, letting his words sink in. When they do, my own eyes widen. "Are you saying they switched me with one of the regulation babies? That whoever this guy is, he's been living out his existence as a natural-born, when there's nothing wrong with him at all?"

"There's nothing wrong with you either," Kilían points out, calm as if I don't have the point of a sverd pressed against his chest. "You're still the same person you've always been."

I suppose I must be. How could it be otherwise? Still, what if I have struggled so much with illicit affection—the friendship, always rebuffed, I offered the other children in the Nursery, the wanting I feel for Eva—because of my flawed genetic code? What if I am broken, less worthy than the rest of my Bellatorum brothers?

Sickened, I press my blade harder against Kilían's bare chest. A bead of blood wells up, but he makes no sound. "Why would they do that?" I say. "What would they stand to gain?"

"I don't know. Presumably they took you away for testing, Ari. And whatever they found—well, it was significant enough to warrant the switch."

"How do you know all this?" The fight is over, and he is talking. With an effort, I suppress my bloodlust, take a step back, and let my blade fall. Kilían pushes off the wall, wiping idly at his chest. His hand comes away red.

"Well," he says, "you're the very image of your father. So, there's that. But as for how I know for sure—we had someone in the records department who confirmed it. Someone with the skill to manipulate the network."

"Had," I echo. "You don't have them anymore?"

He shrugs, looking uncomfortable. "They disappeared shortly after they hacked into your profile. We assume they've been terminated."

That sick feeling twists in my stomach again. "Assume? You don't know?"

Kilían bends over his blade, inspecting it for damage. "They were taken from their post mid-shift. They never turned up in interrogation or anywhere else. We assumed the worst." He straightens up, eyeing my face. "This is a lot to take in, Westergaard. Are you all right?"

"Never better," I tell Kilían, and give him the look the question deserves. "You've kept this from me for nineteen years. Why tell me now unless you want something from me?"

From the way he sets his shoulders, as if bracing for battle, I know I've hit the mark. He turns away, long enough to return his borrowed sverd to its accustomed place on the wall, and I wait, using the hem of my shirt to wipe his blood from my blade. A cloud scuds across the moon, and when Kilían turns back to me, his face is in shadow. "You're not wrong," he says.

I chuckle, the sound devoid of amusement. "Let me spare you the trouble. You want me to join this cursed Brotherhood of yours, and sign my death warrant along with it. Yeah?"

He shrugs again, and I roll my eyes.

"I may be impulsive, Kilían. But I'm not an idiot. Why in the nine hells would I do a thing like that?"

"Are you satisfied, Ari?" he says in response, holding out his hand for my sverd. "Are you happy?"

I pass it to him, tugging at my weapons belt so it hangs evenly from my hips once more. "What kind of virtueless questions are those?"

"Important ones," he says, "and the fact you don't consider them so is indicative of your Commonwealth brainwashing. Happiness is important, Westergaard. As is personal fulfillment and the right to experience a full range of emotions without considering them to be evil or sinful. In the Brotherhood, we believe that." He says it with reverence, as if this misguided little movement of his ought to be pronounced with a capital B.

"You have lost your mind," I tell him, even though the words coming out of his mouth bear an eerie resemblance to the ones I was thinking before—that I am sick of all the rules that govern us, tired of being told what to do. Those were just thoughts, albeit dangerous ones. This is different. "Assuming you're telling the truth, a record-keeper was killed simply for looking at a profile he shouldn't have.

What do you think the Executor would do to someone who tried to bring the entire Commonwealth down?"

Kilían doesn't answer me. He doesn't have to.

Wearily, I run a hand through my sweaty hair. "Thank you for the information, Bellator Bryndísarson, and for the fencing bout. Both have been very instructive. But as for your generous offer, I fear I must decline."

I bow to him politely, as I have been trained, and turn to go. My head is spinning, taking the room with it. Inside I can feel my anger rising, getting closer and closer to the surface, threatening to break free. I want to be long gone from here when it does.

"Wait," Kilían says, and I feel his hand descend on my shoulder. It is too much, and I pivot, glaring.

"Touch me again and forfeit a limb," I spit at him.

"Ease down, Westergaard," he says. "I want to make you an offer."

"There's nothing you've got that I want. Now let me go."

"What about your parents?" He cocks his head to the side, eyebrows raised.

"What about them?" *Wrath is a sin a sin a sin.*

Kilían's hand falls from my shoulder. He takes one careful step backward, then another. "You want to see your parents, don't you, Westergaard?"

"What?"

"Your parents. Work with me, and I'll make sure you meet them. They want that, and I'm sure you do too—or you will, once you've had a chance to think this conversation over. Do what I ask, and I'll make it happen."

All these years, feeling different, desperate for connection and ashamed. And now Kilían is offering me what I've always wanted—wanted so much, I even went looking for it with Eva, knowing the punishment was exile or death. I never thought any temptation would rival what I feel for her—but by the Sins, this comes close.

I regard him, measuring the tilt of his head, the speed of his pulse, his stance. I know Kilían's tells, have studied them for the past two years. He's not exhibiting any now. "How do I know you're not an Informer?"

There is a beat of silence while he considers this. "You'll just have to trust me."

I laugh, the sound echoing in the empty room. "You're a funny man, Kilían Bryndísarson. Say on."

He hands me a photograph. He tells me everything.

17

EVA

All night long, I expect a knock on my door—Ari himself, or maybe Efraím, saying he knows what we did, he sees everything that happens in the Commonwealth and we will pay the price. I barely sleep. At breakfast the next morning, I am exhausted, sipping my tea without a word and ignoring Jakob Riis's dirty looks by the simple expedient of focusing on my plate. This strategy serves a dual purpose: I can't even glance in Ari's direction, for fear of giving myself away. By contrast, Ari is his normal self, inquiring after Riis's scratched cheek with a false air of concern, shoving the basket of toast in my direction before I have to ask, bantering with Karsten about the damage I did to his sword arm. Still, I know better than almost anyone how skilled he is at pretense and disguise.

After assembly, I expect him to order me up to the training room and brace my sore muscles for combat. Instead, he catches Efraím outside and asks for the last thing I'd expect—permission to go down to the vineyards, on the premise of having me taste the varieties of ceremonial wine and learn how to better discern the intricacies of their flavor.

"After yesterday, sir, I don't think it's sparring practice she needs," he says, with a sarcastic smirk that—wonder of wonders—Efraím returns. "I'd like to work with her on honing her senses—the subtleties of battle. If I may?"

Permission granted, Ari strides beside me, not bothering to slow his pace for mine. We've made it through Wunderstrand Square, past the dining hall and the garment factory, and are well on our way down the path to the vineyards before I find the courage to speak. "I'm sorry," I say, pitching my voice low. "Last night—I shouldn't have walked away. It was a coward's retreat, and I owe you an apology."

He clears his throat, then glances down at me. "It's all right, Eva. I'm not upset."

"Really?" I say in disbelief. "Because yesterday, you seemed—"

"I was upset yesterday," he says, cutting me off. "More than upset. But let's just say I got it out of my system."

We cut past a group of white-clad children harvesting grapes, tugging them free of the vines along the arbors and dropping them into buckets. They fall silent at the sight of us, and I remember what it was like to be their age—how intimidating the bellators always seemed, like a separate, predatory species. Now here I am, one of them.

The moment the children are out of earshot, Ari turns to me. "Eva. I have to talk to you."

My heart picks up speed, tapping out an uneven rhythm. "We said everything last night. What else is there to talk about?"

He steps onto the rocky path that leads to the most secluded tasting room, far away from the vineyards themselves. "Plenty," he says over his shoulder. "But not here."

We don't speak again until he pushes open the door to the tasting room, holding it so I can step inside. The room is deserted, except for the barrels of wine that line the walls, the rack of glasses on the counter, and two chairs. Sunlight filters through the windows, illuminating the dust particles that drift in the air, coming to rest on the polished wood floor.

The door swings shut behind us, the latch settling into place with a click. I turn to face Ari, but he isn't looking at me. Instead he has crossed to one of the barrels and is holding a glass underneath the spigot. He fills it and tilts it back, lifting it to his lips. The long muscles of his throat move as he swallows, and I have to admonish myself not to stare.

"Ah," he says after a long moment. "Now, you." Pulling a second glass from the rack on the counter, he fills it and hands it to me, careful not to let our fingers touch.

"Why are we really here?" I ask him, and I'm rewarded with an inscrutable smile.

18

ARI

I made up my mind to tell Eva about the Brotherhood and the circumstances of my birth as soon as I left the training room last night. We already share one dangerous secret; why not another? Besides, whatever strange dynamic has sprung up between us—whatever we might or might not become—I trust her the way I trust few others. She doubted the aims of the Commonwealth before I ever did. If anyone will understand, it's her.

I stayed up until the bell rang for the Oath this morning, thinking about the rest of what Kilían told me—how my parents escaped through a system of tunnels that run beneath the Commonwealth, branching out from the underground passageways containing the prison cells and the interrogation chamber. Kilían brought a photog of my parents as proof—a gift from the leader of the Brotherhood camp —and extended it to me like the rare treasure it was: the two of them together, arms around each other as if touching were the most natural thing in the world.

I stared down at the little square in my hand, evidence Kilían was telling the truth. My father's green eyes matched my own, but the arch of my brows and the sweep of my cheekbones seemed lifted from my mother's face. I had my father's fall of dark hair and my mother's olive skin.

Kilían reclaimed the photog and showed me a handshake to prove

I hailed from the Brotherhood—fingers curled against his palm as his index finger hooked over my own.

"Speak of the wolf, and he will come," he whispered. And taught me how to reply in kind: "So it shall be, Kilían Bryndísarson. A wolf will not bite a wolf."

I stood, silent and still, as Kilían described the entrance to the tunnels that led out of the City—behind an underground passageway dead-ending in a room filled with dusty tomes, maintained by one of the Commonwealth's most respected scholars...and a member of the Brotherhood. If I could talk my way past the scholar, if I could make it to the Outside, I would have accomplished half the battle. The rest would lie in discovering the location of the Brotherhood camp and convincing their leader I was worthy of his trust. And then I would have to decide what to do, where my loyalties stand.

"Let justice be done, even should the world perish," Kilían said at last, voice hoarse from talking.

I took his extended hand, sealing our bargain with the words he'd taught me. "Let justice be done, even should the sky fall." And I walked away, back to my narrow cot and my narrow life, where I lay sleepless until dawn broke over the horizon and I rose, a loyal bellator once more.

The weight of this knowledge is crushing. But it could also set me —*us*—free.

Eva and I are alone in the tasting room, with no one closer than the vineyards to hear. If I am going to tell her, this is the best chance I'll have.

I wait for her to take the first sip. And then I speak.

19

EVA

"Well?" Ari says, his eyes flickering from my face to the half-empty wineglass in his left hand. "Say something."

I lean back against the wall, willing my body not to shake. I'm not sure which topic is more dangerous—this supposed Brotherhood to which Kilían wants to recruit Ari, or the claim he is natural-born. We've been brought up to think of natural-born children as less than worthy, the product of unholy lust. Most languish in menial jobs, stigmatized by their beginnings. They're told who they are from the start, raised with stricter punishments by the Mothers, watched carefully for aberrations, lest they join their parents on the executioner's block or in exile. Their genetic material is flawed, prone to sin and thus excluded from the procreation requirements we are all subject to, one year after the Choosing.

I seize on this, picking one question off the top of multitudes. "Well, to play the Devil's advocate—if you're natural-born, wouldn't they exclude you from the procreation offerings on Donation Day?"

Ari eyes me with disbelief. "Everything I've told you, and *that's* what you choose to focus on?"

"Just answer the question."

He shifts from one foot to the other, shrugging, and doesn't say a word.

"Well?" I press. "They haven't, have they?"

A slow blush heats Ari's cheeks, the first time I've ever seen him look embarrassed. "No," he says shortly. "They haven't."

"I don't understand. What would be the point, if this is really who you are?"

"How do I know?" he snaps, turning away. "Maybe they plan to throw my samples out, Eva. Or use them to study my defective genetics. Or maybe it's a shell game, something to cover up who I really am—since obviously they never intended for me to find out."

"When you went in to fulfill your requirement," I say without thinking, "did you ever notice anything strange in the way they dealt with you? Anything different than the other petitioners?"

Ari sets his glass down on the counter with a thump. His head is bent to hide his face, but I can see a dark flush creeping up the back of his neck nonetheless. "That day," he says, his voice sounding strangled, "you're not thinking about anything but why you're there —what they're sending you into a little room to do."

His voice breaks on the last word, and I feel color begin to heat my own cheeks. Donation Day is one of the few mysteries of the Commonwealth, the subject of endless forbidden speculation. We're not allowed to talk about it amongst ourselves, much less ask the participants to describe their experience. Such curiosity would lead to inappropriate discussions, which might in turn lead to the commission of sin. Better to remove temptation from our paths whenever possible—except here I am, courting it, despite my determination to do otherwise. Why is it when it comes to me and Ari, nothing goes the way it should?

He takes pity on both of us, rocking back on his heels and picking up the glass again. He swallows half of its remaining contents before he speaks. "No one has ever treated me any differently on Donation Day, Eva. But how in all the nine circles of hell would I know what they did with my sample after I put it into that cubby in the wall? If they had something to hide, they'd hide it, wouldn't they? Not flaunt it in my face so I'd get suspicious."

"I suppose," I say, on safer ground. "But then how did Kilían find out? And why tell you now?"

He cradles the bowl of the glass in one hand, running a finger along the rim. "Kilían says he found out from my parents. It could hardly be otherwise—the records are sealed. You'd need a master hacker to break into them."

"I could do it," I say impulsively.

One of his eyebrows creeps upward, a black arch above the moss-green of his eyes. "You're that good?"

I give him the eyebrow right back. "You want the truth, or false modesty?"

His expression alters subtly, absorbing this. "Hmmm. You have many worthwhile talents, apprentice mine. A gift with edged weapons, a flair for distraction, uncanny aim, speed to rival my own. Few fears. And now this. What else are you hiding?"

"I'm not hiding anything," I retort, affronted. "It just wasn't relevant before. I volunteered the information, didn't I?"

"I suppose you're right." He sets the glass down again, his fingers drumming a broken rhythm on the wooden counter. "I'll keep that in mind, Eva. It might come in handy sometime. But to your other question—if Kilían's to be believed, he told me now because he's been keeping an eye on me, at my parents' behest, and he thought I was ready. Before—well, I was too young. I wasn't trained, I would have been a liability." He shrugs. "He said the Brotherhood is building an army to rival the Bellatorum, composed of the best warriors they can find. They're camped outside the Commonwealth, waiting."

I snort, amused. "Don't flatter yourself overmuch, Bellator Westergaard. You're gifted, sure—but that's not the only reason they're trying to recruit you."

Ari's fingers pause in their assault on the countertop. "What do you mean?"

"It's obvious, isn't it? They have something over you. Your desire to find your parents, now you know they exist—that you weren't conceived in a test tube like the rest of us—assuming Kilían is telling you the truth. As long as they have something you want, you're less likely to run screaming to the High Priests and the Executor than your average bellator, sworn to uphold his oath and devoted to the cause."

Ari bares his teeth at me, eyes narrowing again. "I'll not be easily foresworn, Eva. Not for a handful of hollow promises. But if there's any truth to what Kilían told me—I have to find out. And if he is right

—then my oath means nothing, for I have sworn it to a cause that doesn't exist, save in the minds of delusional, power-hungry zealots."

Treason, I think, but the word holds less weight than it ought to. All my life, I've felt that at the heart of the Commonwealth is not the purity we've been led to believe, but rather an insidious, infectious rot. I felt it when the Mothers told us stories of the selkies, stripped of their skins and abandoned on the shores; when the High Priest ordered a man put to death for stealing wine; when Instruktor Bjarki was shamed for wanting to learn. But why should I trust Kilían or Ari, who might well be positioned to sniff out any scent of sedition? I have always been alone in my convictions—except, it occurs to me, for the moment in Clockverk Square when Ari held my gaze.

If the Priest had noticed his defiance, Ari would have been cruelly punished. Why did he chance it? From a soon-to-be-warrior's appreciation of the risk I'd taken? Pity? Or empathy, because down deep, he felt the same?

THEN THERE'S THE WAY THE EXECUTOR IS SO CLOSELY GUARDED, IN THE absence of any visible threats—why? And the malice and competition amongst the bellators—as if we are being trained for war, not the maintenance of a civil society. Seen in the context of this resistance, the pieces suddenly fit.

"Why tell me?" I ask, my voice little more than a breath of air. "Aren't you afraid I'll betray you?"

"You won't," he says, his finger tracing the whorls in the wood.

"Sure of yourself, aren't you? May I remind you of the last time you decided to act on your hubris where I'm concerned?"

He chuckles, remembering, as I am, the moment I knocked him from the tree and pinned him to the wet ground. The smile fades from his face as he thinks, doubtless, of what came afterward—if he's ever stopped thinking about it. I know I haven't been able to.

"I'm not likely to forget anytime soon," Ari says, clearing his throat. "But this isn't pride, Eva—it's faith."

"In *me*?" My voice arches upward, cracking. "Why?"

"Oh, a thousand reasons. Because I remember a little girl who stood up to the High Priest on her first execution day. Who ordered oatmeal when she could have had skyr and cinnamon apples, rather than see a woman suffer. But if you want the simplest one—you're curious, aren't you? You want to know the truth, just as I do. Admit it." His eyes are on me, his gaze coolly amused.

A shiver runs through me at his words. Manipulation—or the truest insight I've ever had into his heart? "All right," I say irritably, concealing my fear. "But they do say curiosity killed the cat, Ari Westergaard. How are you so sure this will be any different?"

Ari tilts his head to one side, considering me. "It'd be worth it," he says, so softly it's hard to hear, "dying with you."

Unnerved, I look down at my hands, resting on my chakram and the hilt of my dagur. Would I say the same—that I'd sacrifice my own life with peace of mind, if Ari were with me? I can't say I'd go willingly to my death, no matter my companion. It seems the worst kind of foolishness—and whatever else Ari Westergaard might be, I have never figured him for a fool.

But then—why?

When I glance upward, having found no answer, he's still watching me. "So you'll come?" he says in that same quiet voice.

"You want me to come with you? My voice cracks with surprise. "Into the tunnels—and out, into what lies beyond the fence? The ruins and the hordes?"

He lifts one shoulder and lets it fall. "Who else?"

"By the Sins, Ari—"

"It's a simple question, apprentice mine. Yes or no. You choose."

Could it be Kilían is telling the truth? And if so—if there's a world where I'm not alone in my belief that mercy may outweigh justice— how can I refuse to see such a place with my own eyes?

Suddenly there isn't enough air in the room. With what's left to me, I try to formulate a solid defense. "Listen to yourself. If there really is a resistance—and we leave the Commonwealth to find it— then what? What if Kilían is a plant, designed to test our loyalty, and we creep through those damned tunnels only to be slaughtered on the other end? What happens if we can't get back in, and we're stranded…out there? Or if we do get back in, and get caught?"

Ari folds his arms across his chest. "I don't think Kilían's lying, Eva. And what if we do get stranded? Would that be so bad?"

"What in the nine hells are you talking about? We have no idea what's out there! The drowned cities—the exiles bent on vengeance and sin—the Outsiders whose idea of morality is corrupt at best—you want to be stuck out there with them?"

He looks down at me, frowning. "How do we know that's what's on the other side of the fence? Because the Priests told us so? We've always believed them, Eva. We took for granted this was how things had to be. But what if we've been lied to? What if there's more?"

His words are like the fairytales the Mothers used to tell us when they tucked us in—the cursed girl who pricked herself with a needle on account of her beauty and was doomed to sleep for a hundred years, the scullery maid who was saved by a dance and a glass slipper, only to spend the rest of her days locked away in the castle she sought to rule, mourning the price of her vanity. Like Lachlan and the Selkie—a warning against the dangers of attachment, of surrendering to our baser emotions and indulging the weaknesses of the flesh—they are a warped version of reality, a seed of honesty grown wild, too wayward to be true.

"More?" I say hoarsely. "More—what?"

"I don't know," he says, meeting my eyes. "Just—more. Don't you feel things could be different, Eva? Better? What you said to me about how we can't erase what happened between us—I've been thinking about it ever since. That, and what Kilían said about how there are people out there who believe there's another way to live. That the world we're living in is wrong, skewed. I know it sounds crazy. But if there's the slightest possibility it's real—don't you think we owe it to ourselves to find out?"

Though it's treachery to think it, I can't help but wonder if leaving the Commonwealth for good would be the answer to all my problems. No struggle to reconcile my conscience with the inexplicable joy I feel when I take a blade in my hand, the sense of triumph that washed through me when I sliced Riis's belt and carved Karsten's arms to bits. No terror Efraím will divine I've begun to feel far more for Ari than an apprentice should feel for her mentor.

We are already Outsiders, he and I. Look at what we've done.

He brushes my cheek with his fingertip, sending that now-familiar electricity searing through my veins. "Be brave," he whispers. "Not for the sake of what's between us. Not for me. But for yourself."

I draw a deep breath, taking in the scent of wine and metal, of the aged oak of the barrels and Ari. And then I straighten and meet his gaze with my own. "You're my mentor. If you're determined to do this, then I will stand by your side."

"Drink to it, then. To seal our bargain." He gestures to my glass and I tilt it back, closing my eyes. The wine slides down my throat, redolent of grapes and sunlight.

"What do you taste?" It's a mentor's question, innocent enough— but the tone of his voice is anything but. It's as if he's asking two questions at once, the second one hidden inside the first like one of those nesting dolls we used to play with in the Nursery.

Startled, I blink. He is standing inches from me, close enough to see the flecks of brown in his green eyes and smell the salt on his skin. Remembering how he shivered beneath me in the woods when I held my knife to his throat, how he gripped my hand under the cover of darkness at Black Falls, I have to fight to hold myself still.

"I taste violets," I say softly. "Chocolate. Pepper. The earth itself. And light."

"Ah." His eyes on mine, he takes the glass, his lips sliding over the rim where mine have touched. And then he drains it, his throat moving as he swallows. He sets it down on the counter and licks his lips, his eyes never leaving my face.

A tingling feeling rushes through me, setting off every alarm bell I have. "We should go." I take a hasty step backward. "I'll think about everything you said—and I won't tell anyone. We'll talk about the details and come up with a strategy that will give us the greatest chance of success. But we shouldn't be here alone any longer. It's not safe."

"I have to ask you a question," Ari says, as if he hasn't heard a word. "And to tell you something. Not necessarily in that order."

"Maybe you shouldn't—"

That sardonic smile is back, transforming his face to something distant, almost cruel. "Oh, I know I shouldn't. But that's beside the point. I'm going crazy, Eva." His voice is inflectionless. "I can't think about my training. I can barely think about what Kilían wants me to do—and the Virtues know I can't afford to walk down *that* road without my wits intact. Every time I shut my eyes, there you are." His eyes narrow, the way they do when he is about to call me out in training. "Am I alone with this? Tell me."

His words could have just as easily come from my lips…if I'd had the foolishness to utter them. I do my best to save us both, offering a plausible excuse. "You're my mentor," I say, trying to keep my teeth from chattering. "Of course I have an—an attachment to you. But that's only natural. We work together every day. It would be strange if I didn't feel closer to you than the rest. What happened last night— it was a mistake."

"Natural?" he echoes. "Is it *natural* for you to ask me about Donation Day, then? And for me to answer, in detail I've never shared with another human being?" His voice lowers, an intimate whisper that slides over my skin. "You know what it felt like to answer you, Eva? It felt like touching you again, with my words instead of my hands. Can you deny that?"

I don't say a word. To speak would be to incriminate myself.

Ari clears his throat. "That was a question. Answer it, please."

I think of the months of watching him train with his shirt off, wanting against all reason to trace his scars with my fingers. Of the nameless desire that wells up in me at the sight of one of his rare, true smiles, a brushfire that flared into a conflagration in the woods against that tree. "It doesn't matter what it felt like," I tell him, willing this to be true. "It's wrong. You know that as well as I do."

"So you do feel something." There's triumph in his voice, an unmistakable vindication. "Last night—when we were together—it changed something in me, Eva. I've never felt that way. Like I'd been asleep for years, and I finally woke up. Or—" He shakes his head in frustration. "I'm not saying it right. All I know is I'd do almost anything to feel that way again. I dream about kissing you, the way you feel, the way you taste. I have, ever since that morning at Black Falls. Since before that, even, if I'm being honest." His voice breaks, but he doesn't look away. "I don't know what to do about it. At least tell me I'm not in it alone."

He steps closer, and now I can feel the warmth emanating from his skin. I want to turn and run, but his gaze holds me and I cannot move. "When we were lying on the ground in the rain..." he says, eyes traveling over me the way they did last night, lazy and sure. "You had your hand pressed to my chest. And your blade to my throat. Remember?"

"*Je me rends,*" I say before I can help myself, and am rewarded with his slow smile.

"I may be your mentor," he says, "but you've got my heart in your hand, Eva Marteinn. And I'm not inclined to let you close your fist, warrior that you are. So as far as I'm concerned—*we* have a problem."

I want to deny what he's saying, to pretend his words don't ignite a slow-burning flame inside me. But that would be a coward's choice, and though I may be a sinner and now a traitor, I'm not a coward. And so I lift my chin and speak my mind.

"If we go through with this, Ari, we may wind up as exiles or prisoners. Or dead." I swallow hard, wishing for more wine. Drink enough of it, I have heard, and it will give you the nerve to do what you most fear. "The way you feel—you're *not* alone. But if we risk this —escaping the Commonwealth to seek the counsel of a band of rebels —how you and I feel about each other will be the least of our problems. And if I'm worrying about what's between us, I won't be able to think clearly."

The light has returned to Ari's eyes, but his voice is cautious. "What are you saying?"

"One betrayal at a time is all I can handle. Let's figure this part out first...how we'll make it through the tunnels and back without being discovered or killed. Accomplish that, and I promise—we can talk about the rest."

Ari looks me over, assessing my sincerity. Then he crosses to the barrels once more, wine glasses in hand. He presses the spigot, and the heady scents of chocolate and pepper fill the air.

Handing my glass to me, he regards me levelly over the rim of his own. "Swear it on your honor as a bellator. And drink."

I draw the wine into my mouth, seeking courage in its depths. "On my honor as a bellator, I do so swear."

Ari tosses half of his glass back in one gulp. He upends the rest, and it splashes to the floor, red as spilled blood. "All right, little warrior," he says. "You have a deal."

20

ARI

We choose Idle Day to venture into the unknown world beyond the fence. It's the only occasion that—unless we're assigned a specific duty—our time is more or less our own, our absence most likely to go unnoticed.

We don't talk much on our way through the woods, to the hollow tree where we've stashed packs filled with enough food and water to last us a couple of days. After that, if we're stuck Outside—or decide to stay—we'll have to hunt.

I stand with my back to the tree, keeping watch, as Eva digs the packs out and slings hers over her shoulder. She shoves mine into my chest, hard enough to hurt. "It took us a *week* to gather all this stuff. Every single time, I thought we were going to get caught and interrogated. So I want to ask you again—are you sure this is worth the risk?"

I think of Kilían, his hand warm in mine, whispering *Speak of the wolf, and he will come.* "It better be," I say, stepping out from between the trees. "Come on—this way."

Neither of us speaks as we find our way down into the underground tunnels that run beneath the City. I concentrate on following the directions Kilían gave me: *Enter the tunnels near Marketor Square, left at the first fork, walk for a quarter mile, bear right, then left, then right again. Then walk for another half-mile down the tunnel*

that appears to have been used the least. It will dead-end in a door. Knock.
And then wait.

I've been in the tunnels before—have done my share of guard duty and interrogation down here—but I had no idea they stretched beyond the Commonwealth's walls. How could I? I've had no occasion to visit the room at the end of the tunnel Kilían described. And even if I had, how would I have known what lay beyond?

Still, I feel foolish, gullible. My annoyance quickens my pace, and beside me, Eva gives a reluctant chuckle. "Eager to meet your fate, I see," she says.

I shoot her a sideways glance, drawing in a lungful of the damp underground air. It's dark, lit only by torches that burn along the walls, but I can see the wry expression on her face clearly enough. "No point in prolonging the agony, is there?" I say.

She shrugs, kicking up a spray of gravel. "I suppose that's a matter of opinion."

The tunnels have narrowed, the air colder now. Far away, I can hear water dripping steadily. I bear right as Kilían instructed, toward the two tunnels that branch before us. "We're supposed to walk down the one that looks neglected," I say. But it's not like either one looks set to host an Idle Day picnic. They're both nicely decorated with wall slime and moldering rock. "How are we supposed to know which one to choose?"

Eva surveys the two tunnels. Then she takes a deep breath and holds it, letting it out in stages as if she's sampling the air. "That one," she says, pointing to the tunnel on the left.

"How do you know?"

She shrugs, looking discomfited. "I can't explain it. It just smells as if fewer people have used it lately. And the scents it does hold are strong, as if the same people have gone there over and over, with a specific purpose in mind."

"I don't understand how you're picking all that up," I say, perplexed and annoyed. I'm her mentor; how is it she can read a scent trail better than I can?

Eva shrugs again, meeting my eyes with a defiant expression. "I can't explain it, and don't ask me to. I'm just telling you what I smell."

"Fine," I say curtly. "The tunnel on the left it is. The worst that can happen is we retrace our steps. Or we go the wrong way and end up getting our heads sliced off."

"We won't have to retrace a thing," Eva mutters, affronted. She steps ahead of me, leading the way down the left-hand tunnel.

The tunnel narrows further, and soon it's only wide enough for us to walk single-file. I wish I were in front—this is my mission, and I am the senior bellator—but it's too late. Instead I follow Eva into the ever-darkening gloom. The wall torches are fewer and further apart here, and my eyes adjust to the darkness. I suppose we could use the solar-powered flashlights we have brought with us, but I have no idea whether there will be any light at all in the tunnels that stretch beyond the Commonwealth, and it seems wiser to save them until we have no choice.

We walk forever down the virtueless tunnel, Eva's shape one of a hundred shifting shadows, the only sounds the crunch of our footsteps, the rasp of our breath, and the endless, mind-numbing drip of water. Finally the tunnel opens up again and we are once more able to stand side by side, in an area lit by three torches. I have to blink several times before I realize we're facing a wooden door set into the stone wall of the tunnel as Kilían had promised it would be.

I look at Eva, and she at me. And then she raises her hand and knocks.

2 1

EVA

A voice comes, harsh with the clear ring of authority. "Who goes?"

Ari draws himself up, straightening to his full six feet. One of his hands reaches over his shoulder, resting on the hilt of the blade along his spine. The other finds mine, fingers pressing hard, and even in the musty dark I can't suppress the feeling that spreads through me—as if my blood has alchemized into the frivolous bubbly drink people used to mark celebrations before the Fall, the one they called Champagne. I squeeze back, and I'm rewarded with one of his rare smiles. He gestures to my own blade, and lets me go.

"Ari Westergaard and Eva Marteinn," he says as my fingers close around the hilt. Immediately, to my shame, I feel better. Just as the small children in the Nursery have their worn stuffed creatures for comfort, passed down from one generation to the next to discourage greed and attachment to material things, so I have my sverd. It may be cold comfort, but it is comfort all the same. "Of the Bellatorum Lucis. We seek safe passage."

The voice behind the door speaks again, skeptical now. "Bellatorum Lucis. You bring danger into our midst. Why should we let you pass?"

I step forward, past Ari. He touches my arm in warning, but I ignore him. "We have information," I say, lifting my chin. "Let us through."

The man laughs, a sound of true surprise. "Does she speak for you, Ari Westergaard?"

Next to me, Ari has come to full alert. I can feel the tension rolling off him in waves, feel his muscles coil. But his voice is calm as still water as it always is, as it was trained to be, when he says, "She does."

"Interesting," the man says. "We have heard of you, Eva Marteinn. The first female warrior to stand with the Bellatorum. We've been waiting, biding our time. That you should approach us is a gift. But you, Westergaard—you are a risk. State your purpose."

"We seek a trade," Ari says in the formal language of the man behind the door, the speech of the scholars. "Our information for safe passage through the tunnels. Eva stands with the Bellatorum, and I stand with her. I mean no harm."

"Really," the man says, amused. "And yet you come to us armed, Ari Westergaard. Don't bother to lie. I can smell the oil on your blade."

Next to me I feel Ari start, a twitch of his muscles stilled and concealed as quickly as it began. He sets his feet, the way he always does before a match, finding his balance. I hear him draw a deep breath, there in the dark. "Speak of the wolf," he says, "and he will come."

Silence falls, and in it, Ari's hand finds mine again. His fingers are rough with grime from the rock walls, gritty with crumbled dirt. For an instant, I see us as if from above—a boy and a girl, clad in black, gripping each other for strength, as if our touch will serve to protect us more than the razor-sharp, gleaming blades strapped to our backs. Trained as hawks to throw into the faces of our enemies, talons slashing and beaks sinking deep. To cleave through a circle without mercy, when discussion has done its best and been found wanting.

The man behind the door speaks, his voice as toneless as our own. "A wolf does not bite a wolf."

And then the door swings wide.

ARI

As the door creaks open, I yank my hand free of Eva's. Our presence here is disadvantage enough without handing this man the ammunition he needs to destroy us.

He is nondescript, the kind of man I could pass on the street a thousand times without taking notice. His hair is short and light brown, his features even. He wears dark pants and a gray shirt. Even his build is average—two or three inches shorter than I am, his shoulders neither narrow nor broad. When his eyes travel over us, though, he smiles—mirthless, anticipatory. His teeth gleam in the dim light.

"Well met, Ari Westergaard," he says. "Let justice be done, even should the world perish."

I extend my hand to him, curl my fingers against his palm the way Kilían showed me, feel his index finger hook over mine in response. "Let justice be done, even should the sky fall."

Beside me, Eva is motionless and silent—the stillness of a predator, determining whether to strike. I hear her breathing, deep and slow, the way the Bellatorum taught us to center ourselves before battle.

She is my weapon, I realize, as I am hers.

She is my weakness.

"We seek passage," I say for the last time. "Do you grant it, or no?"

The man's smile fades, his thin lips flattening into inscrutability. He lifts his hand, wipes it clean against the gray cotton of his shirt. And then he steps away from the door, allowing us entry.

"Welcome, Wolf's Brother," he says. "And you, Eva Marteinn."

The scholar's chamber is a small cavern carved of rock, lined with books that face spine-out from built-in shelves—volumes written before the Fall, perhaps, guarded from unclean fingers and prying eyes. I think, stupidly, that keeping paper copies of precious artifacts down here, where the moisture level is so high, is asking for trouble—but then I notice a small device humming away in the corner, the same kind we keep in the weapons room to protect our blades, designed to suck water from the air. There is a tall ladder that leans up against one of the shelves, a high-backed chair, and a wooden desk. Otherwise, the room is empty.

The man stands aside, gesturing at a door set in the back wall, between shelves. "There," he says.

I know time is of the essence, that we cannot linger here, but curiosity gets the better of me. "What are these books? Why aren't they in the library with the others?"

He gives me a beatific smile. "That knowledge is not for you, Ari Westergaard, blade or no blade."

"If you won't answer his question, maybe you'll answer mine," Eva says, an edge to her voice. "You said you were waiting for me. What were you waiting for?"

The man's smile doesn't change, but a sense of menace emanates from him at her words. "Ask me again when you return, assuming you do so. Ask then, and you may receive your answer."

"What is that supposed to mean—" Eva begins, but I step in front of her, blocking her view.

"Don't bother. He won't tell us anything, unless you plan to torture it out of him. We have to go."

Brow creased in annoyance, she gives a curt nod. We pass through the door, leaving the man, his infuriating smile, his mysterious books, and his worrisome intentions behind.

23

EVA

The tunnels that lead to the Outside are dark, the only illumination emanating from our flashlights, and silent, except for the crunch of our boots and the steady drip of water. I track our footsteps, calculating time and distance the way Ari has taught me. We've gone a quarter of a mile when the tunnel opens into a large, high-ceilinged cavern. I snap my fingers, letting the sound echo, and sweep my flashlight across the room to confirm what both of us already know. There are three tunnels branching out from the other side: Two leading deeper into the labyrinth under the mountain, the other upward, toward fresh air and the Outside.

"That man was disturbing," I say, starting across the cavern, to the closest tunnel. "I don't trust him at all."

Ari shines his flashlight into the tunnel beside mine, looking for the chalked outline of the wolf's face Kilían promised would mark the way to the Outside. "You think?"

"What do you think those books are doing down there?" I say, backing out of my tunnel. "And what does he want from me?"

Ari snorts. "Honestly, Eva, if we pull this off and our worst problem is dealing with that bastard of a scholar, I think we can count ourselves lucky. There it is," he adds, shifting so I can see the sketched outline of a wolf chalked onto the tunnel wall. "This way."

We creep through three tunnels, each one damper and darker than the next. Two are wide enough that we can walk side by side; the third is so narrow that I have to press my arms against my body to wriggle through. Thirty minutes later, we come to a fork in our path. I aim my flashlight into the tunnel on my left, and see nothing—but when I shine it into the one on my right, the beam picks out the faint outline of a wolf's face.

This tunnel is like all the others—water seeping down the pockmarked walls, the damp crunch of gravel beneath my feet—but it narrows at the end, and I can make out a hint of light. One hand resting on the hilt of my dagur, the other tight around the rubberized grip of the flashlight, I move cautiously forward.

Ari follows me, the beam of his flashlight tracing mine, then skirting upward, washing over the ceiling of the tunnel. "This one's different," he whispers, coming to stand next to me.

I nod, realize he probably can't see me very well, and try again, pitching my voice as low as his. "Yes. It feels more open, somehow. I think—I think maybe this is it."

"Yeah, me too," he says. "I—"

Whatever he is about to say is interrupted by a noise that sends my heart rocketing into my throat—the rattle of metal from the other end of the tunnel. Ari's body stiffens, and then he is gone, his flashlight dimmed, his shape melding into the shadows that flank the wall. I do the same, flattening myself on the opposite side of the tunnel, listening for all I am worth.

There are no footsteps or voices, nothing to signal the presence of other human beings—let alone a horde of barbarian Outsiders. A current of air moves past me, and I inhale, sampling it as I have been taught. I smell pine needles and crushed bracken, wet leaves and the musty, close confines of the tunnel—but no scent of unwashed bodies or roasted meat.

The air gusts again, and with it comes the rattling noise—a grate, I realize with relief, vibrating with the force of the wind. I open my mouth to tell Ari this, and jump as his hand closes on my shoulder. "Easy," he whispers. "It's just me."

"Don't *do* that," I hiss into his ear, and feel him laugh silently. "You can let go now," I say, unnerved.

Instead, he spins me toward him and ducks his head, his lips slanting over mine. He tastes like the mint leaves from the garden behind the Bellatorum's quarters—and a taste that is simply Ari, a burnt-sugar heat. His mouth is soft but insistent, urging me forward, and my body gravitates toward his, a moon toward its planet, a plant toward the sun.

Then he pulls away and lets his hand drop. To my surprise I feel his absence keenly, as if something essential has been stolen from me. I stare up at him, trying to gather the wherewithal to speak—but he beats me to it.

"Luck," he says simply, and flicks his flashlight on again, leading the way toward the Outside.

24

ARI

We are met by a pair of scouts halfway down the path that leads away from the tunnel. It would have been easy to avoid them—we can hear them long before they appear in our line of sight—but since we're trying to act in good faith, we merely hide in the trees long enough to be assured of their identity.

Whoever they might be, it's immediately clear to me who they are not—members of the Commonwealth come to drag us back to face our fate. Their clothes are like nothing I've ever seen—green-and-yellow camouflage designed to blend with the leaves and shifting shadows. The woman's skin is a burnished brown, and her eyes slant upward at the corners. No one in the Commonwealth looks like that —as if they've absorbed the light of the sun into themselves. Stunned, I have to force myself not to stare.

As for the man, he has a headful of tangled blond hair and an untrimmed beard. Both of them have weapons holstered at their hips that I recognize from vids of before the Fall: Guns, outlawed in the Commonwealth as barbaric implements of murder whose usage requires little courage and less skill.

Having assessed their weapons, I do a quick physical inventory. The man appears to be in his mid-twenties, the woman a little younger. He stands taller than I do, about six-foot-three, with a stocky build. The thick camouflage pants and loose green shirt he's wearing make it hard for me to tell much more.

His companion looks like the more dangerous of the two. Her shirt is conspicuously lacking in sleeves—it looks like she ripped them off deliberately—and her pants only cover her to the knee. Every inch of her I can see—which is far more than would ever be allowed in the Commonwealth—is muscular and toned. She moves more quietly than the man, scanning the forest as she goes. Of course, she doesn't spot me and Eva, but that is only to be expected.

Barbarians, I think reflexively, but the word holds little bite. There is intelligence in their eyes and a clear sense of teamwork in the way they move together. Here are only two; we were taught to believe they moved in hordes, mindlessly seeking their targets.

Drawing a deep breath, I step out into the sunlight, gesturing for Eva to stay put. I'm pretty sure these two are just an advance team, but their weapons make me uneasy. I've never seen a gun in person, don't know enough about their mechanics to counter an assault. My first impression is that I'm fast and skilled enough to disarm the two of them, but I'd rather not put both of us in the line of fire.

I step hard on the leaves, making enough noise so the scouts will hear me and turn around. When they do, I stand still, hands out at my sides. "Hello," I say.

The woman's hand drops to her holster. "Identify yourself."

"My name is Ari Westergaard. I mean you no harm."

The man places a hand on her bare arm, a casual gesture indicative of familiarity and an intent to soothe. It's a mistake; I could use both of them as leverage against each other and have them on the ground in an instant. I relax infinitesimally—if they'd make this kind of rookie mistake, how well trained can they be?

"It's all right, Zoya," the man says. "This is the one Ronan told us to expect."

"I know," the woman named Zoya replies, an edge to her voice. "But still—how do we know he doesn't have an army of those creepy Commonwealth fighters with him?"

"Come on, Zoya. You don't think we would've noticed an army making their way through the woods?"

Zoya snorts. "Did you bring an army with you?" she asks me.

I have to refrain from smirking at the irony. Here we are, expecting them to be the advance party of a horde of barbarians; and here they are, anticipating that I've got a full military force at my back. "If by that you mean the Bellatorum, then the answer is no," I say, endeavoring to sound genial. "I did bring a friend, though. Eva, come out where they can see you."

There's rustling, and then Eva steps out from behind a tree and takes her place at my side. She doesn't say a word, just eyes the scouts warily.

"That's it?" Zoya says.

I shift my weight, my left hand brushing my throwing knife. "Yes. Just the two of us."

"Ronan said you'd be alone."

"I don't know who Ronan is. And the two of us are a package deal. Take us or leave us. It's up to you." I don't bother saying the rest —that we can go with them or we can go through them. I haven't come this far to be turned back by a pair of Outsiders who don't like my choice of companion.

"You'll meet Ronan soon enough," the man says. "Zoya, stop giving them a hard time."

"That's my job," the woman says, without the slightest bit of humor.

The man sighs. "Why don't we introduce ourselves? I'm Adrien, and that even-tempered, trusting soul is Zoya."

"I'm Eva," my apprentice says, lifting her chin. "But you know that already. Let's not waste time on the civilities. I assume Ronan is in charge? Bring us to him or do your best to shoot us, it makes no difference to me. Either way, we're going to your camp today."

The woman named Zoya laughs. "Ooooh, I like her," she says, giving Eva an appreciative look.

"You would," Adrien says, sounding disgruntled. "Okay, you want to play it that way? We've heard all about the Bellatorum. I'm sure you're armed to the teeth. Fair warning: Don't try anything out of line." His hand drops to his holster, resting on his gun.

Eva gives him the look the comment deserves. "You think we went to all this trouble to hurt you? If that's what we wanted, you would've been dead before you ever heard us coming." There's no arrogance in her words, just a cool statement of fact.

Adrien flinches. It's not much—just a tightening of the muscles that bracket his lips—but I see it, and Eva does too. She smiles, pressing her advantage. "Ronan. Now. Let's go."

The four of us walk silently through the woods until a series of structures come into view, unlike any I've seen before—thin green material stretched across rounded poles so they form a dome. The structures blend with the trees and foliage, an effective camouflage.

"Welcome to Tent City," Adrien says, the first time he's spoken since he threatened to shoot us if we misbehaved. "A humble home, but our own."

Close up, I can see at least twenty of the dome-like structures, people scurrying in and out of them. Adrien and Zoya move aside, flanking us. "Ronan," she calls. "We brought visitors."

Heads turn at the sound of her voice. Then the structure in front of us unzips, and a man steps out. He's tall, about my height, with skin the rich color of soil after it's been turned over for the harvest and hair twisted into thick, graying braids. His eyes are black and hard as obsidian, as if he's seen too much.

"Ah," he says, seeing us, and straightens. "So you have. Well done. Dismissed."

Eva and I stare at him, wordless. We'd heard the southerners had darker complexions, but neither of us has seen anyone who looks like Zoya, let alone this man. He is no barbarian, and he is in charge here; that much is clear. If there's one thing I am trained to recognize and respect, it is a chain of command. Authority radiates from him the way it does from Efraím—effortless and earned.

Ronan looks us over carefully, unsurprised by our silence. "Bellatorum," he says.

"Your scouts called us members of a 'creepy army,'" Eva offers at last, her voice neutral. "If you can't call us by our names, then I suppose getting our title right is a satisfactory improvement."

For the Architect's sake, I think, giving her a dry look. We need this man. Aggravating him from the start is a dicey strategy.

Eva gives me the look right back and turns her eyes on Ronan. I half-expect the man to retaliate, but instead he laughs, a full-throated chuckle that takes me by surprise.

"Ah. Well, they were born in what you would call the Borderlands. What do they know of bellators?" He shrugs. "It's all rumors and legends to them. Whereas I, like you, was raised in a Commonwealth. Not the Commonwealth of Ashes, of course—nothing so grand as that—but the Commonwealth of Scribes, a hundred miles west of here. Your ways used to be my own."

"You escaped a Commonwealth?" Eva says, respect warring with skepticism in her tone.

"Not escaped, as such. Exiled," Ronan says, frowning. "It was a long time ago. I've been in the Brotherhood since I wasn't much older than you are now. But I don't think I've had the pleasure of your names. I am Ronan Blair, leader of this encampment."

"Eva Marteinn. And this is Ari."

"Ari Westergaard," he says, turning to me. "I've been expecting you. But Kilían didn't say you planned to bring a friend."

I lift one shoulder and let it fall. "It seemed foolish to undertake an endeavor of this scope without backup."

Ronan's mouth twitches in what might be a smile. "I see. Well, we have a lot to talk about, and not a lot of time in which to do it. Come into my tent, if you would, and we'll discuss."

He holds the flap aside and Eva and I step through, scanning the interior for danger. But there's nothing inside except for a small comp on a tree stump, a rucksack, and some hand-drawn maps. The place is bare, the temporary home of someone who expects to have to move at a moment's notice, and now the fabric structures with their bendable poles—tents, Ronan and Adrien called them—make sense. They must be easily collapsible, and just as easily abandoned if need be.

Ronan steps through after us and lets the flap fall closed. He zips it shut, sets the comp on the ground, and gestures to the sleeping mat. "Please have a seat," he says. "I apologize for the Spartan quality of the accommodations."

Gingerly, we settle onto the mat. Ronan sits down on the stump in turn, his hands dangling between his legs, and squares his shoulders. "So. Do you want to speak first, or should I?"

"Go ahead," I tell him. It's standard interrogation technique—get your subject talking, and reveal as little of yourself as possible. I'm not interrogating Ronan—but I'll be damned if I'll give away anything he can use against me without gaining something first.

"Well," he begins, "let's get the elephant in the room out of the way first, shall we?"

I glance around the tent, puzzled. I've seen images of elephants before: Giant beasts, gray, with a long trunk and an affinity for peanuts. What one of those creatures has to do with our present situation, I can't imagine—but for all I know, the Brotherhood expects to rise to victory on the backs of massive mammals, shelling nuts as they go.

Ronan laughs, seeing our confusion. "It's an expression. Never mind. What I meant to say is—you've noticed, obviously, that I don't look like you. Nor does Zoya, or many of the people in this camp."

Eva opens her mouth, then shuts it again, at a loss. Forestalling whatever either one of us might say, Ronan holds up a hand, adjuring silence. "You've been taught, doubtless, that those who resemble us—whose skin is darker, whose eyes take a different shape, or whose hair holds a rougher texture—are savages. That we form greedy mobs, massing beyond your gates in an eternal effort to penetrate security, at which point we'll fall upon you, massacring one and all and taking your resources for our own—after we roast small children over pyres and lick our fingers clean." His tone is wry, sardonic—but beneath the surface I can hear an old hurt.

"Is this not the case, then?" Eva says.

Ronan's dark eyes shift to her, taking her measure. "Not in the least. As with so much you have been told about the Fall and its aftermath, that's a lie. We prize children. There aren't enough to go around. I assure you, I would never compromise our resources by devouring one."

Eva ignores his sarcasm. "Is that why you were exiled—for the color of your skin?"

"The Commonwealth breeds us, as you know, for the purity of our genetic material. Yet sometimes, an unexpected fluke sneaks through," he says, shrugging. "That was the case with me. The Priests assigned me to increasingly menial tasks, alongside the natural born. The other children mocked me. When I was fourteen, they stoned me in the square, for no crime other than my appearance. The Priests exiled me then, saying I was a disruption to the peace. I might have died—had not the ones who lived beyond my Commonwealth's fence found me and kept me safe."

I can hear the truth in his words; so, I am sure, can Eva. Whatever Ronan is telling us, he believes it.

"I expected the barbarians Outside to set on me," he continues, "to rip me limb from limb. But they were not barbarians at all—just people, trying to survive. They cared for me. They took me in. And when I grew old enough, I dedicated my life to fighting for their cause."

I weigh his words, considering. "Go on," I say.

Ronan braces his hands on his knees. "Long ago," he says, "in what you think of as before the Fall, it was not as they told you. The southern rainforests were decimated, that much is true, and the land drained of its resources. The southerners came north, seeking sanctuary. Instead, they found a massive wall—and when they sought to surmount it, dehydrated and starving, they were met with guns. Threatened, they fought back. And so the War began."

He clears his throat. "By then, the ocean's waters were already rising. Resources were at a premium. The northerners had a superior arsenal...and the leadership of the men who grew to call themselves the Priests. They imprisoned the southerners that remained, but many escaped, bent on freedom and revenge. And then something else happened—an event that will take more time to explain than the brief period you and I have together. Threatened in its aftermath, the Priests formed the Commonwealths—to keep their citizens in, and others out. And there you've lived, ever since."

His eyes flicker from me to Eva, assessing. "As Bellatorum, you're not the holy warriors you've been led to believe, trained to enforce the wages of sin and keep the peace. You're trained instead to be the Commonwealths' weapon against change and rebellion, to keep the people in line through threats of retribution. You're their greatest weapon against the Brotherhood. And as such, you're also positioned to be our greatest asset."

He pauses, waiting for Eva or me to say something. Neither of us says a word, so he continues, as if it's perfectly normal to be directing a stream of words at two mute, shocked individuals who are staring at you as if the stump on which you sit has suddenly begun to speak.

"As you know, the Commonwealths control reproduction artificially, through the work they do in the gen labs. In the Commonwealth of Ashes, the high-level techs also engage in genetic manipulation, under the auspices of the Priests. We have reason to believe they may be working on new, highly sensitive technology that will enable them to enhance preferred genetic traits—speed, strength. That's one reason we're here—to learn if this is true."

Eva pales. "Go on," she says, her voice a croak. I want to ask her if she's all right, but I don't want to insinuate any sort of vulnerability in front of Ronan—who has taken her at her word and is still speaking.

"The Brotherhood is mobile. We have a series of bases across the country—what you call the Empire—with small advance groups settled temporarily near each Commonwealth to establish communication."

"Where are these bases?" Eva asks at once. Geography is relatively meaningless to us, other than what we have been taught—but information is power.

Ronan shakes his head. "I can't tell you that."

"Why not?" I counter. "Because they aren't real?"

"Oh, they're real enough. But to put information like that in your hands, without knowing where your loyalties lie—" His mouth flattens into a grim line. "It's worth more than my life."

"Give us something," Eva says, leaning forward. "Or we leave, now."

"We're already putting our lives on the line by being here, Ms. Marteinn. Should the Executor of your Commonwealth find out we're camped nearby, he'd put a swift end to us. We don't stay in one place more than two days for that very reason, even when we must remain near a single Commonwealth. We don't light fires. When we leave a campground, we do our best to give no evidence we were ever here."

"You mean," Eva says, "that Commonwealth patrols go out here, beyond the fence?" She leans down, poking at something on the ground, near her foot. I can only imagine she wants to hide the shock I'm doing my best to conceal.

"That's a smoke grenade," Ronan says, sounding uneasy. "Safe enough, as long as you don't pull the pin. It won't hurt your opponent, but it does a great job of obscuring your position. Still, I'd prefer if you didn't set it off in my tent."

Eva picks up the grenade, toying with it as if she hasn't heard a word he's said. "What patrols?" she asks. "When?"

Ronan gives her an exasperated glance. "You didn't think Kilían was the only one to know about that tunnel system, did you? All the Commonwealths have them. It's an alternate form of egress, in the event of an attack. But it also forms a most convenient means to patrol your perimeter without being noticed by those who remain inside the City."

As Efraím's apprentice or a mentor in my own right, no one ever told me about the tunnels. Is this what the Thirty does, when they disappear on missions—venture to the Outside? Try as I might to maintain an indifferent façade, the slight rankles. If Efraím hasn't told me about the tunnels, what else is he keeping from me?

"What you're saying," I say, staying doggedly on task, "is the Executor and the High Priests know the Brotherhood exists. And they'd wipe you all out, just because you threaten their way of life." I knot my hands around my knee, squeezing until the knuckles whiten.

Ronan shrugs. "They've done their best before."

"What do you want from us?" I say, when it's clear he doesn't intend to elaborate. "To defect? To fight for you?"

A smile curves his mouth, creasing the laugh lines that bracket it. "If you decide the cause is a worthy one, we would be honored to have two esteemed bellators at our backs."

I raise an eyebrow, dismissing his flattery. "I've fulfilled my part of the bargain—I've come here, willing to hear you out. But what about yours? Do you actually have any information as to the whereabouts of my parents, or was that a lie designed to get me where you want me?"

Ronan folds his arms across his chest. "I wouldn't lie to you."

"Oh? Where are my parents, then? Halfway across the country, in a camp like this one, awaiting your summons before they rush to their son's side? In the wreckage of one of the ruined cities, building a home where we'll all live in happy harmony?"

My mocking tone is meant to goad him, and it does. He straightens up, his eyes meeting mine, a challenge asked and answered. "Your mother's here," he says, each word measured. "In this camp. And your father—he's serving the Brotherhood to the north. In a place called Banabrekkur."

Dimly, I register his last two sentences, wonder what Banabrekkur is and where, exactly it might be—but the majority of my attention is focused elsewhere. I stride toward the tent flap and step through it, emerging into the dappled sunlight with Eva right behind me. "Ari—" she begins, but I shake my head fiercely, not trusting my voice. All my life, I've had a deep-seated desire to be *someone's*—a desire that drove me to make those overtures of friendship to the other children in the Nursery, to take Eva's hand at Black Falls. To belong somewhere, if not with the Commonwealth and the Bellatorum, then to the parents who were sentenced to death, escaped against all odds, and then came back for me—nineteen years later, but still.

I palm my favorite knife, draw myself up to my full height, and turn to face Ronan, who's followed us and is standing a foot away, regarding me as if I am a dangerous animal. "Where is she?" My voice is a growl. "I want to meet her. Now."

He looks me up and down, assessing. "Of course," he says at last, and turns toward the far end of the clearing. "Miriam," he calls.

Adrien and Zoya are standing in front of one of the tents, their postures stiff. At the sound of Ronan's voice, they glance at each other, and then Zoya leans over to unzip the flap. A woman's voice rises from inside, agitated and jagged-edged: "He's my son. My *son*! I don't care if Ronan said to wait. The hell with your protocols. Let me go!"

The tent trembles as if it will come apart at the seams, and then a woman emerges from the flap, a man right behind her. I take him in, performing an automatic threat assessment—middling height, brown hair, muscular build, a few years older than I—but then my eyes settle on the woman and stay there.

Even at a distance of sixty feet, I can see it's the woman from the photograph, blonde hair, olive skin, and all the rest. In person, there are even more similarities: She has the same stubborn set to her jaw I get when I'm determined to have my way, and the air of impatience that rolls off her is all too familiar. Her face shows the marks of a hard life, but it still bears the high cheekbones I see every morning in the mirror, in the ninety seconds allotted to me to shave.

I stare at her, and she at me. My heart pounds skips speeds breaks.

I want to go to her, but I can't move. I am paralyzed and she is staring at me and her lips curve up in a smile and I recognize it though I've never seen it before and in it there is a quality I can only define as love.

"By the Architect," Eva whispers, sounding awed.

Her words release me. I start forward, toward the woman who is my mother, and she breaks away from the man who's holding onto her and she's running toward me with that smile still on her face, her arms open wide as if to embrace me. Her lips form words but I can't understand them and she is forty feet from me thirty twenty and then there's a horrible noise and the world goes up in smoke and flames and she's gone.

At first I think Eva's thrown the smoke grenade, though why she would do such a thing I don't understand. I turn my head toward her and she's screaming my name but I can't hear her anymore and there is blood everywhere and pieces of people, I'm staring down into someone's sightless eyes and the ground is moving or maybe I am, everything slides sideways and then the world shudders.

Shakes.

Stills.

25

EVA

W e're running.

I've got Ari's hand in mine, pulling him behind me. He's resisting—he wants to go back for his mother and the other people in the camp—but there's no point. Either they got away or they didn't. Whatever the case, there's nothing we can do for them now.

Ari hasn't come to the same conclusion. He tugs on my hand, his lips moving, his free hand gesturing frantically. My ears are still ringing from the aftermath of the blast, but I know what he's saying nonetheless. *Let go of me. Let me go back.* He twists his hand in mine, trying to get free, but I am stronger than I should be, stronger than he is, and I won't loosen my grip.

I've jammed that damned useless grenade thing into my belt so I have both hands free, but I can only hang onto him with one as I run, and he drags us to a halt in a clearing halfway back to the tunnels. My hearing's coming back, his voice breaking through in fits and starts over the high-pitched whine in my ears.

"By the nine hells, Eva!" he says, and then his lips move but his voice fades out, like a vid projection with poor sound quality. His face is covered with dirt and soot, his gear ripped by flying debris. I'm sure I look much the same way, though I couldn't care less. My only concern is getting us to safety. I pull on Ari's arm again, but he won't budge.

"I have to g—" he says, his voice fading, and then, "Maybe we could save…you don't know they all…who are you to decide…my mother…just left to die…!"

I shake my head furiously, wincing at the small hail of detritus that flies from it. My braid has long since come undone, and strands of hair stick to my face, plastered with sweat and blood. "It's over," I tell him. "The Commonwealth—or whomever—they know the Brotherhood is here. We have to save ourselves. We have to run."

A cut has opened on his cheek, and blood drips from it, splashing onto me. His eyes are wild, and he pulls hard, yanking his hand free. "You…go then. But I…look for her…can't just…"

He gives me a desperate look over his shoulder and then takes off through the woods, back toward the camp. With a muttered curse, I chase after him. For all we know, this whole thing was a trap, and we're running right back into it. I can hardly think of a worse idea, but there's no way I'll let Ari go alone. If he's determined to die, then I'll stand with him, and face whatever comes.

We haven't gone ten feet when another explosion rocks the woods. It knocks us off our feet, wipes out what little hearing I've managed to regain. The air fills with smoke, the smell of burning wood and flesh. On my knees, I gag and choke, wiping my eyes to clear them. *Ari*, I think, feeling around desperately. *Where is he?*

I clear my throat, trying to call his name, but all that comes out is a raspy croak. Fighting waves of dizziness, I push myself to my feet. I scrub at my eyes again and again, but all I see is a fog of gray smoke, backlit by the harsh glow of flames. They've bombed the camp again —whoever *they* are—and if there were survivors before, there aren't now.

I wish I could tell where the bombs were coming from. Not from overhead—we don't have air transport in the Commonwealth. At least, I don't think we do. If Ronan was telling the truth—if the northerners won the War through superior firepower, and the Commonwealths are the result—then for all I know, the Thirty have access to a private arsenal.

If the bombs are being dropped, there's nothing I can do. But if not —could whoever is doing this be launching them from behind the fence? Are they in the woods with us, yards away? Tracking us, right this second?

Terrified that Ari has managed to make it back to the camp despite the second blast, I stagger forward. I can't see a damned thing, but the wind is blowing strongly, carrying the smell of charred flesh, and I can tell where the camp lies easily enough. I take five uneven steps, and then a hand closes around my arm.

I suck in a surprised breath that sears my lungs, and my hand drops to my belt for a weapon. But before I can pull one free, the grip on my arm yanks me forward. Ari presses me against him, chest heaving, clutching me as if I'm the only thing in the world that matters, all he has left to hold on to. I hold him the same way, relief coursing through my blood like a drug. I knot my hands in his shirt until the material strains beneath my fingers, and he drops his face into my hair. I can feel the gasp of his breath against my neck, the pound of his heart against my body. "Okay," he whispers. "Okay, I'll go."

He steps away, taking my hand in his. Then he tugs, and we are running again.

My plan is to escape—to flee both the Commonwealth and the resistance, into whatever lies beyond. The Brotherhood camp's in tatters, and trying to get back into the City seems a fool's errand. I'm sure Ari's come to the same conclusion; it's the only strategy that makes sense.

The further away from the center of the blast we run, the clearer the air. The only drawback is, now that I get a good look at Ari's face, I realize he's even more of a mess than I am. His eyes aren't wild anymore. They're vacant, as if he's retreated far inside himself, somewhere I can't follow. He runs through the woods as he's been trained, leaping over logs, looking instinctively for gaps in the foliage, scanning each sector for threats, but I can tell it's only habit. He isn't really here, with me—he's somewhere inside his head, present enough only to issue instructions for his body to follow. I've never seen him look this way, and it scares me more than anything that's come before or lies ahead.

What lies ahead, though—or the possibility of it—is frightening enough. With every step, I expect a knife to come flying down from the trees or out from the brush. I can't understand why no one's come after us. Was it really just an attack on the Brotherhood camp—did they not know Ari and I were there? The timing seems highly suspect —right when Ari and his mother were about to speak for the first time. Can it be a coincidence? A terrible uneasiness settles in my stomach, intensifying when I hear footsteps coming toward us through the woods, fast.

"Ari," I hiss, tugging on his hand, "do you hear that?"

He shakes his head. "What is it?"

I have never been more grateful for those little pink pills. Because the lightness of the newcomers' steps—the smell of them, flooding my nose with the oil we use to clean our blades—there is no doubt in my mind. "Bellatorum."

They're still far away, but there are many, coming from more than one direction.

The Thirty, boxing us in.

Whether they are looking specifically for me and Ari, or just for resistance fighters, I have no idea. Either way, I have no intention of sticking around to find out. "The tunnels," I say in desperation. "Out here, they'll catch us for sure. If we go back, we have a chance."

"We won't intercept them?"

"No." I'm already in motion, with him right behind me. "There are at least two parties, coming from the north and south. Go east to the tunnels and we should be able to give them the slip."

Adrenaline spurs me onward, and I find myself having to hold back so Ari can keep up. He's panting when we find the entrance to the tunnels again, but he drops to his knees anyhow, dragging the grate aside so I can slip through.

"Ari—" I say when he lands on the damp gravel beside me.

He turns his strange new empty face toward me, but doesn't speak.

"What if—" I manage, trying to put words to my anxiety. We're moving fast, away from the square of sunlight afforded by the grate. If I'm going to say anything, now is the time. "What if we're heading right into an ambush?"

"We'll fight." His tone is flat, dead.

Alarmed, I dig my fingers into his upper arms through the battered remains of his shirt.

"What?" he says in that same mild voice, raising his eyebrows.

"Stop this," I say, digging my nails in harder. "I need you, Ari. I need you to think before we do something really stupid. Please come back to me."

He stares at me, his eyes wide and unfocused. At a loss for what to do, I rise onto my toes, pressing my lips to his. For a moment he is still, wooden under my touch. Then his mouth opens, yielding to mine, tasting like fire and blood. His eyes flutter shut, his hands fist in my hair, and then he's kissing me back, all tongue and teeth and desperation. His muscles tense, and his hands tighten so hard in my hair that I gasp in pain and pull away.

Then I feel him gentle himself, with an effort that vibrates all through his body. His hands loosen, and his tongue strokes into my mouth with a slow, lazy sensuality that bears no resemblance to the fury that came before. He bites my lower lip, draws a shuddering breath, and lets me go.

"I hurt you," he says, his voice hoarse. "I couldn't help it, but still —I'm sorry."

"Don't be sorry," I say, my own voice trembling only a little. "Just be here. With me."

"I am here." His eyebrows lift, and he gives me a wry attempt at a smile. "I swore an oath, remember? You're stuck with me, apprentice mine. I'll never leave you—not unless you send me away."

I draw a deep breath. "I just want to be sure we're making the right decision. What if they're waiting for us when we get back? What if there are too many of them?"

He straightens, looking down at me. "I hate to break it to you, Eva, but there are no good choices here. Only survivable ones and ones that'll get us killed."

"I'm not arguing with that," I mutter, pulling my dagur free. "Fine. Let's go."

We set off running down the tunnels again, a punishing pace we only slow long enough to shine our flashlights on the walls, looking for the chalked image of the wolf. Outside the door that leads to the scholars' room, I look at Ari and he at me. He presses his ear against the door and shakes his head, hearing nothing.

The door has no knob on this side. There's no way to dislodge it except to shove, and so that's what Ari does. He puts his shoulder against it and pushes, hard.

He's got a shuriken in one hand and his knife in the other. I, too, am armed. But none of that makes any difference against what we see when the door swings wide.

26

EVA

There are twelve of the Thirty in this room, waiting for us. Later I will think I should have smelled them, door or no. But I was nose-blind, choked with the aftermath of the explosion, and so their presence is the surprise they mean it to be.

There's an awful moment when I think Ari did this—that he set me up to be captured as a traitor—but when I cast my eyes sideways to look at him, his face is pale and set. "Hello, Efraím," he says, the use of his former mentor's first name a deliberate insult.

Efraím ignores him, stalking forward until he comes to a halt in front of me. His lips curve upward in a pleased smile. "Excellent work, Bellator Marteinn," he says. "As always, I couldn't ask for more."

I'd expected him to do any number of things—accuse me, hurt me, try to kill me—but praise me for an imaginary task well executed was not one of them. I stare at him, my mind racing through a vast array of responses, and he covers my confusion by continuing to talk. "The tracker doesn't work as well as we'd hoped in those tunnels. All that stone. But once you were out in the open—it was like a dream, so it was. We could follow you easier than tracking a buck in rutting season. Congratulations, Bellator Marteinn. Thanks to you, we destroyed those rebels easier than stamping out an anthill. You've done your service to the Commonwealth this day."

I can feel Ari's gaze on my face, heavy with disbelief. "What are you talking about?" he says, his voice cracking, and Efraím turns on him.

"Shut up, you. Don't speak. You've done enough damage, don't you think? Trying to see your pathetic, sinful excuse for a mother—by the Architect, you don't think we'd really let that happen, do you? So sorry to have interrupted your little reunion, Westergaard. Please accept my apologies."

The rage that rolls off Ari is a palpable thing. He doesn't try to suppress it—what would be the point?—and I can feel myself flinch backward. Efraím just laughs. "Come, Eva," he says, and holds out his hand, beckoning to me.

In the vids from before the Fall, they talk about heartbreak. I never really understood what they meant—but standing next to Ari, my eyes on Efraím's outstretched hand, I feel a fissure crack my chest, painful as if a blade has sunk between my ribs, cleaving the beating heart beneath in two.

I'd promised myself I would stay with him, whatever came our way. That if he were determined to die, I wouldn't leave him to do so alone.

But this is different. He didn't walk into this room planning his death or mine—even though the risk loomed large. He came here in good faith, because it was the only way he saw for both of us to live. Well, now I see another way. It will break our hearts, if he feels for me as I do for him. But it's our only hope.

If they've been tracking me, following me, then I have value to them. They could have blown me up along with everyone else—but they didn't. I think of the explosion destroying the camp twenty feet from where we stood, the second blast landing after we were well away in the woods, and wonder.

What if they'd done it because they needed me?

If they need me, they won't kill me. But Ari's another story. They're regarding him with cold contempt, as if he's dispensable. Even Efraím, who mentored Ari from the moment he entered the Bellatorum, won't hold his gaze.

Cold certainty settles over me, sure as the feel of my dagur in my hand. They didn't save Ari for his own sake. They saved him—both times—because he was standing next to me.

He means nothing to them. They mean to kill him in front of me, and make me watch the blood run out of him till it bathes the stones on which we stand.

That won't happen, as long as there's breath in my body. I will fight for him, with the only means left to me if need be.

And so I step to Efraím's side.

"Very good," he says, gracing me with another of his rare smiles before he turns back to Ari. "Against the wall," he hisses. "Weapons on the floor. On your knees. Hands behind your head." When Ari doesn't move, he snaps, "Do it, soldier. Or die at the point of my blade."

Ari's eyes shift sideways, toward me. "Eva?" he says, betrayal clear in his voice.

"Do you take orders from the girl now?" The words are chips of ice.

"No," Ari says, not budging. "But I don't know that I take orders from you either, Bellator Stinar. Not when you want me to get on my knees and surrender my sword."

"Insurrectionist fool." Efraím motions at him with his blade, gesturing to the wall. "This is my last warning. Surrender of your own accord, Ari Westergaard. Or I'll offer you a suitable inducement, and I guarantee you won't find it nearly as pleasant."

For a heartbeat, Ari stands, motionless, framed in the doorway that forms the entrance to the tunnels. Then he nods and comes forward, sinking gracefully to his knees in front of Efraím. He unbuckles his weapons belt, lets the contents of his hands fall into the dirt, and pulls the sheath of his sverd loose. "Is this acceptable to you?" he says, his voice inflectionless.

"Not quite." Efraím kicks the fallen weapons and the belt and sheath away, out of his reach. "Go ahead. Say it."

Ari's head bows. And then he looks up, staring straight into my eyes. "*Je me rends,*" he says, imbuing the words with an awful, bitter sarcasm.

Hearing him say this is a crossbow bolt shot straight into my heart —but I know I cannot let my feelings show. I stare back at him as coldly as Efraím, hoping he'll be taken in by this demonstration of indifference. For me to fool the rest of them, I must fool Ari too—no matter how badly it hurts. It's our only chance of survival. *I'll never leave you*, he'd said. *Not unless you send me away.* Well, then that's what I will have to do.

"Nicely done," I tell Efraím, coming to stand at his side. As his apprentice, this would normally be Ari's place of honor. It is a grave insult for me to be standing here, even though Ari serves him no more. Not only does it insinuate I've taken Ari's place—it's a clear declaration of where my loyalties lie.

"I'm pleased to hear you approve," Efraím says. "I was beginning to think you were playing your part a little too well, girl. That you'd formed an unnatural attachment to this virtueless excuse for a fighter."

I force a laugh. It feels like broken glass in my throat. "You don't think I'd waste my time on a natural-born? I understood my orders, sir. If I interpreted them too effectively, let that be a testament to my dedication to the cause we all serve."

Broken though it might be, my heart is still beating, an adrenaline-fueled fusillade that threatens to betray my panic and fear. I force it to slow, gazing down at Ari with disgust that mirrors the expression I see on Efraím's features and that of every other bellator in this room. Kilían is conspicuously absent, but Riis is here, and Daníel Eleazar. Eight others, as well, all of Efraím's most trusted soldiers and the Bellatorum's best fighters. The man from behind the door, the scholar, who has conspired to betray us. And in the shadows, someone else.

I listen intently, careful to be sure my expression displays only indifference, colored by a hint of satisfaction at a job well done. And then I hear it.

The uneven, distinctive thump of the Executor's heart.

ARI

I turn my head to look at Eva, the echo of that awful laugh and her light, amused voice echoing in the dim cavern. Beneath the gray smudges of ash, her cheeks are flushed. She stares back at me, eyes wide, breathing hard.

I've been an exemplary member of the Bellatorum, a laudable warrior, a good soldier. Efraím always praised me for my quick reflexes, the way I could tell when subjects were lying, how I never let my emotions get in the way of what needed to be done. *You see clearly, Westergaard,* he'd told me more than once. It was his highest compliment.

But not this time. This time, I have been blind.

"How could you do this?" I say to Eva, as if we are alone. "I trusted you. And you led them straight to me."

If her loyalty lay with the Commonwealth all along, everything that passed between us—the way she kissed me after the bombing, how she clutched my hand for strength on the wrong side of the scholar's door—all of it's been a lie.

I wonder if they put her up to that, too.

Eva's mouth opens as if she's about to speak. And then it closes again. I regard her icily, thinking about how I'd imagined we might run away together, leave the Commonwealth behind. What an idiot I've been, to think she truly shared my curiosity about the world beyond our borders, my faith there must be something more, something better. What a fool, to imagine a girl like this could be anything but a spy inserted into the very heart of the Bellatorum, an informer planted to ferret out its weakest links. To imagine she craved my touch the way I crave hers, an addiction that's never satisfied.

The fact of her betrayal hurts more than anything ever has—the lash of the High Priest's whip against my back, the icy water of the Austari seeping through my clothes and deep beneath my skin. They're nothing compared to the tightening in my chest, the pain that pierces my heart, sharp as my blade.

But I am a warrior. So I will stand. And I will fight.

There are at least two men in each corner, most of them Bellatorum. Three men between me and the door, all of them armed. This is a suicide mission, pure and simple. But I see no other way. If I run back into the tunnels, they'll catch me. If I let them take me, they'll kill me.

Better to die an honorable death, even in defense of the impossible.

I let the fear run out of me, settle into the focused state that's my only hope of survival. My eyes scan the rutted walls of the cavern for handholds, assess the furniture and the lighting fixtures for anything that can be used as a weapon or a point of balance. I take in the men one by one, considering their weight, what I know of their success in training, their muscularity and the extent to which they're armed.

My best hope—my only hope, really—is to disarm the ones who stand between me and the door, then rely on speed and my knowledge of the tunnels to escape. The only way out is through, and I'll need to strike fast and without mercy. Most likely I'll die in the trying.

But maybe I'll take some of them with me, I think, and I'm disturbed to find the idea doesn't trouble me the way it should.

Efraím sees me scouting the room and raises one dark eyebrow in derision. "Don't bother, Westergaard," he says, his voice clear and cold—as if all the time we've spent together, sparring and debating and studying, means nothing. As if I am a stranger. "You can't win. Why make this difficult? It'll end the same, either way."

"Why did you bomb the encampment?" I ask, ignoring this. In my heart, I know Ronan was telling the truth, but I need to ask. To be sure.

His mouth twists. "The bombing was for the good of the Commonwealth."

A tremor runs through me. "In the name of the Architect, Efraím, why? People died. Innocent people."

"They weren't innocent. They were outlaws, criminals. Threats to everything we have worked so hard to build." His eyes travel over me, disgust in their depths, and I hear what he has left unsaid: *As are you.*

"They've done nothing to you." I think of the longing expression on my mother's face before the smoke swallowed her whole, and fail to keep the anger from my voice. "Your actions are indefensible."

"Mind yourself, Bellator Westergaard." The words are a whisper, issuing from the shadows behind Efraím. It is the voice of the Executor.

I am on my feet, my sverd snatched from the ground, bare in my hand. I didn't mean to draw it, don't remember pulling it from its sheath. But I hold it nonetheless, its familiar weight giving me the confidence I need to take one step forward, then another. "I am Bellatorum Lucis. I walk in the light." My voice rises, echoing off the stone walls of the scholars' chamber. "The Bellatorum administer justice—but we're not conscienceless killers. If you condone the murder of the innocent, then I cannot stand with you."

Efraím draws in his breath in a long hiss. He hesitates, regarding me with an unreadable expression. But when he speaks, his voice does not waver. "You will not stand with the brotherhood, Ari Westergaard? Not even in death?"

The air in the room trembles. There is a bright line here, and with the next sentence I will cross it. What began when I first took Eva's hand, when I heard Kilían out, when Ronan called my mother's name and I saw her face—it ends now. I'll die a traitor, executed for the benefit of the people, my body dumped into the pit. But at least I'll die with my honor intact.

I try not to look at Eva when I speak, but I can't help myself. Her face is blanched, her expression horrified. Infinitesimally, she shakes her head, and her index finger moves against her thigh, signing

169

something to me. I try to decipher it, but at this distance it's useless. Why would she signal me, anyhow? She betrayed me. For all I know, this is yet another trick…unless it isn't.

Dismissing the prospect, I shake off my doubts. I must remain focused if I'm to survive.

Doggedly, I lift my head and look straight into Efraím's eyes. He raised me to be what I am, has mentored and trained me. Yet despite the hours we've spent together, sparring and debating the finer points of strategy—despite the regret I saw in his eyes—there's nothing left between us but this: a traitor and the warrior chosen to bring about his end. It is my flaw, my sin that I cannot help but wish for more.

I made that mistake with Eva; I won't make it again. "*Non serviam,*" I say, the words that sever me from the brotherhood of the Bellatorum—from everything I am, everything I've worked so hard to become. "I will not serve."

A low rumble of incredulity moves through the room. I can't remember the last time someone left the Bellatorum voluntarily. Not in my lifetime.

Efraím nods, resolute. "Then you stand alone," he says, and charges me, blade in hand.

If I wasn't so familiar with the way he fights, attuned to every movement of his body, he might have run me through. Instead I feint right, push off the opposite wall, and use the momentum to flip over his head, landing behind him. He wheels, panting, and I bare my teeth. "You want to kill me, Efraím?" I taunt him. "You'll have to try harder than that."

"You always were insolent, Westergaard," he snarls. "I should've known."

I lift my free hand and crook a finger at him. The exhilaration of battle rises through me, muting my misery at Eva's betrayal, the loss I feel at severing my bond with the Bellatorum—the only family I have ever known. "Come and get me, Bellator Stinar. If you can."

With a low growl, he comes. This time I let him, then parry his blade and foot-sweep him, sending him staggering back against a shelf of books, which cascade to the floor. Efraím is fast and strong, but I'm faster. Stronger. He's telegraphing his every move; all I have to do is deflect it and return the favor.

Flanked by two of the Bellatorum, the Executor claps, as if this is a show designed for his entertainment. "Oh, very good," he says. "Such a shame to lose this one. One of your best, is he not?"

"My apprentice," Efraím says bitterly. "Soon to be named one of my Thirty. I trained him myself."

"Ah." The Executor nods. "A cruel turn of events. There's no worse betrayal than one committed by those we trust. Is that not so, Eva Marteinn?"

Out of the corner of my eye, I see Eva wince. "Yes, Executor," she says obediently. The girl who conspired with me and kissed me is gone. Maybe she was never there at all.

"You'll not reconsider?" the Executor says to me. "Given your talents, even these...indiscretions...might be forgiven. You can rededicate yourself to the service of the Commonwealth, endure the Trials anew. I'm sure redemption can be arranged."

For me to believe that, I'd have to be even more of a fool than I've already demonstrated on this cursed day. "I'm sorry, sir," I say, without taking my gaze from Efraím—feeling my dream of becoming one of the Thirty, everything I've worked toward all my life, slip away. "But I have renounced my oath."

The Executor sighs. "A great loss," he says. "The Commonwealth grieves for you." And then he nods to Efraím, giving him permission to loose his blade again. I see what he has in mind—a fight to the death, here in the cavern. There will be no trial for me, no public execution. I'll die here, and my blood will run out on the stones. They'll burn my body and scatter my ashes in the dark.

I breathe deep, commending my soul to the Architect—if indeed he exists. There are thirteen of them, counting Eva, and one of me. I cannot fight all of them, not and win.

Then Eva steps forward, and I have to suppress a shudder. Will she request the privilege of dueling me herself? Perhaps she'd consider it a mercy for hers to be the last face I see, for her blade to be the one that pierces my heart.

That would be no mercy, as far as I'm concerned, but the blackest kind of end. Could I kill Eva, if I had to?

Would I be willing to sacrifice my own life, to save hers?

I'm all too afraid I know the answer to this question, and as she turns to face the line of black-clad men, I steel myself for what is to come. But all she says is, "I apologize, Executor."

His brow furrows. "For what, Bellator Marteinn?"

"For this," Eva says, and she drops her hand to her weapons belt, yanking a small gray object free. Efraím lunges for her, but he is too late. She pulls the pin and lobs it straight into the middle of the room.

In the seconds before it detonates, I see a number of puzzling things. Efraím has tackled Eva and is doing his best to pin her to the ground, his knee in the middle of her back. She's bucking wildly to dislodge his grip, and, recognizing my tutelage in the way she moves, I feel an incongruous satisfaction—every time he tries to grab her, she anticipates it, so his knee slides off her spine and his hands close on air. She struggles to her feet, and two more of the Bellatorum surround her, trapping her hands behind her.

I don't understand why Eva has created this diversion—Eva, who tricked me into believing in her. Is it another trick? A trap? Warily, I shift my weight, my blade bare in my hand.

Efraím forces Eva to her knees, his dagur at her throat. "Surrender," he hisses, and she shakes her head, a tiny movement that causes a bead of blood to well up on her skin. This is what Efraím would call a rookie mistake. You never, ever move your head with a blade at your throat. You could sever your carotid. The fact is drilled into us over and over again during the first week of training. Eva knows better than this.

Then her eyes meet mine, and I realize she's done it on purpose. "Run," she mouths. Efraím has his hand fisted in her hair, forcing her head down, but she fights him, arching her back away from the blade. "Run!" she mouths again, and on her face I see a pure, clear desperation. "Now!"

A haze of smoke swallows the room. I snatch my weapons belt from the ground and disappear into the tunnel.

EVA

"Wake up."

At the sound of Efraím's voice, I come to consciousness to find I'm exactly where he left me last night—in the dim corner of an underground prison cell. I hadn't intended to sleep, but after the third hour of staring blearily at the locked cell door, waiting for a summons that never came, I'd decided my best advantage was to be well-rested...or as well-rested as I can be, considering I spent the night on a damp, hard floor, wondering if I was going to be put to death in the morning. I blink, look up at Efraím, and start to rise, ignoring the stiffness in my limbs.

"No, don't get up." His voice is cold, hard. "That's not an invitation, it's an order. Don't move an inch unless I say you can. Think of it as a game of *Executor, May I,* with extraordinarily high stakes."

I blink at him again, puzzled by the mention of the childhood game we all used to play—three steps forward, one back, always with an imaginary Executor's permission. "What do you want from me?"

His expression is stony. "That was quite the show you put on last night, Bellator Marteinn. Renouncing the exile, then staging his escape. But the hour for playtime's come and gone. We're going to find out what you know."

"I don't know anything," I say, shifting my weight on the cold stone. It takes everything I have to keep my face blank, not to betray the worry and longing and regret I feel for Ari. But my life depends on it.

"Such a pretty liar you are. But that's the problem, isn't it? Or two of them, anyhow."

"I don't know what you're talking about."

"You don't think you actually meant anything to Westergaard, do you? It was a temptation, a test. Which he failed miserably, I might add."

"Why would I care what I mean to Ari Westergaard?" I say, shrugging. "He's nothing to me. It's in our best interests if he finds his way back to the Brotherhood. I know how Ari thinks, what he'll do. We can track him that way." I hold my hands out, palms up. "Take my pulse. Listen to my heartbeat. You'll see I'm not lying."

"Ah, but as I said, that's the problem, Eva. You're such a good liar. Too good." He stalks closer, glaring. "I can't kill you, that's problem number three. You're too valuable. But I can break you, and make no mistake, I'll do it with pleasure."

Fear floods my veins, icy, and my breath comes short. "You won't break me."

"Ah, Eva." His voice is heavy with false sadness. "Everybody breaks. It's just a matter of how and when. You will shatter at my hands, splintering into a thousand sniveling, pathetic pieces. You'll beg for mercy before I'm done with you."

He turns and strides out of the cell, locking the door behind him. I hear him talking to the bellators who are stationed out of my line of sight. And then he's gone.

I try calling to the other bellators, but they don't answer. So I wait, anticipation being its own torture, as Efraím has intended. I amuse myself by counting my heartbeats, the passing seconds, the number of paces from one side of the cell to the other (fifteen length-wise, ten across). By thinking what I'll do to Efraím when I manage to get free. I'm very careful not to think about Ari. Wherever he is, whatever he's doing, it is better than being dead.

They come for me two hours later—Efraím himself, with Jakob Riis by his side, backed by two other bellators. Efraím grabs me by the arm and hauls me to my feet, his dagur pressed against my neck. I feel the tip of Jakob's knife between my shoulder blades. "Walk," Efraím says, and so I do, past the other cells, all of which are empty.

Efraím drags me down the hallway in grim silence, until we stop in front of the prisoners' door to the interrogation chamber. He gestures for Jakob to unlock it, and then we step through, leaving the two bellators on the other side. We go down the hall to one of the small rooms, and Efraím shoves me into a chair, twists my arms behind me, and cuffs my wrists to the back of the chair. I pull on the metal cuffs experimentally, but no luck.

Despite my determination to stay calm, I can feel my heartbeat in my throat, thudding in an effort to break free. I make myself meet Efraím's eyes. As much as the cuffs will allow, I lean back in the chair in a pretense of insouciance, as if I have nothing to hide.

Efraím looks me over, his eyes narrowed in disgust. I can only imagine how I must look—my gear torn and stained, my face filthy despite my best attempts to scrub it clean—but I hold his gaze, and finally he turns to Jakob. "Leave us," he says, and Jakob backs hastily out of the room, shutting the door behind him.

"So," Efraím says, settling into the chair on the other side of the scarred wooden table. "I'll give you one more chance. Do you want to talk and get this over with, or do we have to do this the hard way?"

I set my jaw and lift my chin. "I have nothing to hide. It was important to get close to the exile, to gain his confidence and make him believe I was on his side. It was equally important no one in the Commonwealth know about his plans or my attempt to subvert them. If I played my part a little too well, I have only my Bellatorum training to blame."

"So you said." He leans back, his chair teetering on two legs, and snaps his fingers at the vid camera in the corner. "The hard way it is, then."

Twenty seconds later the bellator who took Samúel's place, a quiet guy in his fourth year of training named Noél Falk, comes in holding the lie detector machine, complete with its snaking electrodes and pheromone receptors. Efraím takes it from him and attaches the electrodes all over me, sticks the pheromone receptor pads to my skin. He sits back down at the table, in front of the machine with its vid screens and needles and dials. And then the questions begin.

What do you know about the Brotherhood? Does your true allegiance lie with the Commonwealth, or the Outsiders? What were you doing in the tunnels that day? What is your relationship with the exile Ari Westergaard? Why did you throw the smoke grenade that allowed Westergaard to escape? Why did you feign compliance with us, only to resist at the last minute? Why did you not inform your superiors of Westergaard's betrayal? What information does Westergaard have that led him to the tunnels and the Brotherhood camp that day? Who was he looking for? Who told him such a resistance exists?

Ari put me through my paces with the lie detector test, on the premise you can't truly understand how to break a subject to your will until you've been in their shoes. I know how sensitive the test is, programmed to decipher the slightest flutter in a subject's heart rate and the lightest dew of sweat on their skin. So I keep my answers short, breathing slowly in between responses to ensure my heartbeat does not change. I think of the most calming images I can imagine—sunlight striking the water of a small brook below the falls, the shady spot at the edge of the woods where I liked to sit and catch my breath after training. And I reply.

I only know what Ari told me—that such a resistance exists. I'm loyal to the Commonwealth. Ari Westergaard was my mentor. I threw the grenade because I believed he was more valuable to us alive than dead. I feigned compliance in order to take the exile by surprise. I didn't inform my superiors because I feared it would compromise the quality of the intelligence I was gathering. Westergaard wanted to go to the camp because he was informed his mother was there. I don't know who told him about the Brotherhood. He never shared that information with me.

As the questions wear on, Efraím begins using the electrodes to administer a jolt of electricity after each unsatisfactory reply. The shocks prickle through my body, stinging my skin and arching my spine so my wrists dig into the cuffs. He waits for my heartbeat to return to normal, then interrogates me again and shocks me when he doesn't care for the answer. Each one is more painful than the next as he cranks the current higher, and it is all I can do not to scream. I grit my teeth and glare at him through the hair that has fallen into my eyes and say I've told him everything I know.

After what feels like several hours, Efraím rips off the electrodes, grabs me by the scruff of my neck, and marches me out of the room again. Jakob, who is waiting outside the door, falls into formation and follows us. I am sweating and shaking, but I do my best not to let it show. I know how Efraím works. If I show him where my vulnerability lies, he'll be all over it, exploiting it in every way he can think of. So I straighten my spine and limp along next to him, trying to ignore the vestiges of electricity that ripple through my limbs.

I've made up my mind not to fight, not yet. But when he drags me into a room down the hall from the interrogation chamber and I see what lies inside, it's all I can do not to pry my arm loose from his grasp and go shrieking down the hallway.

The room itself is large, the walls carved from the same gray stone as the rest of the underground complex, including the prison. At one end stands a tank that stretches from floor to ceiling—twelve feet tall and four feet wide, crafted from reinforced glass. A hose runs from an opening in the tank to a faucet jutting from the wall. And next to the tank stands a team of five bellators and the Executor himself.

"Uncuff her," the Executor says, flicking his hand in my direction.

Next to me, I feel Efraím stiffen. "Are you sure, sir? Because she—"

"That's an order, Bellator Stinar." The Executor's voice is steel.

"Yes, sir." Doubtless Efraím would like to protest further, but refusing an order from the Executor isn't a mistake anyone lives long enough to make twice. He jerks his head at Jakob, who unlocks the cuffs.

I let my hands fall to my sides, fighting the urge to rub the spots where the metal has chafed my wrists. "What is this? What are you going to do?"

Efraím smiles. "Afraid, girl? You're right to be. Tell us the truth, and you'll never need to know."

"I am telling you the truth."

Efraím cocks his head. "Your heartbeat's sped up now, all right, but I can't tell if it's because you're lying or you're spooked. Well, I guess we'll find out."

He drags me forward, past the team of bellators and the watchful gaze of the Executor, toward the tank. They mean to shut me in there as it fills, to ask their questions again and drive the level of the water higher and higher until I give the answers they want to hear. And otherwise—what? Do they mean to kill me?

Terror floods my body, and with it, adrenaline. I twist free of Efraím's grip and run for the door. He grabs my shoulder, but I kick his blade from his hand and send it spinning across the stones. Driven by desperation, I head-butt Jakob when he tries to grab me, spearhand-strike one of the five bellators who comes after me with a knife, kick a second one in the stomach, throw a third into the wall, and elbow a fourth in the solar plexus hard enough to make him double over, at which point I manage to liberate one of his knives. I'm sprinting for the door again when someone tackles me from behind, knocking me face-first onto the stones and planting their knee in my back. I thrash and fight, but to no avail; a second warrior has joined the first, and then a third.

"Enough," Efraím says, and I realize he's the one who is kneeling on top of me. I turn my head and see Jakob pinning one of my shoulders, blood trickling from his nose. The bellator I didn't manage to damage must have my other shoulder. I can't move an inch.

Grimly, Efraím hauls me to my feet. The room is in chaos; the bellator I threw into the wall is slumped on the ground, unconscious, the one I elbowed in the solar plexus is red-faced and panting, and the man I kicked in the stomach is dry-heaving with one of his hands braced on the wall. The other bellator has reclaimed his knife and is standing in front of the Executor, arms outstretched to protect him.

"Very good," the Executor says from behind his bodyguard. And then he laughs.

It occurs to me that maybe he is insane.

Efraím, Jakob, and the other bellator—Benedikt, his name is—drag me closer to the tank, one step at a time. I buck and kick but it makes no difference, not with the three of them holding onto me. Efraím grabs me by the hair, immobilizing my head, as the bellator next to the Executor presses a button on a panel set into the stone. Part of the glass front of the tank slides upward, and the three of them shove me through. The door closes again, sealing me inside, and icy water begins to pool around my ankles.

I stare at Efraím, wide-eyed and furious. On his face there is a look of triumph. "Ask your questions, Executor," he says. Even through the glass that separates us I can hear him clearly. There must be a speaker system inside the tank, projecting his voice—which means this isn't a special torture they've invented for me. This is something they've done before, in the name of preserving the Commonwealth's status quo and their personal positions of power.

Rage mounts in me, icy as the water licking at my ankles. I don't know how I'll get out of here, but get out of here I will. I'll get out of here, escape, find Ari, and bring this whole place down.

The Executor comes to stand in front of the tank in his pristine white robes, his beetle eyes taking me in. "Hello, Eva," he says. "You've looked better."

"Hello, Executor," I reply, allowing the slightest hint of derision to color my voice. "Always a pleasure."

Efraím clears his throat, low and menacing. "Watch your mouth, girl."

"Why, Bellator Stinar? Are you going to hurt me? Because it looks like things have already turned out poorly, if you don't mind me saying so. I put my life on the line for the Commonwealth, compromise myself by spending time with a natural-born, nearly get blown up, and what do I get for my pains? Dumped in a cell, interrogated and electroshocked, and now you plan to drown me for telling you the truth. At this point, I feel at liberty to speak my mind. What are you going to do? Drown me faster?"

Efraím takes a step closer, his face reddening. "How dare you speak to the Executor this way?" he hisses. "How dare you speak to me this way? You have no idea what you—"

The Executor raises a hand, cutting him off. "It's all right, Efraím. Don't worry about it. The poor girl's had a difficult time of it. Haven't you, Eva dear?"

The water has reached my shins, creeping ever higher. The cold is seeping into my bones, so it is all I can do not to shake. Ignoring the Executor, I throw myself against the tank again and again to no avail. I brace my legs on opposite sides and climb up to the top, seeking a weakness in the glass, but there's nothing. So I take the best option open to me, wedging myself near the ceiling, out of the freezing water, and turn my gaze back to my interrogators.

The Executor begins, asking many of the same questions Efraím did earlier. I answer them the same way. Betraying myself is one thing; I'll be damned if I betray Ari or, by extension, Kilían and the Brotherhood. The resistance is Ari's best hope of survival. I won't take that away from him, no matter what happens to me.

By the time the Executor is finished, the water's up to my waist, even in my tenuous position at the top of the tank, and I'm shivering uncontrollably. The Executor regards me with pity. "Come now, Eva," he says. "Tell us what we need to know, and we can have you out of there in a minute. You'll be wrapped up in a warm blanket, sitting in front of a fire and drinking tea, and all this will feel like a bad dream."

My teeth are chattering so hard it's a challenge to force words through them. "I've. Told. You. Everything."

"Ah, Eva," he says sadly, and gestures to the bellator standing by the faucet.

The water flows faster. Up to my chest. My collarbones. My neck.

"Have you noticed anything different about yourself in the past few months, Eva?" the Executor asks. "Wouldn't you like to know why that is? Tell us what we need to know, and we'll repay you in kind. An exchange of information between allies, if you will."

Even through the awful, paralyzing cold, his words penetrate. For a moment, I consider confessing everything—but he can't be trusted. "No," I say, glaring at him defiantly. "You saved me for a reason, Executor. You value me too much to kill me now."

The water is up to my chin. I suck in a deep breath, and it closes over my head.

I hold my breath forever, longer than ought to be possible. I count the seconds, higher and higher: *121-122-123-124-125*. My lungs burn with the need to breathe, but if I do, I'll die. I clench my jaw, picture Ari's face, fight the choking sensation that threatens to consume me. By the Architect, I have never been so cold. The freezing water of the rapids was nothing compared to this.

379-380-381-382-383

Outside the tank I hear a commotion, Efraím's voice raised in protest, the deeper voice of the Executor. Underwater, their voices blur, reaching me in a slow-motion, indecipherable surge of sound.

535-536-537-538-539

The voices grow louder, tension audible even through the thick glass walls of the tank and the confining press of water. I force my eyes open and see Efraím inches from the front of the tank, peering in at me. The moment my eyes meet his, he leaps backward in startlement, the most telling gesture of surprise I've ever seen from him. He turns to the Executor, gesticulating wildly.

777-778-779-780-781

Summoning what strength remains to me, I beckon at Efraím, splashing the surface of the water to get his attention until he leaves the Executor's side and approaches me again. As soon as he stands in front of the glass, I lift both hands and fold all my fingers down but one, making an unmistakably rude gesture.

892-893-894-895-896

Efraím slaps the tank with an open hand and swivels to face the Executor again. I'm having a hard time hanging onto consciousness, but even in my sorry state I can decipher most of what he is screaming. "...awake in there...impossible...owe me an explanation... it's unnatural...should be dead...how can I control what I don't understand...!"

909-910-911-912-913

The water is crushing me from all sides. Efraím and the Executor are barely visible, obscured by a dense carpet of stars that cloud my vision. I bite my tongue hard enough to draw blood, praying the pain will keep me awake. Unconscious, I will inhale, and all this will be over.

1080-1081-1082-1083-1084

Maybe I was wrong about the Executor. Maybe I was wrong about everything.

1110-1111-1112-1113-1114

"What kind of game is this?" Efraím is yelling, totally undone. "What are you playing at?"

*1222-1223-1224-1225-1226 I can't do this anymore I can't breathe I can't breathe I can't **breathe***

"I am not playing, Efraím." The Executor sounds as implacable as always. "I have never been more serious in my life."

I've stopped counting. My eyes widen and my chest heaves. In desperation, I bang feebly on the glass with my fists. Opening my mouth to breathe won't help, but I don't care anymore. I am suffocating. The world in front of me is narrowing, growing dark. *Ari,* I think with what volition is left to me. *Be free. Be safe. I'm sorry.*

It's probably a side effect of drowning, but the water no longer seems so cold. Inside my starved lungs there's a terrible scorching, a fire that threatens to devour me from the inside out. My body quakes, slamming against the glass. The fire is a live thing, consuming me, trying to break free. I claw at my throat, desperate, but my hands feel strange, rubbery. I am freezing and I am burning and I can't *breathe—*

"All right," the Executor says. "I think she's had enough. Drain the tank."

The glacial water begins to retreat, but not fast enough. The reptilian part of my brain has kept counting, and now the voice starts up again: *1333-1334-1335-1336—by the Architect my lungs my lungs my lungs—*

Suddenly the water drains from beneath me with a gush. The force of it sends me hurtling to the bottom of the tank, then through the door and out onto the stones, where I lie, gasping. Efraím and the Executor are still talking, but I pay no heed to their words. All I care about is breathing.

Then Efraím is standing over me. My eyes are closed, but I can smell him—soap and sweat and an acrid scent I could swear is fear. "How did you do that?" he growls. "Answer me."

I have no answer for him. But what I do have is an immeasurable well of fury. I play possum, lying still until he bends over me, jabbing me with the handle of his dagur. And then I launch myself at him, grabbing him by the collar and pulling him down into the puddle on the stones alongside me. We slip and slide in the icy water, him doing his best to subdue me, me calling him every bad name I can think of, raking my nails down his cheekbones in an attempt to gouge out his eyes.

I am exhausted and starving and weakened by my time in the tank, not to mention unarmed. But I am also filled with rage. I fight him with every bit of strength I have, knocking him off-balance again and again, straining to reach his weapons belt, until he rears up, eyes blazing, and cold-cocks me in the head with his fist. I hiss with pain, still grabbing for him, but my fingers close uselessly on the fabric of his shirt and slip free.

The world goes a deep, dull red and then passes into darkness.

29

ARI

It takes me most of the night and into the morning to find what remains of the resistance. I can't track them well in the dark, especially because all I'm going on is the hope some of them—especially my mother—survived. Eventually I have to abandon the effort and wait for dawn to come. Once it does, I'm able to pick up their trail—which is not good, because if I can find it, so could any of the bellators who might still be looking for them...including Eva.

I trained her, though, taught her everything she knows about hunting a quarry and bringing it to ground. If she's on my trail, I have to believe I will sense it. And if my presence endangers the Brotherhood, I will strike out elsewhere, on my own.

All my life I've been punished for caring too much, and here is the proof that I shouldn't.

Except I can't understand why she tossed that grenade. It surprised the hell out of Efraím, I'd guarantee that; his reaction was genuine. Facilitating my escape might have cost her his goodwill. So —why do it?

I entertain the notion that she'd acted because she feels for me as I do for her—but that's absurd, no matter how much I want it to be true. Of the two of us, I'm the one who spent my childhood being punished for inappropriate attachments. I'm the one who took her hand, who kissed her that first time in the woods, who couldn't keep my virtueless mouth shut.

So, what's the alternative? Did she feel guilty about betraying me, and figure the least she could do is give me a shot at freedom? Or are her motives more complex, even sinister? Does she think she can use me to track the movements of the Brotherhood—in which case she can justify her actions to Efraím by telling him the ruse occurred to her on the spur of the moment, and she had to make it as believable as possible so I would take the bait?

Cursing myself for trusting her, I concentrate on the task at hand —finding the resistance and trying to undo some of the damage I've caused by bringing Eva into their midst. I come upon their new makeshift camp after daybreak and find Ronan sitting on a stump at the edge of the woods outside the small clearing where they've pitched their remaining tents. His face is grim, his eyes reddened. He's got a gun in one hand and something else I can't make out in the other.

"Westergaard," he says, rising, the word smoke-rough. "I hoped we might see you again."

I drop my hands to my sides, showing I mean no harm. "You have no reason to believe me," I say, my voice as raw as his, "but I didn't have anything to do with the bombing. I swear it on the Architect and my honor as a bellator." I swallow hard. "Well, as a former bellator, anyhow. I may have foresworn my vow, but the intention behind it remains."

"You don't have to explain yourself. Kilían told us what happened."

Kilían—who wasn't present in the scholar's room. Which begs the question...where was he? Was he the one who engineered the attack on the camp?

"What exactly did he tell you?" The words fall into the air sharp as razors, cutting my throat as they go, and Ronan's eyes flick warily to my face before he replies.

"He told us about Eva. What she did—and where her loyalties truly lay. I'm sorry."

"You're sorry?" A harsh chuckle escapes me. "I think I should be saying that to you, yeah? How many did you lose yesterday?"

Ronan's eyes drop to the ground. "Too many," he says, his voice thick.

It takes all my remaining courage to ask the only question that still matters. "My mother?"

He steps forward and presses the contents of the hand that isn't holding his gun into mine. "Here," he says.

Puzzled, I open my hand. I am holding a series of photogs of myself, profile pictures the record-keepers take each year for our files. Here I am at three, all dark hair and big green eyes. At five, wearing my white Under-School uniform, my hair beaten into submission by the Mother's comb. At ten, long-limbed and gawky. At fourteen, the first hint of dark stubble tracing my cheekbones and an indecipherable expression on my face. At seventeen, looking much like I do now, wearing the black uniform of the Bellatorum and staring directly into the camera. The last photog is the one Kilían showed me—my parents together, their arms wrapped around each other, smiling into the lens.

A sinking sensation in my stomach, I look away from the photogs and up at Ronan's face. "Where's my mother?"

"She died in the second wave," he says, his eyes flickering downward. "I'm so sorry. She went back for the wounded. I told her not to, that it was a fool's errand. But she said if we didn't try to go back for them, we were as guilty as the officials who'd ordered the bombings, and the bellators who'd seen it done. I got hold of her arm, but she twisted away from me and went running back into the clearing. Right when the second bombs fell."

"My fault," I say, my voice as numb as I feel. "I led Eva straight to you."

"You're not to blame, Ari." He folds his arms across his chest for emphasis. "The Executor, the Bellatorum, and Eva, for allowing them to implant a tracker to lead them here. But not you, and don't you ever think it."

"A tracker? How do you know?"

"Kilían got word to me. He feels a considerable amount of guilt. Had he known such a thing existed, he would have taken steps to eliminate it before it could do us harm."

Eliminate it. He means, eliminate *her*—kill Eva. Why doesn't the thought fill me with satisfaction? Her actions led to the death of most of the people in the encampment—of my mother. She betrayed me. Shouldn't I want her dead?

My thoughts must show on my face, because he gives me a pained smile. "People aren't one thing or another, Ari—good or evil. Eva used you to further the Executor's ends, sure—but if she hadn't cared for you, she never would have tossed that grenade to facilitate your escape."

I shake my head, dismissing this with an effort. "It doesn't matter. The people who betrayed me and cast me out, the ones who slaughtered your camp and killed my mother—I will make them pay at the point of my sword, until they beg for mercy."

Ronan raises a soot-smudged eyebrow. "All by yourself, really? We'll lose a fighter and you'll make no difference to our cause."

"What's my life, into the bargain? I've already lost everything else."

He grips my shoulder—a gesture that, in the Commonwealth, would have to be earned through years of solidarity. I have to force myself not to flinch. "No," he says quietly. "You haven't."

Without another word, he turns. One hand on the hilt of my dagur, I follow him into what remains of the Brotherhood's camp.

I huddle on the floor of the cell, shivering. I'd come to in here, still wearing my drenched clothes, with no idea of the time. When I'd asked Paul, one of the bellators stationed outside the door, he'd told me it was past midnight. And then he'd shoved a heel of bread and some water through the bars and stalked away without another word.

I eat the food, use the toilet in the corner, and then try to sleep—but it's no use. One of the guards approaches the cell every time I doze off, sticks an electrical prod through the bars, and shocks me. After the third time, I give up and sit with my back against the wall and my knees drawn up to my chest, waiting for morning.

As the night passes, so does the cold, transmuting itself into a slow-burning, simmering heat that creeps through my muscles, making them twitch without warning. Even my eyeballs feel hot, scorching my lids whenever I close them. At first I think it is a lingering side effect from the electroshock—but as time wears on, I begin to wonder if I have a fever. Hugging my knees to my chest to keep myself still, I peer into the red haze that blankets the inside of my eyelids and imagine I can see Ari's face.

I'm still awake hours later, when I hear the Executor and Efraím conversing in low voices out of sight of my cell. "I trust you'll explain what I saw yesterday afternoon, sir," Efraím is saying stiffly. "I apologize for losing control of my temper. That was unforgivable."

"No need to apologize, Bellator Stinar. I'm sure I would have been equally taken aback. And yes—when the time comes, I shall most definitely explain."

"Is there anything else I should know, sir? So I can prepare myself —and my bellators—"

"Ah, Efraím." The Executor gives a mirthless chuckle. "Citizen Marteinn is special. Unique. Even I don't know everything she might be capable of."

"I see," Efraím says, sounding as if he doesn't see in the slightest. "Is this why you recommended her for the Bellatorum, sir?"

"It is, yes. And she has performed admirably, has she not?"

"She has, sir. But if what I saw yesterday is any indication, she can be said to have some unusual advantages."

I am listening for all I am worth, fever forgotten, inching toward the cell door. The changes in my perception—the way everything looks brighter and more detailed, my superior night vision, my ability to run and jump and fall, the way I was able to hold my breath in the tank yesterday—I'm sure this is what he is talking about. So what's the answer? What's wrong with me? Am I finally about to discover the secret of the little pink pills?

As if I've spoken aloud, the Executor chuckles again. "Advantages, yes. You could say that. But perhaps disadvantages, too —it's too early to tell. It is most important we keep an eye on her— hence the molecular trackers that we put in those pills we have been including with her vitamins. And a good thing, too, otherwise we would have fallen short of the opportunity to destroy the Brotherhood's forward party and catch the seditionist Westergaard in the act."

I sag back against the wall of the cell, feeling the rough outline of the stone through my clothes. They're close to dry now, spurred by the waves of heat that have deluged me all night. I was right to be suspicious of the pink pills. They had nothing to do with my supposed anemia—nor are they behind the enhancement of my senses. They were trackers, meant to apprise the Executor of my whereabouts. Which means—what? That the Bellatorum has succeeded in stripping me of my civility, shaping me into one of them —a savage warrior—without chemical assistance? That my ability to track Ari through the branches of a tree by scent and see in the dark, my victory over Riis and Karsten—it is a learned skill?

All the Bellatorum are trained to bolster their senses. They rely on them in interrogation and in a fight. But what's happening to me is different. I think of the time I heard people approaching in the woods before Ari did, the way I was able to find the right path through the tunnels to the scholar's room when he couldn't smell a thing—not to mention how I held my breath in the ice tank—and shudder. And then there's the night of the Choosing, when I jumped from the window of the Rookery and landed without a scratch...before I had an ounce of Bellatorum training. If the pink pills aren't making this possible, then what is?

What if what Ronan told us was true? Have the gen techs tampered with my DNA somehow, enhanced it?

I shudder at the thought—then at another one, right on its heels. What the pink pills *did* make possible—that the bellators found the location of the resistance camp—means something else: I'm responsible for Ronan and his fighters, for whatever's happening to Ari now. Guilt stabs me, and I wrap my arms around myself, trying to ignore the memory of Ari's mother making her way toward him, hand outstretched, before a horrible sound split the stillness and the woods went up in flames.

I'm sorry, I mouth, so the bellators who are guarding me can't hear. *I'm so sorry.*

But I have no time to dwell on this terrible realization, because the Executor is talking again. "Of course, there's no need to administer that pill anymore," he says briskly. "No need to track our little rebel. She's not leaving anytime soon."

"Begging your pardon, Executor," Efraím says, sounding uncomfortable, "but the girl maintains she was acting on behalf of the Commonwealth. She's held true to that position this entire time. You don't suppose she could be telling the truth—"

"Unlikely. But we'll have her at our mercy tomorrow, will we not? Together, we will separate fact from fiction."

"Yes sir," Efraím replies, and then I hear their footsteps moving away.

I drift into an uneasy sleep, plagued by nightmares. First I dream I am back in the ice tank, struggling for breath, burning with fever despite the cold. I try to bang on the glass, to smash my way to freedom, but it is no use. My hand has become a flipper, and all it does is slap uselessly against the surface of the tank, again and again.

Fury fills me, but when I scream, my voice emerges as a harsh, inhuman bark. I lunge at the glass, throwing my body against it, and somehow break through. Then I am flying, my flippers transformed into wings, soaring out of that horrible room and through the tunnels, up the stairs and into the crisp outdoor air. I spread my wings wide, cawing in victory, heading for the woods.

The forest is mine. The world is mine.

I'm free.

My eyes blink open. I'm lying on the floor of the cell, the ground blessedly cold beneath my cheek. Something is wrong. I know it, I can feel it—

I try to sit up, but my hand skids along the stone, making a horrible screeching noise—as if my nails have grown exponentially while I slept. My palm feels strange, leathery.

I turn my head, afraid to look. When I do, I have to stifle a scream. The thing at the end of my arm no longer resembles a hand. It is yellow-gray and scaly, tipped with curved black talons—a bird's claw.

Nightmare, I think, clenching my eyes shut. *Not real.*

The fever grabs hold of me, sinking its jaws into my bones, and drags me back down into sleep. When I wake, my hand is its normal self again. The relief that washes over me is so profound, for a moment I forget to be afraid.

Then someone says my name, and my heart starts pounding all over again.

"Get up, Eva." The voice is rough in my ear, accompanied by the bite of fingers into my upper arm. I blink and twist away, rolling onto my knees.

Kilían crouches next to me, his expression grim. "Good evening," he says. "Or should I say good morning? It's three a.m.—the hour of the ill-doer. You decide."

My eyes flick over him, assessing the proximity of his weapons, and he shifts backward, shaking his head. "Don't even try it. I've heard every bit of what happened in the ice tank chamber, not to mention your little performance in interrogation." His hand drops to his belt, and when he lifts it again, he's holding a syringe. "So I brought a gift to entice you to cooperate. You don't want to know what this will do to you, Eva. You really don't."

My gaze must linger on the syringe a few seconds too long, because he gives a reluctant chuckle. "I see you're thinking of using this against me, Bellator Marteinn. Don't bother. There's an antidote, and I've already taken it. You'll just get yourself in even more trouble."

I glance upward, at his face. "What do you want from me, Kilían?"

"That's the question, isn't it," he muses. "What do I want from you, indeed? A fair query, as you've already done more than enough."

It occurs to me that Kilían believes what Ari must—that I was opposed to the Brotherhood all along, that I used my relationship with my mentor as leverage to gather information. It's ironic, really— the two people who I need to convince I have no investment in the resistance, that I am committed to upholding the Commonwealth, don't believe me in the slightest. And here's Kilían, convinced I undermined the Brotherhood and triggered the bombing. That whatever tracker they utilized to follow me to the resistance camp was implemented with my knowledge and consent.

My only consolation is that he can't kill me, not without angering the Executor, who seems to believe I am valuable—or take drastic action without exposing himself as a Brotherhood spy. I want desperately to give him a sign I'm on his side, to ask if he's seen Ari. To find out what happened to Ronan and Ari's mother and the other members of the resistance. But I don't know how.

I glance down, hoping to compose myself. But that does me no good, because carved into the stone I see the impossible: Four shallow furrows, exactly where the talons from my nightmare scraped along the floor of my cell.

By the Architect, what is happening to me?

I'm still staring at the grooves in the stone when Kilían digs his fingers into my shoulders. "Am I boring you, Bellator Marteinn?"

I can't afford to think about my nightmare, about the fever and the claw. Kilían holds my life in his hands. With a supreme effort, I force myself to focus.

"What are you doing here?" I do my best not to sound as frightened as I feel. "I'm surprised they let you in. Efraím and the Executor seem intent on having me all to themselves."

"Oh, they are," he says, rocking back on his heels. "But I have my ways."

"You did something to the guards outside my cell, didn't you." It isn't a question.

He shrugs. "They'll be fine. Unlike the majority of the people in that camp you helped to destroy. Nice work, by the way. I think the boy really believed you."

A chill runs through me, attributable to more than my still-damp clothing and the conditions of the underground. "Ari?" I say stupidly, as if there's another boy he might mean.

"Who else? I must say, the Executor and Stinar are being very secretive about the origins of their plan. I'd be happy if you could shed some light on it." He grabs me by the arm again and stands, hauling me to my feet. I think of struggling, but feel the pressure of the needle against my upper arm and reconsider.

"Walk," Kilían snaps at me.

"Where are we going?"

"Don't ask questions. Move." He pushes me forward.

"Kilían," I say, "I don't think you understand—"

"Oh, I understand more than you know. But not nearly as much as I'd like to. Now move. We don't have all night."

He shoves me again and this time I comply. My mind is churning, trying to find a way to communicate with him, but there are ears everywhere. Maybe wherever he is taking me will be soundproof. In the meantime my best course of action is to go along with what he wants, and not compromise the only ally I have—not that he thinks he's any ally of mine.

The two guards are slumped outside my cell, leaning against the wall. Kilían steers me around them and down the passageway, in the direction of the interrogation chamber. He unlocks the door and pushes me through.

"Efraím already interrogated me," I say, twisting to look at him. "I don't know what you think you're going to accomplish—"

"Shut up," he says. "You traitor."

"No," I protest. "I'm not, Kilían, I swear. Not the way you think."

"I told you to shut up." He locks the door behind us and grabs my upper arm again. "I'm not interrogating you, Bellator Marteinn. Oh, no. You'll do that all on your own."

"What are you talking about?"

"You'll see." Fingers digging into my arm, he marches me through the interrogation chamber and into a smaller room I've never seen before. Illuminated by wall-mounted torches, it's empty save for a jute mat and a large fireplace, piled high with branches. Dark blue berries cling to the tightly woven green needles.

"That's juniper," I say to Kilían, who has locked the door behind us and is standing with his back against it, as if to prevent my escape. The torchlight casts grotesque shadows on his face, transforming his features into elongated, monstrous shapes. His hair gleams red, then auburn, then brown as he turns to face me.

"Very good, Marteinn," he says, and, moving forward, pulls one of the torches from the wall. "The Bellatorum use it to induce trance states, to achieve a higher sense of discipline and focus. But you'll find it's also excellent at rendering one more susceptible to the questions and suggestions of others. It's what Stinar and the Executor have in mind for you next—but I've usurped the privilege."

He strides across the room and tosses the torch onto the stack of branches. Immediately they begin to smolder, white smoke drifting up the chimney and out into the room. "You're trained in resisting interrogation techniques, Marteinn," he says, swiveling to face me. "But no one taught you how to withstand this."

The smoke fills my lungs, making me dizzy, and I struggle to keep my feet. I consider holding my breath, the way I did in the tank—but then I change my mind. If this is what it takes for him to believe me, I'll marinate myself in juniper fumes, and welcome.

"Ask me whatever you want, Kilían," I manage. "I have nothing to hide from you." *Aside from the fact that I'm transforming into some kind of beast.* "I'm on your side."

He digs in his weapons belt for a mask, which he hooks over his ears, covering his nose and mouth. "You'll say anything, won't you? No conscience whatsoever. What a bellator you would have made."

Try as I might to stay standing, I lose the battle. My knees buckle, and I sink onto the jute mat. My eyes blink, then flutter closed. The resinous smell of burning juniper singes my throat, and a strange sensation floods my body, as if I'm floating.

Kilían's voice comes to me from a great distance, echoing throughout the room. "What is your name?"

Without conscious volition I feel my mouth move, forming a reply. "Eva Marteinn."

"And who are you, Eva Marteinn?"

"I am—I *was*—a bellator."

"Are you not anymore?" His voice betrays only mild curiosity.

"I followed Ari to the resistance camp. I listened to Ronan. And then—then the Commonwealth bombed them." I hear my voice break, catch. "When we fled back through the tunnels, seeking sanctuary, the bellators confronted us. They would have killed Ari. They wanted me, so I pretended to go along with their plan. Then I threw the grenade. I helped Ari escape. I don't know what they want from me. But I can't endorse what they have done."

"What they have done." His tone is quiet, considering. "Westergaard's mother is dead. So are seventeen others. Their deaths are on your heads."

"No," I say, shaking my head violently. "Not the way you mean."

"Do you support the Brotherhood, Eva?" The voice is a needle, sinking through the haze of the juniper smoke, prodding me to reply.

"I support what they represent. I cannot stand with the Commonwealth any longer."

"Why did you help Ari Westergaard escape?"

"Ari is my friend."

"I see. Why did you lead the Commonwealth to the resistance camp?"

I shift on the mat, fighting the grip of the smoke. Each of my limbs weighs a thousand pounds. "I didn't mean to. They were using me as a tracking device. I overheard Efraím and the Executor talking. It was in my vitamins. They tricked me. They used me."

"But you've done your utmost to persuade them you do, indeed, stand with them. That you were playing Westergaard for a fool. How do you justify this?"

I force my eyes open. Kilían is standing on the mat in front of me, his features obscured by the mask, hands clasped behind his back. "At first," I say, the words thick on my awkward tongue, "I did what I had to, so they would let Ari go. After that, maintaining my original story was safest. I wouldn't endanger the Brotherhood. They were victims, trying to build a better life. Also, to endanger them is to endanger Ari. I would never do that. I want him to be safe. To get away, even if it means I never leave this place."

Holding my eyes open is too much effort. They sink closed again, and a minefield of tiny pinpricks, bright holes in the darkness, lines the inside of my eyelids. Kilían speaks into the dark. "What do you see? Describe it for me. Every detail."

Somehow, I am standing, unarmed, in the middle of Clockverk Square. The air around me is silent except for the call of a hawk from the top of the tower; sun glints off the windows of the dining hall, the Rookery and library.

I stand warily in the middle of the square, scanning the perimeter for threats. And then, between one heartbeat and the next, it happens: A wall of fire springs up around the square, solid and as high as I can see, hemming me in. Heat singes my face, bakes into my clothes. My eyes dart from one corner to the other, seeking a way out—but there is nothing.

The fire creeps closer, encircling me. If I reached out my hands, I could touch it.

In the small circle where I stand, a fellow bellator appears, armed for battle. A weapons belt crisscrosses his hips; a sverd is strapped to his back. His face is turned away from me, concealed by a hood. He stands, backlit by fire, but does not speak.

"Who are you?" I demand. "What do you want?"

Next to me, the bellator stirs, shifting his weight. And then he turns toward me and pushes back his hood, revealing Ari's face.

I can't help it—my pulse starts pounding, fluttering wildly. I want to throw my arms around him, to let him know I will do whatever it takes to make things right. That if I have to die here, in the flames, I would consider it an honor for his face to be the last one I see.

He stares down at me, his green eyes solemn, and I know what I have to do.

"He threatens the innocent who spares the guilty," I say.

"Either by meeting or by the sword," he replies in that achingly familiar voice. And he pulls his blade free.

The flames close around us as I sink to my knees, bare my neck, and wait for the blade to fall. A fitting sacrifice, for the loss of his mother and all she held dear.

A hand grabs my wrist, gripping tight. "Enough, Eva. Can you hear me?" Kilían says.

I open my eyes, trying to focus on his face through the haze of smoke. "I hear."

"With attachment comes chaos." The words resonate within my skull, as if it is not his voice at all, but my own. "He threatens the innocent who spares the guilty, indeed. How came you to bare your neck to Ari Westergaard?"

"Chaos is all around us," I reply. "Lack of attachment will not keep it at bay."

Kilían huffs out a muffled laugh. "You claim you stand with the Brotherhood, Eva Marteinn. You could have told Efraím all you know about my involvement, and spared yourself much pain. Yet you have kept my secrets and your silence. Why?"

"A wolf will not bite a wolf, Kilían Bryndísarson. So, too, will I do you no harm."

Even from behind the mask, I hear Kilían's startled intake of breath. "Why do you matter so much to the Executor?" he presses me. "What happened in the ice tank—how did you hold your breath that way?"

"I don't know. The Executor told Efraím I was unique. I don't understand why."

"Why did you not hold your breath in this room, with me, to avoid the effects of the smoke?"

"I wanted you to know the truth. I wanted you to believe me. Efraím and the Executor are different. They punished me. They are my enemies. But I'll keep your secrets, on my honor as a bellator. I won't betray your cause."

"Is that so? And what do you want? What would you do, had you your freedom?"

"I'd find Ari," I say immediately. "I'd rejoin what remains of the camp, and fight by their side. If I am to be a weapon, I'll choose the hand that holds the blade."

Kilían kneels down next to me and takes my shoulders in his hands. I struggle to focus on his face through the fog of smoke that shrouds the room. "Let justice be done even should the world perish," he whispers. "What say you to that, Eva Marteinn?"

Casting my mind back to the conversation between Ari and the scholar before we entered the tunnels for the first time—before so much—I muster a response. "Let justice be done, Bellator Bryndísarson, even should the sky fall."

Kilían's hands tighten on my shoulders. His masked face, inches from my own, is the last thing I see before the smoke overwhelms me and the world tips, sending me sideways. From far away, I hear Kilían say my name. Then there is nothing but the dark.

ARI

Ronan has moved the camp twice since I arrived two days ago. I don't know why he doesn't leave this area; staying seems a fool's errand.

Of the nine members of the Brotherhood who survived the bombing, only five are warriors. There is Adrien, the scout who met us when we emerged from the tunnels—Zoya, his companion, is dead. Then there's Fadel, another scout, who goes by Fade; Camila, their weapons expert, with almond-shaped eyes and a lilting accent I've never heard before; Ronan himself; and Jaxon, his second in command—a tall guy in his early twenties with pale skin, hair as black as a selkie's pelt, eyes to match, and a watchful attitude. Jaxon does not like me.

The first time we met, he was sitting on the ground, turning a small object over and over in his hands. There were deep purple bruises beneath his eyes, and a nasty burn on his forearm. When he saw me, he got to his feet, closing his fist around the object he held. I caught the deep blue gleam of a gemstone before he shoved whatever it was into his pocket.

I opened my mouth to speak, but Jaxon beat me to it. "Ronan trusts you," he said, his voice a harsh croak. "He believes everything that guy Kilían said to him about your girl Eva and the bombing. But me—all I know is you got eighteen of my friends killed. You come from a society of savages. And I'll be watching you."

Which he has. Every time I turn around, his eyes are on me, dark and haunted. I am glad when Ronan assigns me patrol duty of the camp's eastern perimeter on my second evening with the Brotherhood. My guilt is heavy enough without having to shoulder the accusation that's clear enough in Jaxon's gaze. Once again, the irony does not escape me—in his eyes, Eva and I are the barbarians. It's the inverse of what I've always been taught to believe.

Ronan has trained me on the basics of how to use a gun, cracking his apart to show me how to load the bullets, lifting it to teach me how to aim, but I prefer to use my own weapons. I'm patrolling the border, prowling through the trees with my blade unsheathed, when I hear footfalls. They're a long way off, but closing fast. Whoever it is, they are moving with assurance, making no effort to conceal their approach—which means they are a friend who doesn't wish to get stabbed by mistake, or an enemy who believes they are so well guarded they have nothing to lose. Regardless, my strategy is the same: Patience and vigilance. I step behind the gnarled trunk of a giant oak, and wait.

I smell Kilían before I see him: the clean sweat of a man who has been exerting himself, the faint moldering odor of the tunnels, and beneath that, the neutral trace of Commonwealth soap. The top note to these layered scents is what gives him away—juniper. He has marked himself with oil, so I won't mistake him for a threat.

Two feet from my hiding place he comes to a halt. "Ari?" he says, his voice carrying in the silence of the woods, broken only by the fall of branches and the scurrying of small animals. "I know you're here. You might as well come out."

"How are you armed?" I reply, and he laughs.

"What has happened to your manners, boy? What, not even so much as a hello?"

"Hello, Kilían. How are you armed?"

He gives an exasperated chuckle. "I'm armed for battle, Ari. But I'm not here to fight with you. Come out, would you, for the Architect's sake? Time's of the essence."

Carefully, I step from the shadows and clear my throat. Clad in black gear, his red hair tucked under a cap to conceal its telltale shade, he turns in a circle, his face lighting with a relieved smile when his eyes find mine. "Not dead," he says lightly. "Nor maimed. The night is looking up."

"Is it? What do you want?"

"Why so hostile?" he says, taking a step toward me. "I'm on your side, Westergaard. Or rather, we're on the same side. Have you forgotten?"

"And what side is that?" My voice is tight.

"The side of justice. Fairness. And freedom." He steps closer still, and I don't like it. My hand falls to my belt in warning, and he stops. "Freedom comes with a cost, Westergaard."

He regards me with narrowed eyes, and I sigh. "So. Eva." Her name is barbed wire in my throat. "Is she living the high life, or what? Have they appointed her to the council of High Priests, or made her the Executor's new right hand? I bet she's their prize pet, huh?"

An odd look passes across Kilían's face. "Well," he says slowly, "not unless you keep your pets on a very short leash."

I feel my eyebrows knit. "What do you mean?"

"They have her in a cell, Ari. Have had her there, ever since she threw that smoke grenade. I tell you, what I would've given to see that…"

"In a cell?" I say, cutting him off mid-sentence. "Who does?"

He takes a step back, eyeing me with caution. "All of them. The Executor, Efraím. They keep her under heavy guard. It was all I could do to work myself into the rotation."

"You've seen her, then?" Despite myself, I feel eagerness surge up inside me.

Kilían frowns, shaking his head. "Don't even think about it. You'll never get to her. Even if you could make it back inside, she's heavily guarded, like I said. There's two bellators on her door at all times, never mind the guards for the prison itself." His voice drops lower, into a cadence meant to be soothing. "I know she led them here, Ari. That she's to blame for the bombing and your mother's death. But believe me, they're having their revenge on her, Commonwealth loyalist or no. There's no need for you to risk yourself."

"What are they doing to her?" I say, my tone neutral.

He snorts. "What aren't they doing, that would be a better question. Lie detector tests, electroshock, ice tank immersion, sleep deprivation, the works." He spins his knife over his knuckles, the edge of the blade catching moonlight. "Quite frankly, I'm surprised they'd treat her like this, after she's been such a valuable informant. She must've really displeased them, tossing that grenade. I'm telling you, Westergaard—that girl's got stones."

"Yeah, she does." Against my better judgment, I envision Eva trapped in a shatterproof tank, filling minute by minute with icy water until only the smallest air pocket remains. I've seen people tortured this way, seen them sink into hypothermia, limbs braced against the sides of the tank for the leverage that will afford them a few precious sips of air, fingers clawing at the glass in a bid for freedom. It's a punishment reserved for the worst of the Commonwealth's criminals. No matter what heinous acts Eva has committed, I can't stand to think about her suffering like that. Better to kill her and have done.

"Lie detector tests?" I say, clearing my throat roughly. "Why would they need those?"

Kilían shrugs. "*No dissension will be tolerated*, and all that. She was their nice little marionette, she played along with them—right up until it looked like your life was on the line. And then she fought back, just enough to cover your escape. So now they have it in for her." He raises an eyebrow. "She must have known what the consequences would be."

I stare at him, giving him nothing.

He sighs. "It's none of my business."

"No," I say. "It's not."

"You don't have to look at me that way. I won't say it again."

"Say what? That a girl who cared about me enough to endanger her own life would maybe balk at murdering my mother?" I give a harsh laugh. "Don't bother, Kilían. I have no desire to explore what a twisted little piece Eva Marteinn must be. She made her choices; I'll make mine. Regardless, it's not any of your concern."

"No," he says. "Except—well, forget it."

"What?"

"Never mind," he says, examining the blade of his knife. "I came to see that you were all right, and here you are. I need to get back. The camp will be moving on, I suppose, so this is goodbye. Stand strong, Ari Westergaard."

He turns to go, and I am on him, kicking his knife free and pinning him up against the trunk of a tree, my blade at his throat. "Don't play with me, Kilían," I say.

In the light of the harvest moon, I see him smile, as if I have pleased him. "By the Architect, you are fast, boy."

"You knew that. Now speak, or bleed."

His smile broadens. "I thought you didn't want to talk about Eva anymore. What did you call her? A twisted little piece? Imaginative, Westergaard, even for you."

"Do you *want* me to hurt you?" The words emerge from between gritted teeth.

Unbelievably, the bastard laughs. "No, no," he says. "Of course not. I'll tell you what I was going to say. But in the meantime, perhaps you could remove your knife from my throat? It's a bit uncomfortable, especially if we're going to be having a little chat."

"I bet it is," I say, but I let up on the blade anyhow, stepping back from him. "Happy?"

"Overjoyed," he says, rubbing his throat gingerly.

"Fantastic. Pray continue."

Kilían bends to pick up his knife, keeping a cautious eye on me. "It's strange, is the thing. Everything I know about the tests they ran on her is secondhand. They won't let anyone in there. Almost as if they're afraid to have the wrong person overhear what she might say."

"Yet *you* know," I observe. "How might that be?"

"I have my sources. Someone has to conduct the tests. And even the strongest soldier has a weakness." His gaze rests on me, considering. "My source says every test they gave her—the lie detector, everything—she passed with flying colors."

"So she's not lying," I say impatiently. "So what?"

"Not just the lie detector test. The ice tank—they kept her in there for twenty minutes before they pulled her out. And aside from slight hypothermia—*slight*, mind you—she was fine. Held her breath the whole time, and came out swinging. It took two of them to hold her back, is what I heard."

"For twenty minutes? Your source is playing you, Kilían. There's no way."

"That's what I thought. But it made me curious. So I took her out of her cell myself, to the juniper chamber. They would've had me put her under anyhow, but I wanted to do it without a witness. And so I did." He pauses, clearing his throat. "She denied everything she'd told Efraím and the Executor, claimed she was on your side all along. That she did what she did to protect you. And then, when I put her further under—she saw the strangest things."

It takes everything I have to maintain my indifferent expression. "Such as?"

"Well, to begin with—execution in the Square at your hands."

"What?" My voice comes low, filled with shock. "Eva had *me* kill her?"

Kilían nods grimly. "That was the only time her heartbeat did anything out of the ordinary—when the bellator pushed back his hood and she saw your face. I had my fingers on her pulse; it spiked sky-high. But the next thing I knew it was back to normal again—slow, even, like she was pacing it. And she knelt and bent her head and waited for the blade to fall."

"She—what? She knelt there and let me—" Try as I might, I can't keep the agitation from my voice. "Eva would never let that happen. She would fight me until the end, even if she knew she couldn't win."

"That's what I thought," Kilían says, his voice careful. "Yet she threw the grenade. Her heart rate spiked. She let you kill her. Why would that happen?"

"Why does Eva do anything?" My left hand creeps downward, toward my weapons belt. With an effort, I still it.

Kilían's gaze follows the movement of my hand, and he smiles wryly. "I trained you, Bellator Westergaard. Are you lying to me, or to yourself?"

Silence is my only possible defense. So I don't speak, and he continues. "Wherever the truth lies, I don't believe you would willingly have put the encampment in danger, or put in motion the chain of events that led to your mother's death. But something's not right here." He looks me over, the set of his shoulders tightening. "You're hiding something."

He isn't wrong—but for him to guess what it is might be disastrous. I don't trust anyone, not anymore. Exiled from the Commonwealth or no, I have no intention of telling him about my feelings for Eva—much less what's transpired between us. If there's the slimmest chance what she told him was the truth—well, then I don't care to think of what she's given up...for me. And so I draw a deep breath, brace myself, and lie.

"You're right, I did have every intention of coming back through the tunnels to take her life. And I don't believe she's telling the truth now, no matter what the juniper trance showed. But you know what? She's not worth my time, not worth another thought. I have dedicated my blade to the service of the Brotherhood. Let the girl rot. I'll trouble her no more."

His gaze rests on my face, then widens to take in my hand resting on the knife, the tension in my stance. He is examining me, assessing me for weaknesses. Well, two can play his little game. I straighten my spine, drop my hands to my sides the way I do during inspections, and stand at attention. And then I give him a slow, sardonic smile, daring him to find fault. "I'll not carry her betrayal with me. Perhaps she did me a favor—for now I'm free."

"Free to run," he says, his mouth twisting. "Free to die."

"If that's what you really believe, then why are you doing this? That's what I can't figure out. What's in this for you?"

Kilían's mouth compresses. "My reasons are my own."

I tilt my head, considering, and bait him. "You may devalue my freedom, Bellator Bryndísarson, but at least the choice is mine. Wish you could say the same?"

"I serve the resistance in my own way," he snaps, tension thrumming through him. "My role is just as important. Perhaps more so. As for the girl, perhaps she's telling the truth. Or perhaps she's playing a deeper game, manipulating the two of us against each other to achieve her own means. She could have betrayed us both to the Executor and saved herself considerable pain. Either way, something's amiss. And I intend to find out what it is."

He turns without another word and vanishes into the dark. I watch him go, weaving soundlessly between the trees, his form blending in and out of the shadows until he merges with them and I can't see him anymore. Only then do I allow myself to sink down at the base of the giant oak, head in my hands and breath coming hard.

Kneeling like that—baring her neck for me—it can only mean one thing.

Je me rends, she was saying. I surrender.

Which in turn means—whatever game she's playing, it's over.

"Damn her to Belial and back again," I mutter into my hands. If what she told Kilían was true, she's played all of us—the Commonwealth, the resistance, and me—for fools. And for what? An agenda of her own? Or some ridiculous, noble reason?

Either way, I have no intention of leaving her in that cell, to be interrogated and experimented upon like an animal. The Executor knows she's lying—but he can't crack her, and despite myself I feel a bright flash of pride. Then I realize that out here, it's not forbidden, and let the feeling spread, filling my chest with warmth, chasing back the awful emptiness.

"Twenty minutes underwater, Eva?" I murmur, as if she were here beside me. "Coming out of the ice tank swinging? You're full of surprises, apprentice mine."

With those words, I can *see* her—her fall of black hair, her wide-spaced eyes, dark as chocolate, her arched brows and pointed chin, that delicious mouth, her lips a deep shade of pink, and her pale skin, gorgeously flushed the way it had been when I'd broken away from her in the woods that night. I suck in air, striving desperately for equilibrium, and her scent floods me—soap and salt and that sweet, sharp richness.

Now that the bone-deep sense of rage and betrayal that has accompanied me for days is gone, I realize what I ought to have known all along: I miss Eva. She has become as essential to me as breathing, as necessary as food or water or air. I want her back—and more than that, I need her. As much as I hate to admit this, it's the truth.

I feel wetness on my face and pull my hands away, puzzled. Gingerly, I run a finger down my cheek, and realize the moisture's coming from my eyes.

For the first time in as long as I can remember, I'm crying.

I push myself to my feet, sheathing my blade. Roughly, I wipe the tears away.

I will get her back. No matter what Kilían says, I'll find a way. And if that means the resistance moves on without me—so be it. We'll make it on our own.

For the first time in days, the sick, empty feeling inside me begins to retreat. The horrible weight on my chest lifts, and I can breathe again. I find my way back to camp, careful to keep to the shadows, beginning to formulate a plan.

3 2

EVA

"Hey!" I wrap my hands around the bars of my cell, rattling them. "I know you're out there, Benedikt. I want to talk to the Executor. Now."

A few hours have passed since Kilían interrogated me. I woke up on the floor of my cell, my back propped against the wall and my head filled with the remnants of a juniper haze. My body is my own again—no claws, talons, beaks, or flippers. Still, if I had any doubt about what I saw, those shallow grooves in the stone put paid to it. I want answers—and there's one person who I'm sure can give them to me.

"Benedikt!" I yell, shaking the bars again. I can smell him—sweat and metal and the dried figs he likes to eat. Nasty, shriveled things. I can't stand them.

He appears in my line of vision, taking his sweet time strolling over, his sverd loose in his hand. "Yell a little louder, Marteinn, why don't you. There might be a few citizens asleep in the Rookery who haven't heard you yet."

"I wouldn't have had to yell if you'd come when I called you the first time," I tell him, and bare my teeth in a facsimile of a smile. My face is streaked with mud and blood—I can feel it caking my skin—and Benedikt takes a step back before he can stop himself.

"The Executor isn't at your beck and call," he says.

I stand my ground. "I want to talk to him. Get. Him."

He flares his nostrils at me in disgust—whatever, it isn't as if he smells like a rose—and stalks off. Ten minutes later, he is back, Efraím in tow.

"Marteinn," is all Efraím says. His lips are a thin seam of disapproval.

"May I please speak with the Executor." It isn't a question.

He tilts his head. "What gives you the right to make demands?"

I don't say a word. I don't have to. Somewhere in the darkness behind him, I can hear the limping beat of the Executor's heart. Sure enough, the man himself steps from the shadows, a leather bag slung over one shoulder.

"I'll speak with her, Efraím," he says.

"Sir—"

"You may leave." He swivels to face Efraím and Benedikt. "Both of you."

"She's dangerous." Efraím's voice comes low, a warning.

"I know what she is. Better than you do. Now go." His tone doesn't brook refusal.

They obey, backs stiff, walking off down the long hall that leads away from the cells. The Executor and I stare at each other. I fight the urge to drop my eyes, and win.

Inexplicably, his stern mouth curves upward, as if my defiance has pleased him. "So," he says. "You wished to speak with me."

My hands are still curled around the bars of my cell. I shake them, just a little, and see his eyes narrow as the metal trembles. I can't wrench the bars apart—the Architect knows I've tried, when my guards' backs were turned—but it doesn't do any harm for the Executor to think I could. "I don't suppose you'd consider letting me out so we could have this conversation in a more civilized fashion."

His bottomless eyes narrow still further. "I don't suppose," he says, "that I would."

"Or," I say, "you could come in. The accommodations are poor, but there's enough space for two."

He smiles at me, that shark's smile that I've dreaded and detested in equal measure since the first time I saw it. "I think we both know I'm wise enough to know better."

I step back, hands open to show my willingness to refrain from throttling him. "Tell me the truth, then. What's happening to me?"

The smile is back, but this time it's different—anticipatory, with what I'd swear is genuine happiness lurking around the edges. "You're becoming what you are meant to be."

To the nine hells and back with not throttling him. If I wasn't confined in this cell, I'd pin him to the wall and choke the information out of him, Executor or no. "In the past twenty-four hours, I've been electroshocked, beaten, and nearly drowned," I say, feeling that prickling heat rush over my body again. "I'm not in the mood for riddles."

He opens the leather bag that's slung across his shoulder, reaches in, and pulls out a portable comp. "Here," he says simply, and passes the comp through the bars.

I take it and flip it open, fingers clenching on the plastic cover. The screen comes up immediately, login information bypassed. I see my name. My date of birth. And then a flurry of information that makes no sense. Words that can't possibly have anything to do with me, with who I am.

It can't be. It's a ploy. A trick. A lie.

I rearrange the letters in my mind, wishing I could make them say something else. But no matter how hard I try, they are still there, an undeniable reality in black and white.

Eva Marteinn. Deliberate mutation, Trial 12.

Parents: Mixed parentage. Genetic fracturing employed to maximize intellectual and physical capacities. Blueprint incorporates Panthera pardus *(leopard)*, Canis lupus arctos *(Arctic wolf)*, Hydrurga leptonyx *(leopard seal), and* Falco peregrinus *(peregrine falcon). Human genetic material harvested as per typical extraction procedures. Human progenitors—*

That's as far as I get before the comp falls from my shaking hands to the floor.

My worst fear. Everything I've worked so hard to combat.

"No," I hear myself say, small and cold and not like me at all. "It's not true. No."

"It's a gift," the Executor says, his eyes bright with excitement. "So many died. So many were not strong enough. But you, Eva—you are the end result of years of hard work and sacrifice. You are my prize."

"Your prize experiment, you mean." My voice is thin with shock. "Where did you—how did you even—"

"It wasn't easy. There were so many failures. Dreadful, terrible things." He shudders. "But you lived, Eva. To protect you, we encoded a trigger in your genes that wouldn't allow the shifting process to begin until the time of your Choosing. We watched you, though—*I* watched you—more closely than you can imagine."

My leap from the window of the Rookery, my speed in training, my skill in scenting Ari that night in the woods, my ability to hold my breath in the ice tank, even my dreams—they coalesce into an impossible, irrefutable image. I lunge, throwing myself against the bars. *"What have you done to me?"*

He steps back, cocking an eyebrow. "Why, Eva," he says, "we haven't done anything to you at all. This is who you've been. From the very beginning."

I think about the shadows I saw when I was a small child in the Nursery—the way they'd writhed on the wall, the way no one else could see them. *Teeth and claws and talons.*

"'The shifting process,'" I say, each word a growl. "Meaning —what?"

That gleeful smile is back again. "Eventually," he says, "you'll be able to take the shape of each of the animals whose genes you share. And oh, what a weapon you will be. There will be no one inside any of the Commonwealths or outside our borders who will dare to challenge us then."

I want to call him a liar. But all I can think of is how I'd woken to find my hand gone, replaced with a bird's claw. "This is about defeating the resistance?" I say, my voice shaking. "You corrupted my DNA—killed who knows how many others—for the sake of *power*?"

The smile fades. "There are things you don't know, Eva. Threats whose existence you cannot begin to imagine."

"Enlighten me then," I snarl, and hurl the comp back through the bars, so it lands, shattering, at his feet.

"One day," he says, his voice serene.

Questions flood my head, too many to sort through. "Like the fables?" I say, remembering the old stories the Mothers used to tell. "Lachlan and the Selkie? The beasts that ruled the Houses? You've made me into one of them?"

The Executor's thin lips twitch, as if I've irritated him. "In a way."

"Are there others? Or am I the only one?"

"Just you. Once we see how the process works—what the dangers are, and the risks—we will proceed."

The dangers. The risks. "How am I supposed to change into four different kinds of animals? A *seal*, for the Architect's sake? I'm not a selkie. I'm a *person*. You'll kill me!"

"Oh," he says, nudging bits of plastic and wiring out of his way with his foot, "on the whole, I think not."

"What do you mean, *you think not?*" The waves of heat come again, making sweat break out on my skin. "I'm a bellator, not a shapeshifter. I know how to fight. Not to..." Words fail me, and I slump against the bars, my forehead against the cool metal.

"You are both. Designed to be the perfect warrior." His voice vibrates with conviction. "And we had the perfect partner for you, to anchor you during your first shift and all the ones to come. Too bad you had to go and screw it up. Not to worry, I'll find you a substitute before it's too late—but I was so pleased with my choice."

I lift my head, staring at him. "What partner? Are you talking about Ari?"

"Did you think," he says, his beady gaze fixed on me, "that I didn't notice how Westergaard met your eyes all those years ago in the Square, when you committed your little act of rebellion? I knew then he would be a match for you."

Our secret, the one I'd thought belonged to us alone—it hadn't been a secret at all. "He was my mentor," I say, feeling my body tremble.

"Certainly. Hand-picked for you, for the strength of his spirit and his gifts as a bellator. And when the time came, he would have been your anchor, meant to tether you when you shift. We tested him at birth for the aptitude, which is quite rare."

I think of the story Kilían told Ari—how he was switched with a regulation-born child shortly after birth. This must be the reason why. "I don't understand. An aptitude for what?"

"Shapeshifting comes with a price." He shrugs. "You may have the genetic raw material for it, but it takes tremendous energy. That energy has to come from somewhere. In your case, Westergaard would have acted as your anchor. You'd pull energy from the earth, through him, and he'd keep you from destroying yourself in the process. Alas, now I need to find someone else for you—and soon. Luckily, we have one other with the ability. Otherwise, I'd be forced to expend valuable energy chasing Westergaard down—and I have no need of a traitor."

"How?" My brain feels as if it's melting. "How would Ari know how to do such a thing?"

The Executor lifts a shoulder, looking uncomfortable for the first time since he arrived outside my cell. "He has the aptitude, as I said. The two of you were compatible in training, in battle. You would have figured it out when the time came—as you will do with his replacement."

It occurs to me that he has no idea how Ari or whoever he has in mind to take his place is meant to do this—if, indeed, he's telling me the truth at all. I swallow hard. "You're insane."

Anger flashes across his face, quickly concealed. "I know how it must sound, Eva. But believe me, in a few short weeks—maybe even days—you'll see for yourself."

"And Ari?" His name is a razor blade in my mouth. "If he were to successfully serve as my—what did you call it? My anchor?—what would happen to him?"

"Ah, well. That's a bit of an interesting situation. Physically, he would remain unharmed. But otherwise, I suspect serving as your anchor would force him to subsume his will to yours. If you gave him an order, he couldn't disobey you. His life—his purpose—would be to serve you."

My jaw drops. "I would control him? He'd be my slave?"

The Executor shrugs, as if Ari's free will—or the lack thereof—is immaterial. "He is a bellator, after all. Perhaps it wouldn't work that way for him. At any rate, it doesn't matter, as he's gone."

"*Perhaps?*" I wish, harder than anything I've ever wished for in my life, that these bars would vanish so I could get my hands around his throat. "What in the nine hells is wrong with you?"

"Wrath is a sin," he reminds me.

I'm about to tell him how little I care when something else occurs to me. "If I'm the first," I say, each word a chip of ice, "how do you know all this?"

"I never said you were the first, Eva. Just the only one at my disposal. As I said, there are threats in the world of which you know nothing."

Rage curdles inside me, sins be damned. "I am not at your disposal!"

"Really?" He gestures at the cell. "What do you call this?"

"This," I say from between clenched teeth, "is a temporary inconvenience. Make no mistake, I will get out. And when I do, I will take great pleasure in killing you for what you've done."

He rolls his eyes, as if my threats amuse him. "You won't hurt me. I'll tell you exactly what I want you to do, and you'll stay right here and carry out my orders."

It's all I can do to keep my voice from shaking. "Why would I help you?"

"Because," he says, running a finger along the bars, "if you don't, I'll devote all of the resources at my disposal to dragging Ari Westergaard back where he belongs. I'll torture him every day, and make you watch. Until finally, I'll have Efraím finish what he started in the scholar's room." He smiles at me, that cold shark's grin. "Efraím will slit the exile's throat in front of you, and when he dies, you'll know it's all your fault. That you could have saved him, if only you'd cooperated when I asked."

He turns his back and walks off down the shadowed hallway, my curses trailing in his wake.

33
ARI

I n training, they drill us on *The Art of War*, a thin book by an ancient writer named Sun Tzu. Efraím used to quote the damn thing at me all the time. One of his favorite lines was this: "Let your plans be dark and impenetrable as night, and when you move, fall like a thunderbolt."

Making my way through the damp tunnels that will lead me back to the Commonwealth, I think of this and have to laugh. I hadn't told anyone where I was going, just written Ronan a note saying I'd left of my own volition and he shouldn't waste resources looking for me. That I'd be back if I could. Well, the tunnels are dark enough, and I suppose failing to reveal any details about what I have in mind falls under the category of 'impenetrable.' Still, I can't imagine this singlehanded stealth attack is what Efraím had in mind.

I do have a plan, however shaky: Disable and silence whoever stands between me and my goal, question Eva, and liberate her from her cell. Then find our way back to the tunnels and flee for safety, either with the Brotherhood or, if they have moved on, deeper into the Borderlands. Make our way north, toward Banabrekkur, where my father is.

The plan sounds simple enough—but tactically speaking, it's a disaster waiting to happen. There are too many unknowns, too many variables waiting to trip me up—what if Eva isn't in her cell? What if there's someone waiting to ambush me in the tunnels? What if she is too damaged to move? What if—

I shake my head hard to dislodge these unproductive thoughts. Dwell on them and I'll be stymied before I've even properly begun. By the Architect, I am so mad at her for risking herself, for making me believe everything we shared was an act for the Commonwealth's benefit.

The tunnels smell as wet and nasty as they did a few days ago—maybe worse, because every passing minute brings me closer to a bloody confrontation. "Damn you, Eva," I mutter under my breath, and keep walking...left, right, then left again. The dank air of the tunnels fills my lungs, and without a flashlight, I have to squint to peer through the gloom.

Twenty minutes later, I hear the sound of water dripping, and increase my pace. Five minutes after that, I find myself in the cavern where we'd first found the wolf's face.

I don't hear anything when I press my ear against the door that leads to the scholar's chamber, but I'm not foolish enough to fall for the same gambit twice. My sverd in one hand and my shuriken in the other, I kick the door in.

The scholar is nowhere to be seen. Instead, there are two Bellatorum guards—Austmar Bantok and Grímar Hjalvi, who I've trained alongside for the past two years. They're good fighters, but they're no match for me. I'm on them before they have a chance to raise the alarm, slitting Bantok's throat as he opens his mouth to speak and driving my blade into Hjalvi's chest as he lunges toward me. It's over before it even began, the stones awash in blood.

Bantok's lying facedown on the ground, at the center of a spreading pool of liquid, black in the dimness. This is good; I don't want to have to look at what I've done to him. Hjalvi, however, is on his knees, gasping his last as I yank my blade free. He would have killed me, I'm sure of it—but still, he was a fellow warrior, a brother. I don't enjoy watching the light fade from his eyes.

"I'm sorry," I mutter as he pitches forward onto the stones, although I'm the only one who hears. "*Integer vitae scelerisque purus.*"

The blessing is the most I can give them, pitifully inadequate as it is. I wipe my blade clean on the back of Hjalvi's shirt, drag both him and Bantok out of the line of sight of the doorway, and slip silently from the room.

The underground is quiet this time of night. I'd hoped for that, timed my attack this way on purpose. Still, I'm on edge as I creep down the tunnels that lead to the prison cells, concealing myself in the shadows. I hope they're keeping Eva separate from the other prisoners, so breaking her out won't cause too much of a commotion. The last thing I want is to kill or maim the other people locked in the cells when they start yelling for the guards—and they will. No loyalty exists between the Commonwealth's prisoners. They'll inform on each other in a heartbeat if they think it will grant them a measure of clemency.

As I round the final corner, I hear voices. I freeze, backing against the wall, and listen hard. Two men are talking, their tone the desultory banter of people who don't expect to be overheard.

"—don't know why the Executor has it in for her," one of them says. I recognize his voice. It's Benedikt Mundahl, one of the four bellators who were recruited along with me. "She was his golden girl a couple months ago."

There's the scraping sound of shoes moving over stone, and then the other man replies. "Who can say, Mundahl. I always told you it wasn't natural, the way they let a female in. There's something twisted at work there, no mistake."

Anger flares in me, but I stay still, assessing. The second man is Gídeon Falk, a broad-shouldered beast who's been paired with Benedikt for guard duty before. He outweighs me by forty pounds. I'm faster, though, not to mention smarter. As for Benedikt, I have nothing to worry about. Efraím used to pit the two of us against each other all the time, and I always kicked his ass. Together, though, they represent a force to reckon with. I knot my hand around the hilt of my sverd, and try to figure out what to do.

In the end, I decide my best bet is to divide and conquer. Drawing a deep breath, I look down at the ground, find a loose pebble, and kick it, hard.

As I intended, this gets the immediate attention of Falk and company. "What was that?" Gídeon says, sounding more alert.

"Sounded like a rock shaking loose to me."

"A rock being kicked loose, more likely." I hear the hiss as Falk's blade comes free of its sheath. "You stay here."

Then he's stalking toward me, his footsteps growing louder as he approaches the bend in the tunnel where I stand, concealed from view. "Show yourself," he growls.

And so I do.

This fight is not as easy as the others. For one thing, it is noisier. Falk gets half my name out of his mouth before I kick him in the stomach, silencing him. He surges toward me, blade outstretched, trying to pin me against the wall, but I dodge and knock him into it instead, headfirst. He comes back at me, slashing with his knife, and I duck under his arm. As he spins and lunges for me again, I stab him in the gut, twisting the blade. He opens his mouth to scream, and that's when I cut his throat.

The whole thing's over in thirty seconds. I bend over him, muttering the blessing again, and yank his set of keys free. Then I straighten up, and realize I'm not alone.

"You exile bastard." It's Benedikt, standing a foot away, his mouth open in shock and his sverd in his hand. "You won't get away with this."

"Hello, Benedikt," I say, wiping my blade clean for the second time tonight. "If you don't want to meet a similar fate, I would suggest you unlock Eva Marteinn's cell and pretend you never saw me."

"The girl?" he says, stepping to the side to avoid the river of Falk's blood that has begun trickling toward him. "You came back here for your apprentice? By the Architect, Westergaard, you must be even dumber than I thought."

"Is that a no?" I say in the same polite voice. "It sounds kind of like a no to me."

"You're not getting past me," he says, doing his best to block my way.

"Oh, Benedikt. If that's the way you want to play it," I say, backing up. He's still talking when I give myself a running start and vault over his head, using the sides of the tunnel for leverage. I land on the other side of him and take off running, in the direction of the cells. I know Benedikt; he won't go for help. The bastard's prideful—

after all the times he's fought me and lost, he'll want to be the one who brings me down. He'll come after me, and a good thing, too. If I can't find Eva on my own, I may need to coerce him into sharing what he knows.

She isn't in the first cell, or the second. In fact, all the cells are empty, a lucky—and suspicious—fact I realize as I race by them, Benedikt hard on my heels. I yank the unlocked doors open behind me as I go, and hear him swear as he dodges one after the other. Finally I'm at the end of the cell block, Benedikt just feet away. I peer into the last cell on the left and see Eva gripping the bars, her clothes ripped and her dark eyes wide, the truth stamped all over her face.

The sight of her is a sharpened blade, piercing straight through me. Even filthy and caged like an animal, she's the loveliest thing I've ever seen. More than that—she is air, filling my chest where that awful weight used to be. Her lips form my name as Benedikt comes pounding up behind me, blade gripped in his hand. "Get away from her," he barks.

I lean back, against the bars, and face him. "Whatever you say," I drawl.

His eyes narrow, and then he launches himself. I spin, letting his momentum carry him past me. He smacks into the bars of Eva's cell, panting. His eyes meet mine, and then Eva uses the dagur she's liberated from my belt to reach through the bars and cut his throat.

He claws at her, trying to get free, but it's too late. Blood gushes over her hand where it grips the knife. In the half-light of the cell, her face is bone-white, her breath coming in harsh, uneven gasps. Benedikt's body sinks to the ground and I push him out of the way with my foot, shoving key after key into the lock until I find the right one. Finally the door swings open, and then Eva is in my arms.

34

EVA

Ari holds me close, gripping me as if he doesn't believe I'm real, his heart pounding against me. He smells like blood and fighting and the dampness of the tunnels, but he also smells like him —that ineffable, intoxicating scent of burnt sugar. I bury my face in his chest and breathe him in. "You came back," I whisper.

His hand twines in my hair, pulling me tighter against him. Then he lets go and steps away. "Are you all right? Did they—what did they do to you?"

I shrug, feeling infinitely better now he's here—despite what the Executor told me about my true nature, and his. *Selfish*, I think. "Nothing that really matters. I'm all right."

His eyes darken. "I wish I could kill every one of them that hurt you."

Now that we're not touching, I feel awkward in his presence, clumsy and stiff. There's so much I have to explain, and no time in which to do it. At the very least, I owe him an apology.

"I'm sorry, Ari," I blurt out, kneeling next to Benedikt to divest him of his weapons belt and the blade down his back. I'm unprepared for the boneless way his lifeless body moves, and have to fight a shiver of revulsion as I slide the belt and the blade free. "Your mother —I'm so sorry. I never meant this to happen. I had no idea. You have to believe me."

Ari kneels next to me, rolling Benedikt over so I don't have to look at him anymore. "I know," he says, getting to his feet and turning to scout the hallway for intruders.

"That day at the camp...I didn't—I wouldn't—I never—" The words catch on each other, so that I can't complete the sentence, and I give up trying. Instead I buckle Benedikt's belt around my hips, slide his ill-fitting sheath onto my back, and find the courage to look at Ari. He's turned from the hallway and is staring down at me, his green eyes troubled.

"I know, Eva," he says again.

"I tried to tell Kilían—and then I passed out and the next thing I knew, I woke up here again..."

"It's all right," he says. "Eva. It's okay."

"But I—"

He reaches out and presses a finger against my lips. His skin tastes like other people's spilled blood, but his touch is gentle. "Not now," he says, dropping his hand and setting off down the aisle between the cells at a brisk pace. "We'll talk about it later, if we live that long. Any minute, they're going to find the trail of corpses I've left behind. When they find out you're gone, there will be hell to pay, and the two of us will be first in line."

35

ARI

We run out of the cellblock and back into the tunnel where Falk's body lies, scanning the hallway. We've been lucky so far, but unlike skill, luck cannot be trusted. Lady Luck is capricious; she gives as she wills, and takes away when the spirit pleases her.

Sure enough, footsteps come pounding down the tunnel, blocking our only escape route. Eva pales. She looks left and right, desperately —then up. "The ventilation shaft," she says. "Hurry!"

I kneel and she climbs onto my shoulders, knife out to pry the grid loose. It swings free with a creak and clatter of metal, opening on rusty hinges.

"Boost me up, Ari," she says, but I'm already standing, providing her with the height she needs to wriggle into the shaft. I pull myself up, drop the grid shut behind us, and crawl after her into darkness.

36

EVA

We crawl as fast as we can through dirt and dust. I concentrate on what I can remember of the ventilation tunnel blueprints the guard showed me that day in the gen lab, but at last, despite my best efforts, we come to a dead end.

Drawing a deep breath, I reach forward and slide my knife around the edge of the grid, then push it outward. I lean forward, enough to see over the edge.

We are in the hallway of the skól, where the Instruktors teach. It is deserted, only the emergency lights illuminating the corridors. The swinging doors at the end of the hallway are shut. But when I breathe deep, I can pick up a scent that doesn't belong here—well-oiled metal. A Bellatorum blade.

"They're coming," I say, leaping down to the floor.

Ari lands next to me, yanking a coil of rope from his weapons belt. "We don't have time to make it to a stairwell. Come on."

He shoves the door of the nearest classroom open and points at one of the windows. I push it up, the swollen wood protesting, as he knots the rope around the stanchion that supports the ceiling and gestures to me to go first.

As I climb through, I hear the hallway door judder open, hear Efraím's voice raised in inquiry, then in demand. We have seconds, no more. I grip the rope tight and start scaling down the outside wall, my feet braced against the brick. The rough fibers burn my palms, but

I ignore the pain, use it to goad me onward. If they catch us, a few abrasions will be the least of my problems.

The rope jerks, and I look up to see Ari above me, climbing down as fast as my pace will allow. I redouble my speed, and he responds, pushing off the wall to give him as much momentum as possible. We have almost reached the ground when the rope goes slack, and then we are falling. It's only about five feet, but when I hit on my back, hard, with Ari on top of me, it knocks the air out of my body.

He scrambles to his feet and pulls his blade, looking upward. In the lighted frame of the window stands Efraím, the severed end of the rope in his hands. He gazes down at us, and the look on his face is all threat.

"Come on," Ari says, but I'm already on my feet, heading for the alleyway that snakes between the food market and the garment factory, emptying out into Wunderstrand Square. The only reason Efraím would cut the rope is to give himself an advantage; otherwise he would've come rappelling down after us. Which in turn means he has bellator reinforcements on the ground.

The wind picks up as we disappear into the confines of the alley, howling through the narrow passage and whipping around the buildings. A squall is coming, one of the fall thunderstorms that descends quickly in the mountains. Above the damp scent of moss-covered cobblestones, the far-off acridity of the trash fires, I smell the men who are on our trail, borne to me on the rising breeze.

"There," I say to Ari, pointing. Beyond the mouth of the alley, at the edge of the square, I can make them out—four bellators lying in wait, hidden in the shadowed arch of the temple. If I hadn't scented them on the wind, I would have been hard-pressed to find them until it was too late. Efraím would expect us to retreat that way; it's the most direct route away from the skól, plus it's got the hidden crypts beneath the sacristy floor, a perfect place for hiding. He has set us a trap. No wonder he was so confident about cutting the rope; it's fed us right into his hands.

"By the Sins," Ari swears under his breath. Behind us I hear the rest of the Bellatorum guard making their approach, blocking the entrance to the alley, the way we've come.

They are boxing us in—again.

"Can they still track you?" he hisses, and I shake my head with relief, remembering what the Executor said to Efraím.

"All right," he says, running his palm over the wall of the garment factory. "We'll have to climb. You first, Eva. Go."

"Climb *this*?" I say, my voice squeaking. "How?"

"You can do it. I've seen you." His tone is firm, refusing to admit the possibility of failure, and despite the gravity of our situation, I feel his confidence seep into me. "Now go." He boosts me, hard, and I grab for the wall, digging in my hands and feet, finding purchase on the rough stone. I haul myself upward by sheer force of will, jamming the toes of my boots into the crevices between the rocks and ignoring the sensation of flesh shredding from my fingers, already abused from their encounter with the rope.

Beneath me I hear a grunt as Ari leaps for the wall, then a thud as his foot collides with flesh. I spare a glance downward, and he shakes his head furiously. "Climb, Eva," he demands. "Don't look down."

Training or no training, the last thing I want is to be a liability that puts us in even more danger. So for once I obey him, turning my entire sense of purpose to the task. I ignore the shouts from below, the sounds of knives clattering uselessly against rock, and climb as fast as I can, until the pain in my bloodied fingers fades into numbness and the pounding of my heart blurs with the thud of my boots against the stone, the scrape and snag of my clothes as I drag myself upward.

To my surprise, I reach the roof well before Ari. I pull myself over the edge and look down to see him six feet below me, Daníel and another bellator in hot pursuit. One of them grabs for his legs, and he kicks out, connecting with a thump that knocks the man loose. The bellator he's kicked—Jakob Riis, I see as moonlight illuminates his face—loses his grip and falls to the cobblestones below, landing with a sickening crack that portends broken limbs, a fractured skull, or worse. He's no longer a threat, but Daníel is still climbing, gaining steadily on Ari. I consider throwing my knife or one of my chakrams to shake him loose, but with the wind kicking up the way it is, I could miss...and then I'd be out a weapon, not to mention having given the bellators on the ground something to use against me.

I can't just stand here. If Daníel doesn't succeed in pulling Ari down, they'll have soldiers in the building soon, racing up the stairs to the rooftop door. Desperately, I look around, searching for a solution, finding none. And then in a moment of inspiration, I uncoil the rope from Benedikt's weapons belt, anchor it to one of the smokestacks that rises from the rooftop, and toss the remaining length over the side. "Ari!" I yell.

His head jerks up in time to see the rope sway to the left of him, then the right. His eyes meet mine. And then, in an act of perfect trust, he lets go and grabs for it.

The rope snaps taut as it takes his full weight, making a high-pitched whining sound audible even over the rising cry of the wind. I'm petrified it won't hold him, that it will pull me over the edge too, both of us hurtling down to die on the stones. Grimly, I dig in my feet, haul back on the rope with everything I have, and pray. *By the Architect, don't let me lose him.*

It holds, and I let out a harsh breath. My lungs ache from climbing, from our dash through the alleyway, but I pay them little mind. I will need more from them before this night is done; it will do me no good to dwell on the ways in which I am already compromised. I grit my teeth against the pain in my chest, the needle-sharp jab of the rope fibers into my palms.

Then some of the weight is gone. I look down and see Ari leaning out from the wall, his feet braced hard on the stone, climbing upward for all he's worth. For a brief instant I feel relief—and then the rope jerks again, and I realize what I've done. Below him, Daníel has also gotten hold of it and is making his way upward at an alarming pace. Ari kicks at him, trying to dislodge him the way he did Jakob, but Daníel is a far better climber—as I know from the hours we've spent in training, watching him scale cliffs as effortlessly as if he was walking across flat ground. He takes evasive action, swinging to the left and right in an attempt to shake Ari free, then plants his feet and renews his assault.

The weight on the rope has doubled, pulling me closer to the edge. I have to brace my feet against the low wall at the edge of the roof to keep myself from going over, but I can still see the top of Ari's head, getting closer as he pulls himself stubbornly upward. His hands come into view just as he lifts his boot and stomps down on Daníel's face, breaking his nose. Blood streams everywhere, but Daníel doesn't let go.

Bracing myself against the knee wall, I reach out with both hands and pull Ari over the top. The moment he lands, I yank my dagur free. And then I lean over and look down at Daníel. He stares up at me, the flesh beneath his eyes already blackening. Blood masks the lower half of his face.

"You wouldn't," he says as I raise the knife.

"The Commonwealth grieves for you, Daníel Eleazar," I reply. And then I slice the rope and watch him fall.

37

ARI

As we race across the rooftop of the garment factory, I feel the first drops of rain hit my face. Soon it's pelting down without mercy, drenching both of us. Eva rubs at her eyes to clear them and points at the roof of the cannery. There's about a ten-foot gap between the buildings. "You think we can make it?" she shouts over the rising wind.

I nod, not wanting to waste my breath on a reply. Squinting through the sheets of rain, I gauge the distance, suck in air, and break into a sprint. Beside me, I see Eva do the same. We are both running full out, Eva pacing me easily despite her shorter stride. *By the Architect*, I pray, *let it be enough.*

My feet skid on the asphalt, straining for purchase. Fifteen feet from the edge, I glance sideways at Eva. Her fists are clenched, her braid streaming out behind her. Rain plasters her torn clothes to her body, cuts patterns into the dirt streaking her face, but she has never looked more beautiful. We are meant for each other, Eva and I, and I promise myself if we survive this mess, I will find the courage to tell her so.

Twelve feet. Ten.

"On my signal," I tell her, forcing the words out between breaths. She nods to show she understands, and bares her teeth in a fierce grin.

Eight feet. Six. Five.

"Now!" I yell, and on command she launches her body into the air, hurling herself into the gap between the buildings as if she was born for the purpose. I follow, and for an awful, exhilarating moment we are weightless, borne by momentum and battered by the wind. Then we are over the cannery, and falling. The roof comes rushing up and smacks me, hard. For a second I can't breathe. On my hands and knees, I fight for air. "Eva?"

"Here." The voice comes from above me, and, startled, I lift my head to see her standing there, soaked but otherwise uncompromised. I gape, bewildered.

"How—"

"It doesn't matter." She grabs one of my bloodied hands, dragging me to my feet. "They'll be up here in a second. Run."

Even as the practical part of me wonders how in the nine hells she managed to make that jump and land on her feet without a scratch, the rest of me is already in motion, sprinting across the roof toward the looming gray form of the education center. My hand tightens on Eva's, and she squeezes back, her grip so tight, I feel my bones grate. "Where can we go?" she shouts.

"I'm thinking," I yell back, and yank my hand free as we approach the edge of the cannery's roof. "Three...two...one...*now*."

She leaps on my signal, the perfect apprentice. I have a second to see she's landed in a crouch, fingertips touching the ground, before I barrel into her, knocking her off-balance. For a moment she is under me, wide dark eyes staring up into mine, eyelashes studded with raindrops like a thousand tiny stars. Then we're up and running again, weaving across the roof of the education center, through jutting chimneys and the skeletal structures the fifth-formers built this past week to study the impact of wind energy. All around us they whir and buzz and turn, metallic propellers spinning and joints creaking with the force of the storm. We race across the roof and I think about what the Bellatorum will expect—for us to make a stand? For us to flee?

They outnumber us, have better weapons and the Commonwealth's cameras at their disposal. We can't make it into the tunnels, that's for sure. And even if we could, we'd be trapped like rats in a barrel. Which leaves us with only one option.

We will have to attempt an overland escape, through the forest, where the Bastarour patrol. I've seen them, of course, but from afar. I've never had to fight one, don't know anyone who has and lived. There's a reason the Commonwealth sends exiles into the forest—if they don't opt for death by the sword, they can take their chances and risk being torn apart by monsters.

The exiles die every time. I ought to know; I've helped drag their bodies free, or what's left of them, as a warning to the rest of us. The Bastarour bring their kills back to the edge of the woods—they can't go any further, confined by their solar-powered shock collars—like a cat rewarding its owner with the present of a mouse. The Executor always seemed to find it endearing. *Things,* I'd tell myself as we wrapped shredded torsos and ragged-edged bones in white plastic. *Not people. Objects. Not real not real not real.*

"All right," I say to Eva, surprised by how calm I sound. "We go down here, on the fire escape. It's concealed from the street, which should give us a chance. When we make it to the ground, we'll run for the woods. It's the only way."

If this surprises Eva, she doesn't show it. She nods once, and drops my hand. Her nails have broken the skin; the rainwater stings where it hits the cuts. "Let's go," she says.

We make our way down the rickety fire escape, keeping to the shadows. Each creak and groan of the old iron ladder sounds loud as a scream, but there's nothing we can do about it but climb faster and hope the storm will mask our descent. The wet metal is slick under my hands, and I have to wipe my palms on my pants to keep from slipping. There used to be railings here, but they have long since crumbled away. No one uses these fire escapes anymore, and they've fallen into horrible disrepair.

I climb as fast as I dare, descending into the darkness of the narrow, twisted alley. Above me, metal rattles as Eva follows. The wind batters the fire escape, and beneath my hands the last ladder shudders, the metal shrieking as it struggles to support our combined weight. I reach the bottom, five feet above the ground, grasp the bar below the last rung, and jump.

Behind me, Eva lands in a puddle, spraying water and mud over both of us, then grabs my arm and pulls. My back smacks into the rough stone of the library hard enough to drive the air out of my body, but I don't fight her. Beside me, she has gone still, an animal hunted in the woods.

I squint, peering through the rain, but see nothing except the confines of the alley, its cobblestones cracked and its walls rain-slick, trash cans lined up at its mouth like squat, weary sentinels. And then I hear what must've warned Eva: Soldiers thundering by in search of us, splashing through the mud and then thumping on the concrete. The air-raid siren starts up in long, loud whoops, the one they always use for evacuation drills—except this time it is no drill. This time they're hunting us, and we'll be lucky to escape.

The siren gives five long, ululating cries. Then there are ten seconds of silence, as there always are, and in them Efraím's voice rings out across the square. "Bellator Marteinn, Exile Westergaard, show yourselves. It will be easier for all of us if you do."

Exile Westergaard, I think, and wince. Of course that's what they're calling me; I wouldn't expect anything else. Still, it hurts to hear. I thought I was beyond caring what Efraím thought of me, but the ingrained need for his approval is not so easily dismissed.

I am not weak, I tell myself. *I am not his.*

Standing in the murky dark, flattened against the building, I let go of my fear. Tapping Eva's arm, I tilt my head toward the warren of buildings that indicate the nursery, the playground, and gardens. They'll expect us to go this way, but it's the best cover we have. If we can make it into the hills between where we stand and the woods where the Bastarour roam, we can lose them. And if we make it into the forest, then we may lose ourselves—but I am reasonably certain they won't follow...or if they do, they'll be facing the same dangers we are. They won't kill the Bastarour—that would be foolish, compromising their own security. Which means they'll have to evade them, just like us.

Cautiously I edge toward the mouth of the alley. The siren has stopped shrieking; it was a warning, no more. In the comparative silence I listen, hard, but hear nothing other than the renewed fury of the storm. On the Library's outdoor screen, our faces play in a continuous loop, below them the words *Wanted for treason. Extremely dangerous. Do not attempt to apprehend. Alert nearest bellator immediately.*

Clearly they view us as the greatest of threats. It would be flattering if they didn't want to kill us.

We keep to the shadows, ducking between buildings, using the alleyways to our advantage. But the people tracking us are the same ones who have trained us, and there is only so much we can do. I know the moment the bellators catch sight of us, past the alley that skirts the machine shop, at the edge of Clockverk Square. There are shouts, and then a knife comes flying toward me. I duck and it pierces the vid screen that covers the southwest wall of the machine shop, slicing straight through the 'a' in treason, its handle shuddering with the force of the throw.

I glance around for the source of the weapon and see no one. In fact, I am alone. Eva has faded into the darkness, giving herself the advantages of camouflage and surprise.

There is a noise on the other side of Clockverk Square, the scraping of shoes against stone. I pivot, slower than usual in my sodden clothes, and see Efraím standing under the streetlight, making no effort to conceal himself. Our eyes meet, and in his I see nothing but a vast, indifferent emptiness. His hands move to his belt, going for his shuriken. No matter what his orders might be, he has no intention of taking us alive.

It is a war of wills, as it has always been between us. Determination, tempered by cunning and skill. And I'll be damned if I'll let him win.

The other Bellatorum flank their leader, fanning out behind him. He is the tip of the arrowhead, the sharp point that will cut us to bits if we let him.

Let justice be done, even should the world perish, I think. And pull my chakram free.

Efraím's hand rises, the shuriken gripped tight in his fist. I hold my breath, steadying myself, and let my vision narrow to its target. Deep inside, I feel a pang of regret. It's different to kill a man in a fight than to take his life in cold blood, much less a man who mentored me and molded me into a warrior. But I cannot let that interfere with what I have to do.

I draw back my arm to let the chakram fly—and see a flash of silver slice through the air, heading straight for Efraím. It hits his weapon hand straight on and sends the shuriken hurtling into the night, where it embeds harmlessly in a tree.

Efraím's hand is bleeding. He cradles it to his chest, looking around for his assailant. "Hold!" he says sharply to the bellators behind him. "To me, the lot of you."

I look down at my hand, wondering if I have thrown the chakram without intending to. But no, I am still clutching it, my knuckles white and streaming water. Efraím and I stare at each other across the expanse of the square, and in my heart I feel a small spark of triumph.

Then Eva emerges from the shadows behind me. Her hair is down, torn from its braid, and the wind takes it, blowing it around her head. She comes to a stop beside me, just outside the glow of the streetlamp. Her eyes are fierce, her lips set.

"Let justice be done, even should the sky fall," she whispers to me, though I don't think I have spoken aloud.

She grabs my hand and yanks me after her, into the shadows. The bellators give chase as we tear through the garden plots behind the nursery and into the woods, following the sound of the stream. Pounding up the bank without a word, we run for the rapids. Eva frees one raft from the trees, then another, slicing at moorings with her knife. Without the rafts, the bellators will have a much harder time following us. They'll have to leap down the falls, and who knows how many of them will survive the descent?

Eva cuts the rafts free and I pitch one after the other over the edge, watching them careen down the drop through the whitewater, until we run out of time. I can hear Efraím and the others crashing through the bracken behind us, heedless of stealth or disguise. We vault onto the last remaining raft together, and I feel the familiar sickening vertigo as we hurtle down the falls.

The journey to the bottom's even more bone-rattling than usual, what with the wind and the full force of the Bellatorum in pursuit. But we make it, with a full minute's head start. The moment we're close enough to shore to touch bottom, I abandon the raft and run for the treeline, Eva at my side. Always before we had begun the arduous climb up the cliffs, or the long hike around to the path. Now we head straight for the pines that stand sentry at the edge of the forest, demarcating the edge of the Commonwealth's territory. Inside the forest there are no lights, no paths, nothing but trees and dirt and dark. And the Bastarour, of course, prowling silent and hungry.

I wouldn't willingly confront one of them, had I the choice. But it's either do so, or die.

Eva and I spare a glance at each other, and then her hand finds mine, pressing hard. "Luck," she whispers, and I remember it's what I said to her back in the tunnels, before we shoved aside the grill that led to the Outside.

My heart squeezes, hard and tight. Like doomed children in that ancient legend about the wanderers, the breadcrumbs, and the witch, we disappear into the murk.

38

EVA

A s we race through the windswept forest toward the electric fence, the first of the Bastarour's howls sound in the distance. Unless we can figure out how to neutralize the fence or open the gate, it will be a toss-up whether we die in the beasts' jaws or at the hands of the Bellatorum, our backs to the electric fence, inches from freedom.

We flee through the woods, the trees catching at our clothes and tearing at our skin. Maybe it's nerves—or what the Executor told me about my true nature—but I feel as if I could outrun Ari easily, as if I am holding myself back to wait for him to catch up. My skin tingles with the sense of danger, and the eerie howls rise from all sides, hemming us in.

"Let me," I say, pushing past Ari. "I see better in the dark than you do."

He allows this without comment, and I take the lead, hacking through the dense, waterlogged brush and then sighting open space and breaking into a dead run. I have never been in this part of the forest before; I have no idea how far it stretches or how long it may be until we reach the fence.

I burst through the treeline into the open clearing and scan desperately for something—*anything*—that will help us. Then I see a gleam of silver no more than five feet ahead and come to a halt so abrupt that Ari slams into my back. "What?" he says.

"Look right there—the fence—" My breath sobs in my throat, and Ari peers over my shoulder in the direction I'm pointing.

"Which way?" he pants. "The gate?"

I have no idea, but no matter which way we go, it has to be better than staying here. I take off to the left, through the cleared land that runs parallel to the fence as far as I can see, and he follows. We run, and the howls get louder, and I am terrified I have made the wrong choice—that after all this, we'll die because I made a wrong turn.

We race along the fence, the rain pelting us. Any moment, I expect to feel the bite of a blade sinking deep into muscle, or the inexorable pressure of the beasts' teeth on my neck. But just when I'm beginning to despair, I see it—a massive sliding metal gate. And next to it, a keypad, mounted on a separate pole next to a speaker. There is no handprint pad; no reason to bother with the extra layer of security out here, where someone would have to brave the threat of the Bastarour if they wanted to escape.

"By the Architect," Ari says, doubling over, hands on his knees.

I dash for the keypad and shove the dripping mass of my hair out of my eyes just as Efraím's voice rises from the woods less than a hundred yards away. "Bellator Marteinn. Exile Westergaard. This is a useless game. We have darts that will tranquilize the beasts; they're no threat to us. You have no such protection. If they don't kill you, we will. Surrender and you'll be dealt with humanely."

"Hurry!" Ari hisses at me, as if I'm not. I won't let us die here in the woods, torn limb from limb by animals, murdered by our brethren, no matter what the odds. *It's just another code to break. Just like one of the puzzles in the comp lab.* Except the punishment for failing to solve one of those was never death.

I stab my fingers at the keypad, remembering the day the Executor came to the gen lab. I'd committed his password to memory, thinking such information could prove useful—though how, I couldn't imagine. Well, now I know...maybe.

I try the password. Nothing. The howls grow closer, and my heart pounds so hard I can taste my pulse in my mouth.

And then inspiration strikes. I type the password backward. And by the Virtues, it works.

The light goes green under my fingers, but I don't open the gate.

Instead I let it fade to red again, then motion to Ari. He comes, backing toward me, trusting me to guard his blind side.

"Do you have it?" he hisses.

"I do."

"Then open the gate, for the Architect's sake!"

"No," I tell him, eyes on the treeline. "Not yet."

"Are you crazy? What are you waiting for?"

"They're coming," I say, watching the shift of shadows in the trees, the changing patterns of leaves outlined by the scrim of moon. The storm rages on, bending limbs to its will, pelting us with water. I can smell the scorch of ozone as lightning streaks down on not-so-distant mountains.

"Really? I had no idea." His eyes are fixed on a Bastarour that has come to crouch at the treeline thirty feet away, its head lowered and its pale eyes focused on both of us. The beast tilts back its head and howls, doubtless summoning its companions. It is even larger than I'd imagined, its body a solid block of black muscle. This close, I can see the cross-breeding clearly, based on images in textbooks from before the Fall—it has the sleek dark body and gleaming green eyes of a panther, the striped face and massive shoulders of a tiger, the upright, pointed ears and long muzzle of a wolf. Its tail curves upward, bushy and bristling. The thing must weigh three hundred pounds.

It is horrifying—but I feel a kind of odd kinship with it, all the same. If what the Executor told me was true, doubtless the same technology was used to create us both.

"Do you trust me?" I ask.

Ari gives a low, dissatisfied growl. "Do I have a choice?"

The Bastarour howls again. I can hear its fellow beasts coming closer, hear the difference between their padding footsteps and the quick, light echoes of the Bellatorum, moving on two legs rather than four. Thank the Architect for my ability to distinguish between the fury of the storm and these smaller, subtle sounds. Tonight, this may mean the difference between life and death.

"You always have a choice," I say softly, eyes roving the shadowy woods. There are three of the identical beasts crouched at the treeline, regarding us. They are growling steadily, but make no effort to advance, not yet. I clutch a knife in each hand, facing them, and wonder what holds them in abeyance. A signal from their leader? The arrival of the Bellatorum?

"I hope you know what you're doing," Ari mutters, gaze flicking to the locked gate.

One of the creatures turns toward me, paws scuffling impatiently in the dirt. I glare at it, and it ducks its head, breaking our staring contest in a peculiar gesture of submission. Its behavior puzzles me. We are alone here, isolated. We are prey. Why doesn't it attack?

Maybe because it recognizes its own kind. A dull pain throbs in my chest.

"Eva," Ari hisses, "you'd better have a plan."

I want to roll my eyes at him, but I don't dare glance away. "Whatever you do, don't take your eyes off them. Don't look down."

"Oh, thank you so much," he says acidly. "That would never have occurred to me. Any other brilliant tips you feel the need to impart, before we're devoured or stabbed? Since you refuse to open the virtueless gate, and all?"

"Yes," I say. "Since you ask. Duck." And throw my body on top of his, knocking us both to the saturated ground, as the first knife flies out of the shadows.

"Are you all right?" Eva says, scrambling off me.

"I thought," I manage, spitting dirt out of my mouth, "that you said not to look down."

She's on her feet now, as am I, weapons gripped in our hands. "Yes, well," she says, scanning the shadows beneath the swaying trees as the first of the Bellatorum burst into the clearing, "sometimes plans change."

What remains of the Thirty are lining up at the edge of the woods, Efraím out in front. Behind him is Kilían, who looks through me as if my demise holds no more interest to him than a sparring match between two ill-prepared recruits. I hope I don't have to kill him tonight. That would be unfortunate.

The Bastarour's heads move in unison between the Bellatorum and the two of us. Efraím moves a step closer, and they growl louder. One bares its teeth in menace, and he freezes where he stands.

I grip my sverd tightly, trying to figure out what to do. Attack Efraím, and every one of the Bellatorum will return the favor. Do nothing, and they'll kill us anyhow. Provoke the Bastarour, and they will probably lunge at us en masse.

The nearest beast makes the decision for me and charges. I crouch low, swinging my blade in a wide arc. My knife punches hard through the thick hide and slides into the flesh beneath, ricocheting off the bone. The animal bellows and shakes its head, blood spraying everywhere. And then it charges me again.

Efraím and his henchmen haven't moved. They are conserving their energy, waiting to see if the Bastarour is going to finish me off so they won't have to. And perhaps it will, because when the infuriated beast comes after me this time, it knocks me flat on my back in the mud, snarling and snapping.

The creature's matted, wet fur is in my mouth, its hot breath on my face. Drool pours onto my arms as I raise them to protect my head, slashing at the thing with my blade. Pain flares as the beast sinks its claws into my arm. Even over the racket of the fight, I hear the unmistakable sound of Efraím's mocking laughter.

Then something slams into the beast and it shudders all over, shaking its head violently as if to rid itself of an infestation of horseflies. Its body jerks, then jerks again. Blood pours from it, drenching me. And then it goes limp, crushing me under its weight.

Disgusted, I push the creature to the side and crawl out from underneath it. When I blink the blood and rain out of my eyes, I see Eva standing above the beast, her sverd gripped in both hands, breathing hard. There is a gaping wound on its back and its head lolls at an unnatural angle: Eva has nearly severed its spine. "Are you all right?" she says, her eyes roving over me in search of damage. "Is any of that yours?"

On my hands and knees, I shake my head. "All...the beast's," I manage. The pain in my arm is nothing—I can ignore it long enough to fight.

Satisfied, Eva's eyes flick away from me to the other two Bastarour, who have stopped prowling and are staring at us with an assessing expression. I am willing to bet they have never seen someone slaughter one of their kind before. They sink to their haunches in front of Eva and make a strange chuffing sound. I get to my feet and they settle back into that threatening growl—but they don't come any closer, which is good enough for me. I spit blood out of my mouth, wipe my blade on my dirt-splattered pants, and face the men who used to be my brothers.

"Let us go, Efraím," I say.

"Or...what? We'll be next?" He laughs again, as if the prospect amuses him. "That was an impressive bit of butchery. But butchery was all it was. You'll find we're not nearly as easily disposed of as that poor hunk of meat."

"Really?" Eva says. "Tell that to Jakob and Daníel Eleazar. I think they might have a different opinion, don't you?"

"You bitch." The rain has plastered Efraím's hair to his face and his clothes to his skin, but he glares at Eva as if they're alone in the training room and he's about to teach her a lesson of the most painful kind. "By the time I'm done with you, you'll wish you never swore an oath to me."

Eva opens her mouth to answer, just as thunder booms overhead and the wind shifts so the rain strikes my face dead-on, carving a path through the blood. The intensity of the storm unsettles the two remaining creatures, which shift uneasily on their haunches and then rise again, pacing the clearing. This is not a good sign. Spooked animals are unpredictable, and the two Bastarour were already unpredictable enough.

In my opinion, it is high time to get the hell out of here. Eva, on the other hand, remains unperturbed. "Remember the ice tank, Bellator Stinar? I think you'll find I am capable of much more than you realize."

Her face is serene in the moonlight, her expression empty. If she is bluffing, she is doing a stellar job. Even I cannot tell the truth.

"Capable or not," Efraím sneers, "there are two of you and twenty-seven of us. Westergaard will die here tonight, and I'll drag you back to your cell to pay the price of your insolence. You'll pay over and over again, Eva Marteinn, until you are broken and at my mercy. And then you'll pay some more."

At this, Eva gives a savage smile, ruthless and wintry. "Ah, Bellator Stinar," she says, "I told you before. You will not break me."

Still smiling, she takes a step forward and throws her dagur high. It flies end over end, silhouetted against the grim face of the moon. As it reaches its apex, lightning strikes, streaking down toward the earth. Eva lunges for the keypad, punching in the code to open the gate. It slides to the left slowly—too slowly.

"Gate opening," an automated voice announces, emanating from a speaker affixed to the post by the keypad. "Step through. Stand clear."

The Bastarour sense freedom. They abandon their pacing and charge for the gate, just as Eva does the same. She wraps her fingers around my hand, tugging me with her, pulling me through the narrow opening. Linked like we are, we squeeze past, but barely. I feel the metal skim my skin, sending a faint shock through me: Eva has managed to open the gate without disarming it. Given the right conditions, it'll become a formidable weapon.

The dagur falls, tumbling end over end, until it thunks into the ground. Throwing it was a distraction, but a good one: It diverted the bellators' attention long enough for us to make it through the gate. The Bastarour charge after us, deprived of their prey and desperate for freedom, and Efraím charges after them.

"Bellator Stinar!" I hear Kilían yell, but Efraím isn't listening. His eyes are slitted with rage, his attention all for us, so he fails to realize what is happening until it is too late.

Cut off the snake's head, he'd always told us in training, *and the rest of the beast will fall.* Well, here's Eva, implementing a textbook illustration of how bellators are meant to prevail when the odds don't favor victory.

She's taken his lessons to heart.

Lightning streaks from the sky, striking the fence as Efraím and one of the remaining Bastarour collide midway through the gate, the space hardly large enough to accommodate both of them. They struggle, entwined, as the creature gets hold of Efraím's arm and shakes its head viciously, seeking to sever the bone. He fights, trying to get free, but the beast has him pinned.

The fence sparks wildly, bright blue against the backdrop of the night, and I hear it crackle as electricity pours through the conducting strands, amplified to what is likely a fatal level. The two of them—beast and man—aren't touching the gate, not yet. But if they should, I can't imagine either one of them will survive.

Eva lunges for the keypad mounted on our side of the fence. I scream her name and grab for her, but she slips through my grasp. Inches from the blazing fence, she presses a sequence of buttons and darts backward, taking her place at my side once more.

"Gate closing," the automated voice says. "Ten seconds until lockdown. Please stand clear."

On the other side of the fence, all is chaos. The bellators are screaming, the remaining beast is howling, and the fence has caught fire, blazing up into the night. I hear Kilían give the order to use the tranquilizer darts and hurl myself flat, pulling Eva down with me. But the storm is raging too furiously to account for the trajectory of the wind. The darts go wide, missing again and again.

"Eight seconds until lockdown," says the implacable voice. "Stand clear."

I turn my head and blink the rain from my eyes. Efraím and the Bastarour are caught, helpless in the maw of the heavy gate as it inches shut, their limbs enmeshed, neither of them able to break free from the other. Intent on killing its prey, the creature is either unaware or indifferent to the danger of the closing gate. Efraím, on the other hand, is under no such illusion. I see his eyes flick toward the gate, and then he fights even harder to get loose.

The Bastarour snaps its teeth, shredding the fabric of his sleeve, sinking deep into flesh. His blood sizzles as it hits the fence, bubbling up and dripping toward the ground. Efraím slashes at the beast with his dagur, bellowing curses. His blade sinks home, but the creature howls as its jaws close on the hand that holds the knife, in brutal retaliation. The two of them are wedded together, caught in a vicious dance, stabbing and snapping at each other with no hope of release.

"Five seconds until lockdown. All personnel, step away and stand clear."

From the other side of the gate I watch, stunned into immobility, Eva silent beside me. And then Efraím's rolling eyes find my face.

"Ari," he cries. "Help me!"

I know what he's asking of me. Not to save his life—it is too late for that—but to offer him the departure he deserves. To die in battle, rather than crushed to death by a few thousand pounds of electrified metal, entwined with a genetically modified beast.

"Lockdown commencing. In three...two...one..."

There is a fraction of a second where I could have cut the throat of the Bastarour, or dragged them both free, to settle the matter on the ground at my feet. But in the end I stand there, motionless. The rain blurs my vision, but not so much that I cannot see the beast sink its great teeth into Efraím's neck, offering him the merciful end I could not—just as his knife jabs deep into its throat, sending arterial spray across his face. It is a warrior's death.

"The Commonwealth grieves for you, Bellator Stinar," I say, my voice a whisper. "As will I."

"Ari," he mouths one last time, his eyes fixed on mine. Then the gate slams home, the world goes up in blood and fire, and we run.

40

EVA

W e hike through the night, barely speaking except for the brief answers I give Ari about what happened while I was imprisoned. The further we get from the Commonwealth, the more a tremendous sense of relief and an abiding guilt consumes me. I have to tell Ari what I know. How can I, though? Once I tell him the truth, it'll be over between us. He won't want to be with someone whose DNA was spliced with that of four other animals, who is on the verge of transforming into a beast. And if the Executor told the truth about him serving as my anchor, I have to let him go before I break him to my will. But I can't bear to lose him yet.

Surely we can work it out. This can't be the end of us. Not like this, after everything.

I'll see him to the Brotherhood, see him safe. I can't think beyond that. No matter what else happens, he has to survive.

Close to sunset on the next afternoon, while Ari is crouched on the ground, studying the pattern of crushed leaves and branches, the wind shifts, bringing with it the scent of people. I nudge him with my foot, and he straightens up, eyebrows raised.

"That way," I tell him, pointing in the direction of a grove of spruce trees. "If it's not them, it's someone."

He nods, and we start off again, more slowly this time. "How far off?" he asks over his shoulder. "Can you tell?"

I breathe in again, sampling the air. "Half a mile?" I say, uncertain. "Not far."

"If it's them, Eva, I'll go in first. Explain to Ronan what happened. You follow when I say."

"And if it's not?"

He shrugs one shoulder. "We run. Or we fight. Does it matter?"

I hear what he's left unsaid—that from now on, our lives are going to be comprised of one or the other, or maybe both at once. What I did to Efraím has bought us time, but the Executor and the other bellators are looking for us, that much is for sure. They won't let a traitorous act of this magnitude go unavenged—and the Executor will be furious that his prize experiment has escaped. "I guess not," I tell him, trying to keep the hopelessness from my voice, and we keep walking.

The scent intensifies as we get closer—dried meat, unwashed bodies, the sharp reek of medicinal salve. We hike up a final rise through a mountain pass. The trail bottlenecks, cliffs rising on both sides to hem us in. It's the perfect spot, clearly chosen for ease of defense—evoking the battle of Thermopylae. As we approach, I take note of the Brotherhood's traps: a tripwire, laid across the trail and disguised by leaves; a hail of rocks, set to be triggered by a hastily placed foot. A less observant individual—or one approaching under cover of darkness—might be taken in.

We edge through the bottleneck unharmed. The path drops down into a clearing in a valley, surrounded by woods on three sides and hemmed in by the cliff on the fourth. In the clearing is what remains of the camp, the tents concealed beneath cut branches. I can see a few figures moving around, lugging water, huddled on the ground in conversation.

"That's all that's left?" I whisper to Ari, unable to keep the horror from my voice.

"That's it," he says, expressionless. "You stay here."

Then he is gone, moving fleet-footed and silent down the rise. A few yards from the edge of camp, he gives a long, low whistle. Immediately all the figures stand, and I see one of them separate himself from the rest: Ronan. He comes striding toward the perimeter as Ari steps into view.

"Westergaard," I hear him say. "I thought you were a dead man."

Ari gives a rough chuckle. "Closer than I would have liked. But no."

"You went back for her. Didn't you?" His tone isn't accusatory, but I flinch back from it anyhow.   He thinks what they all do—that I deliberately caused the bombing. That their friends are dead because of me.

"I did," Ari says evenly. He tells them, then—how I was on their side the whole time, how I did what I did to make sure he escaped. About the tracker, and the torture.

"Kilían told me as much." Ronan's tone is dry. "But he wasn't sure Eva spoke the truth."

Ari says nothing, and Ronan raises an eyebrow. "I haven't heard from Kilían since you left. I was growing concerned. Should I be?"

"Well," Ari says, "probably. But he's all right, as far as I know. If you're able to contact him, he'll vouch for what I have to say."

The other people in the camp have been staying back, letting their leader speak. Now one of them, a tall man a few years older than Ari, with ink-dark hair and eyes set in a pale, grim face, comes up behind Ronan. "I can't believe you're listening to this," he says. "It's a trick, a trap. I say we shoot him and be done with it."

"Be quiet, Jaxon." Ronan doesn't raise his voice, but it cracks like a whip just the same. "Where is she, then?"

"Up the path," Ari replies. "Waiting." He raises his arm, giving the Bellatorum's signal for 'follow me.' Cautiously, I step over the rise and make my way down the scree of pebbles and loose dirt.

I come to a stop next to Ari and nod my head to Ronan in greeting. He returns the favor. "Eva," he says, his voice grave.

"I'm very sorry for your loss," I tell him, which is what we are taught to say in the Commonwealth when a death occurs. Here's hoping it's appropriate on the Outside as well. "It's true, what Ari said. I really didn't know."

He looks me up and down, as if he's assessing my sincerity. Or maybe he is trying to figure out where I've concealed my weapons— which is a joke. Since I lost my borrowed weapons belt somehow in the skirmish with the beast, all I have left is my sverd. I feel naked and underequipped, and I hate it. "Thank you," he says at last.

"I know you don't have a good reason to believe Ari," I say, the words spilling over each other in my haste to get them out. "But please, don't punish him on my behalf. I didn't ask him to come after me. Not that I'm not grateful," I say, giving Ari a sideways glance in time to see his mouth twitch. "I wouldn't trust me either, if I were you. Just—it wasn't his fault."

Ronan regards me, his face expressionless. "We don't punish people here. Not in the manner to which you're accustomed."

The dark-haired man—Jaxon—gives a nasty laugh. "You must be the great Eva Marteinn. The girl that launched a thousand bombs," he says. "Why wouldn't they kill you? What makes you so special? Obviously you had something to bargain with. I'd like to know what it is."

I smile at Jaxon in an effort to disarm him—or at least to lessen his hostility. Efraím used to tell the new recruits that smiling would make people trust us, if we could manage it sincerely enough. But apparently I'm all out of sincerity, because Jaxon just glares, unmoved.

"The two of you are responsible for that bombing. Or at least, you are." He jabs an index finger in my direction. "And you"—he jerks his head at Ari—"you're foolish enough to be taken in by her lies a second time, because you want to get in her pants."

I've never heard the saying before, but it's clear enough what it must mean. My face flames red, and I don't dare look at Ari.

"Jaxon!" Ronan sounds appalled. "That was out of line. Apologize."

"The hell I will. How did you two get away, with so many of your kind focused on killing one of you and locking the other one up for safekeeping? I assume you were locked up, huh?" he says, turning to me.

"I was," I say, my voice tight. "We escaped, like Ari said. Efraím—Ari's mentor, the lead bellator—he led a hunt for us. But we outsmarted him, in the end."

"Ha." Jaxon imbues the word with more sarcasm than I would have believed possible. "How?"

"I killed him." I give Jaxon the most guileless look I can manage. "Indirectly, I must admit—but the end result's the same."

Ronan sighs and runs a hand through his hair again. He looks exhausted. "I think," he says, stepping back to let us pass, "you'd better tell me the whole story."

41

ARI

An hour later, as darkness falls on the Brotherhood's small campsite, Eva and I finish talking. Aside from the two scouts—Adrien and Fade—who are out on patrol, everyone listens with rapt attention. Mateo and Isobel don't say a word, and Camila, the weapons expert, uses the time to take apart, clean and reload all the camp's guns. Still, publicly sharing the events of the past few days is not pleasant, especially with Jaxon giving us the evil eye every other sentence and Mei—the camp's botanist and healer—gasping in horror as punctuation, clapping her hand over her mouth and tossing her sleek dark hair over her shoulders in surprise.

Ronan listens quietly, interrupting only to clarify a point or to ask a question. Midway through our account, since we can't risk lighting a fire and giving our presence away, he hands out more dried meat and fruit for dinner. Mei serves up some dandelion greens she found growing by the stream that runs close to the camp, and the scouts, on their way back from patrol, come bearing flasks full of water. It's not a bad meal, although by this point I'm so hungry, I bet my weapons belt would taste good.

Eva sits next to me on the log that serves as our chair, her body taut. I've got my dagur in one hand; I fight the urge to put the other arm around her, to draw her in against my side and make sure she is real. Now that I have her back again, I don't ever want to let her go. But she's been by turns as skittish as a wild animal and as remote as she'd been when we waited for the door to the scholar's chamber to swing open, with no real knowledge of what lay on the other side. It's a strange conundrum: The more I keep my distance, trying to respect her space, the more aware of her presence I become. I swear I can feel her beside me, a disturbance in the air.

Noticing how easy the Brotherhood are with each other only makes things worse: Mei eats on the ground, leaning back against Mateo's legs, and Camila nudges Adrien with the butt of her gun when he makes an offhand comment that strikes her the wrong way. Next to them, Eva and I are at a loss in this new world, strangers to the laws that govern it.

Aggravated, I clear my throat and turn to Ronan. "Is there anything else you want to know?"

He shakes his head, looking around at the group for confirmation. "No. I think you've been through enough...for now."

"All right. So, then—do you mind if we ask a few questions?"

"About what?" Jaxon says, sounding wary. He's sitting on Eva's other side, methodically shredding a piece of jerky into bits and shoving them into his mouth.

"About what's next," Eva says, speaking for the first time in several minutes. "It's not safe to stay here—but you've stuck around as long as you have for a reason. You're waiting for something, am I right?"

A smile spreads across Ronan's face. "You're an intelligent one, Eva Marteinn. A real asset to the Brotherhood—if you'll join us."

"They're here, aren't they?" Mateo says. He's gotten to his feet and is dusting off his hands. In the growing dusk, the blue of his eyes is unnervingly bright.

"Being here and committing to being part of our effort are two different things," Ronan says mildly. "But yes. We are waiting—despite what some among us believe is wise—to hear from Kilían. If things have gone badly, then perhaps he's in such significant danger he must run. And if he does—I'll not abandon him."

Jaxon makes a disdainful sound deep in his throat, and this time I feel it might be warranted. "I don't think Kilían will leave unless he has to," I say, recalling our last conversation. "He hasn't told me why he's helping the Brotherhood—nor do I expect *you* to—but whatever his reasons, seeking freedom for himself isn't among them. And the last time we saw him"—firing tranquilizer darts at the creature ripping out Efraím's throat—"none of the bellators seemed to suspect a thing."

"Be that as it may," Ronan says, "we'll wait twenty-four hours. Then we'll continue on to the next Commonwealth to the east, to recruit more members to the resistance, unless—well. We've heard a rumor—but the content of it isn't something I'm free to share as yet, until you make your decision and we can be certain of your loyalty." His gaze flicks toward Eva.

I nod, fighting back my exhaustion. "Before the bombing," I say, the words catching in my throat, "you started to tell us about the origins of the Commonwealth, and the locations of the Brotherhood's bases. You didn't trust us enough to finish then, but now—we deserve to know."

The wind rustles through the pines, and Eva lifts her head, as if scenting the air. Satisfied, she fixes her gaze on Ronan's face as he says, face grim, "You do. And I intend to tell you—in the morning, after all of us have had some sleep."

"And that's my cue. Goodnight, all," Mei says, boosting herself to her feet and walking toward one of the tents. Mateo's eyes are trained on her as she disappears into the shadows, and I wait automatically for the consequences, but of course there are none. Out here, looking at a girl like that isn't forbidden. No one would judge me for kissing Eva, or holding her hand. It's hard to imagine, but I know it's the truth.

One by one, except for Ronan and Jaxon, the rest of the Brotherhood party bids us goodnight. Adrien and Fade, the two scouts, are last, making arrangements for Ronan to wake them when it's their turn to stand guard.

"We'll take our turn watching the camp," I tell Ronan after the two of them have gone. "Or scouting, like I was doing before. We'll pull our weight. Just tell us what you need."

He inclines his head in acknowledgement. "The two of you need *sleep*. You look exhausted. We'll wake you tonight if we need you, but I'd rather you get some rest."

"We're Bellatorum," Eva says, offering him a half-smile. "We're trained to operate without sleep. Don't worry about us. We won't be a liability and we won't let you down."

Next to her, Jaxon, who has been mercifully silent, gives a mocking laugh. "Bellatorum. You know what we call you in the real world, boys and girls? Assassins, plain and simple. You think love makes you weak, that it's the first step toward destroying life as we know it? Hate to disillusion you, but normal human beings believe the opposite. Caring about other people is what makes the world go 'round."

"Jaxon." Ronan's voice is a warning.

"What, boss? Just trying to enlighten them, before someone else does the job." He shifts his weight on the log, hands dangling between his knees.

"I don't think love makes you weak," Eva says, shooting him an irritated look. "But I do think it's dangerous. For love, people will take risks they'd never dream of otherwise."

She doesn't glance at me—but then again, she doesn't have to. I feel like she's stripped me bare, revealing my deepest vulnerabilities for everyone to see. I do my best to keep my face blank, but Jaxon can't resist.

"Ah. Like loverboy here, charging back into the lion's den to rescue you, you mean. How many lives did you take to bring her back, Westergaard? How many men did you kill?"

My voice comes even, controlled, betraying no hint of how much I'd like to punch him. "I did what I had to do."

"It doesn't even make a difference to you, does it? How many people die, as long as you have what you want—"

I ball the hand that's not holding the knife into a fist. "Of course it makes a difference. But in war, there's always collateral damage. People who get hurt because they're in the wrong place at the wrong time."

"Ah," Jaxon says, his eyes on my face. "Like your mother."

At this, I surge to my feet. Enough is enough. "Yes," I say, stalking toward him. "Like her. War is unpredictable. You never know who's going to be a casualty until it's too late."

Now Jaxon is on his feet too, with Ronan right behind him.

"What's the matter with you?" he hisses at his second-in-command. "Why are you provoking him?"

This is a fair question, and I myself am curious to hear the answer to it. But instead, Jaxon turns on him. "Why aren't *you*, Ronan? Why are you so accepting of the two of them? Everything was fine before they showed up, operating right on schedule. Then they come into camp, and before you know it, half of our people are *dead*." His voice breaks on the last word, and he clears his throat viciously.

"That wasn't their fault," Ronan insists. "Westergaard's right—we knew the risks when we agreed to do this. Either we support each other, or everything falls apart. They gave me their explanation. I accepted it. You have to make your own decisions, but I'm still the leader of this expedition and as long as you operate under my command, you'll respect what I say." His voice is as even as ever, but there is no mistaking the air of authority it carries.

Jaxon gives me a hard look. Then he mutters, "Yes, sir," and stalks off toward the edge of the clearing, in the direction of the woods.

Ronan watches him go. Then he turns back to us. "I apologize for his behavior," he says wearily. "Jaxon was born in Vik, our capital city, to parents who were never part of any Commonwealth. Everything he knows about your ways, he's learned secondhand, and to outsiders—well, Commonwealth habits can seem restrictive, to say the least. Jaxon's not an easy person by any means, but he lost someone he cared about very much in the bombing. Someone he loved. He's grieving, and looking for a person to blame."

"Oh," Eva says, sounding uncharacteristically apologetic. I'm sure she's thinking about my mother. "Oh, no. Should we—I could tell him how sorry we are—"

"Just leave him be," Ronan says. "He'll be all right...if you can refrain from doing him in."

"I would never—" Eva begins hotly, before it occurs to her Ronan is joking. A blush washes over her face, visible even in the deepening darkness.

"Go to bed," Ronan says, resting a hand on her arm. I can't help but notice she doesn't pull away from *him*. "We've got an extra tent for the two of you, staked over there at the edge of the woods. I dug up a sleeping mat, too. It's nothing special, but it's better than the ground."

Eva thanks Ronan for his generosity and wishes him goodnight. Then she turns and walks off toward the tent he indicated, and, commending my soul to the Architect, I follow her.

My heart is pounding by the time we unzip the tent flap and duck inside. It's empty, save for the sleeping mat Ronan mentioned—but when I enter after Eva and pull the zipper shut behind me, I feel as if the walls are closing in. I stand, unmoving, as Eva shrugs off Benedikt's sheath and lets the blade fall to the ground.

"Are you all right?" she asks.

"I'm fine."

"Really? Because you're just standing there—"

"There's not a lot of places to sit," I tell her, trying to summon some bravado. "It's stand here, or lie down there." I point at the sleeping mat, and even in the dimness of the tent, see her eyes go wide.

"I didn't mean that," she says.

"I'm sure you didn't."

A long silence falls between us. I am searching for something to say when Eva breaks it. "About Jaxon—" she says. "What if he's right? What if we're just assassins? Not just how the Bellatorum trained us to be—but who we are?" Her voice is small.

"Jaxon's an idiot," I tell her. "It doesn't matter what he thinks."

"No." She messes with her hair, wrapping an errant curl around one of her fingers. "How about what you think, though?"

"What I think? What do you mean?"

Her gaze falls, and when her voice comes, it's so low I can hardly hear it. "You hate me, don't you? For what I did to Daníel—and to Efraím. You think I'm a monster."

I blink at her, startled. "Of course I don't hate you, Eva. How could you say such a thing?"

"Well, because." She shifts her weight, still toying with her hair. "Since—what I did with the fence—well, you haven't touched me. Not at all. And before…"

Her voice trails off into silence. I stare at her, dumbfounded. And then I laugh. "By the Architect, Eva, is that what you think? That I've been keeping my distance because I'm holding a grudge? Or because I see you differently after everything that's happened?"

Her head snaps up, and she glares at me. "What am I supposed to think?"

"I haven't been touching you out of *respect*. After what you've been through—well, the last thing I want is for you to think the only reason I came after you is because I wanted—" I feel the blood heat my own face, and fight the urge to look away. "It's a two-way street, apprentice mine. The times I've reached out to you, you've acted as if my hand was soaked in poison."

"I don't scare you? What I did—the men I killed—" Her voice breaks. "I meant to take Efraím's life. But how I did it... It was like I understood what the Bastarour would do, like I knew they'd see him as the alpha and go after him if they couldn't get to us. Seeing him ripped apart—it was like the beasts and I worked together to murder him."

She bites her lip, teeth sinking deep. When she speaks again, it's a whisper. "All my life, ever since the thief died in Clockverk Square, I've been afraid I was nothing more than an animal. I never wanted to be a bellator. And now—"

I look her up and down—her torn clothes, the hair straggling loose from her braid, her dark eyes fixed on mine—and have a sudden flash of insight. "I think you scared *yourself*, little warrior. Am I right?"

Her mouth opens, no doubt to deliver a scathing retort. And then it closes. "Maybe," she says.

"Hey." I step closer, so she has to look up at me, and draw a deep breath to steady myself. That is a mistake, though, because as soon as the scent of her floods my lungs, all I can think about is feeling her against me, knotting my fingers in her hair and finishing what we started in the woods that day. The fear I've held so tightly in check ever since I figured out she'd sacrificed herself for me, losing my mother before I'd even met her, my anger at Efraím and the Executor for using Eva, the void that is our future—all of it wells up, shredding my hard-earned control. "What about the ones I killed, apprentice mine? I cut two men's throats. I stabbed another through the heart, all to get to you. Are you not frightened of me, then?"

"No," she says, her voice a whisper. "Never."

"Well," I say, stepping closer still, "I'm not frightened of you, either, little warrior. And I do want you, more than I ever have. If you let me, I'll show you just how much."

A smile curves her lips, the first genuine one since I found her locked in that filthy cell. And then her hand rises to grip my collar, pulling me down to her.

"Please," is all she says.

EVA

My head tilts up and his mouth comes down, sealing over mine. His tongue traces my lips, as soft as I remember. I moan, stepping into him. "Ari—"

"Hmmm?" he murmurs, his breath warm on my neck, then lower. By the time he reaches the torn collar of my shirt, pushing the material apart and skimming the skin beneath with his fingers and then his tongue, I'm trembling all over. Alone in my cell, waiting to see what manner of punishment Efraím and the Executor would devise for me next, I'd dreamed about him touching me like this. It was a secret that had held me together, kept me defiant and strong. But now, with his hands and lips roving over me, the opposite is true —I feel as if I might disintegrate beneath his touch, shattering into a thousand pieces.

I shiver again, and Ari straightens, looking down at me. "Are you cold?"

"No."

"You're shaking."

"Well," I point out, and glance down at his fingers, vibrating ever so slightly where they rest against the top button of my shirt, "so are you."

He follows my gaze, and a surprised expression spreads across his face. Then it fades, replaced by the intense, focused look I remember from our first time together, in the woods. With the lightning-quick reflexes I've seen him demonstrate a hundred times, he seizes my braid in his fist and tugs my head back, baring my neck. I feel the warmth of his lips, trailing from the edge of my mouth to the hollow at the base of my throat, and then the thinly veiled threat of his teeth. "I'm not shaking *now*," he says.

This close, I can smell the lingering smoke of the fence-fire on his clothes, undergirded by blood from the cut on his arm and his own, burnt-sugar scent. His weapons belt digs into my stomach, and the hilt of the dagur presses against my hip, reminding me all too painfully that I'm unarmed.

I almost struggle against his grip, try to put enough space between us to get my hands on his blade. And then, as his lips touch mine, the part of me still capable of rational thought devises an alternate strategy. I remember how he'd made that small, helpless sound the first time I'd kissed him—how the edge of violence had undone his control, so that he'd wrapped his arms around me and driven me back against the tree.

And so I don't try to get free. Instead I take more of his mouth, sinking my teeth into his lower lip, wresting control of the kiss away from him. Sure enough, he makes the noise again, and this time I recognize it for what it is: the unmistakable sound of surrender. Testing a theory, I brush my fingers against his belt, liberating a small throwing knife and slipping it into the waistband of my pants, at the small of my back. Ari doesn't notice. His breath comes faster, and his grip on my hair loosens, letting me move. I tilt my head back enough to look up at him; beneath his dazed expression there is the unmistakable stamp of surprise.

"When we do this—" he says, the ghost of a laugh in his voice, "I'm supposed to end up being the one who's inside you, yeah? So then why can I feel you right here?" He presses my hand against his chest, and just like that night in the woods, his heart pounds under my palm. I try to reclaim my hand, but his fingers knot with mine, holding me still. "I can feel you under my skin, Eva." His voice is a whisper. "You drive me crazy. That virtueless stunt you pulled—what were you thinking? You could have *died*."

"But I didn't, did I?"

"You could have. By the Architect, why are you so stubborn?" His jaw sets, and his hands close around my upper arms, tightening until the pressure of his fingers is just this side of pain. But his eyes—they tell a different story. They are wide, and the look I see in them is wholly unfamiliar—vulnerability, edged with a dangerous heat. "You never listen. I swear, you make me wish for the days that I could pin you to the wall of your room with my blade and keep you right where I want you."

His words send a shiver through me, thinking of the day I'd come back from shadowing the guard in the gen lab to find Ari sitting on my bed, flipping his knife between his fingers. What if there is no way left to us but violence? What if all there can be between us is bloodshed and sin? "That's not really what you want," I say, lifting my chin in challenge.

He shakes me, just a little. "Don't tell me what I want. Right now that sounds just about perfect to me, if you want to know the truth."

"You wouldn't dare."

One side of his mouth creeps upward in a half-smile, and I hear the hiss as his nails caress the hilt of his dagur. "Wouldn't I?"

I swallow hard, my mouth suddenly dry as the barren lava fields they've showed us in the vids. "You could try."

"I could," he says equably, running his index finger down my face, trailing it down my neck to my collarbone so I quiver beneath his touch. "You want to run from me, Eva? Please do, little warrior. You run, and I'll chase. And when I catch you—you are *mine*."

His voice drops lower with each word, so the last one is nearly a growl. He bends his head, his lips brushing against mine, sending a jolt of electricity through me. "Run, Eva," he whispers. "I dare you."

I pull free of his grip, glaring. "I'll not run from you."

Ari straightens up. Color burns high on his cheekbones, and he returns the glare. "Of course you won't. You'll just lie to me, is that it, and treat me like a child who needs protecting? You'll sacrifice yourself to save me, and give yourself over to the Executor like a plaything, and let me believe that you—" He bites off the last syllable, clenching his hands into fists.

"That I *what*?"

He shakes his head, his pulse beating in his throat, hard and fast as a trip-hammer. And then he reaches out, grabs me by the hips, and yanks me tight against him. His mouth slants over mine again, but this time there is no gentleness in it. He presses harder, demanding I open for him, and when I do, his tongue finds its way inside, tangling with mine.

"Damn you, Eva," he says, and in his voice I hear the ragged edge of tears. "Damn you for doing this to me."

I slide my hands underneath his shirt in response, raking my nails over his skin, and he moves against me, rough, so his weapons belt presses into me and his stubble scrapes my face. We are kneeling on the borrowed sleeping mat, and my hands are in his hair and his are on my back, urging me toward him, and we are kissing again, our bodies pressed so tightly together I have a hard time figuring out where he ends and I begin. He is murmuring my name, and I am saying his, and then my mouth is on his neck and his shirt is on the floor and he is fumbling with my buttons, ripping the ruined material free.

"Beautiful," he says reverentially when what's left of my shirt falls to the floor of the tent. "So beautiful."

I give the breath of a laugh. "You can hardly see me."

"I can see well enough." His hands find me, cupping, stroking, and I make a sound like a sob.

"Ari, please—"

"I don't really want to hurt you," he murmurs, his lips against my hair. "I would never hurt you. It's just—I was scared, Eva. So scared." It's a whispered admission, barely audible even in the silence of the tent. The Bellatorum never admit fear, much less Ari, with all his flash and arrogance. I know what it costs him.

"Promise me you'll never do anything like that again." His fingers are under my chin, lifting my face. "Swear it on the Architect."

His scrutiny makes me uncomfortable, and I toss my hair, breaking free. "What? Infiltrate the resistance? Impersonate a Commonwealth loyalist? Pretend to be playing both sides against each other? Throw a smoke grenade into the middle of a room of warriors? I'm afraid you'll have to be a little more specific, Bellator Westergaard."

His growl fills the air between us. "You know what I mean. No more of the self-sacrificing games. I'll have honesty between us, or I'll have nothing. You choose."

At his words, a thread of doubt winds through me. I drop my eyes, trying to hide it, but it's no use; we have been in the interrogation chamber together, Ari and I, and he knows me all too well. "What is it?" he says.

"Nothing."

"Liar. What are you keeping from me, Eva? Still hiding things, even now?"

"I—"

He rocks back on his heels, hands spread on his thighs. "It's never enough, is it? What do I have to say to make you trust me? What do I have to do?"

"I do trust you! That's not it. You've got the wrong idea."

"Oh?" he says in the cold voice he uses to question interrogation subjects. "Enlighten me, then."

There's so much I haven't told him—about who I really am, and who he is to me. But there's something else, too, a nagging worry that's been in the back of my mind since the first time he pinned me to the tree in the woods and pressed his lips to my skin.

I don't know why giving voice to my suspicions is so difficult, in some ways harder than letting the Executor capture me or enduring the ice tank. Maybe it's because we're trained for combat and surrender—but no one ever taught us how to deal with situations like this. It takes everything I have to lift my face and meet Ari's icy gaze. "Are you sure you haven't done this before?"

His head jerks back. "What do you mean? Who would I have done this with?"

"I don't know," I mumble. "People."

Ari reaches out and hugs me, holding me close against his chest. His laugh travels through me, moving us both, and he strokes my hair with a deft hand, pulling it loose from my braid. "Well, that's some small comfort," he muses. "Here I am, wondering if I'm too forward, if my touch disgusts you, if I'm doing everything wrong and you're too mortified to tell me so. And here *you* are, suspecting my superior technique's the result of seducing a multitude of willing Commonwealth seditionists."

I squirm, embarrassed. "It was just a thought."

"And a pleasing one, apprentice mine. Because I do want to please you, more than anything." His voice drops, roughens. "You'll tell me what you like then, yeah?"

I have blushed more with Ari in the past two weeks than I have in the preceding seventeen years. "I don't *know* what I like."

"Mmmm." It's a purr, rumbling in his throat as his lips brush my neck. "We can figure it out together. If you will?"

"Why, Ari Westergaard. Are you asking me to go to the devil with you?"

He laughs again, a low, amused chuckle. "I hate to break it to you, Eva, but I think that ship has long since sailed. But if you're offering…"

"See?" I say, pushing at his chest. "That's it. Right there."

"That's what?" he says, refusing to be pushed.

"Why I think you've done this before. Saying things like that."

"Ah, Eva." The tips of his fingers trace my shoulder blades. "There's only you. You do something to me—make me *feel* —"

"You do something to me too," I whisper, pulling back to look up at his face. His eyes are half-closed, his gaze fixed on me as if I've hypnotized him.

"Do I?" His voice is lazy, curling like smoke into the air. "Well, that's only fair, then." He reaches out and runs a finger along my lower lip. I touch the tip of my tongue to it, tasting salt, and he shudders. "I was so angry with you for lying to me. But then I see you and all I want to do is kneel down and promise you everything I am, everything I have, if only you'll stay with me." He glares at me, his green eyes dark in the faint light. "I can't stand it. It makes me weak. That's why I said what I did about pinning you to the wall with my dagur, if you want to know the truth—to feel, even for a few minutes, as if there's some way—any way—I'm not the one on my knees."

His words have the unmistakable ring of honesty, but I don't understand them. What he's describing—it's the way I feel about *him*, not the other way around. "Well," I say, striving for a tone that mirrors his usual sarcastic detachment, "technically we're both on our knees, Ari. So maybe you could keep your blade to yourself, until the situation requires otherwise."

The familiar smile spreads across his face. "We are, aren't we?" he muses. "Come here, then, apprentice mine." He lunges, bearing me down toward the sleeping mat. I land on my back with him on top of me, his face an inch away. He brushes my nose with his, a teasing, playful touch, and then his mouth comes down on mine.

The kiss starts out gentle, but when I tug at him, urging, it changes, a clash of lips and tongue and teeth almost frightening in its desperation. Ari kisses me like the taste of my mouth is something he needs to survive, as if he's afraid he'll never have a chance to do it again. His urgency is contagious, and I kiss him back the same way, knotting my fingers in his hair and answering his hunger with my own.

These kisses are different, their insistence bordering on savagery— as if we're trying to climb inside each other, breaking through the barriers of heat and flesh to join the souls that lie beneath. He gasps into my mouth, taking my breath for his own, and I press my lips to his, taking it back. Even though he's on top of me, though he must have me by about fifty pounds, though he has a weapons belt and I have none, I don't feel helpless. I can feel him yielding to me, then rising to my touch, just as he'd said. His greater size, his strength—it is an illusion, meaningless between us. I think of him saying, *Everything I am, everything I have, if only you'll stay with me,* and hold him tighter.

He nudges my legs apart with his knee and I shift under him, pulling him closer, digging my nails into his shoulders. Reaching between us, I tug the buckles of his weapons belt free and toss the belt beside us, so it lands with a clatter of metal. Then I wrap my legs around his hips and roll him, ending on top. My hair falls down around us, and he inhales sharply, tracing his way down my back to span my hips. The tips of his fingers brush the hilt of the blade at my back, and he freezes, eyes wide.

"What in the nine hells—"

"You should take better care of your weapons, Bellator Westergaard," I say, my lips curving in a smile.

Ari rolls his eyes. "By the Virtues. I should have known." His fingers warm against my skin, he pulls the blade free and slides out from under me, covering my body with his. Then his hands are moving on me everywhere, and he is murmuring my name, and our bodies are shadows on the wall of the tent that merge with the swaying branches outside, the noises we make swallowed by the wind. "Ah, Eva," he whispers, like the word means something else. "*Je me rends.*"

Deep inside me, I feel a rush of feeling begin to build, the same way it had in the woods. I move against him, seeking, and he moves with me, his body effortlessly following mine. But then he pushes away and rises up on his hands, staring down at me. In the darkness of the tent, his expression is inscrutable.

"This—" he says, sounding breathless. "I—do you want...?"

I struggle to think clearly, but it's not easy, with the taste of him on my lips and the heat of his body inches away. "Are you asking me...what I think you're asking?"

Shyly, he nods. "If you'll have me. Will you?"

I open my mouth to reply and find I can't say a word. A shiver runs through me anew, half fear, half anticipation, resolving into a fine trembling that shakes me from head to toe. Ari must feel it, because suddenly his weight is gone and he is sitting next to me on the mat, arms wrapped around his knees.

"Maybe it's too soon, yeah?" he says, careful not to look at me. "Or maybe—you don't want me. Not like that."

Despite the gravity of the situation, I can't help but laugh. His eyes flash to mine at the sound, the expression in them wounded. "Funny, is it? Glad I could amuse."

With a start, I realize I've hurt his feelings—the last thing I intended. "No," I say, sitting up myself and rubbing my bare arms in an effort to stem my shivering. "Not the way you mean."

"Then what?"

"I'm here, aren't I?" Tentatively, I rest a hand on his arm. His muscles are rock-hard, coiled the way they are before a fight, and I let my hand fall. "I've lost half my clothes," I say in an effort at conciliation. "Or did you not notice?"

Ari snorts. "Oh, I noticed all right. By the Sins, Eva, I'd notice that if I were *dead*. Which I am definitely not. As you may have noticed, yourself."

"So then…" I say, fumbling for the right words, "why would you say that? Have I given any indication I don't want you?"

"No," he says dubiously. "Except when I asked—you didn't say yes. And you're shaking again. You're still doing it, and I'm not even touching you."

"I didn't say *anything*," I point out. "And I'm shaking because—because I'm frightened, if you must know."

"I frighten you?" His mouth is a grim line. "What I want—"

"Not you," I say, forcing the words out, ignoring every instinct I have, all my Commonwealth indoctrination. Efraím is dead, but I can still hear him saying, *Information is fuel for your enemies. The less they know, the better. The more they know, the more they can hurt you.* Mundus vult decipi, *Eva. The world wants to be deceived.* "I frighten myself," I tell Ari. "What I feel for you. What I want to do."

In the darkness of the tent, his eyes widen. "And what's that?" His gaze travels over my body, lingering everywhere it shouldn't, and the intensity in his voice makes me shiver all over again.

"Are you not scared, then?" I ask him, dodging the question.

"Ah, Eva." His eyes settle on my face, and in them there is a haunting tenderness. "Can't you tell? I'm terrified."

"Then—"

"I'm terrified," he continues inexorably, "but not because I think we're making a mistake. Not because I think this is wrong, or a sin, or because we're condemning our souls to a lifetime of eternal damnation." He relinquishes his grip on his knees, presses his palm against my cheek. "I'm terrified because I can't imagine feeling more for you than I already do. I can't imagine feeling closer to you, or more—more *consumed*. You own every part of me, little warrior. And if we do this—I'm terrified there will be nothing left. But I'll take the risk, because I'd rather die with you than live alongside anyone else. And if I were to sacrifice myself, I can think of no greater cause." His other hand rises, cupping my face. I can feel him trembling, but his voice is even when he says, "So speak, Eva Marteinn, and remember between us, there is no more room for lies. Will you have me?"

I close my eyes, lean my face into his hands, let his burnt-sugar scent roll through me like the tide. He deserves the truth —about who I really am, who we might be to each other. If I don't tell him—if I go through with this, knowing with every second, I might be binding him closer to me as my anchor—I am no better than the Executor and the Priests who took our free will away.

Drawing a deep breath for courage, I sit up straight, away from the lure of his touch, and meet his gaze. "There are things you don't know about me, Ari. Things I should tell you before we go any further."

He meets my eyes. "There is nothing you could tell me that would make me think less of you. Nothing that would make me want you less."

There is such confidence in his voice, such faith in the way he looks at me. It shatters me inside—especially when I know what I have to say might shatter him the same way. "Don't be so sure," I tell him, thinking of the way I'd woken on the floor of that freezing cell to find my hand leathery and tipped with claws. If he'd seen me then, would he still say the same?

I am a beast, a monster. The way I looked that morning—what I can become—is the least of it. I could enslave him, steal his soul.

"Hey." His voice is gentle. "We have time now. All the time in the world. We don't need to figure this out tonight."

He wraps his arms around me, guiding me back down to the mat. I let him, reveling in the illusory safety of his touch.

"You're burning up, Eva," he says, pressing his hand to my forehead. "Are you sick?"

Tell him, I think, but I don't have the heart. I want the memory of this night with him—just one perfect night, untainted by ugly truths that might tear us apart. "I'm fine," I tell him, glad that the dark hides my face. "And most importantly, we're free."

He kisses my hair, pulls me close against him, and falls silent. I lie awake, Ari's arm draped over my body, listening to his breathing even out into sleep. I don't dare close my own eyes—what if what happened to me in the cell happens again?

Still, there's comfort in the feel of Ari's body against mine. Tomorrow, we'll leave for the Brotherhood's stronghold. Tomorrow,

I'll have to decide whether to break his heart. Tomorrow, the rest of our lives will begin.

But tonight I lie, secure under the weight of his arm, the knife I liberated from his belt cold in my hand, and allow myself to find peace.

ACKNOWLEDGMENTS

I started this book back in 2016, when the world looked very different. I hadn't yet faced a personal health challenge that would test my strength and resilience beyond anything I'd experienced before—and I've experienced a few daunting things!—nor had I imagined a global society stretched to the breaking point by COVID-19.

As I write these acknowledgments, we are still several weeks away from the projected peak in the state I call home. New York City, where I was born and where my parents still live, is a war zone. My son grieves his inability to see his friends; everything that enters this house does so by delivery, and cardboard boxes sit on the porch for 24 hours before we bring them inside, lest they carry the virus; doctors and nurses face terrifying shortages of personal protective equipment. Each day, I peruse news feeds like a scavenger, sorting through opinion pieces for gleaming scraps of facts from epidemiologists and public health experts who, despite years of work in the field, are only able to hazard their best guesses as to the shape of our collective future.

And yet…if there is one thing these past few months have taught me—even in the darkest of times, there is hope. Sometimes it is blinding, like the glare of a floodlight…and sometimes it is a pale ray, a lifeline whose path you follow, having faith that eventually, it will show you the way home.

More than a few individuals have been my lifeline during the past year. I owe my unending gratitude—and potentially my sanity—to them, especially LaToia Brown, Sarah Carpenter, Carol Crate, Melinda Cummings, Dina Dudas, Anne Firmender, Amy Lyon, Kari Skaar, Jessica Smith, Kris Spangler, and my amazing service dog, Tracy Wilkes. All the folks who brought us delicious meals—I will owe you forever. A special shout-out to my parents, Lois and Michael Colin, who disrupted their own lives to assist with ours when everything went to hell in a handbasket. Huge hugs to my community at DREAMS of Wilmington and the Wilson Center for your support. Bottomless appreciation to Dr. Kenneth Kotz and all of the nurses at the Zimmer Cancer Center; Dr. Elizabeth Weinberg; and Dr. Patrick Maguire. To my fabulous neighbor Traci Johnson—I raise a glass to your kindness. And, of course, all my love to Neil Horne, who stood by my side during the maelstrom. Thank you for being my lighthouse when I couldn't see the shore.

Beyond those who stuck with me during this extraordinary year, I owe a debt of gratitude to several individuals for their contributions to the Seven Sins series. Thanks go out to my beta readers, Anne Firmender and Neil Horne; my agent, Felicia Eth, for supporting me as I ventured into new territory; Emily Hainsworth, whose feedback on an early version of this manuscript was invaluable; Emily Grace Williams and Jessica Bayliss, for their insightful perspectives; and the Weymouth Center for Arts and Humanities, for granting me the time and space to tell Eva and Ari's story. Tremendous appreciation to Lisa Amowitz for designing my lovely Facebook banner and to Sarah Anderson for hosting my Instagram cover reveal. Cake, balloons, and fine wine to Katie Rose Guest Pryal and Lauren Faulkenberry for taking a chance on me and helping me see the manuscript with fresh eyes. You are rock stars.

My ultimate gratitude goes, of course, to my readers. Without your support, I wouldn't have the privilege of continuing to tell the stories I love. If I could hug each and every one of you, I would.

ABOUT THE AUTHOR

Emily Colin is the *New York Times* bestselling author of *The Memory Thief* and *The Dream Keeper's Daughter*. With Blue Crow Books, she is the editor of *Wicked South: Secrets and Lies, Stories for Young Adults* and *The Sword of the Seven Sins,* the first book of the Seven Sins series.

Her diverse life experience includes organizing a Coney Island tattoo and piercing show, hauling fish at the Florida Keys' Dolphin Research Center, roaming New York City as an itinerant teenage violinist, helping launch two small publishing companies, and serving as the associate director of DREAMS of Wilmington, a nonprofit dedicated to immersing youth in need in the arts.

A 2017 Pitch Wars mentor, she is the 2017 recipient of the North Carolina Sorosis Award for Excellence in Creative Writing and the 2018 recipient of the North Carolina Greater Foundation of Women's Clubs Lucy Bramlett Patterson Award for Excellence in Creative Writing. Originally from Brooklyn, she lives in Wilmington, NC, with her family.

CPSIA information can be obtained
at www.ICGtesting.com
Printed in the USA
BVHW030314140820
586344BV00019B/193